· · ·

Contents

• • •

FRANCES HODGSON BURNETT

A Little Princess

AND

The Secret Garden

an imprint of
RUNNING PRESS
Philadelphia • London

The text of *A Little Princess* is reprinted from a first edition, published in
1905 by Charles Scribner's Sons in New York, and made available through the
courtesy of the Free Library of Philadelphia. The text of *The Secret Garden* is
reprinted from a first edition, published in 1911 by Frederick A. Stokes
Company in New York, and made available through the courtesy of the
Houghton Reading Room, Harvard College Library. All spellings and
punctuation are preserved as they appeared in the original editions,
except for obvious typographical errors.

The essay is excerpted from *Happily Ever After: A Portrait of Frances Hodgson
Burnett* by Constance Buel Burnett, © 1965 by Constance Buel Burnett.
Reprinted by permission of Vanguard Press, a division of Random House, Inc.

Cover illustration of *The Secret Garden* by Frances Hodgson Burnett,
1911, Clifton Waller Barrett Library, Special Collections Department,
University of Virginia Library.

9 8 7 6 5 4 3 2 1
Digit on the right indicates the number of this printing

Library of Congress Cataloging-in-Publication Number 96-86285

ISBN 0-7624-0115-X

Cover design by Diane Miljat
Edited by Elaine M. Bucher
Set in ITC Berkeley Oldstyle

Published by Courage Books, an imprint of
Running Press Book Publishers
125 South Twenty-second Street
Philadelphia, Pennsylvania 19103-4399

. . .

A LITTLE PRINCESS

Being the Whole Story of Sara Crewe

Now Told for the First Time

. . .

THE WHOLE OF THE STORY

I do not know whether many people realize how much more than is ever written there really is in a story—how many parts of it are never told—how much more really happened than there is in the book one holds in one's hand and pores over. Stories are something like letters. When a letter is written, how often one remembers things omitted and says, "Ah, why did I not tell them that?" In writing a book one relates all that one remembers at the time, and if one told all that really happened perhaps the book would never end. Between the lines of every story there is another story, and that is one that is never heard and can only be guessed at by the people who are good at guessing. The person who writes the story may never know all of it, but sometimes he knows and wishes he had the chance to begin again.

When I wrote the story of "Sara Crewe" I guessed that a great deal more had happened at Miss Minchin's than I had had time to find out just then. I knew, of course, that there must have been chapters full of things going on all the time; and when I began to make a play out of the book and called it "A Little Princess," I discovered three acts full of things. What interested me most was that I found that there had been girls at the school whose names I had not even known before. There was a little girl whose name was Lottie, who was an amusing little person; there was a hungry scullery-maid who was Sara's adoring friend; Ermengarde was much more entertaining than she had seemed at first; things happened in the garret which had never been hinted at in the book; and a certain gentleman whose name was Melchisedec was an intimate friend of Sara's who should never have been left out of the story if he had only walked into it in time. He and Becky and Lottie lived at Miss Minchin's, and I cannot understand why they did not mention themselves to me at first. They were as real as Sara, and it was careless of them not to come out of the story shadowland and say, "Here I am—tell about me." But they did not—which was their fault and not mine. People who live in the story one is writing ought to come forward at the beginning and tap the writing person on the shoulder and say, "Hallo, what about me?" If they don't, no one can be blamed but themselves and their slouching, idle ways.

After the play of "A Little Princess" was produced in New York, and so many children went to see it and liked Becky and Lottie and Melchisedec, my publishers asked me if I could not write Sara's story over again and put into it all the things and people who had been left out before, and so I have done it; and when I began I found there were actually pages and pages of things which had happened that had never been put even into the play, so in this new "Little Princess" I have put all I have been able to discover.

FRANCES HODGSON BURNETT

CHAPTER 1
SARA

Once on a dark winter's day, when the yellow fog hung so thick and heavy in the streets of London that the lamps were lighted and the shop windows blazed with gas as they do at night, an odd-looking little girl sat in a cab with her father and was driven rather slowly through the big thoroughfares.

She sat with her feet tucked under her, and leaned against her father, who held her in his arm, as she stared out of the window at the passing people with a queer old-fashioned thoughtfulness in her big eyes.

She was such a little girl that one did not expect to see such a look on her small face. It would have been an old look for a child of twelve, and Sara Crewe was only seven. The fact was, however, that she was always dreaming and thinking odd things and could not herself remember any time when she had not been thinking things about grown-up people and the world they belonged to. She felt as if she had lived a long, long time.

At this moment she was remembering the voyage she had just made from Bombay with her father, Captain Crewe. She was thinking of the big ship, of the Lascars passing silently to and fro on it, of the children playing about on the hot deck, and of some young officers' wives who used to try to make her talk to them and laugh at the things she said.

Principally, she was thinking of what a queer thing it was that at one time one was in India in the blazing sun, and then in the middle of the ocean, and then driving in a strange vehicle through strange streets where the day was as dark as the night. She found this so puzzling that she moved closer to her father.

"Papa," she said in a low, mysterious little voice which was almost a whisper, "papa."

"What is it, darling?" Captain Crewe answered, holding her closer and looking down into her face. "What is Sara thinking of?"

"Is this the place?" Sara whispered, cuddling still closer to him. "Is it, papa?"

"Yes, little Sara, it is. We have reached it at last." And though she was only seven years old, she knew that he felt sad when he said it.

It seemed to her many years since he had begun to prepare her mind for "the place," as she always called it. Her mother had died when she was born, so she had never known or missed her. Her young, handsome, rich, petting father seemed to be the only relation she had in the world. They had always played together and been fond of each other. She only knew she was rich because she had heard people say so when they thought she was not listening, and she had also heard them say that when she grew up she would be rich, too. She did not know all that being rich meant. She had always lived in a beautiful bungalow, and had been used to seeing many servants who made salaams to her and called her "Missee Sahib," and gave her her own way in everything. She had had toys and pets and an ayah who worshipped her, and she had gradually learned that people who were rich had these things. That, however, was all she knew about it.

During her short life only one thing had troubled her, and that thing was "the place" she was to be taken to some day. The climate of India was very bad for children, and as soon as possible they were sent away from it—generally to England and to school. She had seen other children go away, and had heard their fathers and mothers talk about the letters they received from them. She had known that she would be obliged to go also, and though sometimes her father's stories of the voyage and the new country had attracted her, she had been troubled by the thought that he could not stay with her.

"Couldn't you go to that place with me, papa?" she had asked when she was five years old. "Couldn't you go to school, too? I would help you with your lessons."

"But you will not have to stay for a very long time, little Sara," he had always said. "You will go to a nice house where there will be a lot of little girls, and you will play together, and I will send you plenty of books, and you will grow so fast that it will seem scarcely a year before you are big enough and clever enough to come back and take care of papa."

She had liked to think of that. To keep the house for her father; to ride with him, and sit at the head of his table when he had dinner-parties; to talk to him and read his books—that would be what she would like most in the world, and if one must go away to "the place" in England to attain it, she must make up her mind to go. She did not care very much for other little girls, but if she had plenty of books she could console herself. She liked books more than anything else, and was, in fact, always inventing stories of beautiful things and telling them to herself. Sometimes she had told them to her father, and he had liked them as much as she did.

"Well, papa," she said softly, "if we are here I suppose we must be resigned."

He laughed at her old-fashioned speech and kissed her. He was really not at all resigned himself, though he knew he must keep that a secret. His quaint little Sara had been a great companion to him, and he felt he should be a lonely fellow when, on his return to India, he went into his bungalow knowing he need not expect to see the small figure in its white smock come forward to meet him. So he held her very closely in his arm as the cab rolled into the big, dull square in which stood the house which was their destination.

It was a big, dull, brick house, exactly like all the others in its row, but that on the front door there shone a brass plate on which was engraved in black letters:

MISS MINCHIN,
Select Seminary for Young Ladies.

"Here we are, Sara," said Captain Crewe, making his voice sound as cheerful as possible. Then he lifted her out of the cab and they mounted the steps and rang the bell. Sara often thought afterward that the house was somehow exactly like Miss Minchin. It was respectable and well furnished, but everything in it was ugly; and the very arm-chairs seemed to have hard bones in them. In the hall everything was hard and polished—even the red cheeks of the moon face on the tall clock in the corner had a severe varnished look. The drawing-room into which they were ushered was covered by a carpet with a square pattern upon it, the chairs were square, and a heavy marble timepiece stood upon the heavy marble mantel.

As she sat down in one of the stiff mahogany chairs, Sara cast one of her quick looks about her.

"I don't like it, papa," she said. "But then I dare say soldiers— even brave ones—don't really *like* going into battle."

Captain Crewe laughed outright at this. He was young and full of fun, and he never tired of hearing Sara's queer speeches.

"Oh, little Sara," he said. "What shall I do when I have no one to say solemn things to me? No one else is quite as solemn as you are."

"But why do solemn things make you laugh so?" inquired Sara.

"Because you are such fun when you say them," he answered, laughing still more. And then suddenly he swept her into his arms and kissed her very hard, stopping laughing all at once and looking almost as if tears had come into his eyes.

It was just then that Miss Minchin entered the room. She was very like her house, Sara felt: tall and dull, and respectable and ugly. She had large, cold, fishy eyes, and a large, cold, fishy smile. It spread itself into a very large smile when she saw Sara and Captain Crewe. She had heard a great many desirable things of the young soldier from the lady who had recommended her school to him. Among other things, she had heard that he was a rich father who was willing to spend a great deal of money on his little daughter.

"It will be a great privilege to have charge of such a beautiful and promising child, Captain Crewe," she said, taking Sara's hand and stroking it. "Lady Meredith has told me of her unusual cleverness. A clever child is a great treasure in an establishment like mine."

Sara stood quietly, with her eyes fixed upon Miss Minchin's face. She was thinking something odd, as usual.

"Why does she say I am a beautiful child," she was thinking. "I am not beautiful at all. Colonel Grange's little girl, Isobel, is beautiful. She has dimples and rose-colored cheeks, and long hair the color of gold. I have short black hair and green eyes; besides which, I am a thin child and not fair in the least. I am one of the ugliest children I ever saw. She is beginning by telling a story."

She was mistaken, however, in thinking she was an ugly child. She was not in the least like Isobel Grange, who had been the beauty of the regiment, but she had an odd charm of her own. She was a slim, supple creature, rather tall for her age, and had an intense, attractive little face. Her hair was heavy and quite black and only curled at the tips; her eyes were greenish gray, it is true, but they were big, wonderful eyes with long, black lashes, and though she herself did not like the color of them, many other people did. Still she was very firm in her belief that she was an ugly little girl, and she was not at all elated by Miss Minchin's flattery.

"I should be telling a story if I said she was beautiful," she thought; "and I should know I was telling a story. I believe I am as ugly as she is—in my way. What did she say that for?"

After she had known Miss Minchin longer she learned why she had said it. She discovered that she said the same thing to each papa and mamma who brought a child to her school.

Sara stood near her father and listened while he and Miss Minchin talked. She had been brought to the seminary because Lady Meredith's two little girls had been educated there, and Captain Crewe had a great respect for Lady Meredith's experience. Sara was to be what was known as "a parlor-boarder," and she was to enjoy even greater privileges than parlor-boarders usually did. She was to have a pretty bedroom and sitting-room of her own; she was to have a pony and a carriage, and a maid to take the place of the ayah who had been her nurse in India.

"I am not in the least anxious about her education," Captain Crewe said, with his gay laugh, as he held Sara's hand and patted it. "The difficulty will be to keep her from learning too fast and too much. She is always sitting with her little nose burrowing into books. She doesn't read them, Miss Minchin: she gobbles them up as if she were a little wolf instead of a little girl. She is always starving for new books to gobble, and she wants grown-up books—great, big, fat ones—French and German as well as English—history and biography and poets, and all sorts of things. Drag her away from her books when she reads too much. Make her ride her pony in the Row or go out and buy a new doll. She ought to play more with dolls."

"Papa," said Sara. "You see, if I went out and bought a new doll every few days I should have more than I could be fond of. Dolls ought to be intimate friends. Emily is going to be my intimate friend."

Captain Crewe looked at Miss Minchin and Miss Minchin looked at Captain Crewe.

"Who is Emily?" she inquired.

"Tell her, Sara," Captain Crewe said, smiling.

Sara's green-gray eyes looked very solemn and quite soft as she answered.

"She is a doll I haven't got yet," she said. "She is a doll papa is going to buy for me. We are going out together to find her. I have called her Emily. She is going to be my friend when papa is gone. I want her to talk to about him."

Miss Minchin's large, fishy smile became very flattering indeed.

"What an original child!" she said. "What a darling little creature!"

"Yes," said Captain Crewe, drawing Sara close. "She is a darling little creature. Take great care of her for me, Miss Minchin."

Sara stayed with her father at his hotel for several days; in fact, she remained with him until he sailed away to India. They went out and visited many big shops together, and bought a great many things. They bought, indeed, a great many more things than Sara needed; but Captain Crewe was a rash, innocent young man and wanted his little girl to have everything she admired and everything he admired himself, so between them they collected a wardrobe much too grand for a child of seven. There were velvet dresses trimmed with costly furs, and lace dresses, and embroidered ones, and hats with great, soft ostrich feathers, and ermine coats and muffs, and boxes of tiny gloves and handkerchiefs and silk stockings in such abundant supplies that the polite young women behind the counters whispered to each other that the odd little girl with the big, solemn eyes must be at least some foreign princess—perhaps the little daughter of an Indian rajah.

And at last they found Emily, but they went to a number of toy-shops and looked at a great many dolls before they finally discovered her.

"I want her to look as if she wasn't a doll really," Sara said. "I want her to look as if she *listens* when I talk to her. The trouble with dolls, papa"—and she put her head on one side and reflected as she said it—"the trouble with dolls is that they never seem to *hear*." So they looked at big ones and little ones—at dolls with black eyes and dolls with blue—at dolls with brown curls and dolls with golden braids, dolls dressed and dolls undressed.

"You see," Sara said when they were examining one who had no clothes. "If, when I find her, she has no frocks, we can take her to a dressmaker and have her things made to fit. They will fit better if they are tried on."

After a number of disappointments they decided to walk and look in at the shop windows and let the cab follow them. They had passed two or three places without even going in, when, as they were approaching a shop which was really not a very large one, Sara suddenly started and clutched her father's arm.

"Oh, papa!" she cried. "There is Emily!"

A flush had risen to her face and there was an expression in her green-gray eyes as if she had just recognized some one she was intimate with and fond of.

"She is actually waiting for us!" she said. "Let us go in to her."

"Dear me!" said Captain Crewe; "I feel as if we ought to have some one to introduce us."

"You must introduce me and I will introduce you," said Sara. "But I knew her the minute I saw her—so perhaps she knew me, too."

Perhaps she had known her. She had certainly a very intelligent expression in her eyes when Sara took her in her arms. She was a large doll, but not too large to carry about easily; she had naturally curling golden-brown hair, which hung like a mantle about her, and her eyes were a deep, clear, gray blue, with soft, thick eyelashes which were real eyelashes and not mere painted lines.

"Of course," said Sara, looking into her face as she held her on her knee—"of course, papa, this is Emily."

So Emily was bought and actually taken to a children's outfitter's shop, and measured for a wardrobe as grand as Sara's own. She had lace frocks, too, and velvet and muslin ones, and hats and coats and beautiful lace-trimmed underclothes, and gloves and handkerchiefs and furs.

"I should like her always to look as if she were a child with a good mother," said Sara. "I'm her mother, though I am going to make a companion of her."

Captain Crewe would really have enjoyed the shopping tremendously, but that a sad thought kept tugging at his heart. This all meant that he was going to be separated from his beloved, quaint little comrade.

He got out of his bed in the middle of the night and stood looking down at Sara, who lay asleep with Emily in her arms. Her black hair was spread out on the pillow and Emily's golden-brown hair mingled with it, both of them had lace-ruffled night-gowns, and both had long eyelashes which lay and curled up on their cheeks. Emily looked so like a real child that Captain Crewe felt glad she was there. He drew a big sigh and pulled his mustache with a boyish expression.

"Heigh-ho, little Sara!" he said to himself. "I don't believe you know how much your daddy will miss you."

The next day he took her to Miss Minchin's and left her there. He was to sail away the next morning. He explained to Miss Minchin that his solicitors, Messrs. Barrow & Skipworth, had charge of his affairs in England and would give her any advice she wanted, and that they would pay the bills she sent in for Sara's expenses. He would write to Sara twice a week, and she was to be given every pleasure she asked for.

"She is a sensible little thing, and she never wants anything it isn't safe to give her," he said.

Then he went with Sara into her little sitting-room and they bade each other good-by. Sara sat on his knee and held the lapels of his coat in her small hands, and looked long and hard at his face.

"Are you learning me by heart, little Sara," he said, stroking her hair.

"No," she answered. "I know you by heart. You are inside my heart." And they put their arms around each other and kissed as if they would never let each other go.

When the cab drove away from the door, Sara was sitting on the floor of her sitting-room, with her hands under her chin and her eyes following it until it had turned the corner of the square. Emily was sitting by her, and she looked after it, too. When Miss Minchin sent her sister, Miss Amelia, to see what the child was doing, she found she could not open the door.

"I have locked it," said a queer, polite little voice from inside. "I want to be quite by myself, if you please."

Miss Amelia was fat and dumpy, and stood very much in awe of her sister. She was really the better-natured person of the two, but she never disobeyed Miss Minchin. She went down-stairs again, looking almost alarmed.

"I never saw such a funny, old-fashioned child, sister," she said. "She has locked herself in, and she is not making the least particle of noise."

"It is much better than if she kicked and screamed, as some of them do," Miss Minchin answered. "I expected that a child as much spoiled as she is would set the whole house in an uproar. If ever a child was given her own way in everything, she is."

"I've been opening her trunks and putting her things away," said Miss Amelia. "I never saw anything like them—sable and ermine on her coats, and real Valenciennes lace on her under-clothing. You have seen some of her clothes. What *do* you think of them?"

"I think they are perfectly ridiculous," replied Miss Minchin, sharply; "but they will look very well at the head of the line when we take the school-children to church on Sunday. She has been provided for as if she were a little princess."

And up-stairs in the locked room Sara and Emily sat on the floor and stared at the corner round which the cab had disappeared, while Captain Crewe looked backward, waving and kissing his hand as if he could not bear to stop.

CHAPTER 2
A FRENCH LESSON

When Sara entered the school-room the next day, everybody looks at her with wide, interested eyes. By that time every pupil—from Lavinia Herbert, who was nearly thirteen and felt quite grown up, to Lottie Legh, who was only just four and the baby of the school—had heard a great deal about her. They knew very certainly that she was Miss Minchin's show pupil and was considered a credit to the establishment. One or two of them had even caught a glimpse of her French maid, Mariette, who had arrived the evening before. Lavinia had managed to pass Sara's room when the door was open, and had seen Mariette opening a box which had arrived late from some shop.

"It was full of petticoats with lace frills on them—frills and frills," she whispered to her friend Jessie as she bent over her geography. "I saw her shaking them out. I heard Miss Minchin say to Miss Amelia that her clothes were so grand that they were ridiculous for a child. My mamma says that children should be dressed simply. She has got one of those petticoats on now. I saw it when she sat down."

"She has silk stockings on!" whispered Jessie, bending over her geography also. "And what little feet! I never saw such little feet."

"Oh," sniffed Lavinia, spitefully, "that is the way her slippers are made. My mamma says that even big feet can be made to look small if you have a clever shoemaker. I don't think she is pretty at all. Her eyes are such a queer color."

"She isn't pretty as other pretty people are," said Jessie, stealing a glance across the room; "but she makes you want to look at her again. She has tremendously long eyelashes, but her eyes are almost green."

Sara was sitting quietly in her seat, waiting to be told what to do. She had been placed near Miss Minchin's desk. She was not abashed at all by the many pairs of eyes watching her. She was interested and looked back quietly at the children who looked at her. She wondered what they were thinking of, and if they liked Miss Minchin, and if they cared for their lessons, and if any of them had a papa at all like her own. She had had a long talk with Emily about her papa that morning.

"He is on the sea now, Emily," she had said. "We must be very great friends to each other and tell each other things. Emily, look at me. You have the nicest eyes I ever saw,—but I wish you could speak."

She was a child full of imaginings and whimsical thoughts, and one of her fancies was that there would be a great deal of comfort in even pretending that Emily was alive and really heard and understood. After Mariette had dressed her in her dark-blue school-room frock and tied her hair with a dark-blue ribbon, she went to Emily, who sat in a chair of her own, and gave her a book.

"You can read that while I am down-stairs," she said; and, seeing Mariette looking at her curiously, she spoke to her with a serious little face.

"What I believe about dolls," she said, "is that they can do things they will not let us know about. Perhaps, really, Emily can read and talk and walk, but she will only do it when people are out of the room. That is her secret. You see, if people knew that dolls could do things, they would make them work. So, perhaps, they have promised each other to keep it a secret. If you stay in the room, Emily will just sit there and stare; but if you go out, she will begin to read, perhaps, or go and look out of the window. Then if she heard either of us coming, she would just run back and jump into her chair and pretend she had been there all the time."

"*Comme elle est drôle!*" Mariette said to herself, and when she went down-stairs she told the head housemaid about it. But she had already begun to like this odd little girl who had such an intelligent small face and such perfect manners. She had taken care of children before who were not so polite. Sara was a very fine little person, and had a gentle, appreciative way of saying, "If you please, Mariette," "Thank you, Mariette," which was very charming. Mariette told the head housemaid that she thanked her as if she was thanking a lady.

"Elle a l'air d'une princesse, cette petite," she said. Indeed, she was very much pleased with her new little mistress and liked her place greatly.

After Sara had sat in her seat in the school-room for a few minutes, being looked at by the pupils, Miss Minchin rapped in a dignified manner upon her desk.

"Young ladies," she said, "I wish to introduce you to your new companion." All the little girls rose in their places, and Sara rose also. "I shall expect you all to be very agreeable to Miss Crewe; she has just come to us from a great distance—in fact, from India. As soon as lessons are over you must make each other's acquaintance."

The pupils bowed ceremoniously, and Sara made a little courtesy, and then they sat down and looked at each other again.

"Sara," said Miss Minchin in her school-room manner, "come here to me."

She had taken a book from the desk and was turning over its leaves. Sara went to her politely.

"As your papa has engaged a French maid for you," she began, "I conclude that he wishes you to make a special study of the French language."

Sara felt a little awkward.

"I think he engaged her," she said, "because he—he thought I would like her, Miss Minchin."

"I am afraid," said Miss Minchin, with a slightly sour smile, "that you have been a very spoiled little girl and always imagine that things are done because you like them. My impression is that your papa wished you to learn French."

If Sara had been older or less punctilious about being quite polite to people, she could have explained herself in a very few words. But, as it was, she felt a flush rising on her cheeks. Miss Minchin was a very severe and imposing person, and she seemed so absolutely sure that Sara knew nothing whatever of French that she felt as if it would be almost rude to correct her. The truth was that Sara could not remember the time when she had not seemed to know French. Her father had often spoken it to her when she had been a baby. Her mother had been a French-woman, and Captain Crewe had loved her language, so it happened that Sara had always heard and been familiar with it.

"I—I have never really learned French, but—but—" she began, trying shyly to make herself clear.

One of Miss Minchin's chief secret annoyances was that she did not speak French herself, and was desirous of concealing the irritating fact. She, therefore, had no intention of discussing the matter and laying herself open to innocent questioning by a new pupil.

"That is enough," she said with polite tartness. "If you have not learned, you must begin at once. The French master, Monsieur Dufarge, will be here in a few minutes. Take this book and look at it until he arrives."

Sara's cheeks felt warm. She went back to her seat and opened the book. She looked at the first page with a grave face. She knew it would be rude to smile, and she was very determined not to be rude. But it was very odd to find herself expected to study a page which told her that "*le père*" meant "the father," and "*la mère*" meant "the mother."

Miss Minchin glanced toward her scrutinizingly.

"You look rather cross, Sara," she said. "I am sorry you do not like the idea of learning French."

"I am very fond of it," answered Sara, thinking she would try again; "but—"

"You must not say 'but' when you are told to do things," said Miss Minchin. "Look at your book again."

And Sara did so, and did not smile, even when she found that "*le fils*" meant "the son," and "*le frère*" meant "the brother."

"When Monsieur Dufarge comes," she thought, "I can make him understand."

Monsieur Dufarge arrived very shortly afterward. He was a very nice, intelligent, middle-aged Frenchman, and he looked interested when his eyes fell upon Sara trying politely to seem absorbed in her little book of phrases.

"Is this a new pupil for me, madame?" he said to Miss Minchin. "I hope that is my good fortune."

"Her papa—Captain Crewe—is very anxious that she should begin the language. But I am afraid she has a childish prejudice against it. She does not seem to wish to learn," said Miss Minchin.

"I am sorry of that, Mademoiselle," he said kindly to Sara. "Perhaps, when we begin to study together, I may show you that it is a charming tongue."

Little Sara rose in her seat. She was beginning to feel rather desperate, as if she were almost in disgrace. She looked up into Monsieur Dufarge's face with her big, green-gray eyes, and they were quite innocently appealing. She knew that he would understand as soon as she spoke. She began to explain quite simply in pretty and fluent French. Madame had not understood. She had not learned French exactly,—not out of books,—but her papa and other people had always spoken it to her, and she had read it and written it as she had read and written English. Her papa loved it, and she loved it because he did. Her dear mamma, who had died when she was born, had been French. She would be glad to learn anything monsieur would teach her, but what she had tried to explain to madame was that she already knew the words in this book—and she held out the little book of phrases.

When she began to speak Miss Minchin started quite violently and sat staring at her over her eye-glasses, almost indignantly, until she had finished. Monsieur Dufarge began to smile, and his smile was one of great pleasure. To hear this pretty childish voice speaking his own language so simply and charmingly made him feel almost as if he were in his native land—which in dark, foggy days in London sometimes seemed worlds away. When she had finished, he took the phrase-book from her, with a look almost affectionate. But he spoke to Miss Minchin.

"Ah, madame," he said, "there is not much I can teach her. She has not *learned* French; she *is* French. Her accent is exquisite."

"You ought to have told me," exclaimed Miss Minchin, much mortified, turning on Sara.

"I—I tried," said Sara. "I—I suppose I did not begin right."

Miss Minchin knew she had tried, and that it had not been her fault that she was not allowed to explain. And when she saw that the pupils had been listening and that Lavinia and Jessie were giggling behind their French grammars, she felt infuriated.

"Silence, young ladies!" she said severely, rapping upon the desk. "Silence at once!"

And she began from that minute to feel rather a grudge against her show pupil.

CHAPTER 3
ERMENGARDE

On that first morning, when Sara sat at Miss Minchin's side, aware that the whole school-room was devoting itself to observing her, she had noticed very soon one little girl, about her own age, who looked at her very hard with a pair of light, rather dull, blue eyes. She was a fat child who did not look as if she were in the least clever, but she had a good-naturedly pouting mouth. Her flaxen hair was braided in a tight pigtail, tied with a ribbon, and she had pulled this pigtail round her neck, and was biting the end of the ribbon, resting her elbows on the desk, as she stared wonderingly at the new pupil. When Monsieur Dufarge began to speak to Sara, she looked a little frightened; and when Sara stepped forward and, looking at him with the innocent, appealing eyes, answered him, without any warning, in French, the fat little girl gave a startled jump, and grew quite red in her awed amazement. Having wept hopeless tears for weeks in her efforts to remember that *"la mère"* meant "the mother," and *"le père,"* "the father,"—when one spoke sensible English,—it was almost too much for her to suddenly find herself listening to a child her own age who seemed not only quite familiar with these words, but apparently knew any number of others, and could mix them up with verbs as if they were mere trifles.

She stared so hard and bit the ribbon on her pigtail so fast that she attracted the attention of Miss Minchin, who, feeling extremely cross at the moment, immediately pounced upon her.

"Miss St. John!" she exclaimed severely. "What do you mean by such conduct? Remove your elbows! Take your ribbon out of your mouth! Sit up at once!"

Upon which Miss St. John gave another jump, and when Lavinia and Jessie tittered she became redder than ever—so red, indeed, that she almost looked as if tears were coming into her poor, dull, childish eyes; and Sara saw her and was so sorry for her that she began to rather like her and want to be her friend. It was a way of hers always to want to spring into any fray in which some one was made uncomfortable or unhappy.

"If Sara had been a boy and lived a few centuries ago," her father used to say, "she would have gone about the country with her sword drawn, rescuing and defending every one in distress. She always wants to fight when she sees people in trouble."

So she took rather a fancy to fat, slow, little Miss St. John, and kept glancing toward her through the morning. She saw that lessons were no easy matter to her, and that there was no danger of her ever being spoiled by being treated as a show pupil. Her French lesson was a pathetic thing. Her pronunciation made even Monsieur Dufarge smile in spite of himself, and Lavinia and Jessie and the more fortunate girls either giggled or looked at her in wondering disdain. But Sara did not laugh. She tried to look as if she did not hear when Miss St. John called *"le bon pain," "lee bong pang."* She had a fine, hot little temper of her own, and it made her feel rather savage when she heard the titters and saw the poor, stupid, distressed child's face.

"It isn't funny, really," she said between her teeth, as she bent over her book. "They ought not to laugh."

When lessons were over and the pupils gathered together in groups to talk, Sara looked for Miss St. John, and finding her bundled rather disconsolately in a window-seat, she walked over to her and spoke. She only said the kind of thing little girls always say to each other by way of beginning an acquaintance, but there was something nice and friendly about Sara, and people always felt it.

"What is your name?" she said.

To explain Miss St. John's amazement one must recall that a new pupil is, for a short time, a somewhat uncertain thing; and of this new pupil the entire school had talked the night before until it fell asleep quite exhausted by excitement and contradictory stories. A new pupil with a carriage and a pony and a maid, and a voyage from India to discuss, was not an ordinary acquaintance.

"My name's Ermengarde St. John," she answered.

"Mine is Sara Crewe," said Sara. "Yours is very pretty. It sounds like a story-book."

"Do you like it?" fluttered Ermengarde. "I—I like yours."

Miss St. John's chief trouble in life was that she had a clever father. Sometimes this seemed to her a dreadful calamity. If you have a father who knows everything, who speaks seven or eight languages, and has thousands of volumes which he has apparently learned by heart, he frequently expects you to be familiar with the contents of your lesson-books at least; and it is not improbable that he will feel you ought to be able to remember a few incidents of history and to write a French exercise. Ermengarde was a severe trial to Mr. St. John. He could not understand how a child of his could be a notably and unmistakably dull creature who never shone in anything.

"Good heavens!" he had said more than once, as he stared at her, "there are times when I think she is as stupid as her Aunt Eliza!"

If her Aunt Eliza had been slow to learn and quick to forget a thing entirely when she had learned it, Ermengarde was strikingly like her. She was the monumental dunce of the school, and it could not be denied.

"She must be *made* to learn," her father said to Miss Minchin.

Consequently Ermengarde spent the greater part of her life in disgrace or in tears. She learned things and forgot them; or, if she remembered them, she did not understand them. So it was natural that, having made Sara's acquaintance, she should sit and stare at her with profound admiration.

"You can speak French, can't you?" she said respectfully.

Sara got on to the window-seat, which was a big, deep one, and, tucking up her feet, sat with her hands clasped round her knees.

"I can speak it because I have heard it all my life," she answered. "You could speak it if you had always heard it."

"Oh, no, I couldn't," said Ermengarde. "I *never* could speak it!"

"Why?" inquired Sara, curiously.

Ermengarde shook her head so that the pigtail wabbled.

"You heard me just now," she said. "I'm always like that. I can't *say* the words. They're so queer."

She paused a moment, and then added with a touch of awe in her voice:

"You are *clever*, aren't you?"

Sara looked out of the window into the dingy square, where the sparrows were hopping and twittering on the wet, iron railings and the sooty branches of the trees. She reflected a few moments. She had heard it said very often that she was "clever," and she wondered if she was,—and *if* she was, how it had happened.

"I don't know," she said. "I can't tell." Then, seeing a mournful look on the round, chubby face, she gave a little laugh and changed the subject.

"Would you like to see Emily?" she inquired.

"Who is Emily?" Ermengarde asked, just as Miss Minchin had done.

"Come up to my room and see," said Sara, holding out her hand.

They jumped down from the window-seat together, and went up-stairs.

"Is it true," Ermengarde whispered, as they went through the hall—"is it true that you have a play-room all to yourself?"

"Yes," Sara answered. "Papa asked Miss Minchin to let me have one, because—well, it was because when I play I make up stories and tell them to myself, and I don't like people to hear me. It spoils it if I think people listen."

They had reached the passage leading to Sara's room by this time, and Ermengarde stopped short, staring, and quite losing her breath.

"You *make up* stories!" she gasped. "Can you do that—as well as speak French? *Can* you?"

Sara looked at her in simple surprise.

"Why, any one can make up things," she said. "Have you never tried?"

She put her hand warningly on Ermengarde's.

"Let us go very quietly to the door," she whispered, "and then I will open it quite suddenly; perhaps we may catch her."

She was half laughing, but there was a touch of mysterious hope in her eyes which fascinated Ermengarde, though she had not the remotest idea what it meant, or whom it was she wanted to "catch," or why she wanted to catch her. Whatsoever she meant, Ermengarde was sure it was something delightfully exciting. So, quite thrilled with expectation, she followed her on tiptoe along the passage. They made not the least noise until they reached the door. Then Sara suddenly turned the handle, and threw it wide open. Its opening revealed the room quite neat and quiet, a fire gently burning in the grate, and a wonderful doll sitting in a chair by it, apparently reading a book.

"Oh, she got back to her seat before we could see her!" Sara exclaimed. "Of course they always do. They are as quick as lightning."

Ermengarde looked from her to the doll and back again.

"Can she—walk?" she asked breathlessly.

"Yes," answered Sara. "At least I believe she can. At least I *pretend* I believe she can. And that makes it seem as if it were true. Have you never pretended things?"

"No," said Ermengarde. "Never. I—tell me about it."

She was so bewitched by this odd, new companion that she actually stared at Sara instead of at Emily—notwithstanding that Emily was the most attractive doll person she had ever seen.

"Let us sit down," said Sara, "and I will tell you. It's so easy that when you begin you can't stop. You just go on and on doing it always. And it's beautiful. Emily, you must listen. This is Ermengarde St. John, Emily. Ermengarde, this is Emily. Would you like to hold her?"

"Oh, may I?" said Ermengarde. "May I, really? She *is* beauti-ful!" And Emily was put into her arms.

Never in her dull, short life had Miss St. John dreamed of such an hour as the one she spent with the queer new pupil before they heard the lunch-bell ring and were obliged to go down-stairs.

Sara sat upon the hearth-rug and told her strange things. She sat rather huddled up, and her green eyes shone and her cheeks flushed. She told stories of the voyage, and stories of India; but what fascinated Ermengarde the most was her fancy about the dolls who walked and talked, and who could do anything they chose when the human beings were out of the room, but who must keep their powers a secret and so flew back to their places "like lightning" when people returned to the room.

"*We* couldn't do it," said Sara, seriously. "You see, it's a kind of magic."

Once, when she was relating the story of the search for Emily, Ermengarde saw her face suddenly change. A cloud seemed to pass over it and put out the light in her shining eyes. She drew her breath in so sharply that it made a funny, sad little sound, and then she shut her lips and held them tightly closed, as if she were determined either to do or *not* to do something. Ermengarde had an idea that if she had been like any other little girl, she might have suddenly burst out sobbing and crying. But she did not.

"Have you a—a pain?" Ermengarde ventured.

"Yes," Sara answered, after a moment's silence. "But it is not in my body." Then she added something in a low voice which she tried to keep quite steady, and it was this: "Do you love your father more than anything else in all the whole world?"

Ermengarde's mouth fell open a little. She knew that it would be far from behaving like a respectable child at a select seminary to say that it had never occurred to you that you *could* love your father, that you would do anything desperate to avoid being left alone in his society for ten minutes. She was, indeed, greatly embarrassed.

"I—I scarcely ever see him," she stammered. "He is always in the library—reading things."

"I love mine more than all the world ten times over," Sara said. "That is what my pain is. He has gone away."

She put her head quietly down on her little, huddled-up knees, and sat very still for a few minutes.

"She's going to cry out loud," thought Ermengarde, fearfully.

But she did not. Her short, black locks tumbled about her ears, and she sat still. Then she spoke without lifting her head.

"I promised him I would bear it," she said. "And I will. You have to bear things. Think what soldiers bear! Papa is a soldier. If there was a war he would have to bear marching and thirstiness and, perhaps, deep wounds. And he would never say a word—not one word."

Ermengarde could only gaze at her, but she felt that she was beginning to adore her. She was so wonderful and different from any one else.

Presently, she lifted her face and shook back her black locks, with a queer little smile.

"If I go on talking and talking," she said, "and telling you things about pretending, I shall bear it better. You don't forget, but you bear it better."

Ermengarde did not know why a lump came into her throat and her eyes felt as if tears were in them.

"Lavinia and Jessie are 'best friends.'" she said rather huskily. "I wish we could be 'best friends.' Would you have me for yours? You're clever, and I'm the stupidest child in the school, but I—oh, I do so like you!"

"I'm glad of that," said Sara. "It makes you thankful when you are liked. Yes. We will be friends. And I'll tell you what"—a sudden gleam lighting her face—"I can help you with your French lessons."

CHAPTER 4
LOTTIE

If Sara had been a different kind of child, the life she led at Miss Minchin's Select Seminary for the next ten years would not have been at all good for her. She was treated more as if she were a distinguished guest at the establishment than as if she were a mere little girl. If she had been a self-opinionated, domineering child, she might have become disagreeable enough to be unbearable through being so much indulged and flattered. If she had been an indolent child, she would have learned nothing. Privately Miss Minchin disliked her, but she was far too worldly a woman to do or say anything which might make such a desirable pupil wish to leave her school. She knew quite well that if Sara wrote to her papa to tell him that she was uncomfortable or unhappy, Captain Crewe would remove her at once. Miss Minchin's opinion was that if a child were continually praised and never forbidden to do what she liked, she would be sure to be fond of the place where she was so treated. Accordingly, Sara was praised for her quickness at her lessons, for her good manners, for her amiability to her fellow-pupils, for her generosity if she gave a sixpence to a beggar out of her full little purse; the simplest thing she did was treated as if it were a virtue, and if she had not had a disposition and a clever little brain, she might have been a very self-satisfied young person. But the clever little brain told her a great many sensible and true things about herself and her circumstances, and now and then she talked these things over to Ermengarde as time went on.

"Things happen to people by accident," she used to say. "A lot of nice accidents have happened to me. It just *happened* that I always liked lessons and books, and could remember things when I learned them. It just happened that I was born with a father who was beautiful and nice and clever, and could give me everything I liked. Perhaps I have not really a good temper at all, but if you have everything you want and every one is kind to you, how can you help but be good-tempered? I don't know"—looking quite serious—"how I shall ever find out whether I am really a nice child or a horrid one. Perhaps I'm a *hideous* child, and no one will ever know, just because I never have any trials."

"Lavinia has no trials," said Ermengarde, stolidly, "and she is horrid enough."

Sara rubbed the end of her little nose reflectively, as she thought the matter over.

"Well," she said at last, "perhaps—perhaps that is because Lavinia is *growing.*"

This was the result of a charitable recollection of having heard Miss Amelia say that Lavinia was growing so fast that she believed it affected her health and temper.

Lavinia, in fact, was spiteful. She was inordinately jealous of Sara. Until the new pupil's arrival, she had felt herself the leader in the school. She had led because she was capable of making herself extremely disagreeable if the others did not follow her. She domineered over the little children, and assumed grand airs with those big enough to be her companions. She was rather pretty, and had been the best-dressed pupil in the procession when the Select Seminary walked out two by two, until Sara's velvet coats and sable muffs appeared, combined with drooping ostrich feathers, and were led by Miss Minchin at the head of the line. This, at the beginning, had been bitter enough; but as time went on it became apparent that Sara was a leader, too, and not because she could make herself disagreeable, but because she never did.

"There's one thing about Sara Crewe," Jessie had enraged her "best friend" by saying honestly,—"she's never 'grand' about herself the least bit, and you know she might be, Lavvie. I believe I couldn't help being—just a little—if I had so many fine things and was made such a fuss over. It's disgusting, the way Miss Minchin shows her off when parents come."

"'Dear Sara must come into the drawing-room and talk to Mrs. Musgrave about India,'" mimicked Lavinia, in her most highly flavored imitation of Miss Minchin. "'Dear Sara must speak French to Lady Pitkin. Her accent is so perfect.' She didn't learn her French at the Seminary, at any rate. And there's nothing so clever in her knowing it. She says herself she didn't learn it at all. She just picked it up, because she always heard her papa speak it. And, as to her papa, there is nothing so grand in being an Indian officer."

"Well," said Jessie, slowly, "he's killed tigers. He killed the one in the skin Sara has in her room. That's why she likes it so. She lies on it and strokes its head, and talks to it as if it was a cat."

"She's always doing something silly," snapped Lavinia. "My mamma says that way of hers of pretending things is silly. She says she will grow up eccentric."

It was quite true that Sara was never "grand." She was a friendly little soul, and shared her privileges and belongings with a free hand. The little ones, who were accustomed to being disdained and ordered out of the way by mature ladies aged ten and twelve, were never made to cry by this most envied of them all. She was a motherly young person, and when people fell down and scraped their knees, she ran and helped them up and patted them, or found in her pocket a bonbon or some other article of a soothing nature. She never pushed them out of her way or alluded to their years as a humiliation and a blot upon their small characters.

"If you are four you are four," she said severely to Lavinia on an occasion of her having—it must be confessed—slapped Lottie and called her "a brat"; "but you will be five next year, and six the year after that. And," opening large, convicting eyes, "it only takes sixteen years to make you twenty."

"Dear me!" said Lavinia; "how we can calculate!" In fact, it was not to be denied that sixteen and four made twenty,—and twenty was an age the most daring were scarcely bold enough to dream of.

So the younger children adored Sara. More than once she had been known to have a tea-party, made up of these despised ones, in her own room. And Emily had been played with, and Emily's own tea-service used—the one with cups that held quite a lot of much-sweetened weak tea and had blue flowers on them. No one had seen such a very real doll's tea-set before. From that afternoon Sara was regarded as a goddess and a queen by the entire alphabet class.

Lottie Legh worshipped her to such an extent that if Sara had not been a motherly person, she would have found her tiresome. Lottie had been sent to school by a rather flighty young papa who could not imagine what else to do with her. Her young mother had died, and as the child had been treated like a favorite doll or a very spoiled pet monkey or lap-dog ever since the first hour of her life, she was a very appalling little creature. When she wanted anything or did not want anything she wept and howled; and, as she always wanted the things she could not have, and did not want the things that were best for her, her shrill little voice was usually to be heard uplifted in wails in one part of the house or another.

Her strongest weapon was that in some mysterious way she had found out that a very small girl who had lost her mother was a person who ought to be pitied and made much of. She had probably heard some grown-up people talking her over in the early days, after her mother's death. So it became her habit to make great use of this knowledge.

The first time Sara took her in charge was one morning when, on passing a sitting-room, she heard both Miss Minchin and Miss Amelia trying to suppress the angry wails of some child who, evidently, refused to be silenced. She refused so strenuously indeed that Miss Minchin was obliged to almost shout—in a stately and severe manner—to make herself heard.

"What *is* she crying for?" she almost yelled.

"Oh—oh—oh!" Sara heard; "I haven't got any mam—ma-a!"

"Oh, Lottie!" screamed Miss Amelia. "Do stop, darling! Don't cry! Please don't!"

"Oh! oh! oh!" Lottie howled tempestuously. "Haven't—got—any—mam—ma-a!"

"She ought to be whipped," Miss Minchin proclaimed. "You *shall* be whipped, you naughty child!"

Lottie wailed more loudly than ever. Miss Amelia began to cry. Miss Minchin's voice rose until it almost thundered, then suddenly she sprang up from her chair in impotent indignation and flounced out of the room, leaving Miss Amelia to arrange the matter.

Sara had paused in the hall, wondering if she ought to go into the room, because she had recently begun a friendly acquaintance with Lottie and might be able to quiet her. When Miss Minchin came out and saw her, she looked rather annoyed. She realized that her voice, as heard from inside the room, could not have sounded either dignified or amiable.

"Oh, Sara!" she exclaimed, endeavoring to produce a suitable smile.

"I stopped," explained Sara, "because I knew it was Lottie,—and I thought, perhaps—just perhaps, I could make her be quiet. May I try, Miss Minchin?"

"If you can. You are a clever child," answered Miss Minchin, drawing in her mouth sharply. Then, seeing that Sara looked slightly chilled by her asperity, she changed her manner. "But you are clever in everything," she said in her approving way. "I dare say you can manage her. Go in." And she left her.

When Sara entered the room, Lottie was lying upon the floor, screaming and kicking her small fat legs violently, and Miss Amelia was bending over her in consternation and despair, looking quite red and damp with heat. Lottie had always found, when in her own nursery at home, that kicking and screaming would always be quieted by any means she insisted on. Poor plump Miss Amelia was trying first one method, and then another.

"Poor darling!" she said one moment; "I know you haven't any mamma, poor—" Then in quite another tone: "If you don't stop,

Lottie, I will shake you. Poor little angel! There—there! You wicked, bad, detestable child, I will smack you! I will!"

Sara went to them quietly. She did not know at all what she was going to do, but she had a vague inward conviction that it would be better not to say such different kinds of things quite so helplessly and excitedly.

"Miss Amelia," she said in a low voice, "Miss Minchin says I may try to make her stop—may I?"

Miss Amelia turned and looked at her hopelessly. "Oh, *do* you think you can?" she gasped.

"I don't know whether I *can*," answered Sara, still in her half-whisper; "but I will try."

Miss Amelia stumbled up from her knees with a heavy sigh, and Lottie's fat little legs kicked as hard as ever.

"If you will steal out of the room," said Sara, "I will stay with her."

"Oh, Sara!" almost whimpered Miss Amelia. "We never had such a dreadful child before. I don't believe we *can* keep her."

But she crept out of the room, and was very much relieved to find an excuse for doing it.

Sara stood by the howling, furious child for a few moments, and looked down at her without saying anything. Then she sat down flat on the floor beside her and waited. Except for Lottie's angry screams, the room was quite quiet. This was a new state of affairs for little Miss Legh, who was accustomed, when she screamed, to hear other people protest and implore and command and coax by turns. To lie and kick and shriek, and find the only person near you not seeming to mind in the least, attracted her attention. She opened her tight-shut streaming eyes to see who this person was. And it was only another little girl. But it was the person who owned Emily and all the nice things. And she was looking at her steadily and as if she was merely thinking. Having paused for a few seconds to find this out, Lottie thought she must begin again, but the quiet of the room and of Sara's odd, interested face made her first howl rather half-hearted.

"I—haven't—any—ma—ma—ma-a!" she announced; but her voice was not so strong.

Sara looked at her still more steadily, but with a sort of understanding in her eyes.

"Neither have I," she said.

This was so unexpected that it was astounding. Lottie actually dropped her legs, gave a wriggle, and lay and stared. A new idea will stop a crying child when nothing else will. Also it was true that while Lottie disliked Miss Minchin, who was cross, and Miss Amelia, who was foolishly indulgent, she rather liked Sara, little as she knew her. She did not want to give up her grievance, but her thoughts were distracted from it, so she wriggled again, and, after a sulky sob, said:

"Where is she?"

Sara paused a moment. Because she had been told that her mamma was in heaven, she had thought a great deal about the matter, and her thoughts had not been quite like those of other people.

"She went to heaven," she said. "But I am sure she comes out sometimes to see me—though I don't see her. So does yours. Perhaps they can both see us now. Perhaps they are both in this room."

Lottie sat bolt upright, and looked about her. She was a pretty, little, curly-headed creature, and her round eyes were like wet forget-me-nots. If her mamma had seen her during the last half-hour, she might not have thought her the kind of child who ought to be related to an angel.

Sara went on talking. Perhaps some people might think that what she said was rather like a fairy story, but it was all so real to her own imagination that Lottie began to listen in spite of herself. She had been told that her mamma had wings and a crown, and she had been shown pictures of ladies in beautiful white night-gowns, who were said to be angels. But Sara seemed to be telling a real story about a lovely country where real people were.

"There are fields and fields of flowers," she said, forgetting herself, as usual, when she began, and talking rather as if she were in a dream—"fields and fields of lilies—and when the soft wind blows over them it wafts the scent of them into the air—and everybody always breathes it, because the soft wind is always blowing. And little children run about in the lily-fields and gather armsful of them, and laugh and make little wreaths. And the streets are shining. And no one is ever tired, however far they walk. They can float anywhere they like. And there are walls made of pearl and gold all round the city, but they are low enough for the people to go and lean on them, and look down on to the earth and smile, and send beautiful messages."

Whatsoever story she had begun to tell, Lottie would, no doubt, have stopped crying, and been fascinated into listening; but there was no denying that this story was prettier than most others. She dragged herself close to Sara, and drank in every word until the end came—far too soon.

When it did come, she was so sorry that she put up her lip ominously.

"I want to go there," she cried. "I—haven't any mamma in this school."

Sara saw the danger-signal, and came out of her dream. She took hold of the chubby hand and pulled her close to her side with a coaxing little laugh.

"I will be your mamma," she said. "We will play that you are my little girl. And Emily shall be your sister."

Lottie's dimples all began to show themselves.

"Shall she?" she said.

"Yes," answered Sara, jumping to her feet. "Let us go and tell her. And then I will wash your face and brush your hair."

To which Lottie agreed quite cheerfully, and trotted out of the room and up-stairs with her, without seeming even to remember that the whole of the last hour's tragedy had been caused by the fact that she had refused to be washed and brushed for lunch and Miss Minchin had been called in to use her majestic authority.

And from that time Sara was an adopted mother.

CHAPTER 5
BECKY

Of course the greatest power Sara possessed and the one which gained her even more followers than her luxuries and the fact that she was "the show pupil," the power that Lavinia and certain other girls were most envious of, and at the same time most fascinated by in spite of themselves, was her power of telling stories and of making everything she talked about seem like a story, whether it was one or not.

Any one who has been at school with a teller of stories knows what the wonder means—how he or she is followed about and besought in a whisper to relate romances; how groups gather round and hang on the outskirts of the favored party in the hope of being allowed to join it and listen. Sara not only could tell stories, but she adored telling them. When she sat or stood in the midst of a circle and began to invent wonderful things, her green eyes grew big and shining, her cheeks flushed, and, without knowing that she was doing it, she began to act and made what she told lovely or alarming by the raising or dropping of her voice, the bend and sway of her slim body, and the dramatic movement of her hands. She forgot that she was talking to listening children; she saw and lived with the fairy folk, or the kings and queens and beautiful ladies, whose adventures she was narrating. Sometimes when she had finished her story, she was quite out of breath with excitement, and would lay her hand on her thin, little, quick-rising chest, and half laugh as if at herself.

"When I am telling it," she would say, "it doesn't seem as if it was only made up. It seems more real than you are—more real than the school-room. I feel as if I were all the people in the story—one after the other. It *is* queer."

She had been at Miss Minchin's school about two years when, one foggy winter's afternoon, as she was getting out of her carriage, comfortably wrapped up in her warmest velvets and furs and looking very much grander than she knew, she caught sight, as she crossed the pavement, of a dingy little figure standing on the area steps, and stretching its neck so that its wide-open eyes might peer at her through the railings. Something in the eagerness and timidity of the smudgy face made her look at it, and when she looked she smiled because it was her way to smile at people.

But the owner of the smudgy face and the wide-open eyes evidently was afraid that she ought not to have been caught looking at pupils of importance. She dodged out of sight like a Jack-in-the-box and scurried back into the kitchen, disappearing so suddenly that if she had not been such a poor, little forlorn thing, Sara would have laughed in spite of herself. That very evening, as Sara was sitting in the midst of a group of listeners in a corner of the school-room telling one of her stories, the very same figure timidly entered the room, carrying a coal-box much too heavy for her, and knelt down upon the hearth-rug to replenish the fire and sweep up the ashes.

She was cleaner than she had been when she peeped through the area railings, but she looked just as frightened. She was evidently afraid to look at the children or seem to be listening. She put on pieces of coal cautiously with her fingers so that she might make no disturbing noise, and she swept about the fire-irons very softly. But Sara saw in two minutes that she was deeply interested in what was going on, and that she was doing her work slowly in the hope of catching a word here and there. And realizing this, she raised her voice and spoke more clearly.

"The Mermaids swam softly about in the crystal-green water, and dragged after them a fishing-net woven of deep-sea pearls," she said. "The Princess sat on the white rock and watched them."

It was a wonderful story about a princess who was loved by a Prince Merman, and went to live with him in shining caves under the sea.

The small drudge before the grate swept the hearth once and then swept it again. Having done it twice, she did it three times; and, as she was doing it the third time, the sound of the story so lured her to listen that she fell under the spell and actually forgot that she had no right to listen at all, and also forgot everything else. She sat down upon her heels as she knelt on the hearth-rug, and the brush hung idly in her fingers. The voice of the story-teller went on and drew her with it into winding grottos under the sea, glowing with soft, clear blue light, and paved with pure golden sands. Strange sea flowers and grasses waved about her, and far away faint singing and music echoed.

The hearth-brush fell from the work-roughened hand, and Lavinia Herbert looked round.

"That girl has been listening," she said.

The culprit snatched up her brush, and scrambled to her feet. She caught at the coal-box and simply scuttled out of the room like a frightened rabbit.

Sara felt rather hot-tempered.

"I knew she was listening," she said. "Why shouldn't she?"

Lavinia tossed her head with great elegance.

"Well," she remarked, "I do not know whether your mamma would like you to tell stories to servant girls, but I know *my* mamma wouldn't like *me* to do it."

"My mamma!" said Sara, looking odd. "I don't believe she would mind in the least. She knows that stories belong to everybody."

"I thought," retorted Lavinia, in severe recollection, "that your mamma was dead. How can she know things?"

"Do you think she *doesn't* know things?" said Sara, in her stern little voice. Sometimes she had a rather stern little voice.

"Sara's mamma knows everything," piped in Lottie. "So does my mamma—'cept Sara is my mamma at Miss Minchin's—my other one knows everything. The streets are shining, and there are fields and fields of lilies, and everybody gathers them. Sara tells me when she puts me to bed."

"You wicked thing," said Lavinia, turning on Sara; "making fairy stories about heaven."

"There are much more splendid stories in Revelation," returned Sara. "Just look and see! How do you know mine are fairy stories? But I can tell you"—with a fine bit of unheavenly temper—"you will never find out whether they are or not if you're not kinder to people than you are now. Come along, Lottie." And she marched out of the room, rather hoping that she might see the little servant again somewhere, but she found no trace of her when she got into the hall.

"Who is that little girl who makes the fires?" she asked Mariette that night.

Mariette broke forth into a flow of description.

Ah, indeed, Mademoiselle Sara might well ask. She was a forlorn little thing who had just taken the place of scullery-maid—though, as to being scullery-maid, she was everything else besides. She blacked boots and grates, and carried heavy coal-scuttles up and down stairs, and scrubbed floors and cleaned windows, and was ordered about by everybody. She was fourteen years old, but was so stunted in growth that she looked about twelve. In truth, Mariette was sorry for her. She was so timid that if one chanced to speak to her it appeared as if her poor, frightened eyes would jump out of her head.

"What is her name?" asked Sara, who had sat by the table, with her chin on her hands, as she listened absorbedly to the recital.

Her name was Becky. Mariette heard every one below-stairs calling, "Becky, do this," and "Becky, do that," every five minutes in the day.

Sara sat and looked into the fire, reflecting on Becky for some time after Mariette left her. She made up a story of which Becky was the ill-used heroine. She thought she looked as if she had never had quite enough to eat. Her very eyes were hungry. She hoped she should see her again, but though she caught sight of her carrying things up or down stairs on several occasions, she always seemed in such a hurry and so afraid of being seen that it was impossible to speak to her.

But a few weeks later, on another foggy afternoon, when she entered her sitting-room she found herself confronting a rather pathetic picture. In her own special and pet easy-chair before the bright fire, Becky—with a coal smudge on her nose and several on her apron, with her poor little cap hanging half off her head, and an empty coal-box on the floor near her—sat fast asleep, tired out beyond even the endurance of her hard-working young body. She had been sent up to put the bedrooms in order for the evening. There were a great many of them, and she had been running about all day. Sara's rooms she had saved until the last. They were not like the other rooms, which were plain and bare. Ordinary pupils were expected to be satisfied with mere necessaries. Sara's comfortable sitting-room seemed a bower of luxury to the scullery-maid, though it was, in fact, merely a nice, bright little room. But there were pictures and books in it, and curious things from India; there was a sofa and the low, soft chair; Emily sat in a chair of her own, with the air of a presiding goddess, and there was always a glowing fire and a polished grate. Becky saved it until the end of her afternoon's work, because it rested her to go into it, and she always hoped to snatch a few minutes to sit down in the soft chair and look about her, and think about the wonderful good fortune of the child who owned such surroundings and who went out on the cold days in beautiful hats and coats one tried to catch a glimpse of through the area railing.

On this afternoon, when she had sat down, the sensation of relief to her short, aching legs had been so wonderful and delightful that it had seemed to soothe her whole body, and the glow of warmth and comfort from the fire had crept over her like a spell, until, as she looked at the red coals, a tired, slow smile stole over her smudged face, her head nodded forward without her being aware of it, her eyes drooped, and she fell fast asleep. She had really been only about ten minutes in the room when Sara entered, but she was in as deep a sleep as if she had been, like Sleeping Beauty, slumbering for a hundred years. But she did not look—poor Becky!—like a Sleeping Beauty at all. She looked only like an ugly, stunted, worn-out little scullery drudge.

Sara seemed as much unlike her as if she were a creature from another world.

On this particular afternoon she had been taking her dancing-lesson, and the afternoon on which the dancing-master appeared was rather a grand occasion at the seminary, though it occurred every week. The pupils were attired in their prettiest frocks, and as Sara danced particularly well, she was very much brought forward, and Mariette was requested to make her as diaphanous and fine as possible.

To-day a frock the color of a rose had been put on her, and Mariette had bought some real buds and made her a wreath to wear on her black locks. She had been learning a new, delightful dance in which she had been skimming and flying about the room, like a large rose-colored butterfly, and the enjoyment and exercise had brought a brilliant, happy glow into her face.

When she entered the room, she floated in with a few of the butterfly steps,—and there sat Becky, nodding her cap sideways off her head.

"Oh!" cried Sara, softly, when she saw her. "That poor thing!"

It did not occur to her to feel cross at finding her pet chair occupied by the small, dingy figure. To tell the truth, she was quite glad to find it there. When the ill-used heroine of her story wakened, she could talk to her. She crept toward her quietly, and stood looking at her. Becky gave a little snore.

"I wish she'd waken herself," Sara said. "I don't like to waken her. But Miss Minchin would be cross if she found out. I'll just wait a few minutes."

She took a seat on the edge of the table, and sat swinging her slim, rose-colored legs, and wondering what it would be best to do. Miss Amelia might come in at any moment, and if she did, Becky would be sure to be scolded.

"But she is so tired," she thought. "She *is* so tired!"

A piece of flaming coal ended her perplexity for her that very moment. It broke off from a large lump and fell on to the fender. Becky started, and opened her eyes with a frightened gasp. She did not know she had fallen asleep. She had only sat down for one moment and felt the beautiful glow—and here she found herself staring in wild alarm at the wonderful pupil, who sat perched quite near her, like a rose-colored fairy, with interested eyes.

She sprang up and clutched at her cap. She felt it dangling over her ear, and tried wildly to put it straight. Oh, she had got herself into trouble now with a vengeance! To have impudently fallen asleep on such a young lady's chair! She would be turned out of door without wages.

She made a sound like a big breathless sob.

"Oh, miss! Oh, miss!" she stuttered. "I arst yer pardon, miss! Oh, I do, miss!"

Sara jumped down, and came quite close to her.

"Don't be frightened," she said, quite as if she had been speaking to a little girl like herself. "It doesn't matter the least bit."

"I didn't go to do it, miss," protested Becky. "It was the warm fire—an' me bein' so tired. It—it *wasn't* imperence!"

Sara broke into a friendly little laugh, and put her hand on her shoulder.

"You were tired," she said; "you could not help it. You are not really awake yet."

How poor Becky stared at her! In fact, she had never heard such a nice, friendly sound in any one's voice before. She was used to being ordered about and scolded, and having her ears boxed. And this one—in her rose-colored dancing afternoon splendor—was looking at her as if she were not a culprit at all—as if she had a right to be tired—even to fall asleep! The touch of the soft, slim little paw on her shoulder was the most amazing thing she had ever known.

"Ain't—ain't yer angry, miss?" she gasped. "Ain't yer goin' to tell the missus?"

"No," cried out Sara. "Of course I'm not."

The woful fright in the coal-smutted face made her suddenly so sorry that she could scarcely bear it. One of her queer thoughts rushed into her mind. She put her hand against Becky's cheek.

"Why," she said, "we are just the same—I am only a little girl like you. It's just an accident that I am not you, and you are not me!"

Becky did not understand in the least. Her mind could not grasp such amazing thoughts, and "an accident" meant to her a calamity in which some one was run over or fell off a ladder and was carried to "the 'orspital."

"A' accident, miss," she fluttered respectfully. "Is it?"

"Yes," Sara answered, and she looked at her dreamily for a moment. But the next she spoke in a different tone. She realized that Becky did not know what she meant.

"Have you done your work?" she asked. "Dare you stay here a few minutes?"

Becky lost her breath again.

"Here, miss? Me?"

Sara ran to the door, opened it, and looked out and listened.

"No one is anywhere about," she explained. "If your bedrooms are finished, perhaps you might stay a tiny while. I thought—perhaps—you might like a piece of cake."

The next ten minutes seemed to Becky like a sort of delirium. Sara opened a cupboard, and gave her a thick slice of cake. She seemed to rejoice when it was devoured in hungry bites. She talked and asked questions, and laughed until Becky's fears actually began to calm themselves, and she once or twice gathered boldness enough to ask a question or so herself, daring as she felt it to be.

"Is that—" she ventured, looking longingly at the rose-colored frock. And she asked it almost in a whisper. "Is that there your best?"

"It is one of my dancing-frocks," answered Sara. "I like it, don't you?"

For a few seconds Becky was almost speechless with admiration. Then she said in an awed voice:

"Onct I see a princess. I was standin' in the street with the crowd outside Covin' Garden, watchin' the swells go inter the operer. An' there was one every one stared at most. They ses to each other, 'That's the princess.' She was a growed-up young lady, but she was pink all over—gownd an' cloak, an' flowers an' all. I called her to mind the minnit I see you, sittin' there on the table, miss. You looked like her."

"I've often thought," said Sara in her reflecting voice, "that I should like to be a princess; I wonder what it feels like. I believe I will begin pretending I am one."

Becky stared at her admiringly, and, as before, did not understand her in the least. She watched her with a sort of adoration. Very soon Sara left her reflections and turned to her with a new question.

"Becky," she said, "weren't you listening to that story?"

"Yes, miss," confessed Becky, a little alarmed again. "I knowed I hadn't orter, but it was that beautiful I—I couldn't help it."

"I liked you to listen to it," said Sara. "If you tell stories, you like nothing so much as to tell them to people who want to listen. I don't know why it is. Would you like to hear the rest?"

Becky lost her breath again.

"Me hear it?" she cried. "Like as if I was a pupil, miss! All about the Prince—and the little white Merbabies swimming about laughing—with stars in their hair?"

Sara nodded.

"You haven't time to hear it now, I'm afraid," she said; "but if you will tell me just what time you come to do my rooms, I will try to be here and tell you a bit of it every day until it is finished. It's a lovely long one—and I'm always putting new bits to it."

"Then," breathed Becky, devoutly, "I wouldn't mind *how* heavy the coal-boxes was—or *what* the cook done to me, if—if I might have that to think of."

"You may," said Sara. "I'll tell it *all* to you."

When Becky went down-stairs, she was not the same Becky who had staggered up, loaded down by the weight of the coal-scuttle. She had an extra piece of cake in her pocket, and she had been fed and warmed, but not only by cake and fire. Something else had warmed and fed her, and that something else was Sara.

When she was gone Sara sat on her favorite perch on the end of her table. Her feet were on a chair, her elbows on her knees, and her chin in her hands.

"If I *was* a princess—a *real* princess," she murmured, "I could scatter largess to the populace. But even if I am only a pretend princess, I can invent little things to do for people. Things like this. She was just as happy as if it was largess. I'll pretend that to do things people like is scattering largess. I've scattered largess."

CHAPTER 6
THE DIAMOND-MINES

Not very long after this a very exciting thing happened. Not only Sara, but the entire school, found it exciting, and made it the chief subject of conversation for weeks after it occurred. In one of his letters Captain Crewe told a most interesting story. A friend who had been at school with him when he was a boy had unexpectedly come to see him in India. He was the owner of a large tract of land upon which diamonds had been found, and he was engaged in developing the mines. If all went as was confidently expected, he would become possessed of such wealth as it made one dizzy to think of; and because he was fond of the friend of his school-days, he had given him an opportunity to share his enormous fortune by becoming a partner in his scheme. This, at least, was what Sara gathered from his letters. It is true that any other business scheme, however magnificent, would have but small attraction for her or for the school-room; but "diamond-mines" sounded so like the "Arabian Nights" that no one could be indifferent. Sara thought them enchanting, and painted pictures, for Ermengarde and Lottie, of labyrinthine passages in the bowels of the earth, where sparkling stones studded the walls and roofs and ceilings, and strange, dark men dug them out with heavy picks. Ermengarde delighted in the story, and Lottie insisted on its being retold to her every evening. Lavinia was very spiteful about it, and told Jessie that she didn't believe such things as diamond-mines existed.

"My mamma has a diamond ring which cost forty pounds," she said. "And it is not a big one, either. If there were mines full of diamonds, people would be so rich it would be ridiculous."

"Perhaps Sara will be so rich that she will be ridiculous," giggled Jessie.

"She's ridiculous without being rich," Lavinia sniffed.

"I believe you hate her," said Jessie.

"No, I don't," snapped Lavinia. "But I don't believe in mines full of diamonds."

"Well, people have to get them from somewhere," said Jessie. "Lavinia,"—with a new giggle,—"what do you think Gertrude says?"

"I don't know, I'm sure; and I don't care if it's something more about that everlasting Sara."

"Well, it is. One of her 'pretends' is that she is a princess. She plays it all the time—even in school. She says it makes her learn her lessons better. She wants Ermengarde to be one, too, but Ermengarde says she is too fat."

"She *is* too fat," said Lavinia. "And Sara is too thin."

Naturally, Jessie giggled again.

"She says it has nothing to do with what you look like, or what you have. It has only to do with what you *think* of, and what you *do*."

"I suppose she thinks she could be a princess if she was a beggar," said Lavinia. "Let us begin to call her Your Royal Highness."

Lessons for the day were over, and they were sitting before the school-room fire, enjoying the time they liked best. It was the time when Miss Minchin and Miss Amelia were taking their tea in the sitting-room sacred to themselves. At this hour a great deal of talking was done, and a great many secrets changed hands, particularly if the younger pupils behaved themselves well, and did not squabble or run about noisily, which it must be confessed they usually did. When they made an uproar the older girls usually interfered with scoldings and shakes. They were expected to keep order, and there was danger that if they did not, Miss Minchin or Miss Amelia would appear and put an end to festivities. Even as Lavinia spoke the door opened and Sara entered with Lottie, whose habit was to trot everywhere after her like a little dog.

"There she is, with that horrid child!" exclaimed Lavinia, in a whisper. "If she's so fond of her, why doesn't she keep her in her own room? She will begin howling about something in five minutes."

It happened that Lottie had been seized with a sudden desire to play in the school-room, and had begged her adopted parent to come with her. She joined a group of little ones who were playing in a corner. Sara curled herself up in the window-seat, opened a book, and began to read. It was a book about the French Revolution, and she was soon lost in a harrowing picture of the prisoners in the Bastille—men who had spent so many years in dungeons that when they were dragged out by those who rescued them, their long, gray hair and beards almost hid their faces, and they had forgotten that an outside world existed at all, and were like beings in a dream.

She was so far away from the school-room that it was not agreeable to be dragged back suddenly by a howl from Lottie. Never did she find anything so difficult as to keep herself from losing her temper when she was suddenly disturbed while absorbed in a book. People who are fond of books know the feeling of irritation which sweeps over them at such a moment. The temptation to be unreasonable and snappish is one not easy to manage.

"It makes me feel as if some one had hit me," Sara had told Ermengarde once in confidence. "And as if I want to hit back. I have to remember things quickly to keep from saying something ill-tempered."

She had to remember things quickly when she laid her book on the window-seat and jumped down from her comfortable corner.

Lottie had been sliding across the school-room floor, and, having first irritated Lavinia and Jessie by making a noise, had ended by falling down and hurting her fat knee. She was screaming and dancing up and down in the midst of a group of friends and enemies, who were alternately coaxing and scolding her.

"Stop this minute, you cry-baby! Stop this minute!" Lavinia commanded.

"I'm not a cry-baby—I'm not!" wailed Lottie. "Sara, Sa—ra!"

"If she doesn't stop, Miss Minchin will hear her," cried Jessie. "Lottie darling, I'll give you a penny!"

"I don't want your penny," sobbed Lottie; and she looked down at the fat knee, and, seeing a drop of blood on it, burst forth again.

Sara flew across the room and, kneeling down, put her arms round her.

"Now, Lottie," she said. "Now, Lottie, you *promised* Sara."

"She said I was a cry-baby," wept Lottie.

Sara patted her, but spoke in the steady voice Lottie knew.

"But if you cry, you will be one, Lottie pet. You *promised*."

Lottie remembered that she had promised, but she preferred to lift up her voice.

"I haven't any mamma," she proclaimed. "I haven't—a bit—of mamma."

"Yes, you have," said Sara cheerfully. "Have you forgotten? Don't you know that Sara is your mamma? Don't you want Sara for your mamma?"

Lottie cuddled up to her with a consoled sniff.

"Come and sit in the window-seat with me," Sara went on, "and I'll whisper a story to you."

"Will you?" whimpered Lottie. "Will you—tell me—about the diamond-mines?"

"The diamond-mines?" broke out Lavinia. "Nasty, little spoiled thing, I should like to *slap* her!"

Sara got up quickly on her feet. It must be remembered that she had been very deeply absorbed in the book about the Bastille, and she had had to recall several things rapidly when she realized that she must go and take care of her adopted child. She was not an angel, and she was not fond of Lavinia.

"Well," she said, with some fire, "I should like to slap you— but I don't want to slap you!" restraining herself. "At least I both want to slap you—and I should *like* to slap you,—but I *won't* slap you. We are not little gutter children. We are both old enough to know better."

Here was Lavinia's opportunity.

"Ah, yes, your royal highness," she said. "We are princesses, I believe. At least one of us is. The school ought to be very fashionable now Miss Minchin has a princess for a pupil."

Sara started toward her. She looked as if she were going to box her ears. Perhaps she was. Her trick of pretending things was the joy of her life. She never spoke of it to girls she was not fond of. Her new "pretend" about being a princess was very near to her heart, and she was shy and sensitive about it. She had meant it to be rather a secret, and here was Lavinia deriding it before nearly all the school. She felt the blood rush up into her face and tingle in her ears. She only just saved herself. If you were a princess, you did not fly into rages. Her hand dropped, and she stood quite still a moment. When she spoke it was in a quiet, steady voice; she held her head up, and everybody listened to her.

"It's true," she said. "Sometimes I do pretend I am a princess. I pretend I am a princess, so that I can try and behave like one."

Lavinia could not think of exactly the right thing to say. Several times she had found that she could not think of a satisfactory reply when she was dealing with Sara. The reason of this was that, somehow, the rest always seemed to be vaguely in sympathy with her opponent. She saw now that they were pricking up their ears interestedly. The truth was, they liked princesses, and they all hoped they might hear something more definite about this one, and drew nearer Sara accordingly.

Lavinia could only invent one remark, and it fell rather flat.

"Dear me!" she said; "I hope, when you ascend the throne, you won't forget us."

"I won't," said Sara, and she did not utter another word, but stood quite still, and stared at her steadily as she saw her take Jessie's arm and turn away.

After this, the girls who were jealous of her used to speak of her as "Princess Sara" whenever they wished to be particularly disdainful, and those who were fond of her gave her the name among themselves as a term of affection. No one called her "princess" instead of "Sara," but her adorers were much pleased with the picturesqueness and grandeur of the title, and Miss Minchin, hearing of it, mentioned it more than once to visiting parents, feeling that it rather suggested a sort of royal boarding-school.

To Becky it seemed the most appropriate thing in the world. The acquaintance begun on the foggy afternoon when she had jumped up terrified from her sleep in the comfortable chair, had ripened and grown, though it must be confessed that Miss Minchin and Miss Amelia knew very little about it. They were aware that Sara was "kind" to the scullery-maid, but they knew nothing of the certain delightful moments snatched perilously when, the up-stairs rooms being set in order with lightning rapidity, Sara's sitting-room was reached, and the heavy coal-box set down with a sigh of joy. At such times stories were told by instalments, things of a satisfying nature were either produced and eaten or hastily tucked into pockets to be disposed of at night, when Becky went up-stairs to her attic to bed.

"But I has to eat 'em careful, miss," she said once; "'cos if I leaves crumbs the rats come out to get 'em."

"Rats!" exclaimed Sara, in horror. "Are there *rats* there?"

"Lots of 'em, miss," Becky answered in quite a matter-of-fact manner. "There mostly is rats an' mice in attics. You gets used to the noise they makes scuttling about. I've got so I don't mind 'em s' long as they don't run over my piller."

"Ugh!" said Sara.

"You gets used to anythin' after a bit," said Becky. "You have to, miss, if you're born a scullery-maid. I'd rather have rats than cockroaches."

"So would I," said Sara; "I suppose you might make friends with a rat in time, but I don't believe I should like to make friends with a cockroach."

Sometimes Becky did not dare to spend more than a few minutes in the bright, warm room, and when this was the case perhaps only a few words could be exchanged, and a small purchase slipped into the old-fashioned pocket Becky carried under her dress skirt, tied round her waist with a band of tape. The search for and discovery of satisfying things to eat which could be packed into small compass, added a new interest to Sara's existence. When she drove or walked out, she used to look into shop windows eagerly. The first time it occurred to her to bring home two or three little meat-pies, she felt that she had hit upon a discovery. When she exhibited them, Becky's eyes quite sparkled.

"Oh, miss!" she murmured. "Them will be nice an' fillin'. It's fillin'ness that's best. Sponge-cake's a 'evingly thing, but it melts away like—if you understand, miss. These'll just *stay* in yer stummick."

"Well," hesitated Sara, "I don't think it would be good if they stayed always, but I do believe they will be satisfying."

They were satisfying,—and so were beef sandwiches, bought at a cook-shop,—and so were rolls and Bologna sausage. In time, Becky began to lose her hungry, tired feeling, and the coal-box did not seem so unbearably heavy.

However heavy it was, and whatsoever the temper of the cook, and the hardness of the work heaped upon her shoulders, she had always the chance of the afternoon to look forward to—the chance that Miss Sara would be able to be in her sitting-room. In fact, the mere seeing of Miss Sara would have been enough without the meat-pies. If there was time only for a few words, they were always friendly, merry words that put heart into one, and if there was time for more, then there was an instalment of a story to be told, or some other thing one remembered afterward and sometimes lay awake in one's bed in the attic to think over. Sara—who was only doing what she unconsciously liked better than anything else, Nature having made her for a giver—had not the least idea what she meant to poor Becky, and how wonderful a benefactor she seemed. If Nature has made you for a giver, your hands are born open, and so is your heart; and though there may be times when your hands are empty, your heart is always full, and you can give things out of that—warm things, kind things, sweet things,—help and comfort and laughter,—and sometimes gay, kind laughter is the best help of all.

Becky had scarcely known what laughter was through all her poor, little hard-driven life. Sara made her laugh, and laughed with her; and, though neither of them quite knew it, the laughter was as "fillin'" as the meat-pies.

A few weeks before Sara's eleventh birthday a letter came to her from her father, which did not seem to be written in such boyish high spirits as usual. He was not very well, and was evidently overweighted by the business connected with the diamond-mines.

"You see, little Sara," he wrote, "your daddy is not a business man at all, and figures and documents bother him. He does not really understand them, and all this seems so enormous. Perhaps, if I was not feverish I should not be awake, tossing about, one half of the night and spend the other half in troublesome dreams. If my little missus were here, I dare say she would give me some solemn, good advice. You would, wouldn't you, little missus?"

One of his many jokes had been to call her his "little missus" because she had such an old-fashioned air.

He had made wonderful preparations for her birthday. Among other things, a new doll had been ordered in Paris, and her wardrobe was to be, indeed, a marvel of splendid perfection. When she had replied to the letter asking her if the doll would be an acceptable present, Sara had been very quaint.

"I am getting very old," she wrote; "you see, I shall never live to have another doll given me. This will be my last doll. There is something solemn about it. If I could write poetry, I am sure a poem about 'A Last Doll' would be very nice. But I cannot write poetry. I have tried, and it made me laugh. It did not sound like Watts or Coleridge or Shakespeare at all. No one could ever take Emily's place, but I should respect the Last Doll very much; and I am sure the school would love it. They all like dolls, though some of the big ones—the almost fifteen ones—pretend they are too grown up."

Captain Crewe had a splitting headache when he read this letter in his bungalow in India. The table before him was heaped
with papers and letters which were alarming him and filling
him with anxious dread, but he laughed as he had not laughed
for weeks.

"Oh," he said, "she's better fun every year she lives. God grant
this business may right itself and leave me free to run home and
see her. What wouldn't I give to have her little arms round my
neck this minute! What *wouldn't* I give!"

The birthday was to be celebrated by great festivities. The
school-room was to be decorated, and there was to be a party. The
boxes containing the presents were to be opened with great cere-
mony, and there was to be a glittering feast spread in Miss
Minchin's sacred room. When the day arrived the whole house
was in a whirl of excitement. How the morning passed nobody
quite knew, because there seemed such preparations to be made.
The school-room was being decked with garlands of holly; the
desks had been moved away, and red covers had been put on the
forms which were arrayed round the room against the wall.

When Sara went into her sitting-room in the morning, she
found on the table a small, dumpy package, tied up in a piece of
brown paper. She knew it was a present, and she thought she
could guess whom it came from. She opened it quite tenderly. It
was a square pincushion, made of not quite clean red flannel, and
black pins had been stuck carefully into it to form the words,
"Menny hapy returns."

"Oh!" cried Sara, with a warm feeling in her heart. "What
pains she has taken! I like it so, it—it makes me feel sorrowful."

But the next moment she was mystified. On the under side of
the pincushion was secured a card, bearing in neat letters the
name "Miss Amelia Minchin."

Sara turned it over and over.

"Miss Amelia!" she said to herself. "How *can* it be!"

And just at that very moment she heard the door being cautiously pushed open and saw Becky peeping round it.

There was an affectionate, happy grin on her face, and she shuffled forward and stood nervously pulling at her fingers.

"Do yer like it, Miss Sara?" she said. "Do yer?"

"Like it?" cried Sara. "You darling Becky, you made it all yourself."

Becky gave a hysteric but joyful sniff, and her eyes looked quite moist with delight.

"It ain't nothin' but flannin, an' the flannin ain't new; but I wanted to give yer somethin' an' I made it of nights. I knew yer could *pretend* it was satin with diamond pins in. *I* tried to when I was makin' it. The card, miss," rather doubtfully; "'t warn't wrong of me to pick it up out o' the dust-bin, was it? Miss 'Meliar had throwed it away. I hadn't no card o' my own, an' I knowed it wouldn't be a proper presink if I didn't pin a card on—so I pinned Miss 'Meliar's."

Sara flew at her and hugged her. She could not have told herself or any one else why there was a lump in her throat.

"Oh, Becky!" she cried out, with a queer little laugh. "I love you Becky,—I do, I do!"

"Oh, miss!" breathed Becky. "Thank yer, miss, kindly; It ain't good enough for that. The—the flannin wasn't new."

CHAPTER 7
THE DIAMOND-MINES AGAIN

When Sara entered the holly-hung school-room in the afternoon, she did so as the head of a sort of procession. Miss Minchin, in her grandest silk dress, led her by the hand. A man-servant followed, carrying the box containing the Last Doll, a housemaid carried a second box, and Becky brought up the rear, carrying a third and wearing a clean apron and a new cap. Sara would have much preferred to enter in the usual way, but Miss Minchin had sent for her, and, after an interview in her private sitting-room, had expressed her wishes.

"This is not an ordinary occasion," she said. "I do not desire that it should be treated as one."

So Sara was led grandly in and felt shy when, on her entry, the big girls stared at her and touched each other's elbows, and the little ones began to squirm joyously in their seats.

"Silence, young ladies!" said Miss Minchin, at the murmur which arose. "James, place the box on the table and remove the lid. Emma, put yours upon a chair. Becky!" suddenly and severely.

Becky had quite forgotten herself in her excitement, and was grinning at Lottie, who was wriggling with rapturous expectation. She almost dropped her box, the disapproving voice so startled her, and her frightened, bobbing courtesy of apology was so funny that Lavinia and Jessie tittered.

"It is not your place to look at the young ladies," said Miss Minchin. "You forget yourself. Put your box down."

Becky obeyed with alarmed haste and hastily backed toward the door.

"You may leave us," Miss Minchin announced to the servants with a wave of her hand.

Becky stepped aside respectfully to allow the superior servants to pass out first. She could not help casting a longing glance at the box on the table. Something made of blue satin was peeping from between the folds of tissue-paper.

"If you please, Miss Minchin," said Sara, suddenly, "mayn't Becky stay?"

It was a bold thing to do. Miss Minchin was betrayed into something like a slight jump. Then she put her eye-glass up, and gazed at her show pupil disturbedly.

"Becky!" she exclaimed. "My dearest Sara!"

Sara advanced a step toward her.

"I want her because I know she will like to see the presents," she explained. "She is a little girl, too, you know."

Miss Minchin was scandalized. She glanced from one figure to the other.

"My dear Sara," she said, "Becky is the scullery-maid. Scullery-maids—er—are not little girls."

It really had not occurred to her to think of them in that light. Scullery-maids were machines who carried coal-scuttles and made fires.

"But Becky is," said Sara. "And I know she would enjoy herself. Please let her stay—because it is my birthday."

Miss Minchin replied with much dignity:

"As you ask it as a birthday favor—she may stay. Rebecca, thank Miss Sara for her great kindness."

Becky had been backing into the corner, twisting the hem of her apron in delighted suspense. She came forward, bobbing courtesies, but between Sara's eyes and her own there passed a gleam of friendly understanding, while her words tumbled over each other.

"Oh, if you please, miss! I'm that grateful, miss! I did want to see the doll, miss, that I did. Thank you, miss. And thank you, ma'am,"—turning and making an alarmed bob to Miss Minchin,—"for letting me take the liberty."

Miss Minchin waved her hand again—this time it was in the direction of the corner near the door.

"Go and stand there," she commanded. "Not too near the young ladies."

Becky went to her place, grinning. She did not care where she was sent, so that she might have the luck of being inside the room, instead of being down-stairs in the scullery, while these delights were going on. She did not even mind when Miss Minchin cleared her throat ominously and spoke again.

"Now, young ladies, I have a few words to say to you," she announced.

"She's going to make a speech," whispered one of the girls. "I wish it was over."

Sara felt rather uncomfortable. As this was her party, it was probable that the speech was about her. It is not agreeable to stand in a school-room and have a speech made about you.

"You are aware, young ladies," the speech began,—for it was a speech,—"that dear Sara is eleven years old today."

"*Dear* Sara!" murmured Lavinia.

"Several of you here have also been eleven years old, but Sara's birthdays are rather different from other little girls' birthdays. When she is older she will be heiress to a large fortune, which it will be her duty to spend in a meritorious manner."

"The diamond-mines," giggled Jessie, in a whisper.

Sara did not hear her; but as she stood with her green-gray eyes fixed steadily on Miss Minchin, she felt herself growing rather hot. When Miss Minchin talked about money, she felt somehow that she always hated her—and, of course, it was disrespectful to hate grown-up people.

"When her dear papa, Captain Crewe, brought her from India and gave her into my care," the speech proceeded, "he said to me, in a jesting way, 'I am afraid she will be very rich, Miss Minchin.' My reply was, 'Her education at my seminary, Captain Crewe, shall be such as will adorn the largest fortune.' Sara has become my most accomplished pupil. Her French and her dancing are a credit to the seminary. Her manners—which have caused you to call her Princess Sara—are perfect. Her amiability she exhibits by giving you this afternoon's party. I hope you appreciate her generosity. I wish you to express your appreciation of it by saying aloud all together, 'Thank you, Sara!'"

The entire school-room rose to its feet as it had done the morning Sara remembered so well.

"Thank you, Sara!" it said, and it must be confessed that Lottie jumped up and down. Sara looked rather shy for a moment. She made a courtesy—and it was a very nice one.

"Thank you," she said, "for coming to my party."

"Very pretty, indeed, Sara," approved Miss Minchin. "That is what a real princess does when the populace applauds her. Lavinia,"—scathingly,—"the sound you just made was extremely like a snort. If you are jealous of your fellow-pupil, I beg you will express your feelings in some more ladylike manner. Now I will leave you to enjoy yourselves."

The instant she had swept out of the room the spell her presence always had upon them was broken. The door had scarcely closed before every seat was empty. The little girls jumped or tumbled out of theirs; the older ones wasted no time in deserting theirs. There was a rush toward the boxes. Sara had bent over one of them with a delighted face.

"These are books, I know," she said.

The little children broke into a rueful murmur, and Ermengarde looked aghast.

"Does your papa send you books for a birthday present?" she exclaimed. "Why, he's as bad as mine. Don't open them, Sara."

"I like them," Sara laughed, but she turned to the biggest box. When she took out the Last Doll it was so magnificent that the children uttered delighted groans of joy, and actually drew back to gaze at it in breathless rapture.

"She is almost as big as Lottie," some one gasped.

Lottie clapped her hands and danced about, giggling.

"She's dressed for the theatre," said Lavinia. "Her cloak is lined with ermine."

"Oh!" cried Ermengarde, darting forward, "she has an opera-glass in her hand—a blue-and-gold one."

"Here is her trunk," said Sara. "Let us open it and look at her things."

She sat down upon the floor and turned the key. The children crowded, clamoring around her, as she lifted tray after tray and revealed their contents. Never had the school-room been in such an uproar. There were lace collars and silk stockings and hand-kerchiefs; there was a jewel-case containing a necklace and a tiara which looked quite as if they were made of real diamonds; there was a long sealskin and muff; there were ball dresses and walking dresses and visiting dresses; there were hats and tea-gowns and fans. Even Lavinia and Jessie forgot that they were too elderly to care for dolls, and uttered exclamations of delight and caught up things to look at them.

"Suppose," Sara said, as she stood by the table, putting a large, black-velvet hat on the impassively smiling owner of all these splendors—"suppose she understands human talk and feels proud of being admired."

"You are always supposing things," said Lavinia, and her air was very superior.

"I know I am," answered Sara, undisturbedly. "I like it. There is nothing so nice as supposing. It's almost like being a fairy. If you suppose anything hard enough it seems as if it were real."

"It's all very well to suppose things if you have everything," said Lavinia. "Could you suppose and pretend if you were a beg-gar and lived in a garret?"

Sara stopped arranging the Last Doll's ostrich plumes, and looked thoughtful.

"I *believe* I could," she said. "If one was a beggar, one would have to suppose and pretend all the time. But it mightn't be easy."

She often thought afterward how strange it was that just as she had finished saying this—just at that very moment—Miss Amelia came into the room.

"Sara," she said, "your papa's solicitor, Mr. Barrow, has called to see Miss Minchin, and, as she must talk to him alone and the refreshments are laid in her parlor, you had all better come and have your feast now, so that my sister can have her interview here in the school-room."

Refreshments were not likely to be disdained at any hour, and many pairs of eyes gleamed. Miss Amelia arranged the procession into decorum, and then, with Sara at her side heading it, she led it away, leaving the Last Doll sitting upon a chair with the glories of her wardrobe scattered about her; dresses and coats hung upon chair backs, piles of lace-frilled petticoats lying upon their seats.

Becky, who was not expected to partake of refreshments, had the indiscretion to linger a moment to look at these beauties—it really was an indiscretion.

"Go back to your work, Becky," Miss Amelia had said; but she had stopped to reverently pick up first a muff and then a coat, and while she stood looking at them adoringly, she heard Miss Minchin upon the threshold, and, being smitten with terror at the thought of being accused of taking liberties, she rashly darted under the table, which hid her by its table-cloth.

Miss Minchin came into the room, accompanied by a sharp-featured, dry little gentleman, who looked rather disturbed. Miss Minchin herself also looked rather disturbed, it must be admitted, and she gazed at the dry little gentleman with an irritated and puzzled expression.

She sat down with stiff dignity, and waved him to a chair.

"Pray, be seated, Mr. Barrow," she said.

Mr. Barrow did not sit down at once. His attention seemed attracted by the Last Doll and the things which surrounded her. He settled his eye-glasses and looked at them in nervous disapproval. The Last Doll herself did not seem to mind this in the least. She merely sat upright and returned his gaze indifferently.

"A hundred pounds," Mr. Barrow remarked succinctly. "All

expensive material, and made at a Parisian modiste's. He spent money lavishly enough, that young man."

Miss Minchin felt offended. This seemed to be a disparagement of her best patron and was a liberty.

Even solicitors had no right to take liberties.

"I beg your pardon, Mr. Barrow," she said stiffly. "I do not understand."

"Birthday presents," said Mr. Barrow in the same critical manner, "to a child eleven years old! Mad extravagance, I call it,"

Miss Minchin drew herself up still more rigidly.

"Captain Crewe is a man of fortune," she said. "The diamond-mines alone—"

Mr. Barrow wheeled round upon her.

"Diamond-mines!" he broke out. "There are none! Never were!"

Miss Minchin actually got up from her chair.

"What!" she cried. "What do you mean?"

"At any rate," answered Mr. Barrow, quite snappishly, "it would have been much better if there never had been any."

"Any diamond-mines?" ejaculated Miss Minchin, catching at the back of a chair and feeling as if a splendid dream was fading away from her.

"Diamond-mines spell ruin oftener than they spell wealth," said Mr. Barrow. "When a man is in the hands of a very dear friend and is not a business man himself, he had better steer clear of the dear friend's diamond-mines, or gold-mines, or any other kind of mines dear friends want his money to put into. The late Captain Crewe—"

Here Miss Minchin stopped him with a gasp.

"The *late* Captain Crewe!" she cried out; "the *late!* You don't come to tell me that Captain Crewe is—"

"He's dead, ma'am," Mr. Barrow answered with jerky brusqueness. "Died of jungle fever and business troubles combined. The jungle fever might not have killed him if he had not been driven mad by the business troubles, and the business troubles might not have put an end to him if the jungle fever had not assisted. Captain Crewe is dead!"

Miss Minchin dropped into her chair again. The words he had spoken filled her with alarm.

"What *were* his business troubles?" she said. "What *were* they?"

"Diamond-mines," answered Mr. Barrow, "and dear friends— and ruin."

Miss Minchin lost her breath.

"Ruin!" she gasped out.

"Lost every penny. That young man had too much money. The dear friend was mad on the subject of the diamond-mine. He put all his own money into it, and all Captain Crewe's. Then the dear friend ran away—Captain Crewe was already stricken with fever when the news came. The shock was too much for him. He died delirious, raving about his little girl—and didn't leave a penny."

Now Miss Minchin understood, and never had she received such a blow in her life. Her show pupil, her show patron, swept away from the Select Seminary at one blow. She felt as if she had been outraged and robbed, and that Captain Crewe and Sara and Mr. Barrow were equally to blame.

"Do you mean to tell me," she cried out, "that he left *nothing!* That Sara will have no fortune! That the child is a beggar! That she is left on my hands a little pauper instead of an heiress?"

Mr. Barrow was a shrewd businessman, and felt it as well to make his own freedom from responsibility quite clear without any delay.

"She is certainly left a beggar," he replied. "And she is certainly left on your hands, ma'am,—as she hasn't a relation in the world that we know of."

Miss Minchin started forward. She looked as if she was going to open the door and rush out of the room to stop the festivities going on joyfully and rather noisily that moment over the refreshments.

"It is monstrous!" she said. "She's in my sitting-room at this moment, dressed in silk gauze and lace petticoats, giving a party at my expense."

"She's giving it at your expense, ma'am, if she's giving it," said Mr. Barrow, calmly. "Barrow & Skipworth are not responsible for anything. There never was a cleaner sweep of a man's fortune. Captain Crewe died without paying *our* last bill—and it was a big one."

Miss Minchin turned back from the door in increased indignation. This was worse than any one could have dreamed of its being.

"That is what has happened to me!" she cried. "I was always so sure of his payments that I went to all sorts of ridiculous expenses for the child. I paid the bills for that ridiculous doll and her ridiculous fantastic wardrobe. The child was to have anything she wanted. She has a carriage and a pony and a maid, and I've paid for all of them since the last cheque came."

Mr. Barrow evidently did not intend to remain to listen to the story of Miss Minchin's grievances after he had made the position of his firm clear and related the mere dry facts. He did not feel any particular sympathy for irate keepers of boarding-schools.

"You had better not pay for anything more, ma'am," he remarked, "unless you want to make presents to the young lady. No one will remember you. She hasn't a brass farthing to call her own."

"But what am I to do?" demanded Miss Minchin, as if she felt it entirely his duty to make the matter right. "What am I to do?"

"There isn't anything to do," said Mr. Barrow, folding up his eye-glasses and slipping them into his pocket. "Captain Crewe is dead. The child is left a pauper. Nobody is responsible for her but you."

"I am not responsible for her, and I refuse to be made responsible!"

Miss Minchin became quite white with rage.

Mr. Barrow turned to go.

"I have nothing to do with that, madam," he said uninterestedly. "Barrow & Skipworth are not responsible. Very sorry the thing has happened, of course."

"If you think she is to be foisted off on me, you are greatly mistaken," Miss Minchin gasped. "I have been robbed and cheated; I will turn her into the street!"

If she had not been so furious, she would have been too discreet to say quite so much. She saw herself burdened with an extravagantly brought-up child whom she had always resented, and she lost all self-control.

Mr. Barrow undisturbedly moved toward the door.

"I wouldn't do that, madam," he commented; "it wouldn't look well. Unpleasant story to get about in connection with the establishment. Pupil bundled out penniless and without friends."

He was a clever business man, and he knew what he was saying. He also knew that Miss Minchin was a business woman, and would be shrewd enough to see the truth. She could not afford to do a thing which would make people speak of her as cruel and hard-hearted.

"Better keep her and make use of her," he added. "She's a clever child, I believe. You can get a good deal out of her as she grows older."

"I will get a good deal out of her before she grows older!" exclaimed Miss Minchin.

"I am sure you will, ma'am," said Mr. Barrow, with a little sinister smile. "I am sure you will. Good morning!"

He bowed himself out and closed the door, and it must be confessed that Miss Minchin stood for a few moments and glared at it. What he had said was quite true. She knew it. She had absolutely no redress. Her show pupil had melted into nothingness, leaving her only a friendless, beggared little girl. Such money as she herself had advanced was lost and could not be regained.

And as she stood there breathless under her sense of injury, there fell upon her ears a burst of gay voices from her own sacred room, which had actually been given up to the feast. She could at least stop this.

But as she started toward the door it was opened by Miss Amelia, who, when she caught sight of the changed, angry face, fell back a step in alarm.

"What *is* the matter, sister?" she ejaculated.

Miss Minchin's voice was almost fierce when she answered:
"Where is Sara Crewe?"

Miss Amelia was bewildered.

"Sara!" she stammered. "Why, she's with the children in your room, of course."

"Has she a black frock in her sumptuous wardrobe?"—in bitter irony.

"A black frock?" Miss Amelia stammered again. "A *black* one?"

"She has frocks of every other color. Has she a black one?"

Miss Amelia began to turn pale.

"No—ye-es!" she said. "But it is too short for her. She has only the old black velvet, and she has outgrown it."

"Go and tell her to take off that preposterous pink silk gauze, and put the black one on, whether it is too short or not. She has done with finery!"

Then Miss Amelia began to wring her fat hands and cry.

"Oh, sister!" she sniffed. "Oh, sister! What *can* have happened?"

Miss Minchin wasted no words.

"Captain Crewe is dead," she said. "He has died without a penny. That spoiled, pampered, fanciful child is left a pauper on my hands."

Miss Amelia sat down quite heavily in the nearest chair.

"Hundreds of pounds have I spent on nonsense for her. And I shall never see a penny of it. Put a stop to this ridiculous party of hers. Go and make her change her frock at once."

"I?" panted Miss Amelia. "M-must I go and tell her now?"

"This moment!" was the fierce answer. "Don't sit staring like a goose. Go!"

Poor Miss Amelia was accustomed to being called a goose. She knew, in fact, that she was rather a goose, and that it was left to geese to do a great many disagreeable things. It was a somewhat embarrassing thing to go into the midst of a room full of delighted children, and tell the giver of the feast that she had suddenly been transformed into a little beggar, and must go upstairs and put on an old black frock that was too small for her. But the thing must be done. This was evidently not the time when questions might be asked.

She rubbed her eyes with her handkerchief until they looked quite red. After which she got up and went out of the room, without venturing to say another word. When her older sister looked and spoke as she had done just now, the wisest course to pursue was to obey orders without any comment. Miss Minchin walked across the room. She spoke to herself aloud without knowing that she was doing it. During the last year the story of the diamond-mines had suggested all sorts of possibilities to her. Even proprietors of seminaries might make fortunes in stocks, with the aid of owners of mines. And now, instead of looking forward to gains, she was left to look back upon losses.

"The Princess Sara, indeed!" she said. "The child has been pampered as if she were a *queen*."

She was sweeping angrily past the corner table as she said it, and the next moment she started at the sound of a loud, sobbing sniff which issued from under the cover.

"What is that!" she exclaimed angrily. The loud, sobbing sniff was heard again, and she stooped and raised the hanging folds of the table-cover.

"How *dare* you!" she cried out. "How *dare* you! Come out immediately!"

It was poor Becky who crawled out, and her cap was knocked on one side, and her face was red with repressed crying.

"If you please, 'm—it's me, mum," she explained. "I know I hadn't ought to. But I was lookin' at the doll, mum—an' I was frightened when you came in—an' slipped under the table."

"You have been there all the time, listening," said Miss Minchin.

"No, mum," Becky protested, bobbing courtesies. "Not listenin'—I thought I could slip out without your noticin', but I couldn't an' I had to stay. But I didn't listen, mum—I wouldn't for nothin'. But I couldn't help hearin'."

Suddenly it seemed almost as if she lost all fear of the awful lady before her. She burst into fresh tears.

"Oh, please, 'm," she said; "I dare say you'll give me warnin', mum,—but I'm so sorry for poor Miss Sara—I'm so sorry!"

"Leave the room!" ordered Miss Minchin.

Becky courtesied again, the tears openly streaming down her cheeks.

"Yes, 'm; I will, 'm," she said, trembling; "but oh, I just wanted to arst you: Miss Sara—she's been such a rich young lady, an' she's been waited on, 'and and foot; an' what will she do now, mum, without no maid? If—if, oh please, would you let me wait on her after I've done my pots an' kettles? I'd do 'em that quick—if you'd let me wait on her now she's poor. Oh,"—breaking out afresh,—"poor little Miss Sara, mum—that was called a princess."

Somehow, she made Miss Minchin feel more angry than ever. That the very scullery-maid should range herself on the side of this child—whom she realized more fully than ever that she had never liked—was too much. She actually stamped her foot.

"No—certainly not," she said. "She will wait on herself, and on other people, too. Leave the room this instant, or you'll leave your place."

Becky threw her apron over her head and fled. She ran out of the room and down the steps into the scullery, and there she sat among her pots and kettles, and wept as if her heart would break.

"It's exactly like the ones in the stories," she wailed. "Them poor princesses that was drove into the world."

• • •

Miss Minchin had never looked quite so still and hard as she did when Sara came to her, a few hours later, in response to a message she had sent her.

Even by that time it seemed to Sara as if the birthday party had either been a dream or a thing which had happened years ago, and had happened in the life of quite another little girl.

Every sign of the festivities had been swept away; the holly had been removed from the school-room walls, and the forms and desks put back into their places. Miss Minchin's sitting-room looked as it always did—all traces of the feast were gone, and

Miss Minchin had resumed her usual dress. The pupils had been ordered to lay aside their party frocks; and this having been done, they had returned to the school-room and huddled together in groups, whispering and talking excitedly.

"Tell Sara to come to my room," Miss Minchin had said to her sister. "And explain to her clearly that I will have no crying or unpleasant scenes."

"Sister," replied Miss Amelia, "she is the strangest child I ever saw. She has actually made no fuss at all. You remember she made none when Captain Crewe went back to India. When I told her what had happened, she just stood quite still and looked at me without making a sound. Her eyes seemed to get bigger and bigger, and she went quite pale. When I had finished, she still stood staring for a few seconds, and then her chin began to shake, and she turned round and ran out of the room and up-stairs. Several of the other children began to cry, but she did not seem to hear them or to be alive to anything but just what I was saying. It made me feel quite queer not to be answered; and when you tell anything sudden and strange, you expect people will say *something*—whatever it is."

Nobody but Sara herself ever knew what had happened in her room after she had run up-stairs and locked her door. In fact, she herself scarcely remembered anything but that she walked up and down, saying over and over again to herself in a voice which did not seem her own:

"My papa is dead! My papa is dead!"

Once she stopped before Emily, who sat watching her from her chair, and cried out wildly:

"Emily! Do you hear? Do you hear—papa is dead? He is dead in India—thousands of miles away."

When she came into Miss Minchin's sitting-room in answer to her summons, her face was white and her eyes had dark rings around them. Her mouth was set as if she did not wish it to reveal what she had suffered and was suffering. She did not look in the least like the rose-colored butterfly child who had flown about from one of her treasures to the other in the decorated school-room. She looked instead a strange, desolate, almost grotesque little figure.

She had put on, without Mariette's help, the cast-aside black-velvet frock. It was too short and tight, and her slender legs looked long and thin, showing themselves from beneath the brief skirt. As she had not found a piece of black ribbon, her short, thick, black hair tumbled loosely about her face and contrasted strongly with its pallor. She held Emily tightly in one arm, and Emily was swathed in a piece of black material.

"Put down your doll," said Miss Minchin. "What do you mean by bringing her here?"

"No," Sara answered. "I will not put her down. She is all I have. My papa gave her to me."

She had always made Miss Minchin feel secretly uncomfortable, and she did so now. She did not speak with rudeness so much as with a cold steadiness with which Miss Minchin felt it difficult to cope—perhaps because she knew she was doing a heartless and inhuman thing.

"You will have no time for dolls in future," she said. "You will have to work and improve yourself and make yourself useful."

Sara kept her big, strange eyes fixed on her, and said not a word.

"Everything will be very different now," Miss Minchin went on. "I suppose Miss Amelia has explained matters to you."

"Yes," answered Sara. "My papa is dead. He left me no money. I am quite poor."

"You are a beggar," said Miss Minchin, her temper rising at the recollection of what all this meant. "It appears that you have no relations and no home, and no one to take care of you."

For a moment the thin, pale little face twitched, but Sara again said nothing.

"What are you staring at?" demanded Miss Minchin, sharply. "Are you so stupid that you cannot understand? I tell you that you are quite alone in the world, and have no one to do anything for you, unless I choose to keep you here out of charity."

"I understand," answered Sara, in a low tone; and there was a sound as if she had gulped down something which rose in her throat. "I understand."

"That doll," cried Miss Minchin, pointing to the splendid birthday gift seated near—"that ridiculous doll, with all her non-sensical, extravagant things—*I* actually paid the bill for her!"

Sara turned her head toward the chair.

"The Last Doll," she said. "The Last Doll." And her little mournful voice had an odd sound.

"The Last Doll, indeed!" said Miss Minchin. "And she is mine, not yours. Everything you own is mine."

"Please take it away from me, then," said Sara. "I do not want it."

If she had cried and sobbed and seemed frightened, Miss Minchin might almost have had more patience with her. She was a woman who liked to domineer and feel her power, and as she looked at Sara's pale little steadfast face and heard her proud little voice, she quite felt as if her might was being set at naught.

"Don't put on grand airs," she said. "The time for that sort of thing is past. You are not a princess any longer. Your carriage and your pony will be sent away—your maid will be dismissed. You will wear your oldest and plainest clothes—your extravagant ones are no longer suited to your station. You are like Becky—you must work for your living."

To her surprise, a faint gleam of light came into the child's eyes—a shade of relief.

"Can I work?" she said. "If I can work it will not matter so much. What can I do?"

"You can do anything you are told," was the answer. "You are a sharp child, and pick up things readily. If you make yourself use-ful I may let you stay here. You speak French well, and you can help with the younger children."

"May I?" exclaimed Sara. "Oh, please let me! I know I can teach them. I like them, and they like me."

"Don't talk nonsense about people liking you," said Miss

Minchin. "You will have to do more than teach the little ones. You will run errands and help in the kitchen as well as in the school-room. If you don't please me, you will be sent away. Remember that. Now go."

Sara stood still just a moment, looking at her. In her young soul, she was thinking deep and strange things. Then she turned to leave the room.

"Stop!" said Miss Minchin. "Don't you intend to thank me?"

Sara paused, and all the deep, strange thoughts surged up in her breast.

"What for?" she said.

"For my kindness to you," replied Miss Minchin. "For my kindness in giving you a home."

Sara made two or three steps toward her. Her thin little chest heaved up and down, and she spoke in a strange, unchildishly fierce way.

"You are not kind," she said. "You are *not* kind, and it is *not* a home." And she had turned and run out of the room before Miss Minchin could stop her or do anything but stare after her with stony anger.

She went up the stairs slowly, but panting for breath, and she held Emily tightly against her side.

"I wish she could talk," she said to herself. "If she could speak—if she could speak!"

She meant to go to her room and lie down on the tiger-skin, with her cheek upon the great cat's head, and look into the fire and think and think and think. But just before she reached the landing Miss Amelia came out of the door and closed it behind her, and stood before it, looking nervous and awkward. The truth was that she felt secretly ashamed of the thing she had been ordered to do.

"You—you are not to go in there," she said.

"Not go in?" exclaimed Sara, and she fell back a pace.

"That is not your room now," Miss Amelia answered, reddening a little.

Somehow, all at once, Sara understood. She realized that this was the beginning of the change Miss Minchin had spoken of.

"Where is my room?" she asked, hoping very much that her voice did not shake.

"You are to sleep in the attic next to Becky."

Sara knew where it was. Becky had told her about it. She turned, and mounted up two flights of stairs. The last one was narrow, and covered with shabby strips of old carpet. She felt as if she were walking away and leaving far behind her the world in which that other child, who no longer seemed herself, had lived. This child, in her short, tight old frock, climbing the stairs to the attic, was quite a different creature.

When she reached the attic door and opened it, her heart gave a dreary little thump. Then she shut the door and stood against it and looked about her.

Yes, this was another world. The room had a slanting roof and was whitewashed. The whitewash was dingy and had fallen off in places. There was a rusty grate, an old iron bedstead, and a hard bed covered with a faded coverlet. Some pieces of furniture too much worn to be used down-stairs had been sent up. Under the skylight in the roof, which showed nothing but an oblong piece of dull gray sky, there stood an old battered red footstool. Sara went to it and sat down. She seldom cried. She did not cry now. She laid Emily across her knees and put her face down upon her and her arms around her, and sat there, her little black head resting on the black draperies, not saying one word, not making one sound.

And as she sat in this silence there came a low tap at the door—such a low, humble one that she did not at first hear it, and, indeed, was not roused until the door was timidly pushed open and a poor tear-smeared face appeared peeping round it. It was Becky's face, and Becky had been crying furtively for hours and rubbing her eyes with her kitchen apron until she looked strange indeed.

"Oh, miss," she said under her breath. "Might I—would you allow me—jest to come in?"

Sara lifted her head and looked at her. She tried to begin a smile, and somehow she could not. Suddenly—and it was all through the loving mournfulness of Becky's streaming eyes—her faced looked more like a child's not so much too old for her years. She held out her hand and gave a little sob.

"Oh, Becky," she said. "I told you we were just the same—only two little girls—just two little girls. You see how true it is. There's no difference now. I'm not a princess any more."

Becky ran to her and caught her hand, and hugged it to her breast, kneeling beside her and sobbing with love and pain.

"Yes, miss, you are," she cried, and her words were all broken. "Whats'ever 'appens to you—whats'ever—you'd be a princess all the same—an' nothin' couldn't make you nothin' different."

CHAPTER 8
IN THE ATTIC

The first night she spent in her attic was a thing Sara never forgot. During its passing, she lived through a wild, unchildlike woe of which she never spoke to any one about her. There was no one who would have understood. It was, indeed, well for her that as she lay awake in the darkness her mind was forcibly distracted, now and then, by the strangeness of her surroundings. It was, perhaps, well for her that she was reminded by her small body of material things. If this had not been so, the anguish of her young mind might have been too great for a child to bear. But, really, while the night was passing she scarcely knew that she had a body at all or remembered any other thing than one.

"My papa is dead!" she kept whispering to herself. "My papa is dead!"

It was not until long afterward that she realized that her bed had been so hard that she turned over and over in it to find a place to rest, that the darkness seemed more intense than any she had ever known, and that the wind howled over the roof among the chimneys like something which wailed aloud. Then there was something worse. This was certain scufflings and scratchings and squeakings in the walls and behind the skirting boards. She knew what they meant, because Becky had described them. They meant rats and mice who were either fighting with each other or playing together. Once or twice she even heard sharp-toed feet scurrying across the floor, and she remembered in those after days, when she recalled things, that when first she heard them she started up in bed and sat trembling, and when she lay down again she covered her head with the bedclothes.

The change in her life did not come about gradually, but was made all at once.

"She must begin as she is to go on," Miss Minchin said to Miss Amelia. "She must be taught at once what she is to expect."

Mariette had left the house the next morning. The glimpse Sara caught of her sitting-room, as she passed its open door, showed her that everything had been changed. Her ornaments and luxuries had been removed, and a bed had been placed in a corner to transform it into a new pupil's bedroom.

When she went down to breakfast she saw that her seat at Miss Minchin's side was occupied by Lavinia, and Miss Minchin spoke to her coldly.

"You will begin your new duties, Sara," she said, "by taking your seat with the younger children at a smaller table. You must keep them quiet, and see that they behave well and do not waste their food. You ought to have been down earlier. Lottie has already upset her tea."

That was the beginning, and from day to day the duties given to her were added to. She taught the younger children French and heard their other lessons, and these were the least of her labors. It was found that she could be made use of in numberless directions. She could be sent on errands at any time and in all weathers. She could be told to do things other people neglected. The cook and the housemaids took their tone from Miss Minchin, and rather enjoyed ordering about the "young one" who had been made so much fuss over for so long. They were not servants of the best class, and had neither good manners nor good tempers, and it was frequently convenient to have at hand some one on whom blame could be laid.

During the first month or two, Sara thought that her willingness to do things as well as she could, and her silence under reproof, might soften those who drove her so hard. In her proud little heart she wanted them to see that she was trying to earn her living and not accepting charity. But the time came when she saw that no one was softened at all; and the more willing she was to do as she was told, the more domineering and exacting careless housemaids became, and the more ready a scolding cook was to blame her.

If she had been older, Miss Minchin would have given her the bigger girls to teach and saved money by dismissing an instructress; but while she remained and looked like a child, she could be made more useful as a sort of little superior errand girl and maid of all work. An ordinary errand boy would not have been so clever and reliable.

Sara could be trusted with difficult commissions and complicated messages. She could even go and pay bills, and she combined with this the ability to dust a room well and to set things in order.

Her own lessons became things of the past. She was taught nothing, and only after long and busy days spent in running here and there at everybody's orders was she grudgingly allowed to go into the deserted school-room, with a pile of old books, and study alone at night.

"If I do not remind myself of the things I have learned, perhaps I may forget them," she said to herself. "I am almost a scullery-maid, and if I am a scullery-maid who knows nothing, I shall be like poor Becky. I wonder if I could *quite* forget and begin to drop my *h*'s and not remember that Henry the Eighth had six wives."

One of the most curious things in her new existence was her changed position among the pupils. Instead of being a sort of small royal personage among them, she no longer seemed to be one of their number at all. She was kept so constantly at work that she scarcely ever had an opportunity of speaking to any of them, and she could not avoid seeing that Miss Minchin preferred that she should live a life apart from that of the occupants of the school-room.

"I will not have her forming intimacies and talking to the other children," that lady said. "Girls like a grievance, and if she begins to tell romantic stories about herself, she will become an ill-used heroine, and parents will be given a wrong impression. It is better that she should live a separate life—one suited to her circumstances. I am giving her a home, and that is more than she has any right to expect from me."

Sara did not expect much, and was far too proud to try to continue to be intimate with girls who evidently felt rather awkward and uncertain about her. The fact was that Miss Minchin's pupils were a set of dull, matter-of-fact young people. They were accustomed to being rich and comfortable, and as Sara's frocks grew shorter and shabbier and queerer-looking, and it became an established fact that she wore shoes with holes in them and was sent out to buy groceries and carry them through the streets in a basket on her arm when the cook wanted them in a hurry, they felt rather as if, when they spoke to her, they were addressing an under servant.

"To think that she was the girl with the diamond-mines," Lavinia commented. "She does look an object. And she's queerer than ever. I never liked her much, but I can't bear that way she has now of looking at people without speaking—just as if she was finding them out."

"I am," said Sara, promptly, when she heard of this. "That's what I look at some people for. I like to know about them. I think them over afterward."

The truth was that she had saved herself annoyance several times by keeping her eye on Lavinia, who was quite ready to make mischief, and would have been rather pleased to have made it for the ex-show pupil.

Sara never made any mischief herself, or interfered with any one. She worked like a drudge; she tramped through the wet streets, carrying parcels and baskets; she labored with the childish inattention of the little ones' French lessons; as she became shabbier and more forlorn-looking, she was told that she had better take her meals down-stairs; she was treated as if she was nobody's concern, and her heart grew proud and sore, but she never told any one what she felt.

"Soldiers don't complain," she would say between her small,

shut teeth. "I am not going to do it; I will pretend this is part of a war."

But there were hours when her child heart might almost have broken with loneliness but for three people.

The first, it must be owned, was Becky—just Becky. Throughout all that first night spent in the garret, she had felt a vague comfort in knowing that on the other side of the wall in which the rats scuffled and squeaked there was another young human creature. And during the nights that followed the sense of comfort grew. They had little chance to speak to each other during the day. Each had her own tasks to perform, and any attempt at conversation would have been regarded as a tendency to loiter and lose time.

"Don't mind me, miss," Becky whispered during the first morning, "if I don't say nothin' polite. Some un 'd be down on us if I did. I *means* 'please' an' 'thank you' an' 'beg pardon,' but I dass n't to take time to say it."

But before daybreak she used to slip into Sara's attic and button her dress and give her such help as she required before she went down-stairs to light the kitchen fire. And when night came Sara always heard the humble knock at her door which meant that her handmaid was ready to help her again if she was needed. During the first weeks of her grief Sara felt as if she were too stupefied to talk, so it happened that some time passed before they saw each other much or exchanged visits. Becky's heart told her that it was best that people in trouble should be left alone.

The second of the trio of comforters was Ermengarde, but odd things happened before Ermengarde found her place.

When Sara's mind seemed to awaken again to the life about her, she realized that she had forgotten that an Ermengarde lived in the world. The two had always been friends, but Sara felt as if she were years the older. It could not be contested that Ermengarde was as dull as she was affectionate. She clung to Sara in a simple, helpless way; she brought her lessons to her that she might be helped; she listened to her every word and besieged her with requests for stories. But she had nothing interesting to say herself, and she loathed books of every description. She was, in fact, not a person one would remember when one was caught in the storm of a great trouble, and Sara forgot her.

It had been all the easier to forget her because she had been suddenly called home for a few weeks. When she came back she did not see Sara for a day or two, and when she met her for the first time she encountered her coming down a corridor with her arms full of garments which were to be taken down-stairs to be mended. Sara herself had already been taught to mend them. She looked pale and unlike herself, and she was attired in the queer, outgrown frock whose shortness showed so much thin black leg.

Ermengarde was too slow a girl to be equal to such a situation. She could not think of anything to say. She knew what had happened, but, somehow, she had never imagined Sara could look like this—so odd and poor and almost like a servant. It made her quite miserable, and she could do nothing but break into a short hysterical laugh and exclaim—aimlessly and as if without any meaning:

"Oh, Sara! is that you?"

"Yes," answered Sara, and suddenly a strange thought passed through her mind and made her face flush.

She held the pile of garments in her arms, and her chin rested upon the top of it to keep it steady. Something in the look of her straight-gazing eyes made Ermengarde lose her wits still more. She felt as if Sara had changed into a new kind of girl, and she had never known her before. Perhaps it was because she had suddenly grown poor and had to mend things and work like Becky.

"Oh," she stammered. "How—how are you?"

"I don't know," Sara replied. "How are you?"

"I'm—I'm quite well," said Ermengarde, overwhelmed with shyness. Then spasmodically she thought of something to say which seemed more intimate. "Are you—are you very unhappy?" she said in a rush.

Then Sara was guilty of an injustice. Just at that moment her torn heart swelled within her, and she felt that if any one was as stupid as that, one had better get away from her.

"What do you think?" she said. "Do you think I am very happy?" and she marched past her without another word.

In course of time she realized that if her wretchedness had not made her forget things, she would have known that poor, dull Ermengarde was not to be blamed for her unready, awkward ways. She was always awkward, and the more she felt, the more stupid she was given to being.

But the sudden thought which had flashed upon her had made her over-sensitive.

"She is like the others," she had thought. "She does not really want to talk to me. She knows no one does."

So for several weeks a barrier stood between them. When they met by chance Sara looked the other way, and Ermengarde felt too stiff and embarrassed to speak. Sometimes they nodded to each other in passing, but there were times when they did not even exchange a greeting.

"If she would rather not talk to me," Sara thought, "I will keep out of her way. Miss Minchin makes that easy enough."

Miss Minchin made it so easy that at last they scarcely saw each other at all. At that time it was noticed that Ermengarde was more stupid than ever, and that she looked listless and unhappy. She used to sit in the window-seat, huddled in a heap, and stare out of the window without speaking. Once Jessie, who was passing, stopped to look at her curiously.

"What are you crying for, Ermengarde?" she asked.

"I'm not crying," answered Ermengarde, in a muffled, unsteady voice.

"You are," said Jessie. "A great big tear just rolled down the bridge of your nose and dropped off the end of it. And there goes another."

"Well," said Ermengarde, "I'm miserable—and no one need interfere." And she turned her plump back and took out her handkerchief and boldly hid her face in it.

That night, when Sara went to her attic, she was later than usual. She had been kept at work until after the hour at which the pupils went to bed, and after that she had gone to her lessons in the lonely school-room. When she reached the top of the stairs, she was surprised to see a glimmer of light coming from under the attic door.

"Nobody goes there but myself," she thought quickly; "but some one has lighted a candle."

Some one had, indeed, lighted a candle, and it was not burning in the kitchen candlestick she was expected to use, but in one of those belonging to the pupils' bedrooms. The some one was sitting upon the battered footstool, and was dressed in her night-gown and wrapped up in a red shawl. It was Ermengarde.

"Ermengarde!" cried Sara. She was so startled that she was almost frightened. "You will get into trouble."

Ermengarde stumbled up from her footstool. She shuffled across the attic in her bedroom slippers, which were too large for her. Her eyes and nose were pink with crying.

"I know I shall—if I'm found out," she said. "But I don't care—I don't care a bit. Oh, Sara, please tell me. What *is* the matter? Why don't you like me any more?"

Something in her voice made the familiar lump rise in Sara's throat. It was so affectionate and simple—so like the old Ermengarde who had asked her to be "best friends." It sounded as if she had not meant what she had seemed to mean during these past weeks.

"I do like you," Sara answered. "I thought—you see, everything is different now. I thought you—were different."

Ermengarde opened her wet eyes wide.

"Why, it was you who were different!" she cried. "You didn't want to talk to me. I didn't know what to do. It was you who were different after I came back."

Sara thought a moment. She saw she had made a mistake.

"I *am* different," she explained, "though not in the way you think. Miss Minchin does not want me to talk to the girls. Most of

them don't want to talk to me. I thought—perhaps—you didn't.
So I tried to keep out of your way."

"Oh, Sara," Ermengarde almost wailed in her reproachful dis-
may. And then after one more look they rushed into each other's
arms. It must be confessed that Sara's small black head lay for
some minutes on the shoulder covered by the red shawl. When
Ermengarde had seemed to desert her, she had felt horribly lonely.

Afterward they sat down upon the floor together, Sara clasping
her knees with her arms, and Ermengarde rolled up in her shawl.
Ermengarde looked at the odd, big-eyed little face adoringly.

"I couldn't bear it any more," she said. "I dare say you could
live without me, Sara; but I couldn't live without you. I was nearly
dead. So to-night, when I was crying under the bedclothes, I
thought all at once of creeping up here and just begging you to let
us be friends again."

"You are nicer than I am," said Sara. "I was too proud to try and
make friends. You see, now that trials have come, they have shown
that I am *not* a nice child. I was afraid they would. Perhaps"—
wrinkling her forehead wisely—"that is what they were sent for."

"I don't see any good in them," said Ermengarde, stoutly.

"Neither do I—to speak the truth," admitted Sara, frankly.
"But I suppose there *might* be good in things, even if we don't see
it. There *might*"—doubtfully—"be good in Miss Minchin."

Ermengarde looked round the attic with a rather fearsome
curiosity.

"Sara," she said, "do you think you can bear living here?"

Sara looked round also.

"If I pretend it's quite different, I can," she answered; "or if I
pretend it is a place in a story."

She spoke slowly. Her imagination was beginning to work for
her. It had not worked for her at all since her troubles had come
upon her. She had felt as if it had been stunned.

"Other people have lived in worse places. Think of the Count
of Monte Cristo in the dungeons of the Château d'If. And think of
the people in the Bastille!"

"The Bastille," half whispered Ermengarde, watching her and beginning to be fascinated. She remembered stories of the French Revolution which Sara had been able to fix in her mind by her dramatic relation of them. No one but Sara could have done it.

A well-known glow came into Sara's eyes.

"Yes," she said, hugging her knees. "That will be a good place to pretend about. I am a prisoner in the Bastille. I have been here for years and years—and years; and everybody has forgotten about me. Miss Minchin is the jailer—and Becky"—a sudden light adding itself to the glow in her eyes—"Becky is the prisoner in the next cell."

She turned to Ermengarde, looking quite like the old Sara.

"I shall pretend that," she said; "and it will be a great comfort."

Ermengarde was at once enraptured and awed.

"And will you tell me all about it?" she said. "May I creep up here at night, whenever it is safe, and hear the things you have made up in the day? It will seem as if we were more 'best friends' than ever."

"Yes," answered Sara, nodding. "Adversity tries people, and mine has tried you and proved how nice you are."

CHAPTER 9
MELCHISEDEC

The third person in the trio was Lottie. She was a small thing and did not know what adversity meant, and was much bewildered by the alteration she saw in her young adopted mother. She had heard it rumored that strange things had happened to Sara, but she could not understand why she looked different—why she wore an old black frock and came into the school-room only to teach instead of to sit in her place of honor and learn lessons herself. There had been much whispering among the little ones when it had been discovered that Sara no longer lived in the rooms in which Emily had so long sat in state. Lottie's chief difficulty was that Sara said so little when one asked her questions. At seven mysteries must be made very clear if one is to understand them.

"Are you very poor now, Sara?" she had asked confidentially the first morning her friend took charge of the small French class. "Are you as poor as a beggar?" She thrust a fat hand into the slim one and opened round, tearful eyes. "I don't want you to be as poor as a beggar."

She looked as if she was going to cry, and Sara hurriedly consoled her.

"Beggars have nowhere to live," she said courageously. "I have a place to live in."

"Where do you live?" persisted Lottie. "The new girl sleeps in your room, and it isn't pretty any more."

"I live in another room," said Sara.

"Is it a nice one?" inquired Lottie. "I want to go and see it."

"You must not talk," said Sara. "Miss Minchin is looking at us. She will be angry with me for letting you whisper."

She had found out already that she was to be held accountable for everything which was objected to. If the children were not attentive, if they talked, if they were restless, it was she who would be reproved.

But Lottie was a determined little person. If Sara would not tell her where she lived, she would find out in some other way. She talked to her small companions and hung about the elder girls and listened when they were gossiping; and acting upon certain information they had unconsciously let drop, she started late one afternoon on a voyage of discovery, climbing stairs she had never known the existence of, until she reached the attic floor. There she found two doors near each other, and opening one, she saw her beloved Sara standing upon an old table and looking out of a window.

"Sara!" she cried, aghast. "Mamma Sara!" She was aghast because the attic was so bare and ugly and seemed so far away from all the world. Her short legs had seemed to have been mounting hundreds of stairs.

Sara turned round at the sound of her voice. It was her turn to be aghast. What would happen now? If Lottie began to cry and any one chanced to hear, they were both lost. She jumped down from her table and ran to the child.

"Don't cry and make a noise," she implored. "I shall be scolded if you do, and I have been scolded all day. It's—it's not such a bad room, Lottie."

"Isn't it?" gasped Lottie, and as she looked round it she bit her lip. She was a spoiled child yet, but she was fond enough of her adopted parent to make an effort to control herself for her sake. Then, somehow, it was quite possible that any place in which Sara lived might turn out to be nice. "Why isn't it, Sara?" she almost whispered.

Sara hugged her close and tried to laugh. There was a sort of comfort in the warmth of the plump, childish body. She had had a hard day and had been staring out of the windows with hot eyes.

"You can see all sorts of things you can't see down-stairs," she said.

"What sort of things?" demanded Lottie, with that curiosity Sara could always awaken even in bigger girls.

"Chimneys—quite close to us—with smoke curling up in wreaths and clouds and going up into the sky,—and sparrows hopping about and talking to each other just as if they were people,—and other attic windows where heads may pop out any minute and you can wonder who they belong to. And it all feels as high up—as if it was another world."

"Oh, let me see it!" cried Lottie. "Lift me up!"

Sara lifted her up, and they stood on the old table together and leaned on the edge of the flat window in the roof, and looked out.

Any one who has not done this does not know what a different world they saw. The slates spread out on either side of them and slanted down into the rain gutter-pipes. The sparrows, being at home there, twittered and hopped about quite without fear. Two of them perched on the chimney-top nearest and quarrelled with each other fiercely until one pecked the other and drove him away. The garret window next to theirs was shut because the house next door was empty.

"I wish some one lived there," Sara said. "It is so close that if there was a little girl in the attic, we could talk to each other through the windows and climb over to see each other, if we were not afraid of falling."

The sky seemed so much nearer than when one saw it from the street, that Lottie was enchanted. From the attic window, among the chimney-pots, the things which were happening in the world below seemed almost unreal. One scarcely believed in the existence of Miss Minchin and Miss Amelia and the school-room, and the roll of wheels in the square seemed a sound belonging to another existence.

"Oh, Sara!" cried Lottie, cuddling in her guarding arm. "I like this attic—I like it! It is nicer than down-stairs!"

"Look at that sparrow," whispered Sara. "I wish I had some crumbs to throw to him."

"I have some!" came in a little shriek from Lottie. "I have part of a bun in my pocket; I bought it with my penny yesterday, and I saved a bit."

When they threw out a few crumbs the sparrow jumped and flew away to an adjacent chimney-top. He was evidently not accustomed to intimates in attics, and unexpected crumbs startled him. But when Lottie remained quite still and Sara chirped very softly—almost as if she were a sparrow herself—he saw that the thing which had alarmed him represented hospitality, after all. He put his head on one side, and from his perch on the chimney looked down at the crumbs with twinkling eyes. Lottie could scarcely keep still.

"Will he come? Will he come?" she whispered.

"His eyes look as if he would," Sara whispered back. "He is thinking and thinking whether he dare. Yes, he will! Yes, he is coming!"

He flew down and hopped toward the crumbs, but stopped a few inches away from them, putting his head on one side again, as if reflecting on the chances that Sara and Lottie might turn out to be big cats and jump on him. At last his heart told him they were really nicer than they looked, and he hopped nearer and nearer, darted at the biggest crumb with a lightning peck, seized it, and carried it away to the other side of his chimney.

"Now he *knows*," said Sara. "And he will come back for the others."

He did come back, and even brought a friend, and the friend went away and brought a relative, and among them they made a hearty meal over which they twittered and chattered and exclaimed, stopping every now and then to put their heads on one side and examine Lottie and Sara. Lottie was so delighted that she quite forgot her first shocked impression of the attic. In fact, when she was lifted down from the table and returned to earthly things, as it were, Sara was able to point out to her many beauties in the room which she herself would not have suspected the existence of.

"It is so little and so high above everything," she said, "that it is almost like a nest in a tree. The slanting ceiling is so funny. See, you can scarcely stand up at this end of the room; and when the morning begins to come I can lie in bed and look right up into the sky through that flat window in the roof. It is like a square patch of light. If the sun is going to shine, little pink clouds float about, and I feel as if I could touch them. And if it rains, the drops patter and patter as if they were saying something nice. Then if there are stars, you can lie and try to count how many go into the patch. I takes such a lot. And just look at that tiny, rusty grate in the corner. If it was polished and there was a fire in it, just think how nice it would be. You see, it's really a beautiful little room."

She was walking round the small place, holding Lottie's hand and making gestures which described all the beauties she was making herself see. She quite made Lottie see them, too. Lottie could always believe in the things Sara made pictures of.

"You see," she said, "there could be a thick, soft blue Indian rug on the floor; and in that corner there could be a soft little sofa, with cushions to curl up on; and just over it could be a shelf full of books so that one could reach them easily; and there could be a fur rug before the fire, and hangings on the wall to cover up the white-wash, and pictures. They would have to be little ones, but they could be beautiful; and there could be a lamp with a deep rose-colored shade; and a table in the middle, with things to have tea with; and a little fat copper kettle singing on the hob; and the bed could be quite different. It could be made soft and covered with a lovely silk coverlet. It could be beautiful. And perhaps we could coax the sparrows until we made such friends with them that they would come and peck at the window and ask to be let in."

"Oh, Sara!" cried Lottie; "I should like to live here!"

When Sara had persuaded her to go down-stairs again, and, after setting her in her way, had come back to her attic, she stood in the middle of it and looked about her. The enchantment of her imaginings for Lottie had died away. The bed was hard and covered with its dingy quilt. The whitewashed wall showed its broken patches, the floor was cold and bare, the grate was broken

and rusty, and the battered footstool, tilted sideways on its injured
leg, the only seat in the room. She sat down on it for a few minutes and let her head drop in her hands. The mere fact that Lottie
had come and gone away again made things seem a little worse—
just as perhaps prisoners feel a little more desolate after visitors
come and go, leaving them behind.

"It's a lonely place," she said. "Sometimes it's the loneliest
place in the world."

She was sitting in this way when her attention was attracted by
a slight sound near her. She lifted her head to see where it came
from, and if she had been a nervous child she would have left her
seat on the battered footstool in a great hurry. A large rat was sitting up on his hind quarters and sniffing the air in an interested
manner. Some of Lottie's crumbs had dropped upon the floor and
their scent had drawn him out of his hole.

He looked so queer and so like a gray-whiskered dwarf or
gnome that Sara was rather fascinated. He looked at her with his
bright eyes, as if he were asking a question. He was evidently
so doubtful that one of the child's queer thoughts came into
her mind.

"I dare say it is rather hard to be a rat," she mused. "Nobody
likes you. People jump and run away and scream out, 'Oh, a horrid rat!' I shouldn't like people to scream and jump and say, 'Oh, a
horrid Sara!' the moment they saw me. And set traps for me, and
pretend they were dinner. It's so different to be a sparrow. But
nobody asked this rat if he wanted to be a rat when he was made.
Nobody said, 'Wouldn't you rather be a sparrow?'"

She had sat so quietly that the rat had begun to take courage.
He was very much afraid of her, but perhaps he had a heart like
the sparrow and it told him that she was not a thing which
pounced. He was very hungry. He had a wife and a large family in
the wall, and they had had frightfully bad luck for several days. He
had left the children crying bitterly, and felt he would risk a good
deal for a few crumbs, so he cautiously dropped upon his feet.

"Come on," said Sara; "I'm not a trap. You can have them,

poor thing! Prisoners in the Bastille used to make friends with rats. Suppose I make friends with you."

How it is that animals understand things I do not know, but it is certain that they do understand. Perhaps there is a language which is not made of words and everything in the world understands it. Perhaps there is a soul hidden in everything and it can always speak, without even making a sound, to another soul. But whatsoever was the reason, the rat knew from that moment that he was safe—even though he was a rat. He knew that this young human being sitting on the red footstool would not jump up and terrify him with wild, sharp noises or throw heavy objects at him which, if they did not fall and crush him, would send him limping in his scurry back to his hole. He was really a very nice rat, and did not mean the least harm. When he had stood on his hind legs and sniffed the air, with his bright eyes fixed on Sara, he had hoped that she would understand this, and would not begin by hating him as an enemy. When the mysterious thing which speaks without saying any words told him that she would not, he went softly toward the crumbs and began to eat them. As he did it he glanced every now and then at Sara, just as the sparrows had done, and his expression was so very apologetic that it touched her heart.

She sat and watched him without making any movement. One crumb was very much larger than the others—in fact, it could scarcely be called a crumb. It was evident that he wanted that piece very much, but it lay quite near the footstool and he was still rather timid.

"I believe he wants it to carry to his family in the wall," Sara thought. "If I do not stir at all, perhaps he will come and get it."

She scarcely allowed herself to breathe, she was so deeply interested. The rat shuffled a little nearer and ate a few more crumbs, then he stopped and sniffed delicately, giving a side glance at the occupant of the footstool; then he darted at the piece of bun with something like the sudden boldness of the sparrow, and the instant he had possession of it fled back to the wall, slipped down a crack in the skirting board, and was gone.

"I knew he wanted it for his children," said Sara. "I do believe I could make friends with him."

A week or so afterward, on one of the rare nights when Ermengarde found it safe to steal up to the attic, when she tapped on the door with the tips of her fingers Sara did not come to her for two or three minutes. There was, indeed, such a silence in the room at first that Ermengarde wondered if she could have fallen asleep. Then, to her surprise, she heard her utter a little, low laugh and speak coaxingly to some one.

"There!" Ermengarde heard her say. "Take it and go home, Melchisedec! Go home to your wife!"

Almost immediately Sara opened the door, and when she did so she found Ermengarde standing with alarmed eyes upon the threshold.

"Who—who *are* you talking to, Sara?" she gasped out.

Sara drew her in cautiously, but she looked as if something pleased and amused her.

"You must promise not to be frightened—not to scream the least bit, or I can't tell you," she answered.

Ermengarde felt almost inclined to scream on the spot, but managed to control herself. She looked all round the attic and saw no one. And yet Sara had certainly been speaking *to* some one. She thought of ghosts.

"Is it—something that will frighten me?" she asked timorously.

"Some people are afraid of them," said Sara. "I was at first,—but I am not now."

"Was it—a ghost?" quaked Ermengarde.

"No," said Sara, laughing. "It was my rat."

Ermengarde made one bound, and landed in the middle of the little dingy bed. She tucked her feet under her night-gown and the red shawl. She did not scream, but she gasped with fright.

"Oh! oh!" she cried under her breath. "A rat! A rat!"

"I was afraid you would be frightened," said Sara. "But you needn't be. I am making him tame. He actually knows me and come out when I call him. Are you too frightened to want to see him?"

The truth was that, as the days had gone on and, with the aid of scraps brought up from the kitchen, her curious friendship had developed, she had gradually forgotten that the timid creature she was becoming familiar with was a mere rat.

At first Ermengarde was too much alarmed to do anything but huddle in a heap upon the bed and tuck up her feet, but the sight of Sara's composed little countenance and the story of Melchisedec's first appearance began at last to rouse her curiosity, and she leaned forward over the edge of the bed and watched Sara go and kneel down by the hole in the skirting board.

"He—he won't run out quickly and jump on the bed, will he?" she said.

"No," answered Sara. "He's as polite as we are. He is just like a person. Now watch!"

She began to make a low, whistling sound—so low and coaxing that it could only have been heard in entire stillness. She did it several times, looking entirely absorbed in it. Ermengarde thought she looked as if she were working a spell. And at last, evidently in response to it, a gray-whiskered, bright-eyed head peeped out of the hole. Sara had some crumbs in her hand. She dropped them, and Melchisedec came quietly forth and ate them. A piece of larger size than the rest he took and carried in the most businesslike manner back to his home.

"You see," said Sara, "that is for his wife and children. He is very nice. He only eats the little bits. After he goes back I can always hear his family squeaking for joy. There are three kinds of squeaks. One kind is the children's, and one is Mrs. Melchisedec's, and one is Melchisedec's own."

Ermengarde began to laugh

"Oh, Sara!" she said. "You *are* queer,—but you are nice."

"I know I am queer," admitted Sara, cheerfully; "and I *try* to be nice." She rubbed her forehead with her little brown paw, and a puzzled, tender look came into her face. "Papa always laughed at me," she said; "but I liked it. He thought I was queer, but he liked me to make up things. I—I can't help making up things. If I didn't, I don't believe I could live." She paused and glanced round the attic. "I'm sure I couldn't live here," she added in a low voice.

Ermengarde was interested, as she always was. "When you talk about things," she said, "they seem as if they grew real. You talk about Melchisedec as if he was a person."

"He is a person," said Sara. "He gets hungry and frightened, just as we do; and he is married and has children. How do we know he doesn't think things, just as we do? His eyes look as if he was a person. That was why I gave him a name."

She sat down on the floor in her favorite attitude, holding her knees.

"Besides," she said, "he is a Bastille rat sent to be my friend. I can always get a bit of bread the cook has thrown away, and it is quite enough to support him."

"Is it the Bastille yet?" asked Ermengarde, eagerly. "Do you always pretend it is the Bastille?"

"Nearly always," answered Sara. "Sometimes I try to pretend it is another kind of place; but the Bastille is generally easiest—particularly when it is cold."

Just at that moment Ermengarde almost jumped off the bed, she was so startled by a sound she heard. It was like two distinct knocks on the wall.

"What is that?" she exclaimed.

Sara got up from the floor and answered quite dramatically:

"It is the prisoner in the next cell."

"Becky!" cried Ermengarde, enraptured.

"Yes," said Sara. "Listen; the two knocks meant, 'Prisoner, are you there?'"

She knocked three times on the wall herself, as if in answer.

"That means, 'Yes, I am here, and all is well.'"

Four knocks came from Becky's side of the wall.

"That means," explained Sara, "'Then, fellow-sufferer, we will sleep in peace. Good-night.'"

Ermengarde quite beamed with delight.

"Oh, Sara!" she whispered joyfully. "It is like a story!"

"It *is* a story," said Sara. "*Everything's* a story. You are a story—I am a story. Miss Minchin is a story."

And she sat down again and talked until Ermengarde forgot that she was a sort of escaped prisoner herself, and had to be reminded by Sara that she could not remain in the Bastille all night, but must steal noiselessly down-stairs again and creep back into her deserted bed.

CHAPTER 10
THE INDIAN GENTLEMAN

But it was a perilous thing for Ermengarde and Lottie to make pilgrimages to the attic. They could never be quite sure when Sara would be there, and they could scarcely ever be certain that Miss Amelia would not make a tour of inspection through the bedrooms after the pupils were supposed to be asleep. So their visits were rare ones, and Sara lived a strange and lonely life. It was a lonelier life when she was down-stairs than when she was in her attic. She had no one to talk to; and when she was sent out on errands and walked through the streets, a forlorn little figure carrying a basket or a parcel, trying to hold her hat on when the wind was blowing, and feeling the water soak through her shoes when it was raining, she felt as if the crowds hurrying past her made her loneliness greater. When she had been Princess Sara, driving though the streets in her brougham, or walking, attended by Mariette, the sight of her bright, eager little face and picturesque coats and hats had often caused people to look after her. A happy, beautifully cared for little girl naturally attracts attention. Shabby, poorly dressed children are not rare enough and pretty enough to make people turn around to look at them and smile. No one looked at Sara in these days, and no one seemed to see her as she hurried along the crowded pavements. She had begun to grow very fast, and, as she was dressed only in such clothes as the plainer remnants of her wardrobe would supply, she knew she looked very queer, indeed. All her valuable garments had been disposed of, and such as had been left for her use she was expected to wear so long as she could put them on at all. Sometimes, when she passed a shop window with a mirror in it, she almost laughed outright on catching a glimpse of herself, and sometimes her face went red and she bit her lip and turned away.

In the evening, when she passed houses whose windows were lighted up, she used to look into the warm rooms and amuse herself by imagining things about the people she saw sitting before the fires or about the tables. It always interested her to catch glimpses of rooms before the shutters were closed. There were several families in the square in which Miss Minchin lived, with which she had become quite familiar in a way of her own. The one she liked best she called the Large Family. She called it the Large Family not because the members of it were big,—for, indeed, most of them were little,—but because there were so many of them. There were eight children in the Large Family, and a stout, rosy mother, and a stout, rosy father, and a stout, rosy grandmother, and any number of servants. The eight children were always either being taken out to walk or to ride in perambulators by comfortable nurses, or they were going to drive with their mamma, or they were flying to the door in the evening to meet their papa and kiss him and dance around him and drag off his overcoat and look in the pockets for packages, or they were crowding about the nursery windows and looking out and pushing each other and laughing—in fact, they were always doing something enjoyable and suited to the tastes of a large family. Sara was quite fond of them, and had given them names out of books—quite romantic names. She called them the Montmorencys when she did not call them the Large Family. The fat, fair baby with the lace cap was Ethelberta Beauchamp Montmorency; the next baby was Violet Cholmondeley Montmorency; the little boy who could just stagger and who had such round legs was Sydney Cecil Vivian Montmorency; and then came Lilian Evangeline Maud Marion, Rosalind Gladys, Guy Clarence, Veronica Eustacia, and Claude Harold Hector.

One evening a very funny thing happened—though, perhaps, in one sense it was not a funny thing at all.

Several of the Montmorencys were evidently going to a children's party, and just as Sara was about to pass the door they were crossing the pavement to get into the carriage which was waiting for them. Veronica Eustacia and Rosalind Gladys, in white-lace frocks and lovely sashes, had just got in, and Guy Clarence, aged five, was following them. He was such a pretty fellow and had such rosy cheeks and blue eyes, and such a darling little round head covered with curls, that Sara forgot her basket and shabby cloak altogether—in fact, forgot everything but that she wanted to look at him for a moment. So she paused and looked.

It was Christmas time, and the Large Family had been hearing many stories about children who were poor and had no mammas and papas to fill their stockings and take them to the pantomime—children who were, in fact, cold and thinly clad and hungry. In the stories, kind people—sometimes little boys and girls with tender hearts—invariably saw the poor children and gave them money or rich gifts, or took them home to beautiful dinners. Guy Clarence had been affected to tears that very afternoon by the reading of such a story, and he had burned with a desire to find such a poor child and give her a certain sixpence he possessed, and thus provide for her for life. An entire sixpence, he was sure, would mean affluence for evermore. As he crossed the strip of red carpet laid across the pavement from the door to the carriage, he had this very sixpence in the pocket of his very short man-o'-war trousers. And just as Rosalind Gladys got into the vehicle and jumped onto the seat in order to feel the cushions spring under her, he saw Sara standing on the wet pavement in her shabby frock and hat, with her old basket on her arm, looking at him hungrily.

He thought that her eyes looked hungry because she had perhaps nothing to eat for a long time. He did not know that they looked so because she was hungry for the warm, merry life his home held and his rosy face spoke of, and that she had a hungry wish to snatch him in her arms and kiss him. He only knew that she had big eyes and a thin face and thin legs and a common basket and poor clothes. So he put his hand in his pocket and found his sixpence and walked up to her benignly.

"Here, poor little girl," he said. "Here is a sixpence. I will give it to you."

Sara started, and all at once realized that she looked exactly like poor children she had seen, in her better days, waiting on the pavement to watch her as she got out of her brougham. And she had given them pennies many a time. Her face went red and then it went pale, and for a second she felt as if she could not take the dear little sixpence.

"Oh, no!" she said. "Oh, no, thank you; I mustn't take it, indeed!"

Her voice was so unlike an ordinary street child's voice and her manner was so like the manner of a well-bred little person that Veronica Eustacia (whose real name was Janet) and Rosalind Gladys (who was really called Nora) leaned forward to listen.

But Guy Clarence was not to be thwarted in his benevolence. He thrust the sixpence into her hand.

"Yes, you must take it, poor little girl!" he insisted stoutly. "You can buy things to eat with it. It is a whole sixpence!"

There was something so honest and kind in his face, and he looked so likely to be heartbrokenly disappointed if she did not take it, that Sara knew she must not refuse him. To be as proud as that would be a cruel thing. So she actually put her pride in her pocket, though it must be admitted her cheeks burned.

"Thank you," she said. "You are a kind, kind little darling thing." And as he scrambled joyfully into the carriage she went away, trying to smile, though she caught her breath quickly and her eyes were shining through a mist. She had known that she looked odd and shabby, but until now she had not known that she might be taken for a beggar.

As the Large Family's carriage drove away, the children inside it were talking with interested excitement.

"Oh, Donald" (this was Guy Clarence's name), Janet exclaimed alarmedly, "why did you offer that little girl your sixpence? I'm sure she is not a beggar!"

"She didn't speak like a beggar!" cried Nora; "and her face didn't really look like a beggar's face!"

"Besides, she didn't beg," said Janet. "I was so afraid she might be angry with you. You know, it makes people angry to be taken for beggars when they are not beggars."

"She wasn't angry," said Donald, a trifle dismayed, but still firm. "She laughed a little, and she said I was a kind, kind little darling thing. And I was!"—stoutly. "It was my whole sixpence."

Janet and Nora exchanged glances.

"A beggar girl would never have said that," decided Janet. "She would have said, 'Thank yer kindly, little gentleman—thank yer, sir'; and perhaps she would have bobbed a courtesy."

Sara knew nothing about the fact, but from that time the Large Family was as profoundly interested in her as she was in it. Faces used to appear at the nursery windows when she passed, and many discussions concerning her were held round the fire.

"She is a kind of servant at the seminary," Janet said. "I don't believe she belongs to anybody. I believe she is an orphan. But she is not a beggar, however shabby she looks."

And afterward she was called by all of them, "The-little-girl-who-is-not-a-beggar" which was, of course, rather a long name, and sounded very funny sometimes when the youngest ones said it in a hurry.

Sara managed to bore a hole in the sixpence and hung it on an old bit of narrow ribbon round her neck. Her affection for the Large Family increased—as, indeed, her affection for everything she could love increased. She grew fonder and fonder of Becky, and she used to look forward to the two mornings a week when she went into the school-room to give the little ones their French lesson. Her small pupils loved her, and strove with each other for the privilege of standing close to her and insinuating their small hands into hers. It fed her hungry heart to feel them nestling up to her. She made such friends with the sparrows that when she stood upon the table, put her head and shoulders out of the attic window, and chirped, she heard almost immediately a flutter of wings and answering twitters, and a little flock of dingy town birds appeared and alighted on the slates to talk to her and make much of the crumbs she scattered. With Melchisedec she had become so intimate that he actually brought Mrs. Melchisedec with him sometimes, and now and then one or two of his children. She used to talk to him, and, somehow, he looked quite as if he understood.

There had grown in her mind rather a strange feeling about Emily, who always sat and looked on at everything. It arose in one of her moments of great desolateness. She would have liked to believe or pretend to believe that Emily understood and sympathized with her. She did not like to own to herself that her only companion could feel and hear nothing. She used to put her in a chair sometimes and sit opposite to her on the old red footstool, and stare and pretend about her until her own eyes would grow large with something which was almost like fear—particularly at night when everything was so still, when the only sound in the attic was the occasional sudden scurry and squeak of Melchisedec's family in the wall. One of her "pretends" was that Emily was a kind of good witch who could protect her. Sometimes, after she had stared at her until she was wrought up to the highest pitch of fancifulness, she would ask her questions and find herself *almost* feeling as if she would presently answer. But she never did.

"As to answering, though," said Sara, trying to console herself, "I don't answer very often. I never answer when I can help it. When people are insulting you, there is nothing so good for them as not to say a word—just to look at them and *think*. Miss Minchin turns pale with rage when I do it, Miss Amelia looks frightened, and so do the girls. When you will not fly into a passion people know you are stronger than they are, because you are strong enough to hold in your rage, and they are not, and they say stupid things they wish they hadn't said afterward. There's nothing so strong as rage, except what makes you hold it in—that's stronger. It's a good thing not to answer your enemies. I scarcely ever do. Perhaps Emily is more like me than I am like myself. Perhaps she would rather not answer her friends, even. She keeps it all in her heart."

But though she tried to satisfy herself with these arguments, she did not find it easy. When, after a long, hard day, in which she had been sent here and there, sometimes on long errands through wind and cold and rain, she came in wet and hungry, and was sent out again because nobody chose to remember that she was only a child, and that her slim legs might be tired and her small body might be chilled; when she had been given only harsh words and cold, slighting looks for thanks; when the cook had been vulgar and insolent; when Miss Minchin had been in her worst mood, and when she had seen the girls sneering among themselves at her shabbiness—then she was not always able to comfort her sore, proud, desolate heart with fancies when Emily merely sat upright in her old chair and stared.

One of these nights, when she came up to the attic cold and hungry, with a tempest raging in her young breast, Emily's stare seemed so vacant, her sawdust legs and arms so inexpressive, that Sara lost all control over herself. There was nobody but Emily— no one in the world. And there she sat.

"I shall die presently," she said at first.

Emily simply stared.

"I can't bear this," said the poor child, trembling. "I know I shall die. I'm cold; I'm wet; I'm starving to death. I've walked a thousand miles to-day, and they have done nothing but scold me from morning until night. And because I could not find that last thing the cook sent me for, they would not give me any supper. Some men laughed at me because my old shoes made me slip down in the mud. I'm covered with mud now. And they laughed. Do you hear?"

She looked at the staring glass eyes and complacent face, and suddenly a sort of heartbroken rage seized her. She lifted her little savage hand and knocked Emily off the chair, bursting into a passion of sobbing,—Sara who never cried.

"You are nothing but a *doll!*" she cried; "nothing but a doll—

doll—doll! You care for nothing. You are stuffed with sawdust. You never had a heart. Nothing could ever make you feel. You are a *doll!*"

Emily lay on the floor, with her legs ignominiously doubled up over her head, and a new flat place on the end of her nose; but she was calm, even dignified. Sara hid her face in her arms. The rats in the wall began to fight and bite each other and squeak and scramble. Melchisedec was chastising some of his family.

Sara's sobs gradually quieted themselves. It was so unlike her to break down that she was surprised at herself. After a while she raised her face and looked at Emily, who seemed to be gazing at her round the side of one angle, and, somehow, by this time actually with a kind of glassy-eyed sympathy. Sara bent and picked her up. Remorse overtook her. She even smiled at herself a very little smile.

"You can't help being a doll," she said with a resigned sigh, "any more than Lavinia and Jessie can help not having any sense. We are not all made alike. Perhaps you do your sawdust best." And she kissed her and shook her clothes straight, and put her back upon her chair.

She had wished very much that some one would take the empty house next door. She wished it because of the attic window which was so near hers. It seemed as if it would be so nice to see it propped open some day and a head and shoulders rising out of the square aperture.

"If it looked a nice head," she thought, "I might begin by saying, 'Good morning,' and all sorts of things might happen. But, of course, it's not really likely that any one but under servants would sleep there."

One morning, on turning the corner of the square after a visit to the grocer's, the butcher's, and the baker's, she saw, to her great delight, that during her rather prolonged absence, a van full of furniture had stopped before the next house, the front doors were thrown open, and men in shirt sleeves were going in and out carrying heavy packages and pieces of furniture.

"It's taken!" she said. "It really *is* taken! Oh, I do hope a nice head will look out of the attic window!"

She would almost have liked to join the group of loiterers who had stopped on the pavement to watch the things carried in. She had an idea that if she could see some of the furniture she could guess something about the people it belonged to.

"Miss Minchin's tables and chairs are just like her," she thought; "I remember thinking that the first minute I saw her, even though I was so little. I told papa afterward, and he laughed and said it was true. I am sure the Large Family have fat, comfortable arm-chairs and sofas, and I can see that their red-flowery wall-paper is exactly like them. It's warm and cheerful and kind-looking and happy."

She was sent out for parsley to the greengrocer's later in the day, and when she came up the area steps her heart gave quite a quick beat of recognition. Several pieces of furniture had been set out of the van upon the pavement. There was a beautiful table of elaborately wrought teak-wood, and some chairs, and a screen covered with rich Oriental embroidery. The sight of them gave her a weird, homesick feeling. She had seen things so like them in India. One of the things Miss Minchin had taken from her was a carved teak-wood desk her father had sent her.

"They are beautiful things," she said; "they look as if they ought to belong to a nice person. All the things look rather grand. I suppose it is a rich family."

The vans of furniture came and were unloaded and gave place to others all the day. Several times it so happened that Sara had an opportunity of seeing things carried in. It became plain that she had been right in guessing that the new-comers were people of large means. All the furniture was rich and beautiful, and a great deal of it was Oriental. Wonderful rugs and draperies and ornaments were taken from the vans, many pictures, and books enough for a library. Among other things there was a superb god Buddha in a splendid shrine.

"Some one in the family *must* have been in India," Sara

thought. "They have got used to Indian things and like them. I *am* glad. I shall feel as if they were friends, even if a head never looks out of the attic window."

When she was taking in the evening's milk for the cook (there was really no odd job she was not called upon to do), she saw something occur which made the situation more interesting than ever. The handsome, rosy man who was the father of the Large Family walked across the square in the most matter-of-fact manner, and ran up the steps of the next-door house. He ran up them as if he felt quite at home and expected to run up and down them many a time in the future. He stayed inside quite a long time, and several times came out and gave directions to the workmen, as if he had a right to do so. It was quite certain that he was in some intimate way connected with the newcomers and was acting for them.

"If the new people have children," Sara speculated, "the Large Family children will be sure to come and play with them, and they *might* come up into the attic just for fun."

At night, after her work was done, Becky came in to see her fellow-prisoner and bring her news.

"It's a' Nindian gentleman that's comin' to live next door, miss," she said. "I don't know whether he's a black gentleman or not, but he's a Nindian one. He's very rich, an' he's ill, an' the gentleman of the Large Family is his lawyer. He's had a lot of trouble, an' it's made him ill an' low in his mind. He worships idols, miss. He's an 'eathen an' bows down to wood an' stone. I seen a' idol bein' carried in for him to worship. Somebody had oughter send him a trac'. You can get a trac' for a penny."

Sara laughed a little.

"I don't believe he worships that idol," she said; "some people like to keep them to look at because they are interesting. My papa had a beautiful one, and he did not worship it."

But Becky was rather inclined to prefer to believe that the new neighbor was "an 'eathen." It sounded so much more romantic than that he should merely be the ordinary kind of gentleman who went to church with a prayer-book. She sat and talked long that night of what he would be like, of what his wife would be like if he had one, and of what his children would be like if they had children. Sara saw that privately she could not help hoping very much that they would all be black, and would wear turbans, and, above all, that—like their parent—they would all be "'eathens."

"I never lived next door to no 'eathens, miss," she said; "I should like to see what sort o' ways they'd have."

It was several weeks before her curiosity was satisfied, and then it was revealed that the new occupant had neither wife nor children. He was a solitary man with no family at all, and it was evident that he was shattered in health and unhappy in mind.

A carriage drove up one day and stopped before the house. When the footman dismounted from the box and opened the door the gentleman who was the father of the Large Family got out first. After him there descended a nurse in uniform, then came down the steps two men-servants. They came to assist their master, who, when he was helped out of the carriage, proved to be a man with a haggard, distressed face, and a skeleton body wrapped in furs. He was carried up the steps, and the head of the Large Family went with him, looking very anxious. Shortly afterward a doctor's carriage arrived, and the doctor went in—plainly to take care of him.

"There is such a yellow gentleman next door, Sara," Lottie whispered at the French class afterward. "Do you think he is a Chinee? The geography says the Chinese men are yellow."

"No, he is not Chinese," Sara whispered back; "he is very ill. Go on with your exercise, Lottie. 'Non, monsieur. Je n'ai pas le canif de mon oncle.'"

That was the beginning of the story of the Indian gentleman.

CHAPTER 11
RAM DASS

There were fine sunsets even in the square, sometimes. One could only see parts of them, however, between the chimneys and over the roofs. From the kitchen windows one could not see them at all, and could only guess that they were going on because the bricks looked warm and the air rosy or yellow for a while, or perhaps one saw a blazing glow strike a particular pane of glass somewhere. There was, however, one place from which one could see all the splendor of them: the piles of red or gold clouds in the west; or the purple ones edged with dazzling brightness; or the little fleecy, floating ones, tinged with rose-color and looking like flights of pink doves scurrying across the blue in a great hurry if there was a wind. The place where one could see all this, and seem at the same time to breathe a purer air, was, of course, the attic window. When the square suddenly seemed to begin to glow in an enchanted way and look wonderful in spite of its sooty trees and railings, Sara knew something was going on in the sky; and when it was at all possible to leave the kitchen without being missed or called back, she invariably stole away and crept up the flights of stairs, and, climbing on the old table, got her head and body as far out of the window as possible. When she had accomplished this, she always drew a long breath and looked all round her. It used to seem as if she had all the sky and the world to herself. No one else ever looked out of the other attics. Generally the skylights were closed; but even if they were propped open to admit air, no one seemed to come near them. And there Sara would stand, sometimes turning her face upward to the blue which seemed so friendly and near,—just like a lovely vaulted

ceiling,—sometimes watching the west and all the wonderful
things that happened there: the clouds melting or drifting or waiting softly to be changed pink or crimson or snow-white or purple
or pale dove-gray. Sometimes they made islands or great mountains enclosing lakes of deep turquoise-blue, or liquid amber, or
chrysoprase-green; sometimes dark headlands jutted into strange,
lost seas; sometimes slender strips of wonderful lands joined
other wonderful lands together. There were places where it
seemed that one could run or climb or stand and wait to see what
next was coming—until, perhaps, as it all melted, one could float
away. At least it seemed so to Sara, and nothing had ever been
quite so beautiful to her as the things she saw as she stood on the
table—her body half out of the skylight— the sparrows twittering
with sunset softness on the slates. The sparrows always seemed to
her to twitter with a sort of subdued softness just when these
marvels were going on.

There was such a sunset as this a few days after the Indian
gentleman was brought to his new home; and, as it fortunately
happened that the afternoon's work was done in the kitchen and
nobody had ordered her to go anywhere or perform any task, Sara
found it easier than usual to slip away and go up-stairs.

She mounted her table and stood looking out. It was a wonderful moment. There were floods of molten gold covering the
west, as if a glorious tide was sweeping over the world. A deep,
rich yellow light filled the air; the birds flying across the tops of
the houses showed quite black against it.

"It's a Splendid one," said Sara, softly, to herself. "It makes me
feel almost afraid—as if something strange was just going to happen. The Splendid ones always make me feel like that."

She suddenly turned her head because she heard a sound a
few yards away from her. It was an odd sound like a queer little
squeaky chattering. It came from the window of the next attic.
Some one had come to look at the sunset as she had. There was a
head and part of a body emerging from the skylight, but it was
not the head or body of a little girl or a housemaid; it was the

picturesque white-swathed form and dark-faced, gleaming-eyed, white-turbaned head of a native Indian man-servant,—"a Lascar," Sara said to herself quickly,—and the sound she had heard came from a small monkey he held in his arms as if he were fond of it, and which was snuggling and chattering against his breast.

As Sara looked toward him he looked toward her. The first thing she thought was that his dark face looked sorrowful and homesick. She felt absolutely sure he had come up to look at the sun, because he had seen it so seldom in England that he longed for the sight of it. She looked at him interestedly for a second, and then smiled across the slates. She had learned to know how comforting a smile, even from a stranger, may be.

Hers was evidently a pleasure to him. His whole expression altered, and he showed such gleaming white teeth as he smiled back that it was as if a light had been illuminated in his dusky face. The friendly look in Sara's eyes was always very effective when people felt tired or dull.

It was perhaps in making his salute to her that he loosened his hold on the monkey. He was an impish monkey and always ready for adventure, and it is probable that the sight of a little girl excited him. He suddenly broke loose, jumped on to the slates, ran across them chattering, and actually leaped on to Sara's shoulder, and from there down into her attic room. It made her laugh and delighted her; but she knew he must be restored to his master,—if the Lascar was his master,—and she wondered how this was to be done. Would he let her catch him, or would he be naughty and refuse to be caught, and perhaps get away and run off over the roofs and be lost? That would not do at all. Perhaps he belonged to the Indian gentleman, and the poor man was fond of him.

She turned to the Lascar, feeling glad that she remembered still some of the Hindustani she had learned when she lived with her father. She could make the man understand. She spoke to him in the language he knew.

"Will he let me catch him?" she asked.

She thought she had never seen more surprise and delight than the dark face expressed when she spoke in the familiar tongue. The truth was that the poor fellow felt as if his gods had intervened, and the kind little voice came from heaven itself. At once Sara saw that he had been accustomed to European children. He poured forth a flood of respectful thanks. He was the servant of Missee Sahib. The monkey was a good monkey and would not bite; but, unfortunately, he was difficult to catch. He would flee from one spot to another, like the lightning. He was disobedient, though not evil. Ram Dass knew him as if he were his child, and Ram Dass he would sometimes obey, but not always. If Missee Sahib would permit Ram Dass, he himself could cross the roof to her room, enter the windows, and regain the unworthy little animal. But he was evidently afraid Sara might think he was taking a great liberty and perhaps would not let him come.

But Sara gave him leave at once.

"Can you get across?" she inquired.

"In a moment," he answered her.

"Then come," she said; "he is flying from side to side of the room as if he was frightened."

Ram Dass slipped through his attic window and crossed to hers as steadily and lightly as if he had walked on roofs all his life. He slipped through the skylight and dropped upon his feet without a sound. Then he turned to Sara and salaamed again. The monkey saw him and uttered a little scream. Ram Dass hastily took the precaution of shutting the skylight, and then went in chase of him. It was not a very long chase. The monkey prolonged it a few minutes evidently for the mere fun of it, but presently he sprang chattering on to Ram Dass's shoulder and sat there chattering and clinging to his neck with a weird little skinny arm.

Ram Dass thanked Sara profoundly. She had seen that his quick native eyes had taken in at a glance all the bare shabbiness of the room, but he spoke to her as if he were speaking to the little daughter of a rajah, and pretended he observed nothing. He did not presume to remain more than a few moments after he had caught the monkey, and those moments were given to further deep and grateful obeisance to her in return for her indulgence. This little evil one, he said, stroking the monkey, was, in truth, not so evil as he seemed, and his master, who was ill, was sometimes amused by him. He would have been made sad if his favorite had run away and been lost. Then he salaamed once more and got through the skylight and across the slates again with as much agility as the monkey himself had displayed.

When he had gone Sara stood in the middle of her attic and thought of many things his face and his manner had brought back to her. The sight of his native costume and the profound reverence of his manner stirred all her past memories. It seemed a strange thing to remember that she—the drudge whom the cook had said insulting things to an hour ago—had only a few years ago been surrounded by people who all treated her as Ram Dass had treated her; who salaamed when she went by, whose foreheads almost touched the ground when she spoke to them, who were her servants and her slaves. It was like a sort of dream. It was all over, and it could never come back. It certainly seemed that there was no way in which any change could take place. She knew what Miss Minchin intended that her future should be. So long as she was too young to be used as a regular teacher, she would be used as an errand girl and servant and yet expected to remember what she had learned and in some mysterious way to learn more. The greater number of her evenings she was supposed to spend at study, and at various indefinite intervals she was examined and knew she would have been severely admonished if she had not advanced as was expected of her. The truth, indeed, was that Miss Minchin knew that she was too anxious to learn to require teachers. Give her books, and she would devour them and end by knowing them by heart. She might be trusted to be equal to teaching a good deal in the course of a few years. This was what would happen: when she was older she would be expected to drudge in the school-room as she drudged now in various parts of the house; they would be obliged to give her more respectable clothes, but they would be sure to be plain and ugly and to make her look somehow like a servant. That was all there seemed to be to look forward to, and Sara stood quite still for several minutes and thought it over.

Then a thought came back to her which made the color rise in her cheek and a spark light itself in her eyes. She straightened her thin little body and lifted her head.

"Whatever comes," she said, "cannot alter one thing. If I am a princess in rags and tatters, I can be a princess inside. It would be easy to be a princess if I were dressed in cloth of gold, but it is a great deal more of a triumph to be one all the time when no one knows it. There was Marie Antoinette when she was in prison and her throne was gone and she had only a black gown on, and her hair was white, and they insulted her and called her Widow Capet. She was a great deal more like a queen then than when she was so gay and everything was so grand. I like her best then. Those howling mobs of people did not frighten her. She was stronger than they were, even when they cut her head off."

This was not a new thought, but quite an old one, by this time. It had consoled her through many a bitter day, and she had gone about the house with an expression in her face which Miss Minchin could not understand and which was a source of great annoyance to her, as it seemed as if the child were mentally living a life which held her above the rest of the world. It was as if she scarcely heard the rude and acid things said to her; or, if she heard them, did not care for them at all. Sometimes, when she was in the midst of some harsh, domineering speech, Miss Minchin would find the still, unchildish eyes fixed upon her with something like a proud smile in them. At such times she did not know that Sara was saying to herself:

"You don't know that you are saying these things to a princess, and that if I chose I could wave my hand and order you to execution. I only spare you because I *am* a princess, and you are a poor, stupid, unkind, vulgar old thing, and don't know any better."

This used to interest and amuse her more than anything else; and queer and fanciful as it was, she found comfort in it and it was a good thing for her. While the thought held possession of her, she could not be made rude and malicious by the rudeness and malice of those about her.

"A princess must be polite," she said to herself.

And so when the servants, taking their tone from their mistress, were insolent and ordered her about, she would hold her head erect and reply to them with a quaint civility which often made them stare at her.

"She's got more airs and graces than if she come from Buckingham Palace, that young one," said the cook, chuckling a little sometimes; "I lose my temper with her often enough, but I will say she never forgets her manners. 'If you please, cook;' 'Will you be so kind, cook?' 'I beg your pardon, cook;' 'May I trouble you, cook?' She drops 'em about the kitchen as if they was nothing."

The morning after the interview with Ram Dass and his monkey, Sara was in the school-room with her small pupils. Having finished giving them their lessons, she was putting the French exercise-books together and thinking, as she did it, of the various things royal personages in disguise were called upon to do; Alfred the Great, for instance, burning the cakes and getting his ears boxed by the wife of the neatherd. How frightened she must have been when she had found out what she had done. If Miss Minchin should find out that she—Sara, whose toes were almost sticking out of her boots—was a princess—a real one! The look in her eyes was exactly the look which Miss Minchin most disliked. She would not have it; she was quite near her and was so enraged that she actually flew at her and boxed her ears—exactly as the neatherd's wife had boxed King Alfred's. It made Sara start. She wakened from her dream at the shock, and, catching her breath, stood still a second. Then, not knowing she was going to do it, she broke into a little laugh.

"What are you laughing at, you bold, impudent child?" Miss Minchin exclaimed.

It took Sara a few seconds to control herself sufficiently to remember that she was a princess. Her cheeks were red and smarting from the blows she had received.

"I was thinking," she answered.

"Beg my pardon immediately," said Miss Minchin.

Sara hesitated a second before she replied.

"I will beg your pardon for laughing, if it was rude," she said then; "but I won't beg your pardon for thinking."

"What were you thinking?" demanded Miss Minchin. "How dare you think? What were you thinking?"

Jessie tittered, and she and Lavinia nudged each other in unison. All the girls looked up from their books to listen. Really, it always interested them a little when Miss Minchin attacked Sara. Sara always said something queer, and never seemed the least bit frightened. She was not in the least frightened now, though her boxed ears were scarlet and her eyes were as bright as stars.

"I was thinking," she answered grandly and politely, "that you did not know what you were doing."

"That I did not know what I was doing?" Miss Minchin fairly gasped.

"Yes," said Sara, "and I was thinking what would happen if I were a princess and you boxed my ears—what I should do to you. And I was thinking that if I were one, you would never dare to do it, whatever I said or did. And I was thinking how surprised and frightened you would be if you suddenly found out—"

She had the imagined future so clearly before her eyes that she spoke in a manner which had an effect even upon Miss Minchin. It almost seemed for the moment to her narrow, unimaginative mind that there must be some real power hidden behind this candid daring.

"What?" she exclaimed. "Found out what?"

"That I really was a princess," said Sara, "and could do anything—anything I liked."

Every pair of eyes in the room widened to its full limit. Lavinia leaned forward on her seat to look.

"Go to your room," cried Miss Minchin, breathlessly, "this instant! Leave the school-room! Attend to your lessons, young ladies!"

Sara made a little bow.

"Excuse me for laughing if it was impolite," she said, and walked out of the room, leaving Miss Minchin struggling with her rage, and the girls whispering over their books.

"Did you see her? Did you see how queer she looked?" Jessie broke out. "I shouldn't be at all surprised if she did turn out to be something. Suppose she should!"

CHAPTER 12
THE OTHER SIDE OF THE WALL

When one lives in a row of houses, it is interesting to think of the things which are being done and said on the other side of the wall of the very rooms one is living in. Sara was fond of amusing herself by trying to imagine the things hidden by the wall which divided the Select Seminary from the Indian gentleman's house. She knew that the school-room was next to the Indian gentleman's study, and she hoped that the wall was thick so that the noise made sometimes after lesson hours would not disturb him.

"I am growing quite fond of him," she said to Ermengarde; "I should not like him to be disturbed. I have adopted him for a friend. You can do that with people you never speak to at all. You can just watch them, and think about them and be sorry for them, until they seem almost like relations. I'm quite anxious sometimes when I see the doctor call twice a day."

"I have very few relations," said Ermengarde, reflectively, "and I'm very glad of it. I don't like those I have. My two aunts are always saying 'Dear me, Ermengarde! You are very fat. You shouldn't eat sweets,' and my uncle is always asking me things like, 'When did Edward the Third ascend the throne?' and, 'Who died of a surfeit of lampreys?'"

Sara laughed.

"People you never speak to can't ask you questions like that," she said; "and I'm sure the Indian gentleman wouldn't even if he was quite intimate with you. I am fond of him."

She had become fond of the Large Family because they looked happy; but she had become fond of the Indian gentleman because he looked unhappy. He had evidently not fully recovered from some severe illness. In the kitchen—where, of course, the servants, through some mysterious means, knew everything—there was much discussion of his case. He was not an Indian gentleman really, but an Englishman who had lived in India. He had met with great misfortunes which had for a time so imperilled his whole fortune that he had thought himself ruined and disgraced forever. The shock had been so great that he had almost died of brain-fever; and ever since he had been shattered in health, though his fortunes had changed and all his possessions had been restored to him. His trouble and peril had been connected with mines.

"And mines with diamonds in 'em!" said the cook. "No savin's of mine ever goes into no mines—particular diamond ones"— with a side glance at Sara. "We all know somethin' of *them*."

"He felt as my papa felt," Sara thought. "He was ill as my papa was; but he did not die."

So her heart was more drawn to him than before. When she was sent out at night she used sometimes to feel quite glad, because there was always a chance that the curtains of the house next door might not yet be closed and she could look into the warm room and see her adopted friend. When no one was about she used sometimes to stop, and, holding to the iron railings, wish him good night as if he could hear her.

"Perhaps you can *feel* if you can't hear," was her fancy. "Perhaps kind thoughts reach people somehow, even through windows and doors and walls. Perhaps you feel a little warm and comforted, and don't know why, when I am standing here in the cold and hoping you will get well and happy again. I am so sorry for you," she would whisper in an intense little voice. "I wish you had a 'Little Missus' who could pet you as I used to pet papa when he had a headache. I should like to be your 'Little Missus' myself, poor dear! Good night—good night. God bless you!"

She would go away, feeling quite comforted and a little warmer herself. Her sympathy was so strong that it seemed as if it *must* reach him somehow as he sat alone in his arm-chair by the fire, nearly always in a great dressing-gown, and nearly always with his forehead resting in his hand as he gazed hopelessly into the fire. He looked to Sara like a man who had a trouble on his mind still, not merely like one whose troubles lay all in the past.

"He always seems as if he were thinking of something that hurts him *now*," she said to herself; "but he has got his money back and he will get over his brain-fever in time, so he ought not to look like that. I wonder if there is something else."

If there was something else,—something even servants did not hear of,—she could not help believing that the father of the Large Family knew it—the gentleman she called Mr. Montmorency. Mr. Montmorency went to see him often, and Mrs. Montmorency and all the little Montmorencys went, too, though less often. He seemed particularly fond of the two elder little girls—the Janet and Nora who had been so alarmed when their small brother Donald had given Sara his sixpence. He had, in fact, a very tender place in his heart for all children, and particularly for little girls. Janet and Nora were as fond of him as he was of them, and looked forward with the greatest pleasure to the afternoons when they were allowed to cross the square and make their well-behaved little visits to him. They were extremely decorous little visits because he was an invalid.

"He is a poor thing," said Janet, "and he says we cheer him up. We try to cheer him up very quietly."

Janet was the head of the family, and kept the rest of it in order. It was she who decided when it was discreet to ask the Indian gentleman to tell stories about India, and it was she who saw when he was tired and it was the time to steal quietly away and tell Ram Dass to go to him. They were very fond of Ram Dass. He could have told any number of stories if he had been able to speak anything but Hindustani. The Indian gentleman's real name was Mr. Carrisford, and Janet told Mr. Carrisford about the encounter with the little-girl-who-was-not-a-beggar. He was very much interested, and all the more so when he heard from Ram Dass of the adventure of the monkey on the roof. Ram Dass made for him a very clear picture of the attic and its desolateness—of the bare floor and broken plaster, the rusty, empty grate, and the hard, narrow bed.

"Carmichael," he said to the father of the Large Family, after he had heard this description; "I wonder how many of the attics in this square are like that one, and how many wretched little servant girls sleep on such beds, while I toss on my down pillows, loaded and harassed by wealth that is, most of it—not mine."

"My dear fellow," Mr. Carmichael answered cheerily, "the sooner you cease tormenting yourself the better it will be for you. If you possessed all the wealth in all the Indies, you could not set right all the discomforts in the world, and if you began to refurnish all the attics in this square, there would still remain all the attics in all the other squares and streets to put in order. And there you are!"

Mr. Carrisford sat and bit his nails as he looked into the glowing bed of coals in the grate.

"Do you suppose," he said slowly, after a pause—"do you think it is possible that the other child—the child I never cease thinking of, I believe—could be—could *possibly* be reduced to any such condition as the poor little soul next door?"

Mr. Carmichael looked at him uneasily. He knew that the worst thing the man could do for himself, for his reason and his health, was to begin to think in this particular way of this particular subject.

"If the child at Madame Pascal's school in Paris was the one you are in search of," he answered soothingly, "she would seem to be in the hands of people who can afford to take care of her. They adopted her because she had been a favorite companion of their little daughter who died. They had no other children, and Madame Pascal said that they were extremely well-to-do Russians."

"And the wretched woman actually did not know where they had taken her!" exclaimed Mr. Carrisford.

Mr. Carmichael shrugged his shoulders.

"She was a shrewd, worldly Frenchwoman, and was evidently only too glad to get the child so comfortably off her hands when the father's death left her totally unprovided for. Women of her type do not trouble themselves about the futures of children who might prove burdens. The adopted parents apparently disappeared and left no trace."

"But you say 'if' the child was the one I am in search of. You say 'if.' We are not sure. There was a difference in the name."

"Madame Pascal pronounced it as if it were Carew instead of Crewe,—but that might be merely a matter of pronunciation. The circumstances were curiously similar. An English officer in India had placed his motherless little girl at the school. He had died suddenly after losing his fortune." Mr. Carmichael paused a moment, as if a new thought had occurred to him. "Are you *sure* the child was left at a school in Paris? Are you sure it was Paris?"

"My dear fellow," broke forth Carrisford, with restless bitterness, "I am *sure* of nothing. I never saw either the child or her mother. Ralph Crewe and I loved each other as boys, but we had not met since our school-days, until we met in India. I was absorbed in the magnificent promise of the mines. He became absorbed, too. The whole thing was so huge and glittering that we half lost our heads. When we met we scarcely spoke of anything else. I only knew that the child had been sent to school somewhere. I do not even remember, now, *how* I knew it."

He was beginning to be excited. He always became excited when his still weakened brain was stirred by memories of the catastrophes of the past.

Mr. Carmichael watched him anxiously. It was necessary to ask some questions, but they must be put quietly and with caution.

"But you had reason to think the school *was* in Paris?"

"Yes," was the answer, "because her mother was a Frenchwoman, and I had heard that she wished her child to be educated in Paris. It seemed only likely that she would be there."

"Yes," Mr. Carmichael said, "it seems more than probable."

The Indian gentleman leaned forward and struck the table with a long, wasted hand.

"Carmichael," he said, "I *must* find her. If she is alive, she is somewhere. If she is friendless and penniless, it is through my fault. How is a man to get back his nerve with a thing like that on his mind? This sudden change of luck at the mines has made realities of all our most fantastic dreams, and poor Crewe's child may be begging in the street!"

"No, no," said Carmichael. "Try to be calm. Console yourself with the fact that when she is found you have a fortune to hand over to her."

"Why was I not man enough to stand my ground when things looked black?" Carrisford groaned in petulant misery. "I believe I should have stood my ground if I had not been responsible for other people's money as well as my own. Poor Crewe had put into the scheme every penny he owned. He trusted me—he *loved* me. And he died thinking I had ruined him—I—Tom Carrisford, who played cricket at Eton with him. What a villain he must have thought me!"

"Don't reproach yourself so bitterly."

"I don't reproach myself because the speculation threatened to fail—I reproach myself for losing my courage. I ran away like a swindler and a thief, because I could not face my best friend and tell him I had ruined him and his child."

The good-hearted father of the Large Family put his hand on his shoulder comfortingly.

"You ran away because your brain had given way under the strain of mental torture," he said. "You were half delirious already. If you had not been you would have stayed and fought it out. You were in a hospital, strapped down in bed, raving with brain-fever, two days after you left the place. Remember that."

Carrisford dropped his forehead in his hands.

"Good God! Yes," he said. "I was driven mad with dread and horror. I had not slept for weeks. The night I staggered out of my house all the air seemed full of hideous things mocking and mouthing at me."

"That is explanation enough in itself," said Mr. Carmichael. "How could a man on the verge of brain-fever judge sanely!"

Carrisford shook his drooping head.

"And when I returned to consciousness poor Crewe was dead—and buried. And I seemed to remember nothing. I did not remember the child for months and months. Even when I began to recall her existence everything seemed in a sort of haze."

He stopped a moment and rubbed his forehead. "It sometimes seems so now when I try to remember. Surely I must sometime have heard Crewe speak of the school she was sent to. Don't you think so?"

"He might not have spoken of it definitely. You never seem even to have heard her real name."

"He used to call her by an odd pet name he had invented. He called her his 'Little Missus.' But the wretched mines drove everything else out of our heads. We talked of nothing else. If he spoke of the school, I forgot—I forgot. And now I shall never remember."

"Come, come," said Carmichael. "We shall find her yet. We will continue to search for Madame Pascal's good-natured Russians. She seemed to have a vague idea that they lived in Moscow. We will take that as a clue. I will go to Moscow."

"If I were able to travel, I would go with you," said Carrisford; "but I can only sit here wrapped in furs and stare at the fire. And when I look into it I seem to see Crewe's gay young face gazing back at me. He looks as if he were asking me a question. Sometimes I dream of him at night, and he always stands before me and asks the same question in words. Can you guess what he says, Carmichael?"

Mr. Carmichael answered him in a rather low voice.

"Not exactly," he said.

"He always says, 'Tom, old man—Tom—where is the Little Missus?'" He caught at Carmichael's hand and clung to it. "I must be able to answer him—I must!" he said. "Help me to find her. Help me."

•   •   •

On the other side of the wall Sara was sitting in her garret talking to Melchisedec, who had come out for his evening meal.

"It has been hard to be a princess to-day, Melchisedec," she said. "It has been harder than usual. It gets harder as the weather grows colder and the streets get more sloppy. When Lavinia laughed at my muddy skirt as I passed her in the hall, I thought of something to say all in a flash—and I only just stopped myself in time. You can't sneer back at people like that—if you are a princess. But you have to bite your tongue to hold yourself in. I bit mine. It was a cold afternoon, Melchisedec. And it's a cold night."

Quite suddenly she put her black head down in her arms, as she often did when she was alone.

"Oh, papa," she whispered, "what a long time it seems since I was your 'Little Missus'!"

This was what happened that day on both sides of the wall.

CHAPTER 13
ONE OF THE POPULACE

The winter was a wretched one. There were days on which Sara tramped through snow when she went on her errands; there were worse days when the snow melted and combined itself with mud to form slush; there were others when the fog was so thick that the lamps in the street were lighted all day and London looked as it had looked the afternoon, several years ago, when the cab had driven through the thoroughfares with Sara tucked up on its seat, leaning against her father's shoulder. On such days the windows of the house of the Large Family always looked delightfully cosey and alluring, and the study in which the Indian gentleman sat glowed with warmth and rich color. But the attic was dismal beyond words. There were no longer sunsets or sunrises to look at, and scarcely ever any stars, it seemed to Sara. The clouds hung low over the skylight and were either gray or mud-color, or dropping heavy rain. At four o'clock in the afternoon, even when there was no special fog, the daylight was at an end. If it was necessary to go to her attic for anything, Sara was obliged to light a candle. The women in the kitchen were depressed, and that made them more ill-tempered than ever. Becky was driven like a little slave.

"'Twarn't for you, miss," she said hoarsely to Sara one night when she had crept into the attic—"'twarn't for you, an' the Bastille, an' bein' the prisoner in the next cell, I should die. That there does seem real now, doesn't it? The missus is more like the head jailer every day she lives. I can jest see them big keys you say she carries. The cook she's like one of the under-jailers. Tell me some more, please, miss—tell me about the subt'ranean passage we've dug under the walls."

"I'll tell you something warmer," shivered Sara. "Get your coverlet and wrap it round you, and I'll get mine, and we will huddle close together on the bed, and I'll tell you about the tropical forest where the Indian gentleman's monkey used to live. When I see him sitting on the table near the window and looking out into the street with that mournful expression, I always feel sure he is thinking about the tropical forest where he used to swing by his tail from cocoanut-trees. I wonder who caught him, and if he left a family behind who had depended on him for cocoanuts."

"That is warmer, miss," said Becky, gratefully; "but, someways, even the Bastille is sort of heatin' when you gets to tellin' about it."

"That is because it makes you think of something else," said Sara, wrapping the coverlet round her until only her small dark face was to be seen looking out of it. "I've noticed this. What you have to do with your mind, when your body is miserable, is to make it think of something else."

"Can you do it, miss?" faltered Becky, regarding her with admiring eyes.

Sara knitted her brows a moment.

"Sometimes I can and sometimes I can't," she said stoutly. "But when I *can* I'm all right. And what I believe is that we always could—if we practised enough. I've been practising a good deal lately, and it's beginning to be easier than it used to be. When things are horrible—just horrible—I think as hard as ever I can of being a princess. I say to myself, 'I am a princess, and I am a fairy one, and because I am a fairy nothing can hurt me or make me uncomfortable.' You don't know how it makes you forget,"—with a laugh.

She had many opportunities of making her mind think of something else, and many opportunities of proving to herself whether or not she was a princess. But one of the strongest tests she was ever put to came on a certain dreadful day which, she often thought afterward, would never quite fade out of her memory even in the years to come.

For several days it had rained continuously; the streets were chilly and sloppy and full of dreary, cold mist; there was mud everywhere,—sticky London mud,—and over everything the pall of drizzle and fog. Of course there were several long and tiresome errands to be done,—there always were on days like this,—and Sara was sent out again and again, until her shabby clothes were damp through. The absurd old feathers on her forlorn hat were more draggled and absurd than ever, and her downtrodden shoes were so wet that they could not hold any more water. Added to this, she had been deprived of her dinner, because Miss Minchin had chosen to punish her. She was so cold and hungry and tired that her face began to have a pinched look, and now and then some kind-hearted person passing her in the street glanced at her with sudden sympathy. But she did not know that. She hurried on, trying to make her mind think of something else. It was really very necessary. Her way of doing it was to "pretend" and "suppose" with all the strength that was left in her. But really this time it was harder than she had ever found it, and once or twice she thought it almost made her more cold and hungry instead of less so. But she persevered obstinately, and as the muddy water squelched through her broken shoes and the wind seemed trying to drag her thin jacket from her, she talked to herself as she walked, though she did not speak aloud or even move her lips.

"Suppose I had dry clothes on," she thought. "Suppose I had good shoes and a long, thick coat and merino stockings and a whole umbrella. And suppose—suppose—just when I was near a baker's where they sold hot buns, I should find sixpence—which belonged to nobody. *Suppose*, if I did, I should go into the shop and buy six of the hottest buns and eat them all without stopping."

Some very odd things happen in this world sometimes.

It certainly was an odd thing that happened to Sara. She had to cross the street just when she was saying this to herself. The mud was dreadful—she almost had to wade. She picked her way as carefully as she could, but she could not save herself much; only, in picking her way, she had to look down at her feet and the mud, and in looking down—just as she reached the pavement—she saw something shining in the gutter. It was actually a piece of silver—a tiny piece trodden upon by many feet, but still with spirit enough to shine a little. Not quite a sixpence, but the next thing to it—a fourpenny piece.

In one second it was in her cold little red-and-blue hand.

"Oh," she gasped, "it is true! It is true!"

And then, if you will believe me, she looked straight at the shop directly facing her. And it was a baker's shop, and a cheerful, stout, motherly woman with rosy cheeks was putting into the window a tray of delicious newly baked hot buns, fresh from the oven—large, plump, shiny buns, with currants in them.

It almost made Sara feel faint for a few seconds—the shock, and the sight of the buns, and the delightful odors of warm bread floating up through the baker's cellar window.

She knew she need not hesitate to use the little piece of money. It had evidently been lying in the mud for some time, and its owner was completely lost in the stream of passing people who crowded and jostled each other all day long.

"But I'll go and ask the baker woman if she has lost anything," she said to herself, rather faintly. So she crossed the pavement and put her wet foot on the step. As she did so she saw something that made her stop.

It was a little figure more forlorn even than herself—a little figure which was not much more than a bundle of rags, from which small, bare, red muddy feet peeped out, only because the rags with which their owner was trying to cover them were not long enough. Above the rags appeared a shock head of tangled hair, and a dirty face with big, hollow, hungry eyes.

Sara knew they were hungry eyes the moment she saw them, and she felt a sudden sympathy.

"This," she said to herself, with a little sigh, "is one of the pop-ulace—and she is hungrier than I am."

The child—this "one of the populace"—stared up at Sara, and shuffled herself aside a little, so as to give her room to pass. She was used to being made to give room to everybody. She knew that if a policeman chanced to see her he would tell her to "move on."

Sara clutched her little fourpenny piece and hesitated a few seconds. Then she spoke to her.

"Are you hungry?" she asked.

The child shuffled herself and her rags a little more.

"Ain't I jist?" she said in a hoarse voice. "Jist ain't I?"

"Haven't you had any dinner?" said Sara.

"No dinner,"—more hoarsely still and with more shuffling. "Nor yet no bre'fast—nor yet no supper. No nothin'."

"Since when?" asked Sara.

"Dunno. Never got nothin' to-day—nowhere. I've axed an' axed."

Just to look at her made Sara more hungry and faint. But those queer little thoughts were at work in her brain, and she was talking to herself, though she was sick at heart.

"If I'm a princess," she was saying—"if I'm a princess—when they were poor and driven from their thrones—they always shared—with the populace—if they met one poorer and hungrier than themselves. They always shared. Buns are a penny each. If it had been sixpence I could have eaten six. It won't be enough for either of us. But it will be better than nothing."

"Wait a minute," she said to the beggar child.

She went into the shop. It was warm and smelled deliciously. The woman was just going to put some more hot buns into the window.

"If you please," said Sara, "have you lost fourpence—a silver fourpence?" And she held the forlorn little piece of money out to her.

The woman looked at it and then at her—at her intense little face and draggled, once fine clothes.

"Bless us! no," she answered. "Did you find it?"

"Yes," said Sara. "In the gutter."

"Keep it, then," said the woman. "It may have been there for a week, and goodness knows who lost it. *You* could never find out."

"I know that," said Sara, "but I thought I would ask you."

"Not many would," said the woman, looking puzzled and interested and good-natured all at once.

"Do you want to buy something?" she added, as she saw Sara glance at the buns.

"Four buns, if you please," said Sara. "Those at a penny each."

The woman went to the window and put some in a paper bag.

Sara noticed that she put in six.

"I said four, if you please," she explained. "I have only fourpence."

"I'll throw in two for makeweight," said the woman, with her good-natured look. "I dare say you can eat them sometime. Aren't you hungry?"

A mist rose before Sara's eyes.

"Yes," she answered. "I am very hungry, and I am much obliged to you for your kindness; and"—she was going to add, "there is a child outside who is hungrier than I am." But just at that moment two or three customers came in at once, and each one seemed in a hurry, so she could only thank the woman again and go out.

The beggar girl was still huddled up in the corner of the step. She looked frightful in her wet and dirty rags. She was staring straight before her with a stupid look of suffering, and Sara saw her suddenly draw the back of her roughened black hand across her eyes to rub away the tears which seemed to have surprised her by forcing their way from under her lids. She was muttering to herself.

Sara opened her paper bag and took out one of the hot buns, which had already warmed her own cold hands a little.

"See," she said, putting the bun in the ragged lap, "this is nice and hot. Eat it, and you will not feel so hungry."

The child started and stared up at her, as if such sudden, amazing good luck almost frightened her; then she snatched up the bun and began to cram it into her mouth with great wolfish bites.

"Oh, my! Oh, my!" Sara heard her say hoarsely, in wild delight. *"Oh, my!"*

Sara took out three more buns and put them down.

The sound in the hoarse, ravenous voice was awful.

"She is hungrier than I am," she said to herself. "She's starving." But her hand trembled when she put down the fourth bun. "I'm not starving," she said—and she put down the fifth.

The little ravening London savage was still snatching and devouring when she turned away. She was too ravenous to give any thanks, even if she had ever been taught politeness—which she had not. She was only a poor little wild animal.

"Good-by," said Sara.

When she reached the other side of the street she looked back. The child had a bun in each hand and had stopped in the middle of a bite to watch her. Sara gave her a little nod, and the child, after another stare,—a curious lingering stare,—jerked her shaggy head in response, and until Sara was out of sight she did not take another bite or even finish the one she had begun.

At that moment the baker-woman looked out of her shop window.

"Well, I never!" she exclaimed. "If that young un hasn't given her buns to a beggar child! It wasn't because she didn't want them, either. Well, well, she looked hungry enough. I'd give something to know what she did it for."

She stood behind her window for a few moments and pondered. Then her curiosity got the better of her. She went to the door and spoke to the beggar child.

"Who gave you those buns?" she asked her.

The child nodded her head toward Sara's vanishing figure.

"What did she say?" inquired the woman.

"Axed me if I was 'ungry," replied the hoarse voice.

"What did you say?"

"Said I was jist."

"And then she came in and got the buns, and gave them to you, did she?"

The child nodded.

"How many?"

"Five."

The woman thought it over.

"Left just one for herself," she said in a low voice. "And she could have eaten the whole six—I saw it in her eyes."

She looked after the little draggled far-away figure and felt more disturbed in her usually comfortable mind than she had felt for many a day.

"I wish she hadn't gone so quick," she said. "I'm blest if she shouldn't have had a dozen." Then she turned to the child.

"Are you hungry yet?" she said.

"I'm allus hungry," was the answer, "but 't ain't as bad as it was."

"Come in here," said the woman, and she held open the shop door.

The child got up and shuffled in. To be invited into a warm place full of bread seemed an incredible thing. She did not know what was going to happen. She did not care, even.

"Get yourself warm," said the woman, pointing to a fire in the tiny back room. "And look here; when you are hard up for a bit of bread, you can come in here and ask for it. I'm blest if I won't give it to you for that young one's sake."

·   ·   ·

Sara found some comfort in her remaining bun. At all events, it was very hot, and it was better than nothing. As she walked along she broke off small pieces and ate them slowly to make them last longer.

"Suppose it was a magic bun," she said, "and a bite was as much as a whole dinner. I should be overeating myself if I went on like this."

It was dark when she reached the square where the Select Seminary was situated. The lights in the houses were all lighted. The blinds were not yet drawn in the windows of the room where she nearly always caught glimpses of members of the Large Family. Frequently at this hour she could see the gentleman she called Mr. Montmorency sitting in a big chair, with a small swarm round him, talking, laughing, perching on the arms of his seat or on his knees or leaning against them. This evening the swarm was about him, but he was not seated. On the contrary, there was a good deal of excitement going on. It was evident that a journey was to be taken, and it was Mr. Montmorency who was going to take it. A brougham stood before the door, and a big portmanteau had been strapped upon it. The children were dancing about, chattering and hanging on to their father. The pretty rosy mother was standing near him, talking as if she was asking final questions. Sara paused a moment to see the little ones lifted up and kissed and the bigger ones bent over and kissed also.

"I wonder if he will stay away long," she thought. "The portmanteau is rather big. Oh, dear, how they will miss him! I shall miss him myself—even though he doesn't know I am alive."

When the door opened she moved away,—remembering the sixpence,—but she saw the traveller come out and stand against the background of the warmly lighted hall, the older children still hovering about him.

"Will Moscow be covered with snow?" said the little girl Janet. "Will there be ice everywhere?"

"Shall you drive in a drosky?" cried another. "Shall you see the Czar?"

"I will write and tell you all about it," he answered, laughing. "And I will send you pictures of muzhiks and things. Run into the house. It is a hideous damp night. I would rather stay with you than go to Moscow. Good night! Good night, duckies! God bless you!" And he ran down the steps and jumped into the brougham.

"If you find the little girl, give her our love," shouted Guy Clarence, jumping up and down on the door-mat.

Then they went in and shut the door.

"Did you see," said Janet to Nora, as they went back to the room—"the little-girl-who-is-not-a-beggar was passing? She looked all cold and wet, and I saw her turn her head over her shoulder and look at us. Mamma says her clothes always look as if they had been given her by some one who was quite rich— some one who only let her have them because they were too shabby to wear. The people at the school always send her out on errands on the horridest days and nights there are."

Sara crossed the square to Miss Minchin's area steps, feeling faint and shaky.

"I wonder who the little girl is," she thought—"the little girl he is going to look for."

And she went down the area steps, lugging her basket and finding it very heavy indeed, as the father of the Large Family drove quickly on his way to the station to take the train which was to carry him to Moscow, where he was to make his best efforts to search for the lost little daughter of Captain Crewe.

CHAPTER 14
WHAT MELCHISEDEC HEARD AND SAW

On this very afternoon, while Sara was out, a strange thing
happened in the attic. Only Melchisedec saw and heard it; and he
was so much alarmed and mystified that he scuttled back to his
hole and hid there, and really quaked and trembled as he peeped
out furtively and with great caution to watch what was going on.

The attic had been very still all the day after Sara had left it in
the early morning. The stillness had only been broken by the pattering of the rain upon the slates and the skylight. Melchisedec
had, in fact, found it rather dull; and when the rain ceased to
patter and perfect silence reigned, he decided to come out and
reconnoitre, though experience taught him that Sara would not
return for some time. He had been rambling and sniffing about,
and had just found a totally unexpected and unexplained crumb
left from his last meal, when his attention was attracted by a
sound on the roof. He stopped to listen with a palpitating heart.
The sound suggested that something was moving on the roof. It
was approaching the skylight; it reached the skylight. The skylight was being mysteriously opened. A dark face peered into the
attic; then another face appeared behind it, and both looked in
with signs of caution and interest. Two men were outside on the
roof, and were making silent preparations to enter through the
skylight itself. One was Ram Dass, and the other was a young
man who was the Indian gentleman's secretary; but of course
Melchisedec did not know this. He only knew that the men were
invading the silence and privacy of the attic; and as the one with
the dark face let himself down through the aperture with such
lightness and dexterity that he did not make the slightest sound,

Melchisedec turned tail and fled precipitately back to his hole. He was frightened to death. He had ceased to be timid with Sara, and knew she would never throw anything but crumbs, and would never make any sound other than the soft, low, coaxing whistling; but strange men were dangerous things to remain near. He lay close and flat near the entrance of his home, just managing to peep through the crack with a bright, alarmed eye. How much he understood of the talk he heard I am not in the least able to say; but, even if he had understood it all, he would probably have remained greatly mystified.

The secretary, who was light and young, slipped through the skylight as noiselessly as Ram Dass had done; and he caught a last glimpse of Melchisedec's vanishing tail.

"Was that a rat?" he asked Ram Dass in a whisper.

"Yes; a rat, Sahib," answered Ram Dass, also whispering. "There are many in the walls."

"Ugh!" exclaimed the young man; "it is a wonder the child is not terrified of them."

Ram Dass made a gesture with his hands. He also smiled respectfully. He was in this place as the intimate exponent of Sara, though she had only spoken to him once.

"The child is the little friend of all things, Sahib," he answered. "She is not as other children. I see her when she does not see me. I slip across the slates and look at her many nights to see that she is safe. I watch her from my window when she does not know I am near. She stands on the table there and looks out at the sky as if it spoke to her. The sparrows come at her call. The rat she has fed and tamed in her loneliness. The poor slave of the house comes to her for comfort. There is a little child who comes to her in secret; there is one older who worships her and would listen to her forever if she might. This I have seen when I have crept across the roof. By the mistress of the house—who is an evil woman— she is treated like a pariah; but she has the bearing of a child who is of the blood of kings!"

"You seem to know a great deal about her," the secretary said.

"All her life each day I know," answered Ram Dass. "Her going out I know, and her coming in; her sadness and her poor joys; her coldness and her hunger. I know when she sits alone until midnight, learning from her books; I know when her secret friends steal to her and she is happier—as children can be, even in the midst of poverty—because they come and she may laugh and talk with them in whispers. If she were ill I should know, and I would come and serve her if it might be done."

"You are sure no one comes near this place but herself, and that she will not return and surprise us. She would be frightened if she found us here, and the Sahib Carrisford's plan would be spoiled."

Ram Dass crossed noiselessly to the door and stood close to it.

"None mount here but herself, Sahib," he said. "She has gone out with her basket and may be gone for hours. If I stand here I can hear any step before it reaches the last flight of stairs."

The secretary took a pencil and a tablet from his breast pocket.

"Keep your ears open," he said; and he began to walk slowly and softly around the miserable little room, making rapid notes on his tablet as he looked at things.

First he went to the narrow bed. He pressed his hand upon the mattress and uttered an exclamation.

"As hard as a stone," he said. "That will have to be altered some day when she is out. A special journey can be made to bring it across. It cannot be done to-night." He lifted the covering and examined the one thin pillow.

"Coverlet dingy and worn, blanket thin, sheets patched and ragged," he said. "What a bed for a child to sleep in—and in a house which calls itself respectable! There has not been a fire in that grate for many a day," glancing at the rusty fireplace.

"Never since I have seen it," said Ram Dass. "The mistress of the house is not one who remembers that another than herself may be cold."

The secretary was writing quickly on his tablet. He looked up from it as he tore off a leaf and slipped it into his breast pocket.

"It is a strange way of doing the thing," he said. "Who planned it?"

Ram Dass made a modestly apologetic obeisance.

"It is true that the first thought was mine, Sahib," he said; "though it was naught but a fancy. I am fond of this child; we are both lonely. It is her way to relate her visions to her secret friends. Being sad one night, I lay close to the open skylight and listened. The vision she related told what this miserable room might be if it had comforts in it. She seemed to see it as she talked, and she grew cheered and warmed as she spoke. Then she came to this fancy; and the next day, the Sahib being ill and wretched, I told him of the thing to amuse him. It seemed then but a dream, but it pleased the Sahib. To hear of the child's doings gave him entertainment. He became interested in her and asked questions. At last he began to please himself with the thought of making her visions real things."

"You think that it can be done while she sleeps? Suppose she awakened," suggested the secretary; and it was evident that whatsoever the plan referred to was, it had caught and pleased his fancy as well as the Sahib Carrisford's.

"I can move as if my feet were of velvet," Ram Dass replied; "and children sleep soundly—even the unhappy ones. I could have entered this room in the night many times, and without causing her to turn upon her pillow. If the other bearer passes to me the things through the window, I can do all and she will not stir. When she awakens she will think a magician has been here."

He smiled as if his heart warmed under his white robe, and the secretary smiled back at him.

"It will be like a story from the 'Arabian Nights,'" he said. "Only an Oriental could have planned it. It does not belong to London fogs."

They did not remain very long, to the great relief of Melchisedec, who, as he probably did not comprehend their conversation, felt their movements and whispers ominous. The young secretary seemed interested in everything. He wrote down things about the floor, the fireplace, the broken footstool, the old table, the walls—which last he touched with his hand again and again, seeming much pleased when he found that a number of old nails had been driven in various places.

"You can hang things on them," he said.

Ram Dass smiled mysteriously.

"Yesterday, when she was out," he said, "I entered, bringing with me small, sharp nails which can be pressed into the wall without blows from a hammer. I placed many in the plaster where I may need them. They are ready."

The Indian gentleman's secretary stood still and looked round him as he thrust his tablets back into his pocket.

"I think I have made notes enough; we can go now," he said. "The Sahib Carrisford has a warm heart. It is a thousand pities that he has not found the lost child."

"If he should find her his strength would be restored to him," said Ram Dass. "His God may lead her to him yet."

Then they slipped through the skylight as noiselessly as they had entered it. And, after he was quite sure they had gone, Melchisedec was greatly relieved, and in the course of a few minutes felt it safe enough to emerge from his hole again and scuffle about in the hope that even such alarming human beings as these might have chanced to carry crumbs in their pockets and drop one or two of them.

CHAPTER 15
THE MAGIC

When Sara had passed the house next door she had seen Ram Dass closing the shutters, and caught her glimpse of this room also.

"It is a long time since I saw a nice place from the inside," was the thought which crossed her mind.

There was the usual bright fire glowing in the grate, and the Indian gentleman was sitting before it. His head was resting in his hand, and he looked as lonely and unhappy as ever.

"Poor man!" said Sara; "I wonder what *you* are supposing."

And this was what he was "supposing" at that very moment.

"Suppose," he was thinking, "suppose—even if Carmichael traces the people to Moscow—the little girl they took from Madame Pascal's school in Paris is *not* the one we are in search of. Suppose she proves to be quite a different child. What steps shall I take next?"

When Sara went into the house she met Miss Minchin, who had come down-stairs to scold the cook.

"Where have you wasted your time?" she demanded. "You have been out for hours."

"It was so wet and muddy," Sara answered, "it was hard to walk, because my shoes were so bad and slipped about."

"Make no excuses," said Miss Minchin, "and tell no falsehoods."

Sara went in to the cook. The cook had received a severe lecture and was in a fearful temper as a result. She was only too rejoiced to have some one to vent her rage on, and Sara was a convenience, as usual.

"Why didn't you stay all night?" she snapped.

Sara laid her purchases on the table.

"Here are the things," she said.

The cook looked them over, grumbling. She was in a very savage humor indeed.

"May I have something to eat?" Sara asked rather faintly.

"Tea's over and done with," was the answer. "Did you expect me to keep it hot for you?"

Sara stood silent for a second.

"I had no dinner," she said next, and her voice was quite low. She made it low because she was afraid it would tremble.

"There's some bread in the pantry," said the cook. "That's all you'll get at this time of day."

Sara went and found the bread. It was old and hard and dry. The cook was in too vicious a humor to give her anything to eat with it. It was always safe and easy to vent her spite on Sara. Really, it was hard for the child to climb the three long flights of stairs leading to her attic. She often found them long and steep when she was tired; but to-night it seemed as if she would never reach the top. Several times she was obliged to stop to rest. When she reached the top landing she was glad to see the glimmer of a light coming from under her door. That meant that Ermengarde had managed to creep up to pay her a visit. There was some comfort in that. It was better than to go into the room alone and find it empty and desolate. The mere presence of plump, comfortable Ermengarde, wrapped in her red shawl, would warm it a little.

Yes; there Ermengarde was when she opened the door. She was sitting in the middle of the bed, with her feet tucked safely under her. She had never become intimate with Melchisedec and his family, though they rather fascinated her. When she found herself alone in the attic she always preferred to sit on the bed until Sara arrived. She had, in fact, on this occasion had time to become rather nervous, because Melchisedec had appeared and sniffed about a good deal, and once had made her utter a repressed squeal by sitting up on his hind legs and, while he looked at her, sniffing pointedly in her direction.

"Oh, Sara," she cried out, "I *am* glad you have come. Melchy *would* sniff about so. I tried to coax him to go back, but he wouldn't for such a long time. I like him, you know; but it does frighten me when he sniffs right at me. Do you think he ever *would* jump?"

"No," answered Sara.

Ermengarde crawled forward on the bed to look at her.

"You *do* look tired, Sara," she said; "you are quite pale."

"I *am* tired," said Sara, dropping on to the lop-sided foot-stool. "Oh, there's Melchisedec, poor thing. He's come to ask for his supper."

Melchisedec had come out of his hole as if he had been listening for her footstep. Sara was quite sure he knew it. He came forward with an affectionate, expectant expression as Sara put her hand in her pocket and turned it inside out, shaking her head.

"I'm very sorry," she said. "I haven't one crumb left. Go home, Melchisedec, and tell your wife there was nothing in my pocket. I'm afraid I forgot because the cook and Miss Minchin were so cross."

Melchisedec seemed to understand. He shuffled resignedly, if not contentedly, back to his home.

"I did not expect to see you to-night, Ermie," Sara said.

Ermengarde hugged herself in the red shawl.

"Miss Amelia has gone out to spend the night with her old aunt," she explained. "No one else ever comes and looks into the bedrooms after we are in bed. I could stay here until morning if I wanted to."

She pointed toward the table under the skylight. Sara had not looked toward it as she came in. A number of books were piled upon it. Ermengarde's gesture was a dejected one.

"Papa has sent me some more books, Sara," she said. "There they are."

Sara looked round and got up at once. She ran to the table, and picking up the top volume, turned over its leaves quickly. For the moment she forgot her discomforts.

"Ah," she cried out, "how beautiful! Carlyle's 'French Revolution.' I have *so* wanted to read that!"

"I haven't," said Ermengarde. "And papa will be so cross if I don't. He'll expect me to know all about it when I go home for the holidays. What *shall* I do?"

Sara stopped turning over the leaves and looked at her with an excited flush on her cheeks.

"Look here," she cried, "if you'll lend me these books, *I'll* read them—and tell you everything that's in them afterward—and I'll tell it so that you will remember it, too."

"Oh, goodness!" exclaimed Ermengarde. "Do you think you can?"

"I know I can," Sara answered. "The little ones always remember what I tell them."

"Sara," said Ermengarde, hope gleaming in her round face, "if you'll do that, and make me remember, I'll—I'll give you anything."

"I don't want you to give me anything," said Sara. "I want your books—I want them!" Her eyes grew big, and her chest heaved.

"Take them, then," said Ermengarde. "I wish I wanted them—but I don't. I'm not clever, and my father is, and he thinks I ought to be."

Sara was opening one book after the other. "What are you going to tell your father?" she asked, a slight doubt dawning in her mind.

"Oh, he needn't know," answered Ermengarde. "He'll think I've read them."

Sara put down her book and shook her head slowly. "That's almost like telling lies," she said. "And lies—well, you see, they are not only wicked—they're *vulgar*. Sometimes"—reflectively—"I've thought perhaps I might do something wicked,—I might suddenly fly into a rage and kill Miss Minchin, you know, when she was ill-treating me,—but I *couldn't* be vulgar. Why can't you tell your father *I* read them?"

"He wants me to read them," said Ermengarde, a little discouraged by this unexpected turn of affairs.

"He wants you to know what is in them," said Sara. "And if I can tell it to you in an easy way and make you remember it, I should think he would like that."

"He'll like it if I learn anything in *any* way," said rueful Ermengarde. "You would if you were my father."

"It's not your fault that—" began Sara. She pulled herself up and stopped rather suddenly. She had been going to say, "It's not your fault that you are stupid."

"That what?" Ermengarde asked.

"That you can't learn things quickly," amended Sara. "If you can't, you can't. If I can—why, I can; that's all."

She always felt very tender of Ermengarde, and tried not to let her feel too strongly the difference between being able to learn anything at once, and not being able to learn anything at all. As she looked at her plump face, one of her wise, old-fashioned thoughts came to her.

"Perhaps," she said, "to be able to learn things quickly isn't everything. To be kind is worth a great deal to other people. If Miss Minchin knew everything on earth and was like what she is now, she'd still be a detestable thing, and everybody would hate her. Lots of clever people have done harm and been wicked. Look at Robespierre—"

She stopped and examined Ermengarde's countenance, which was beginning to look bewildered. "Don't you remember?" she demanded. "I told you about him not long ago. I believe you've forgotten."

"Well, I don't remember *all* of it," admitted Ermengarde.

"Well, you wait a minute," said Sara, "and I'll take off my wet things and wrap myself in the coverlet and tell you over again."

She took off her hat and coat and hung them on a nail against the wall, and she changed her wet shoes for an old pair of slippers. Then she jumped on the bed, and drawing the coverlet about her shoulders, sat with her arms round her knees.

"Now, listen," she said.

She plunged into the gory records of the French Revolution,

and told such stories of it that Ermengarde's eyes grew round with alarm and she held her breath. But though she was rather terrified, there was a delightful thrill in listening, and she was not likely to forget Robespierre again, or to have any doubts about the Princesse de Lamballe.

"You know they put her head on a pike and danced round it," Sara explained. "And she had beautiful floating blonde hair; and when I think of her, I never see her head on her body, but always on a pike, with those furious people dancing and howling."

It was agreed that Mr. St. John was to be told the plan they had made, and for the present the books were to be left in the attic.

"Now let's tell each other things," said Sara. "How are you getting on with your French lessons?"

"Ever so much better since the last time I came up here and you explained the conjugations. Miss Minchin could not understand why I did my exercises so well that first morning."

Sara laughed a little and hugged her knees.

"She doesn't understand why Lottie is doing her sums so well," she said; "but it is because she creeps up here, too, and I help her." She glanced round the room. "The attic would be rather nice—if it wasn't so dreadful," she said, laughing again. "It's a good place to pretend in."

The truth was that Ermengarde did not know anything of the sometimes almost unbearable side of life in the attic, and she had not a sufficiently vivid imagination to depict it for herself. On the rare occasions that she could reach Sara's room she only saw that side of it which was made exciting by things which were "pretended" and stories which were told. Her visits partook of the character of adventures; and though sometimes Sara looked rather pale, and it was not to be denied that she had grown very thin, her proud little spirit would not admit of complaints. She had never confessed that at times she was almost ravenous with hunger, as she was to-night. She was growing rapidly, and her constant walking and running about would have given her a keen appetite even if she had had abundant and regular meals of a much more nourishing nature than the unappetizing, inferior food snatched at such odd times as suited the kitchen convenience. She was growing used to a certain gnawing feeling in her young stomach.

"I suppose soldiers feel like this when they are on a long and weary march," she often said to herself. She liked the sound of the phrase, "long and weary march." It made her feel rather like a soldier. She had also a quaint sense of being a hostess in the attic.

"If I lived in a castle," she argued, "and Ermengarde was the lady of another castle, and came to see me, with knights and squires and vassals riding with her, and pennons flying; when I heard the clarions sounding outside the drawbridge I should go down to receive her, and I should spread feasts in the banquet-hall and call in minstrels to sing and play and relate romances. When she comes into the attic I can't spread feasts, but I can tell stories, and not let her know disagreeable things. I dare say poor chatelaines had to do that in times of famine, when their lands had been pillaged." She was a proud, brave little chatelaine, and dispensed generously the one hospitality she could offer—the dreams she dreamed—the visions she saw—the imaginings which were her joy and comfort.

So, as they sat together, Ermengarde did not know that she was faint as well as ravenous, and that while she talked she now and then wondered if her hunger would let her sleep when she was left alone. She felt as if she had never been quite so hungry before.

"I wish I was as thin as you, Sara," Ermengarde said suddenly. "I believe you are thinner than you used to be. Your eyes look so big, and look at the sharp little bones sticking out of your elbow!"

Sara pulled down her sleeve, which had pushed itself up.

"I always was a thin child," she said bravely, "and I always had big green eyes."

"I love your queer eyes," said Ermengarde, looking into them with affectionate admiration. "They always look as if they saw such a long way. I love them—and I love them to be green—though they look black generally."

"They are cat's eyes," laughed Sara; "but I can't see in the dark with them—because I have tried, and I couldn't—I wish I could."

It was just at this minute that something happened at the sky-light which neither of them saw. If either of them had chanced to turn and look, she would have been startled by the sight of a dark face which peered cautiously into the room and disappeared as quickly and almost as silently as they had appeared. Not *quite* as silently, however. Sara, who had keen ears, suddenly turned a little and looked up at the roof.

"That didn't sound like Melchisedec," she said. "It wasn't scratchy enough."

"What?" said Ermengarde, a little startled.

"Didn't you think you heard something?" asked Sara.

"N-no," Ermengarde faltered. "Did you?"

"Perhaps I didn't," said Sara; "but I thought I did. It sounded as if something was on the slates—something that dragged softly."

"What could it be?" said Ermengarde. "Could it be—robbers?"

"No," Sara began cheerfully. "There is nothing to steal—"

She broke off in the middle of her words. They both heard the sound that checked her. It was not on the slates, but on the stairs below, and it was Miss Minchin's angry voice. Sara sprang off the bed, and put out the candle.

"She is scolding Becky," she whispered, as she stood in the darkness. "She is making her cry."

"Will she come in here?" Ermengarde whispered back, panic-stricken.

"No. She will think I am in bed. Don't stir."

It was very seldom that Miss Minchin mounted the last flight of stairs. Sara could only remember that she had done it once before. But now she was angry enough to be coming at least part of the way up, and it sounded as if she was driving Becky before her.

"You impudent, dishonest child!" they heard her say. "Cook tells me she has missed things repeatedly."

"'T warn't me, mum," said Becky, sobbing. "I was 'ungry enough, but 't warn't me—never!"

"You deserve to be sent to prison," said Miss Minchin's voice. "Picking and stealing! Half a meat-pie, indeed!"

"'T warn't me," wept Becky. "I could 'ave eat a whole un—but I never laid a finger on it."

Miss Minchin was out of breath between temper and mounting the stairs. The meat-pie had been intended for her special late supper. It became apparent that she boxed Becky's ears.

"Don't tell falsehoods," she said. "Go to your room this instant."

Both Sara and Ermengarde heard the slap, and then heard Becky run in her slip-shod shoes up the stairs and into her attic. They heard her door shut, and knew that she threw herself upon her bed.

"I could 'ave e't two of 'em," they heard her cry into her pillow. "An' I never took a bite. 'T was cook give it to her policeman."

Sara stood in the middle of the room in the darkness. She was clenching her little teeth and opening and shutting fiercely her outstretched hands. She could scarcely stand still, but she dared not move until Miss Minchin had gone down the stairs and all was still.

"The wicked, cruel thing!" she burst forth. "The cook takes things herself and then says Becky steals them. She *doesn't*! She *doesn't*! She's so hungry sometimes that she eats crusts out of the ash-barrel!" She pressed her hands hard against her face and burst into passionate little sobs, and Ermengarde, hearing this unusual thing, was quite overawed by it. Sara was crying! The unconquerable Sara! It seemed to denote something new—some mood she had never known. Suppose—! Suppose—! A new dread possibility presented itself to her kind, slow, little mind all at once. She crept off the bed in the dark and found her way to the table where the candle stood. She struck a match and lit the candle. When she had lighted it, she bent forward and looked at Sara, with her new thought growing to definite fear in her eyes.

"Sara," she said in a timid, almost awe-stricken voice, "are—are—you never told me—I don't want to be rude, but—are *you* ever hungry?"

It was too much just at that moment. The barrier broke down. Sara lifted her face from her hands.

"Yes," she said in a new passionate way. "Yes, I am. I'm so hungry now that I could almost eat *you*. And it makes it worse to hear poor Becky. She's hungrier than I am."

Ermengarde gasped.

"Oh! Oh!" she cried woefully; "and I never knew!"

"I didn't want you to know," Sara said. "It would have made me feel like a street beggar. I know I look like a street beggar."

"No, you don't—you don't!" Ermengarde broke in. "Your clothes are a little queer,—but you *couldn't* look like a street beggar. You haven't a street-beggar face."

"A little boy once gave me a sixpence for charity," said Sara, with a short little laugh in spite of herself. "Here it is." And she pulled out the thin ribbon from her neck. "He wouldn't have given me his Christmas sixpence if I hadn't looked as if I needed it."

Somehow the sight of the dear little sixpence was good for both of them. It made them laugh a little, though they both had tears in their eyes.

"Who was he?" asked Ermengarde, looking at it quite as if it had not been a mere ordinary silver sixpence.

"He was a darling little thing going to a party," said Sara. "He was one of the Large Family, the little one with the round legs—the one I call Guy Clarence. I suppose his nursery was crammed with Christmas presents and hampers full of cakes and things, and he could see I had had nothing."

Ermengarde gave a little jump backward. The last sentences had recalled something to her troubled mind and gave her a sudden inspiration.

"Oh, Sara!" she cried. "What a silly thing I am not to have thought of it!"

"Of what?"

"Something splendid!" said Ermengarde, in an excited hurry. "This very afternoon my nicest aunt sent me a box. It is full of good things. I never touched it, I had so much pudding at dinner, and I was so bothered about papa's books." Her words began to tumble over each other. "It's got cake in it, and little meat-pies, and jam-tarts and buns, and oranges and red-currant wine, and figs and chocolate. I'll creep back to my room and get it this minute, and we'll eat it now."

Sara almost reeled. When one is faint with hunger the mention of food has sometimes a curious effect. She clutched Ermengarde's arm.

"Do you think—you *could?*" she ejaculated.

"I know I could," answered Ermengarde, and she ran to the door—opened it softly—put her head out into the darkness, and listened. Then she went back to Sara. "The lights are out. Everybody's in bed. I can creep—and creep—and no one will hear."

It was so delightful that they caught each other's hands and a sudden light sprang into Sara's eyes.

"Ermie!" she said. "Let us *pretend!* Let us pretend it's a party! And oh, won't you invite the prisoner in the next cell?"

"Yes! Yes! Let us knock on the wall now. The jailer won't hear."

Sara went to the wall. Through it she could hear poor Becky crying more softly. She knocked four times.

"That means, 'Come to me through the secret passage under the wall,'" she explained. "'I have something to communicate.'"

Five quick knocks answered her.

"She is coming," she said.

Almost immediately the door of the attic opened and Becky appeared. Her eyes were red and her cap was sliding off, and when she caught sight of Ermengarde she began to rub her face nervously with her apron.

"Don't mind me a bit, Becky!" cried Ermengarde.

"Miss Ermengarde has asked you to come in," said Sara, "because she is going to bring a box of good things up here to us."

Becky's cap almost fell off entirely, she broke in with such excitement.

"To eat, miss?" she said. "Things that's good to eat?"

"Yes," answered Sara, "and we are going to pretend a party."

"And you shall have as much as you *want* to eat," put in Ermengarde. "I'll go this minute!"

She was in such haste that as she tiptoed out of the attic she dropped her red shawl and did not know it had fallen. No one saw it for a minute or so. Becky was too much overpowered by the good luck which had befallen her.

"Oh, miss! oh, miss!" she gasped; "I know it was you that asked her to let me come. It—it makes me cry to think of it." And she went to Sara's side and stood and looked at her worshippingly.

But in Sara's hungry eyes the old light had begun to glow and transform her world for her. Here in the attic—with the cold night outside—with the afternoon in the sloppy streets barely passed—with the memory of the awful unfed look in the beggar child's eyes not yet faded—this simple, cheerful thing had happened like a thing of magic.

She caught her breath.

"Somehow, something always happens," she cried, "just before things get to the very worst. It is as if the Magic did it. If I could only just remember that always. The worst thing never *quite* comes."

She gave Becky a little cheerful shake.

"No, no! You mustn't cry!" she said. "We must make haste and set the table."

"Set the table, miss?" said Becky, gazing round the room. "What'll we set it with?"

Sara looked round the attic, too.

"There doesn't seem to be much," she answered, half laughing.

That moment she saw something and pounced upon it. It was Ermengarde's red shawl which lay upon the floor.

"Here's the shawl," she cried. "I know she won't mind it. It will make such a nice red table-cloth."

They pulled the old table forward, and threw the shawl over it. Red is a wonderfully kind and comfortable color. It began to make the room look furnished directly.

"How nice a red rug would look on the floor!" exclaimed Sara. "We must pretend there is one.

Her eyes swept the bare boards with a swift glance of admiration. The rug was laid down already.

"How soft and thick it is!" she said, with the little laugh which Becky knew the meaning of; and she raised and set her foot down again delicately, as if she felt something under it.

"Yes, miss," answered Becky, watching her with serious rapture. She was always quite serious.

"What next, now?" said Sara, and she stood still and put her hands over her eyes. "Something will come if I think and wait a little"—in a soft, expectant voice. "The Magic will tell me."

One of her favorite fancies was that on "the outside," as she called it, thoughts were waiting for people to call them. Becky had seen her stand and wait many a time before, and knew that in a few seconds she would uncover an enlightened, laughing face.

In a moment she did.

"There!" she cried. "It has come! I know now! I must look among the things in the old trunk I had when I was a princess."

She flew to its corner and kneeled down. It had not been put in the attic for her benefit, but because there was no room for it elsewhere. Nothing had been left in it but rubbish. But she knew she should find something. The Magic always arranged that kind of thing in one way or another.

In a corner lay a package so insignificant-looking that it had been overlooked, and when she herself had found it she had kept it as a relic. It contained a dozen small white handkerchiefs. She seized them joyfully and ran to the table. She began to arrange them upon the red table-cover, patting and coaxing them into shape with the narrow lace edge curling outward, her Magic working its spells for her as she did it.

"These are the plates," she said. "They are golden plates. These are the richly embroidered napkins. Nuns worked them in convents in Spain."

"Did they, miss?" breathed Becky, her very soul uplifted by the information.

"You must pretend it," said Sara. "If you pretend it enough, you will see them."

"Yes, miss," said Becky; and as Sara returned to the trunk she devoted herself to the effort of accomplishing an end so much to be desired.

Sara turned suddenly to find her standing by the table, looking very queer indeed. She had shut her eyes, and was twisting her face in strange, convulsive contortions, her hands hanging stiffly clenched at her sides. She looked as if she was trying to lift some enormous weight.

"What is the matter, Becky?" Sara cried. "What are you doing?"

Becky opened her eyes with a start.

"I was a-'pretendin',' miss," she answered a little sheepishly; "I was tryin' to see it like you do. I almost did," with a hopeful grin. "But it takes a lot o' stren'th."

"Perhaps it does if you are not used to it," said Sara, with friendly sympathy; "but you don't know how easy it is when you've done it often. I wouldn't try so hard just at first. It will come to you after a while. I'll just tell you what things are. Look at these."

She held an old summer hat in her hand which she had fished out of the bottom of the trunk. There was a wreath of flowers on it. She pulled the wreath off.

"These are garlands for the feast," she said grandly. "They fill all the air with perfume. There's a mug on the wash-stand, Becky. Oh—and bring the soap-dish for a centrepiece."

Becky handed them to her reverently.

"What are they now, miss?" she inquired. "You'd think they was made of crockery,—but I know they ain't."

"This is a carven flagon," said Sara, arranging tendrils of the wreath about the mug. "And this"—bending tenderly over the soap-dish and heaping it with roses—"is purest alabaster encrusted with gems."

She touched the things gently, a happy smile hovering about her lips which made her look as if she were a creature in a dream.

"My, ain't it lovely!" whispered Becky.

"If we just had something for bonbon-dishes," Sara murmured. "There!"—darting to the trunk again. "I remember I saw something this minute."

It was only a bundle of wool wrapped in red and white tissue-paper, but the tissue-paper was soon twisted into the form of little dishes, and was combined with the remaining flowers to ornament the candlestick which was to light the feast. Only the Magic could have made it more than an old table covered with a red shawl and set with rubbish from a long-unopened trunk. But Sara drew back and gazed at it, seeing wonders; and Becky, after staring in delight, spoke with bated breath.

"This 'ere," she suggested, with a glance round the attic—"is it the Bastille now—or has it turned into somethin' different?"

"Oh, yes, yes!" said Sara; "quite different. It is a banquet-hall!"

"My eye, miss!" ejaculated Becky. "A blanket-'all!" and she turned to view the splendors about her with awed bewilderment.

"A banquet-hall," said Sara. "A vast chamber where feasts are given. It has a vaulted roof, and a minstrels' gallery, and a huge chimney filled with blazing oaken logs, and it is brilliant with waxen tapers twinkling on every side."

"My eye, Miss Sara!" gasped Becky again.

Then the door opened, and Ermengarde came in, rather staggering under the weight of her hamper. She started back with an exclamation of joy. To enter from the chill darkness outside, and find one's self confronted by a totally unanticipated board, draped with red, adorned with white napery, and wreathed with flowers, was to feel that the preparations were brilliant indeed.

"Oh, Sara!" she cried out. "You are the cleverest girl I ever saw!"

"Isn't it nice?" said Sara. "They are things out of my old trunk. I asked my Magic, and it told me to go and look."

"But oh, miss," cried Becky, "wait till she's told you what they are! They ain't just—oh, miss, please tell her," appealing to Sara.

So Sara told her, and because her Magic helped her she made her *almost* see it all: the golden platters—the vaulted spaces—the blazing logs—the twinkling waxen tapers. As the things were taken out of the hamper—the frosted cakes—the fruits—the bonbons and the wine—the feast became a splendid thing.

"It's like a real party!" cried Ermengarde.

"It's like a queen's table," sighed Becky.

Then Ermengarde had a sudden brilliant thought.

"I'll tell you what, Sara," she said. "Pretend you are a princess now and this is a royal feast."

"But it's your feast," said Sara; "you must be the princess, and we will be your maids of honor."

"Oh, I can't," said Ermengarde. "I'm too fat, and I don't know how. *You* be her."

"Well, if you want me to," said Sara.

But suddenly she thought of something else and ran to the rusty grate.

"There is a lot of paper and rubbish stuffed in here!" she exclaimed. "If we light it, there will be a bright blaze for a few minutes, and we shall feel as if it was a real fire." She struck a match and lighted it up with a great specious glow which illuminated the room.

"By the time it stops blazing," Sara said, "we shall forget about its not being real."

She stood in the dancing glow and smiled.

"Doesn't it *look* real?" she said. "Now we will begin the party."

She led the way to the table. She waved her hand graciously to Ermengarde and Becky. She was in the midst of her dream.

"Advance, fair damsels," she said in her happy dream-voice, "and be seated at the banquet-table. My noble father, the king, who is absent on a long journey, has commanded me to feast you." She turned her head slightly toward the corner of the room. "What, ho! there, minstrels! Strike up with your viols and bassoons. Princesses," she explained rapidly to Ermengarde and Becky, "always had minstrels to play at their feasts. Pretend there is a minstrel gallery up there in the corner. Now we will begin."

They had barely had time to take their pieces of cake into their hands—not one of them had time to do more, when—they all three sprang to their feet and turned pale faces toward the door—listening—listening.

Some one was coming up the stairs. There was no mistake about it. Each of them recognized the angry, mounting tread and knew that the end of all things had come.

"It's—the missus!" choked Becky, and dropped her piece of cake upon the floor.

"Yes," said Sara, her eyes growing shocked and large in her small white face. "Miss Minchin has found us out."

Miss Minchin struck the door open with a blow of her hand. She was pale herself, but it was with rage. She looked from the frightened faces to the banquet-table, and from the banquet-table to the last flicker of the burnt paper in the grate.

"I have been suspecting something of this sort," she exclaimed; "but I did not dream of such audacity. Lavinia was telling the truth."

So they knew that it was Lavinia who had somehow guessed their secret and had betrayed them. Miss Minchin strode over to Becky and boxed her ears for a second time.

"You impudent creature!" she said. "You leave the house in the morning!"

Sara stood quite still, her eyes growing larger, her face paler. Ermengarde burst into tears.

"Oh, don't send her away," she sobbed. "My aunt sent me the hamper. We're—only—having a party."

"So I see," said Miss Minchin, witheringly. "With the Princess Sara at the head of the table." She turned fiercely on Sara. "It is your doing, I know," she cried. "Ermengarde would never have thought of such a thing. You decorated the table, I suppose—with this rubbish." She stamped her foot at Becky. "Go to your attic!" she commanded, and Becky stole away, her face hidden in her apron, her shoulders shaking.

Then it was Sara's turn again.

"I will attend to you to-morrow. You shall have neither break-fast, dinner, nor supper!"

"I have not had either dinner or supper to-day, Miss Minchin," said Sara, rather faintly.

"Then all the better. You will have something to remember. Don't stand there. Put those things into the hamper again."

She began to sweep them off the table into the hamper herself, and caught sight of Ermengarde's new books.

"And you"—to Ermengarde—"have brought your beautiful new books into this dirty attic. Take them up and go back to bed. You will stay there all day to-morrow, and I shall write to your papa. What would *he* say if he knew where you are to-night?"

Something she saw in Sara's grave, fixed gaze at this moment made her turn on her fiercely.

"What are you thinking of?" she demanded. "Why do you look at me like that?"

"I was wondering," answered Sara, as she had answered that notable day in the school-room.

"What were you wondering?"

It was very like the scene in the school-room. There was no pertness in Sara's manner. It was only sad and quiet.

"I was wondering," she said in a low voice, "what *my* papa would say if he knew where I am to-night."

Miss Minchin was infuriated just as she had been before, and her anger expressed itself, as before, in an intemperate fashion. She flew at her and shook her.

"You insolent, unmanageable child!" she cried. "How dare you! How dare you!"

She picked up the books, swept the rest of the feast back into the hamper in a jumbled heap, thrust it into Ermengarde's arms, and pushed her before her toward the door.

"I will leave you to wonder," she said. "Go to bed this instant." And she shut the door behind herself and poor stumbling Ermengarde, and left Sara standing quite alone.

The dream was quite at an end. The last spark had died out of the paper in the grate and left only black tinder; the table was left bare, the golden plates and richly embroidered napkins, and the garlands were transformed again into old handkerchiefs, scraps of red and white paper, and discarded artificial flowers all scattered on the floor; the minstrels in the minstrel gallery had stolen away, and the viols and bassoons were still. Emily was sitting with her back against the wall, staring very hard. Sara saw her, and went and picked her up with trembling hands.

"There isn't any banquet left, Emily," she said. "And there isn't any princess. There is nothing left but the prisoners in the Bastille." And she sat down and hid her face.

What would have happened if she had not hidden it just then, and if she had chanced to look up at the skylight at the wrong moment, I do not know—perhaps the end of this chapter might have been quite different—because if she had glanced at the skylight she would certainly have been startled by what she would have seen. She would have seen exactly the same face pressed against the glass and peering in at her as it had peered in earlier in the evening when she had been talking to Ermengarde.

But she did not look up. She sat with her little black head in her arms for some time. She always sat like that when she was trying to bear something in silence. Then she got up and went slowly to the bed.

"I can't pretend anything else—while I am awake," she said. "There wouldn't be any use in trying. If I go to sleep, perhaps a dream will come and pretend for me."

She suddenly felt so tired—perhaps through want of food—that she sat down on the edge of the bed quite weakly.

"Suppose there was a bright fire in the grate, with lots of little dancing flames," she murmured. "Suppose there was a comfortable chair before it—and suppose there was a small table near, with a little hot—hot supper on it. And suppose"—as she drew the thin coverings over her—"suppose this was a beautiful soft bed, with fleecy blankets and large downy pillows. Suppose—suppose—"

And her very weariness was good to her, for her eyes closed and she fell fast asleep.

• • •

She did not know how long she slept. But she had been tired enough to sleep deeply and profoundly—too deeply and soundly to be disturbed by anything, even by the squeaks and scamperings of Melchisedec's entire family, if all his sons and daughters had chosen to come out of their hole to fight and tumble and play.

When she awakened it was rather suddenly, and she did not know that any particular thing had called her out of her sleep. The truth was, however, that it was a sound which had called her back—a real sound—the click of the skylight as it fell in closing after a lithe white figure which slipped through it and crouched down close by upon the slates of the roof—just near enough to see what happened in the attic, but not near enough to be seen.

At first she did not open her eyes. She felt too sleepy and—curiously enough—too warm and comfortable. She was so warm and comfortable, indeed, that she did not believe she was really awake. She never was as warm and cosey as this except in some lovely vision.

"What a nice dream!" she murmured. "I feel quite warm. I—don't—want—to—wake—up."

Of course it was a dream. She felt as if warm, delightful bedclothes were heaped upon her. She could actually *feel* blankets, and when she put out her hand it touched something exactly like a satin-covered eider-down quilt. She must not awaken from this delight—she must be quite still and make it last.

But she could not—even though she kept her eyes closed tightly, she could not. Something was forcing her to awaken—something in the room. It was a sense of light, and a sound—the sound of a crackling, roaring little fire.

"Oh, I am awakening," she said mournfully. "I can't help it—I can't."

Her eyes opened in spite of herself. And then she actually smiled—for what she saw she had never seen in the attic before, and knew she never should see.

"Oh, I *haven't* awakened," she whispered, daring to rise to her elbow and look all about her. "I am dreaming yet." She knew it *must* be a dream, for if she were awake such things could not—could not be.

Do you wonder that she felt sure she had not come back to earth? This is what she saw. In the grate there was a glowing, blazing fire; on the hob was a little brass kettle hissing and boiling; spread upon the floor was a thick, warm crimson rug; before the fire a folding-chair, unfolded, and with cushions on it; by the chair a small folding-table, unfolded, covered with a white cloth, and upon it spread small covered dishes, a cup, a saucer, a tea-pot; on the bed were new warm coverings and a satin-covered down quilt; at the foot a curious wadded silk robe, a pair of quilted slippers, and some books. The room of her dream seemed changed into fairyland—and it was flooded with warm light, for a bright lamp stood on the table covered with a rosy shade.

She sat up, resting on her elbow, and her breathing came short and fast.

"It does not—melt away," she panted. "Oh, I never had such a dream before." She scarcely dared to stir; but at last she pushed the bedclothes aside, and put her feet on the floor with a rapturous smile.

"I am dreaming—I am getting out of bed," she heard her own voice say; and then, as she stood up in the midst of it all, turning slowly from side to side,—"I am dreaming it stays—real! I'm dreaming it *feels* real. It's bewitched—or I'm bewitched. I only *think* I see it all." Her words began to hurry themselves. "If I can only keep on thinking it," she cried, "I don't care! I don't care!"

She stood panting a moment longer, and then cried out again.

"Oh, it isn't true!" she said. "It *can't* be true! But oh, how true it seems!"

The blazing fire drew her to it, and she knelt down and held out her hands close to it—so close that the heat made her start back.

"A fire I only dreamed wouldn't be *hot*," she cried.

She sprang up, touched the table, the dishes, the rug; she went to the bed and touched the blankets. She took up the soft wadded dressing-gown, and suddenly clutched it to her breast and held it to her cheek.

"It's warm. It's soft!" she almost sobbed. "It's real. It must be!"

She threw it over her shoulders, and put her feet into the slippers.

"They are real, too. It's all real!" she cried. "I am *not*—I am *not* dreaming!"

She almost staggered to the books and opened the one which lay upon the top. Something was written on the fly-leaf—just a few words, and they were these:

"To the little girl in the attic. From a friend."

When she saw that—wasn't it a strange thing for her to do?—she put her face down upon the page and burst into tears.

"I don't know who it is," she said; "but somebody cares for me a little. I have a friend."

She took her candle and stole out of her own room and into Becky's, and stood by her bedside.

"Becky, Becky!" she whispered as loudly as she dared. "Wake up!"

When Becky wakened, and she sat upright staring aghast, her face still smudged with traces of tears, beside her stood a little figure in a luxurious wadded robe of crimson silk. The face she saw was a shining, wonderful thing. The Princess Sara—as she remembered her—stood at her very bedside, holding a candle in her hand.

"Come," she said. "Oh, Becky, come!"

Becky was too frightened to speak. She simply got up and followed her, with her mouth and eyes open, and without a word.

And when they crossed the threshold, Sara shut the door gently and drew her into the warm, glowing midst of things which made her brain reel and her hungry senses faint.

"It's true! It's true!" she cried. "I've touched them all. They are as real as we are. The Magic has come and done it, Becky, while we were asleep—the Magic that won't let those worst things *ever* quite happen."

CHAPTER 16
THE VISITOR

Imagine, if you can, what the rest of the evening was like. How they crouched by the fire which blazed and leaped and made so much of itself in the little grate. How they removed the covers of the dishes, and found rich, hot, savory soup, which was a meal in itself, and sandwiches and toast and muffins enough for both of them. The mug from the washstand was used as Becky's tea-cup, and the tea was so delicious that it was not necessary to pretend that it was anything else but tea. They were warm and full-fed and happy, and it was just like Sara that, having found her strange good fortune real, she should give herself up to the enjoyment of it to the utmost. She had lived such a life of imaginings that she was quite equal to accepting any wonderful thing that happened, and almost to cease, in a short time, to find it bewildering.

"I don't know any one in the world who could have done it," she said; "but there has been some one. And here we are sitting by the fire—and—and—it's *true!* And whoever it is—wherever they are—I have a friend, Becky—some one is my friend."

It cannot be denied that as they sat before the blazing fire, and ate the nourishing, comfortable food, they felt a kind of rapturous awe, and looked into each other's eyes with something like doubt.

"Do you think," Becky faltered once, in a whisper—"do you think it could melt away, miss? Hadn't we better be quick?" And she hastily crammed her sandwich into her mouth. If it was only a dream, kitchen manners would be overlooked.

"No, it won't melt away," said Sara. "I am *eating* this muffin, and I can taste it. You never really eat things in dreams. You only

think you are going to eat them. Besides, I keep giving myself
pinches; and I touched a hot piece of coal just now, on purpose."

The sleepy comfort which at length almost overpowered them
was a heavenly thing. It was the drowsiness of happy, well-fed
childhood, and they sat in the fire-glow and luxuriated in it until
Sara found herself turning to look at her transformed bed.

There were even blankets enough to share with Becky. The
narrow couch in the next attic was more comfortable that night
than its occupant had ever dreamed that it could be.

As she went out of the room, Becky turned upon the threshold
and looked about her with devouring eyes.

"If it ain't here in the mornin', miss," she said, "it's been here
tonight, anyways, an' I sha'n't never forget it." She looked at each
particular thing, as if to commit it to memory. "The fire was
there," pointing with her finger, "an' the table was before it; an' the
lamp was there, an' the light looked rosy red; an' there was a satin
cover on your bed, an' a warm rug on the floor, an' everythin'
looked beautiful; an'"—she paused a second, and laid her hand
on her stomach tenderly—"there *was* soup an' sandwiches an'
muffins—there *was*." And, with this conviction a reality at least,
she went away.

Through the mysterious agency which works in schools and
among servants, it was quite well known in the morning that Sara
Crewe was in horrible disgrace, that Ermengarde was under pun-
ishment, and that Becky would have been packed out of the
house before breakfast, but that a scullery-maid could not be dispensed with at once. The servants knew that she was allowed to
stay because Miss Minchin could not easily find another creature
helpless and humble enough to work like a bounden slave for so
few shillings a week. The elder girls in the school-room knew that
if Miss Minchin did not send Sara away it was for practical rea-
sons of her own.

"She's growing so fast and learning such a lot, somehow," said
Jessie to Lavinia, "that she will be given classes soon, and Miss
Minchin knows she will have to work for nothing. It was rather

nasty of you, Lavvy, to tell about her having fun in the garret. How did you find it out?"

"I got it out of Lottie. She's such a baby she didn't know she was telling me. There was nothing nasty at all in speaking to Miss Minchin. I felt it my duty"—priggishly. "She was being deceitful. And it's ridiculous that she should look so grand, and be made so much of, in her rags and tatters!"

"What were they doing when Miss Minchin caught them?"

"Pretending some silly thing. Ermengarde had taken up her hamper to share with Sara and Becky. She never invites us to share things. Not that I care, but it's rather vulgar of her to share with servant-girls in attics. I wonder Miss Minchin didn't turn Sara out—even if she does want her for a teacher."

"If she was turned out where would she go?" inquired Jessie, a trifle anxiously.

"How do I know?" snapped Lavinia. "She'll look rather queer when she comes into the school-room this morning, I should think—after what's happened. She had no dinner yesterday, and she's not to have any to-day."

Jessie was not as ill-natured as she was silly. She picked up her book with a little jerk.

"Well, I think it's horrid," she said. "They've no right to starve her to death."

When Sara went into the kitchen that morning the cook looked askance at her, and so did the housemaids; but she passed them hurriedly. She had, in fact, overslept herself a little, and as Becky had done the same, neither had had time to see the other, and each had come down-stairs in haste.

Sara went into the scullery. Becky was violently scrubbing a kettle, and was actually gurgling a little song in her throat. She looked up with a wildly elated face.

"It was there when I wakened, miss—the blanket," she whispered excitedly. "It was as real as it was last night."

"So was mine," said Sara. "It is all there now—all of it. While I was dressing I ate some of the cold things we left."

"Oh, laws! oh, laws!" Becky uttered the exclamation in a sort of rapturous groan, and ducked her head over her kettle just in time, as the cook came in from the kitchen.

Miss Minchin had expected to see in Sara, when she appeared in the school-room, very much what Lavinia had expected to see. Sara had always been an annoying puzzle to her, because severity never made her cry or look frightened. When she was scolded she stood still and listened politely with a grave face; when she was punished she performed her extra tasks or went without her meals, making no complaint or outward sign of rebellion. The very fact that she never made an impudent answer seemed to Miss Minchin a kind of impudence in itself. But after yesterday's deprivation of meals, the violent scene of last night, the prospect of hunger to-day, she must surely have broken down. It would be strange indeed if she did not come down-stairs with pale cheeks and red eyes and an unhappy, humbled face.

Miss Minchin saw her for the first time when she entered the school-room to hear the little French class its lessons and superintend its exercises. And she came in with a springing step, color in her cheeks, and a smile hovering about the corners of her mouth. It was the most astonishing thing Miss Minchin had ever known. It gave her quite a shock. What was the child made of? What could such a thing mean? She called her at once to her desk.

"You do not look as if you realize that you are in disgrace," she said. "Are you absolutely hardened?"

The truth is that when one is still a child—or even if one is grown up—and has been well fed, and has slept long and softly and warm; when one has gone to sleep in the midst of a fairy story, and has wakened to find it real, one cannot be unhappy or even look as if one were; and one could not, if one tried, keep a glow of joy out of one's eyes. Miss Minchin was almost struck dumb by the look of Sara's eyes when she lifted them and made her perfectly respectful answer.

"I beg your pardon, Miss Minchin," she said; "I know that I am in disgrace."

"Be good enough not to forget it and look as if you had come into a fortune. It is an impertinence. And remember you are to have no food to-day."

"Yes, Miss Minchin," Sara answered; but as she turned away her heart leaped at the memory of what yesterday had been. "If the Magic had not saved me just in time," she thought, "how horrible it would have been!"

"She can't be very hungry," whispered Lavinia. "Just look at her. Perhaps she is pretending she has had a good breakfast"— with a spiteful laugh.

"She's different from other people," said Jessie, watching Sara with her class. "Sometimes I'm a bit frightened of her."

"Ridiculous thing!" ejaculated Lavinia.

All through the day the light was in Sara's face, and the color in her cheek. The servants cast puzzled glances at her, and whispered to each other, and Miss Amelia's small blue eyes wore an expression of bewilderment. What such an audacious look of well-being, under august displeasure, could mean she could not understand. It was, however, just like Sara's singular obstinate way. She was probably determined to brave the matter out.

One thing Sara had resolved upon, as she thought things over. The wonders which had happened must be kept a secret, if such a thing were possible. If Miss Minchin should choose to mount to the attic again, of course all would be discovered. But it did not seem likely that she would do so for some time at least, unless she was led by suspicion. Ermengarde and Lottie would be watched with such strictness that they would not dare to steal out of their beds again. Ermengarde could be told the story and trusted to keep it secret. If Lottie made any discoveries, she could be bound to secrecy also. Perhaps the Magic itself could help to hide its own marvels.

"But whatever happens," Sara kept saying to herself all day— "whatever happens, somewhere in the world there is a heavenly kind person who is my friend—my friend. If I never know who it is—if I never can even thank him—I shall never feel quite so lonely. Oh, the Magic was *good* to me!"

If it was possible for weather to be worse than it had been the day before, it was worse this day—wetter, muddier, colder. There were more errands to be done, the cook was more irritable, and, knowing that Sara was in disgrace, she was more savage. But what does anything matter when one's Magic has just proved itself one's friend. Sara's supper of the night before had given her strength, she knew that she should sleep well and warmly, and, even though she had naturally begun to be hungry again before evening, she felt that she could bear it until breakfast-time on the following day, when her meals would surely be given to her again. It was quite late when she was at last allowed to go up-stairs. She had been told to go into the school-room and study until ten o'clock, and she had become interested in her work, and remained over her books later.

When she reached the top flight of stairs and stood before the attic door, it must be confessed that her heart beat rather fast.

"Of course it *might* all have been taken away," she whispered, trying to be brave. "It might only have been lent to me for just that one awful night. But it *was* lent to me—I had it. It was real."

She pushed the door open and went in. Once inside, she gasped slightly, shut the door, and stood with her back against it, looking from side to side.

The Magic had been there again. It actually had, and it had done even more than before. The fire was blazing, in lovely leaping flames, more merrily than ever. A number of new things had been brought into the attic which so altered the look of it that if she had not been past doubting, she would have rubbed her eyes. Upon the low table another supper stood—this time with cups and plates for Becky as well as herself; a piece of bright, heavy, strange embroidery covered the battered mantel, and on it some ornaments had been placed. All the bare, ugly things which could be covered with draperies had been concealed and made to look quite pretty. Some odd materials of rich colors had been fastened against the wall with fine, sharp tacks—so sharp that they could be pressed into the wood and plaster without hammering. Some brilliant fans were pinned up, and there were several large cushions, big and substantial enough to use as seats. A wooden box was covered with a rug, and some cushions lay on it, so that it wore quite the air of a sofa.

Sara slowly moved away from the door and simply sat down and looked and looked again.

"It is exactly like something fairy come true," she said. "There isn't the least difference. I feel as if I might wish for anything—diamonds or bags of gold—and they would appear! *That* wouldn't be any stranger than this. Is this my garret? Am I the same cold, ragged, damp Sara? And to think I used to pretend and pretend and wish there were fairies! The one thing I always wanted was to see a fairy story come true. I am *living* in a fairy story. I feel as if I might be a fairy myself, and able to turn things into anything else."

She rose and knocked upon the wall for the prisoner in the next cell, and the prisoner came.

When she entered she almost dropped in a heap upon the floor. For a few seconds she quite lost her breath.

"Oh, laws!" she gasped, "Oh, laws, miss!" just as she had done in the scullery.

"You see," said Sara.

On this night Becky sat on a cushion upon the hearthrug and had a cup and saucer of her own.

When Sara went to bed she found that she had a new thick mattress and big downy pillows. Her old mattress and pillow had been removed to Becky's bedstead, and, consequently, with these additions Becky had been supplied with unheard-of comfort.

"Where does it all come from?" Becky broke forth once. "Laws! who does it, miss?"

"Don't let us even *ask*," said Sara. "If it were not that I want to say, 'Oh, thank you,' I would rather not know. It makes it more beautiful."

From that time life became more wonderful day by day. The fairy story continued. Almost every day something new was done. Some new comfort or ornament appeared each time Sara opened the door at night, until in a short time the attic was a beautiful little room full of all sorts of odd and luxurious things. The ugly walls were gradually entirely covered with pictures and draperies, ingenious pieces of folding furniture appeared, a book-shelf was hung up and filled with books, new comforts and conveniences appeared one by one until there seemed nothing left to be desired. When Sara went down-stairs in the morning, the remains of the supper were on the table; and when she returned to the attic in the evening, the magician had removed them and left another nice little meal. Miss Minchin was as harsh and insulting as ever, Miss Amelia as peevish, and the servants were as vulgar and rude. Sara was sent on errands in all weathers, and scolded and driven hither and thither; she was scarcely allowed to speak to Ermengarde and Lottie; Lavinia sneered at the increasing shabbiness of her clothes; and the other girls stared curiously at her when she appeared in the school-room. But what did it all matter while she was living in this wonderful mysterious story? It was more romantic and delightful than anything she had ever invented to comfort her starved young soul and save herself from despair. Sometimes, when she was scolded, she could scarcely keep from smiling.

"If you only knew!" she was saying to herself. "If you only knew!"

The comfort and happiness she enjoyed were making her stronger, and she had them always to look forward to. If she came home from her errands wet and tired and hungry, she knew she would soon be warm and well fed after she climbed the stairs. During the hardest day, she could occupy herself blissfully by thinking of what she should see when she opened the attic door, and wondering what new delight had been prepared for her. In a very short time she began to look less thin. Color came into her cheeks, and her eyes did not seem so much too big for her face.

"Sara Crewe looks wonderfully well," Miss Minchin remarked disapprovingly to her sister.

"Yes," answered poor, silly Miss Amelia. "She is absolutely fattening. She was beginning to look like a little starved crow."

"Starved!" exclaimed Miss Minchin, angrily. "There was no reason why she should look starved. She always had plenty to eat!"

"Of—of course," agreed Miss Amelia, humbly, alarmed to find that she had, as usual, said the wrong thing.

"There is something very disagreeable in seeing that sort of thing in a child of her age," said Miss Minchin, with haughty vagueness.

"What—sort of thing?" Miss Amelia ventured.

"It might almost be called defiance," answered Miss Minchin, feeling annoyed because she knew the thing she resented was nothing like defiance, and she did not know what other unpleasant term to use. "The spirit and will of any other child would have been entirely humbled and broken by—by the changes she has had to submit to. But, upon my word, she seems as little subdued as if—as if she were a princess."

"Do you remember," put in the unwise Miss Amelia, "what she said to you that day in the school-room about what you would do if you found out that she was—"

"No, I don't," said Miss Minchin. "Don't talk nonsense." But she remembered very clearly indeed.

Very naturally, even Becky was beginning to look plumper and less frightened. She could not help it. She had her share in the secret fairy story, too. She had two mattresses, two pillows, plenty of bed-covering, and every night a hot supper and a seat on the cushions by the fire. The Bastille had melted away, the prisoners no longer existed. Two comforted children sat in the midst of delights. Sometimes Sara read aloud from her books, sometimes she learned her own lessons, sometimes she sat and looked into the fire and tried to imagine who her friend could be, and wished she could say to him some of the things in her heart.

Then it came about that another wonderful thing happened. A man came to the door and left several parcels. All were addressed in large letters, "To the Little Girl in the right-hand attic."

Sara herself was sent to open the door and took them in. She laid the two largest parcels on the hall table, and was looking at the address, when Miss Minchin came down the stairs and saw her.

"Take the things to the young lady to whom they belong," she said severely. "Don't stand there staring at them."

"They belong to me," answered Sara, quietly.

"To you?" exclaimed Miss Minchin. "What do you mean?"

"I don't know where they come from," said Sara, "but they are addressed to me. I sleep in the right-hand attic. Becky has the other one."

Miss Minchin came to her side and looked at the parcels with an excited expression.

"What is in them?" she demanded.

"I don't know," replied Sara.

"Open them," she ordered.

Sara did as she was told. When the packages were unfolded Miss Minchin's countenance wore suddenly a singular expression. What she saw was pretty and comfortable clothing—clothing of different kinds: shoes, stockings, and gloves, and a warm and beautiful coat. There were even a nice hat and an umbrella. They were all good and expensive things, and on the pocket of the coat was pinned a paper, on which were written these words: "To be worn every day.—Will be replaced by others when necessary."

Miss Minchin was quite agitated. This was an incident which suggested strange things to her sordid mind. Could it be that she had made a mistake, after all, and that the neglected child had some powerful though eccentric friend in the background—perhaps some previously unknown relation, who had suddenly traced her whereabouts, and chose to provide for her in this mysterious and fantastic way? Relations were sometimes very odd—particularly rich old bachelor uncles, who did not care for having children near them. A man of that sort might prefer to overlook his young relation's welfare at a distance. Such a person, however, would be sure to be crotchety and hot-tempered enough to be easily offended. It would not be very pleasant if there were such a one, and he should learn all the truth about the thin, shabby clothes, the scant food, and the hard work. She felt very queer indeed, and very uncertain, and she gave a side glance at Sara.

"Well," she said, in a voice such as she had never used since the little girl lost her father, "some one is very kind to you. As the things have been sent, and you are to have new ones when they are worn out, you may as well go and put them on and look respectable. After you are dressed you may come down-stairs and learn your lessons in the school-room. You need not go out on any more errands to-day."

About half an hour afterward, when the school-room door opened and Sara walked in, the entire seminary was struck dumb with amazement.

"My word!" ejaculated Jessie, jogging Lavinia's elbow. "Look at the Princess Sara!"

Everybody was looking, and when Lavinia looked she turned quite red.

It was the Princess Sara indeed. At least, since the days when she had been a princess, Sara had never looked as she did now. She did not seem the Sara they had seen come down the back stairs a few hours ago. She was dressed in the kind of frock Lavinia had been used to envying her the possession of. It was deep and warm in color, and beautifully made. Her slender feet looked as they had done when Jessie had admired them, and the hair, whose heavy locks had made her look rather like a Shetland pony when it fell loose about her small, odd face, was tied back with a ribbon.

"Perhaps some one has left her a fortune," Jessie whispered. "I always thought something would happen to her. She is so queer."

"Perhaps the diamond-mines have suddenly appeared again," said Lavinia, scathingly. "Don't please her by staring at her in that way, you silly thing."

"Sara," broke in Miss Minchin's deep voice, "come and sit here."

And while the whole school-room stared and pushed with elbows, and scarcely made any effort to conceal its excited curiosity, Sara went to her old seat of honor, and bent her head over her books.

That night, when she went to her room, after she and Becky had eaten their supper she sat and looked at the fire seriously for a long time.

"Are you making something up in your head, miss?" Becky inquired with respectful softness. When Sara sat in silence and looked into the coals with dreaming eyes it generally meant that she was making a new story. But this time she was not, and she shook her head.

"No," she answered. "I am wondering what I ought to do."

Becky stared—still respectfully. She was filled with something approaching reverence for everything Sara did and said.

"I can't help thinking about my friend," Sara explained. "If he wants to keep himself a secret, it would be rude to try and find out who he is. But I do so want him to know how thankful I am to him—and how happy he has made me. Any one who is kind wants to know when people have been made happy. They care for that more than for being thanked. I wish—I do wish—"

She stopped short because her eyes at that instant fell upon something standing on a table in a corner. It was something she had found in the room when she came up to it only two days before. It was a little writing-case fitted with paper and envelopes and pens and ink.

"Oh," she exclaimed, "why did I not think of that before?"

She rose and went to the corner and brought the case back to the fire.

"I can write to him," she said joyfully, "and leave it on the table. Then perhaps the person who takes the things away will take it, too. I won't ask him anything. He won't mind my thanking him, I feel sure."

So she wrote a note. This is what she said:

"I hope you will not think it is impolite that I should write this note to you when you wish to keep yourself a secret. Please believe I do not mean to be impolite or try to find out anything at all; only I want to thank you for being so kind to me—so heavenly kind—and making everything like a fairy story. I am so grateful to you, and I am so happy—and so is Becky. Becky feels just as thankful as I do—it is all just as beautiful and wonderful to her as it is to me. We used to be so lonely and cold and hungry, and now—oh, just think what you have done for us! Please let me say just these words. It seems as if I *ought* to say them. *Thank* you—*thank* you—*thank* you!

"THE LITTLE GIRL IN THE ATTIC"

The next morning she left this on the little table, and in the evening it had been taken away with the other things; so she knew the Magician had received it, and she was happier for the thought. She was reading one of her new books to Becky just before they went to their respective beds, when her attention was attracted by a sound at the skylight. When she looked up from her page she saw that Becky had heard the sound also, as she had turned her head to look and was listening rather nervously.

"Something's there, miss," she whispered.

"Yes," said Sara, slowly. "It sounds—rather like a cat—trying to get in."

She left her chair and went to the skylight. It was a queer little sound she heard—like a soft scratching. She suddenly remembered something and laughed. She remembered a quaint little intruder who had made his way into the attic once before. She had seen him that very afternoon, sitting disconsolately on a table before a window in the Indian gentleman's house.

"Suppose," she whispered in pleased excitement—"just

suppose it was the monkey who had got away again. Oh, I wish it was!"

She climbed on a chair, very cautiously raised the skylight and peeped out. It had been snowing all day, and on the snow, quite near her, crouched a tiny, shivering figure, whose small black face wrinkled itself piteously at sight of her.

"It *is* the monkey," she cried out. "He has crept out of the Lascar's attic, and he saw the light."

Becky ran to her side.

"Are you going to let him in, miss?" she said.

"Yes," Sara answered joyfully. "It's too cold for monkeys to be out. They're delicate. I'll coax him in."

She put a hand out delicately, speaking in a coaxing voice—as she spoke to the sparrows and to Melchisedec—as if she were some friendly little animal herself and lovingly understood their timid wildness.

"Come along, monkey darling," she said. "I won't hurt you."

He knew she would not hurt him. He knew it before she laid her soft, caressing little paw on him and drew him toward her. He had felt human love in the slim brown hands of Ram Dass, and he felt it in hers. He let her lift him through the skylight, and when he found himself in her arms he cuddled up to her breast and took friendly hold of a piece of her hair, looking up into her face.

"Nice monkey! Nice monkey!" she crooned, kissing his funny head. "Oh, I do love little animal things."

He was evidently glad to get to the fire, and when she sat down and held him on her knee he looked from her to Becky with mingled interest and appreciation.

"He *is* plain-looking, miss, ain't he?" said Becky.

"He looks like a very ugly baby," laughed Sara. "I beg your pardon, monkey; but I'm glad you are not a baby. Your mother *couldn't* be proud of you, and no one would dare to say you looked like any of your relations. Oh, I do like you!"

She leaned back in her chair and reflected.

"Perhaps he's sorry he's so ugly," she said, "and it's always on his mind. I wonder if he *has* a mind. Monkey, my love, have you a mind?"

But the monkey only put up a tiny paw and scratched his head.

"What shall you do with him?" Becky asked.

"I shall let him sleep with me to-night, and then take him back to the Indian gentleman to-morrow. I am sorry to take you back, monkey; but you must go. You ought to be fondest of your own family; and I'm not a *real* relation."

And when she went to bed she made him a nest at her feet, and he curled up and slept there as if he were a baby and much pleased with his quarters.

CHAPTER 17
"IT IS THE CHILD!"

The next afternoon three members of the Large Family sat in
the Indian gentleman's library, doing their best to cheer him up.
They had been allowed to come in to perform this office because
he had specially invited them. He had been living in a state of suspense for some time, and to-day he was waiting for a certain event
very anxiously. This event was the return of Mr. Carmichael from
Moscow. His stay there had been prolonged from week to week.
On his first arrival there, he had not been able satisfactorily to
trace the family he had gone in search of. When he felt at last sure
that he had found them and had gone to their house, he had been
told that they were absent on a journey. His efforts to reach them
had been unavailing, so he had decided to remain in Moscow
until their return. Mr. Carrisford sat in his reclining-chair, and
Janet sat on the floor beside him. He was very fond of Janet. Nora
had found a footstool, and Donald was astride the tiger's head
which ornamented the rug made of the animal's skin. It must be
owned that he was riding it rather violently.

"Don't chirrup so loud, Donald," Janet said. "When you come
to cheer an ill person up you don't cheer him up at the top of
your voice. Perhaps cheering up is too loud, Mr. Carrisford?"
turning to the Indian gentleman.

But he only patted her shoulder.

"No, it isn't," he answered. "And it keeps me from thinking
too much."

"I'm going to be quiet," Donald shouted. "We'll all be as quiet
as mice."

"Mice don't make a noise like that," said Janet.

Donald made a bridle of his handkerchief and bounced up and down on the tiger's head.

"A whole lot of mice might," he said cheerfully. "A thousand mice might."

"I don't believe fifty thousand mice would," said Janet, severely; "and we have to be as quiet as *one* mouse."

Mr. Carrisford laughed and patted her shoulder again.

"Papa won't be very long now," she said. "May we talk about the lost little girl?"

"I don't think I could talk much about anything else just now," the Indian gentleman answered, knitting his forehead with a tired look.

"We like her so much," said Nora. "We call her the little *un*-fairy princess."

"Why?" the Indian gentleman inquired, because the fancies of the Large Family always made him forget things a little.

It was Janet who answered.

"It is because, though she is not exactly a fairy, she will be so rich when she is found that she will be like a princess in a fairy tale. We called her the fairy princess at first, but it didn't quite suit."

"Is it true," said Nora, "that her papa gave all his money to a friend to put in a mine that had diamonds in it, and then the friend thought he had lost it all and ran away because he felt as if he was a robber?"

"But he wasn't really, you know," put in Janet, hastily.

The Indian gentleman took hold of her hand quickly.

"No, he wasn't really," he said.

"I am sorry for the friend," Janet said; "I can't help it. He didn't mean to do it, and it would break his heart. I am sure it would break his heart."

"You are an understanding little woman, Janet," the Indian gentleman said, and he held her hand close.

"Did you tell Mr. Carrisford," Donald shouted again, "about the little-girl-who-isn't-a-beggar? Did you tell him she has new nice clothes? P'r'aps she's been found by somebody when she was lost."

"There's a cab!" exclaimed Janet. "It's stopping before the door. It is papa!"

They all ran to the windows to look out.

"Yes, it's papa," Donald proclaimed. "But there is no little girl."

All three of them incontinently fled from the room and tumbled into the hall. It was in this way they always welcomed their father. They were to be heard jumping up and down, clapping their hands, and being caught up and kissed.

Mr. Carrisford made an effort to rise and sank back again into his chair.

"It is no use," he said. "What a wreck I am!"

Mr. Carmichael's voice approached the door.

"No, children," he was saying; "you may come in after I have talked to Mr. Carrisford. Go and play with Ram Dass."

Then the door opened and he came in. He looked rosier than ever, and brought an atmosphere of freshness and health with him; but his eyes were disappointed and anxious as they met the invalid's look of eager question even as they grasped each other's hands.

"What news?" Mr. Carrisford asked. "The child the Russian people adopted?"

"She is not the child we are looking for," was Mr. Carmichael's answer. "She is much younger than Captain Crewe's little girl. Her name is Emily Carew. I have seen and talked to her. The Russians were able to give me every detail."

How wearied and miserable the Indian gentleman looked! His hand dropped from Mr. Carmichael's.

"Then the search has to be begun over again," he said. "That is all. Please sit down."

Mr. Carmichael took a seat. Somehow, he had gradually grown fond of this unhappy man. He was himself so well and happy, and so surrounded by cheerfulness and love, that desolation and broken health seemed pitifully unbearable things. If there had been the sound of just one gay little high-pitched voice in the house, it would have been so much less forlorn. And that a man should be compelled to carry about in his breast the thought that he had seemed to wrong and desert a child was not a thing one could face.

"Come, come," he said in his cheery voice; "we'll find her yet."

"We must begin at once. No time must be lost," Mr. Carrisford fretted. "Have you any new suggestion to make—any whatsoever?"

Mr. Carmichael felt rather restless, and he rose and began to pace the room with a thoughtful, though uncertain face.

"Well, perhaps," he said. "I don't know what it may be worth. The fact is, an idea occurred to me as I was thinking the thing over in the train on the journey from Dover."

"What was it? If she is alive, she is somewhere."

"Yes; she is *somewhere*. We have searched the schools in Paris. Let us give up Paris and begin in London. That was my idea—to search London."

"There are schools enough in London," said Mr. Carrisford. Then he slightly started, roused by a recollection. "By the way, there is one next door."

"Then we will begin there. We cannot begin nearer than next door."

"No," said Carrisford. "There is a child there who interests me; but she is not a pupil. And she is a little dark, forlorn creature, as unlike poor Crewe as a child could be."

Perhaps the Magic was at work again at that very moment— the beautiful Magic. It really seemed as if it might be so. What was it that brought Ram Dass into the room—even as his master spoke—salaaming respectfully, but with a scarcely concealed touch of excitement in his dark, flashing eyes?

"Sahib," he said, "the child herself has come—the child the sahib felt pity for. She brings back the monkey who had again run away to her attic under the roof. I have asked that she remain. It was my thought that it would please the sahib to see and speak with her."

"Who is she?" inquired Mr. Carmichael.

"God knows," Mr. Carrisford answered. "She is the child I

spoke of. A little drudge at the school." He waved his hand to Ram Dass, and addressed him. "Yes, I should like to see her. Go and bring her in." Then he turned to Mr. Carmichael. "While you have been away," he explained, "I have been desperate. The days were so dark and long. Ram Dass told me of this child's miseries, and together we invented a romantic plan to help her. I suppose it was a childish thing to do; but it gave me something to plan and think of. Without the help of an agile, soft-footed Oriental like Ram Dass, however, it could not have been done."

Then Sara came into the room. She carried the monkey in her arms, and he evidently did not intend to part from her, if it could be helped. He was clinging to her and chattering, and the interesting excitement of finding herself in the Indian gentleman's room had brought a flush to Sara's cheeks.

"Your monkey ran away again," she said, in her pretty voice. "He came to my garret window last night, and I took him in because it was so cold. I would have brought him back if it had not been so late. I knew you were ill and might not like to be disturbed."

The Indian gentleman's hollow eyes dwelt on her with curious interest.

"That was very thoughtful of you," he said.

Sara looked toward Ram Dass, who stood near the door.

"Shall I give him to the Lascar?" she asked.

"How do you know he is a Lascar?" said the Indian gentleman, smiling a little.

"Oh, I know Lascars," Sara said, handing over the reluctant monkey. "I was born in India."

The Indian gentleman sat upright so suddenly, and with such a change of expression, that she was for a moment quite startled.

"You were born in India," he exclaimed, "were you? Come here." And he held out his hand.

Sara went to him and laid her hand in his, as he seemed to want to take it. She stood still, and her green-gray eyes met his wonderingly. Something seemed to be the matter with him.

"You live next door?" he demanded.

"Yes; I live at Miss Minchin's seminary."

"But you are not one of her pupils?"

A strange little smile hovered about Sara's mouth. She hesitated a moment.

"I don't think I know exactly *what* I am," she replied.

"Why not?"

"At first I was a pupil, and a parlor-boarder; but now—"

"You were a pupil! What are you now?"

The queer little sad smile was on Sara's lips again.

"I sleep in the attic, next to the scullery-maid," she said. "I run errands for the cook—I do anything she tells me; and I teach the little ones their lessons."

"Question her, Carmichael," said Mr. Carrisford, sinking back as if he had lost his strength. "Question her; I cannot."

The big, kind father of the Large Family knew how to question little girls. Sara realized how much practice he had had when he spoke to her in his nice, encouraging voice.

"What do you mean by 'At first,' my child?" he inquired.

"When I was first taken there by my papa."

"Where is your papa?"

"He died," said Sara, very quietly. "He lost all his money and there was none left for me. There was no one to take care of me or to pay Miss Minchin."

"Carmichael!" the Indian gentleman cried out loudly; "Carmichael!"

"We must not frighten her," Mr. Carmichael said aside to him in a quick, low voice; and he added aloud to Sara: "So you were sent up into the attic, and made into a little drudge. That was about it, wasn't it?"

"There was no one to take care of me," said Sara. "There was no money; I belong to nobody."

"How did your father lose his money?" the Indian gentleman broke in breathlessly.

"He did not lose it himself," Sara answered, wondering still more each moment. "He had a friend he was very fond of—he was *very* fond of him. It was his friend who took his money. He trusted his friend too much."

The Indian gentleman's breath came more quickly.

"The friend might have *meant* to do no harm," he said. "It might have happened through a mistake."

Sara did not know how unrelenting her quiet young voice sounded as she answered. If she had known, she would surely have tried to soften it for the Indian gentleman's sake.

"The suffering was just as bad for my papa," she said. "It killed him."

"What was your father's name?" the Indian gentleman said. "Tell me."

"His name was Ralph Crewe," Sara answered, feeling startled. "Captain Crewe. He died in India."

The haggard face contracted, and Ram Dass sprang to his master's side.

"Carmichael," the invalid gasped, "it is the child—the child!"

For a moment Sara thought he was going to die. Ram Dass poured out drops from a bottle, and held them to his lips. Sara stood near, trembling a little. She looked in a bewildered way at Mr. Carmichael.

"What child am I?" she faltered.

"He was your father's friend," Mr. Carmichael answered her. "Don't be frightened. We have been looking for you for two years."

Sara put her hand up to her forehead, and her mouth trembled. She spoke as if she were in a dream.

"And I was at Miss Minchin's all the while," she half whispered. "Just on the other side of the wall."

CHAPTER 18
"I TRIED NOT TO BE"

It was pretty, comfortable Mrs. Carmichael who explained everything. She was sent for at once, and came across the square to take Sara into her warm arms and make clear to her all that had happened. The excitement of the totally unexpected discovery had been temporarily almost overpowering to Mr. Carrisford in his weak condition.

"Upon my word," he said faintly to Mr. Carmichael, when it was suggested that the little girl should go into another room, "I feel as if I do not want to lose sight of her."

"I will take care of her," Janet said, "and mamma will come in a few minutes." And it was Janet who led her away.

"We're so glad you are found," she said. "You don't know how glad we are that you are found."

Donald stood with his hands in his pockets, and gazed at Sara with reflecting and self-reproachful eyes.

"If I'd just asked what your name was when I gave you my sixpence," he said, "you would have told me it was Sara Crewe, and then you would have been found in a minute."

Then Mrs. Carmichael came in. She looked very much moved, and suddenly took Sara in her arms and kissed her.

"You look bewildered, poor child," she said. "And it is not to be wondered at."

Sara could only think of one thing.

"Was he," she said, with a glance toward the closed door of the library—"was *he* the wicked friend? Oh, do tell me!"

Mrs. Carmichael was crying as she kissed her again. She felt as

if she ought to be kissed very often because she had not been
kissed for so long.

"He was not wicked, my dear," she answered. "He did not
really lose your papa's money. He only thought he had lost it; and
because he loved him so much his grief made him so ill that for a
time he was not in his right mind. He almost died of brain-fever,
and long before he began to recover your poor papa was dead."

"And he did not know where to find me," murmured Sara.
"And I was so near." Somehow, she could not forget that she had
been so near.

"He believed you were in school in France," Mrs. Carmichael
explained. "And he was continually misled by false clues. He has
looked for you everywhere. When he saw you pass by, looking so
sad and neglected, he did not dream that you were his friend's poor
child; but because you were a little girl, too, he was sorry for you,
and wanted to make you happier. And he told Ram Dass to climb
into your attic window and try to make you more comfortable."

Sara gave a start of joy; her whole look changed.

"Did Ram Dass bring the things?" she cried out; "did he tell
Ram Dass to do it? Did he make the dream that came true!"

"Yes, my dear—yes! He is kind and good, and he was sorry for
you, for little lost Sara Crewe's sake."

The library door opened and Mr. Carmichael appeared, calling
Sara to him with a gesture.

"Mr. Carrisford is better already," he said. "He wants you to
come to him."

Sara did not wait. When the Indian gentleman looked at her as
she entered, he saw that her face was all alight.

She went and stood before his chair, and with her hands
clasped together against her breast.

"You sent the things to me," she said, in a joyful emotional
little voice—"the beautiful, beautiful things? *You* sent them!"

"Yes, poor, dear child, I did," he answered her. He was weak
and broken with long illness and trouble, but he looked at her
with the look she remembered in her father's eyes—that look of

loving her and wanting to take her in his arms. It made her kneel down by him, just as she used to kneel by her father when they were the dearest friends and lovers in the world.

"Then it is you who are my friend," she said; "it is you who are my friend!" And she dropped her face on his thin hand and kissed it again and again.

"The man will be himself again in three weeks," Mr. Carmichael said aside to his wife. "Look at his face already."

In fact, he did look changed. Here was the "little missus," and he had new things to think of and plan for already. In the first place, there was Miss Minchin. She must be interviewed and told of the change which had taken place in the fortunes of her pupil.

Sara was not to return to the seminary at all. The Indian gentleman was very determined upon that point. She must remain where she was, and Mr. Carmichael should go and see Miss Minchin himself.

"I am glad I need not go back," said Sara. "She will be very angry. She does not like me; though perhaps it is my fault, because I do not like her."

But, oddly enough, Miss Minchin made it unnecessary for Mr. Carmichael to go to her, by actually coming in search of her pupil herself. She had wanted Sara for something, and on inquiry had heard an astonishing thing. One of the housemaids had seen her steal out of the area with something hidden under her cloak, and had also seen her go up the steps of the next door and enter the house.

"What does she mean!" cried Miss Minchin to Miss Amelia.

"I don't know, I'm sure, sister," answered Miss Amelia. "Unless she has made friends with him because he has lived in India."

"It would be just like her to thrust herself upon him and try to gain his sympathies in some such impertinent fashion," said Miss Minchin. "She must have been in the house two hours. I will not allow such presumption. I shall go and inquire into the matter, and apologize for her intrusion."

Sara was sitting on a footstool close to Mr. Carrisford's knee, and listening to some of the many things he felt it necessary to try to explain to her, when Ram Dass announced the visitor's arrival.

Sara rose involuntarily, and became rather pale; but Mr. Carrisford saw that she stood quietly, and showed none of the ordinary signs of child terror.

Miss Minchin entered the room with a sternly dignified manner. She was correctly and well dressed, and rigidly polite.

"I am sorry to disturb Mr. Carrisford," she said; "but I have explanations to make. I am Miss Minchin, the proprietress of the Young Ladies' Seminary next door."

The Indian gentleman looked at her for a moment in silent scrutiny. He was a man who had naturally a rather hot temper, and he did not want it to get too much the better of him.

"So you are Miss Minchin?" he said.

"I am, sir."

"In that case," the Indian gentleman replied, "you have arrived at the right time. My solicitor, Mr. Carmichael, was just on the point of going to see you."

Mr. Carmichael bowed slightly, and Miss Minchin looked from him to Mr. Carrisford in amazement.

"Your solicitor!" she said. "I do not understand. I have come here as a matter of duty. I have just discovered that you have been intruded upon through the forwardness of one of my pupils—a charity pupil. I came to explain that she intruded without my knowledge." She turned upon Sara. "Go home at once," she commanded indignantly. "You shall be severely punished. Go home at once."

The Indian gentleman drew Sara to his side and patted her hand.

"She is not going."

Miss Minchin felt rather as if she must be losing her senses.

"Not going!" she repeated.

"No," said Mr. Carrisford. "She is not going *home*—if you give your house that name. Her home for the future will be with me."

Miss Minchin fell back in amazed indignation.

"With *you*! With *you*, sir! What does this mean?"

"Kindly explain the matter, Carmichael," said the Indian gentleman; "and get it over as quickly as possible." And he made Sara sit down again, and held her hands in his—which was another trick of her papa's.

Then Mr. Carmichael explained—in the quiet, level-toned, steady manner of a man who knew his subject, and all its legal significance, which was a thing Miss Minchin understood as a business woman, and did not enjoy.

"Mr. Carrisford, madam," he said, "was an intimate friend of the late Captain Crewe. He was his partner in certain large investments. The fortune which Captain Crewe supposed he had lost has been recovered, and is now in Mr. Carrisford's hands."

"The fortune!" cried Miss Minchin; and she really lost color as she uttered the exclamation. "Sara's fortune!"

"It *will* be Sara's fortune," replied Mr. Carmichael, rather coldly. "It *is* Sara's fortune now, in fact. Certain events have increased it enormously. The diamond-mines have retrieved themselves."

"The diamond-mines!" Miss Minchin gasped out. If this was true, nothing so horrible, she felt, had ever happened to her since she was born.

"The diamond-mines," Mr. Carmichael repeated, and he could not help adding, with a rather sly, unlawyer-like smile: "There are not many princesses, Miss Minchin, who are richer than your little charity pupil, Sara Crewe, will be. Mr. Carrisford has been searching for her for nearly two years; he has found her at last, and he will keep her."

After which he asked Miss Minchin to sit down while he explained matters to her fully, and went into such detail as was necessary to make it quite clear to her that Sara's future was an assured one, and that what had seemed to be lost was to be restored to her tenfold; also, that she had in Mr. Carrisford a guardian as well as a friend.

Miss Minchin was not a clever woman, and in her excitement she was silly enough to make one desperate effort to regain what she could not help seeing she had lost through her own worldly folly.

"He found her under my care," she protested. "And I have done everything for her. But for me she would have starved in the streets."

Here the Indian gentleman lost his temper.

"As to starving in the streets," he said, "she might have starved more comfortably there than in your attic."

"Captain Crewe left her in my charge," Miss Minchin argued. "She must return to it until she is of age. She can be a parlor-boarder again. She must finish her education. The law will interfere in my behalf."

"Come, come, Miss Minchin," Mr. Carmichael interposed, "the law will do nothing of the sort. If Sara herself wishes to return to you, I dare say Mr. Carrisford might not refuse to allow it. But that rests with Sara."

"Then," said Miss Minchin, "I appeal to Sara. I have not spoiled you, perhaps," she said awkwardly to the little girl; "but you know that your papa was pleased with your progress. And— ahem!—I have always been fond of you."

Sara's green-gray eyes fixed themselves on her with the quiet, clear look Miss Minchin particularly disliked.

"Have you, Miss Minchin?" she said; "I did not know that."

Miss Minchin reddened and drew herself up.

"You ought to have known it," said she; "but children, unfortunately, never know what is best for them. Amelia and I always said you were the cleverest child in the school. Will you not do your duty to your poor papa and come home with me?"

Sara took a step toward her and stood still. She was thinking of the day when she had been told that she belonged to nobody, and was in danger of being turned out into the street; she was thinking of the cold, hungry hours she had spent alone with Emily and Melchisedec in the attic. She looked at Miss Minchin steadily in the face.

"You know why I will not go home with you, Miss Minchin," she said; "you know quite well."

A hot flush showed itself on Miss Minchin's hard, angry face.

"You will never see your companions again," she began. "I will
see that Ermengarde and Lottie are kept away—"

Mr. Carmichael stopped her with polite firmness.

"Excuse me," he said; "she will see any one she wishes to see.
The parents of Miss Crewe's fellow-pupils are not likely to refuse
her invitations to visit her at her guardian's house. Mr. Carrisford
will attend to that."

It must be confessed that even Miss Minchin flinched. This
was worse than the eccentric bachelor uncle who might have a
peppery temper and be easily offended at the treatment of his
niece. A woman of sordid mind could easily believe that most
people would not allow their children to remain friends with a little heiress of diamond-mines. And if Mr. Carrisford chose to tell
certain of her patrons how unhappy Sara Crewe had been made,
many unpleasant things might happen.

"You have not undertaken an easy charge," she said to the
Indian gentleman, as she turned to leave the room; "you will discover that very soon. The child is neither truthful nor grateful.
I suppose"—to Sara—"that you feel now that you are a princess again."

Sara looked down and flushed a little, because she thought her
pet fancy might not be easy for strangers—even nice ones—to
understand at first.

"I—tried not to be anything else," she answered in a low
voice—"even when I was coldest and hungriest—I *tried* not to be."

"Now it will not be necessary to try," said Miss Minchin,
acidly, as Ram Dass salaamed her out of the room.

• • •

She returned home and, going to her sitting-room, sent at
once for Miss Amelia. She sat closeted with her all the rest of the
afternoon, and it must be admitted that poor Miss Amelia passed
through more than one bad quarter of an hour. She shed a good
many tears, and mopped her eyes a good deal. One of her unfor-
tunate remarks almost caused her sister to snap her head entirely
off, but it resulted in an unusual manner.

"I'm not as clever as you, sister," she said, "and I am always afraid to say things to you for fear of making you angry. Perhaps if I were not so timid it would be better for the school and for both of us. I must say I've often thought it would have been better if you had been less severe on Sara Crewe, and had seen that she was decently dressed and more comfortable. I *know* she was worked too hard for a child of her age, and I know she was only half-fed—"

"How dare you say such a thing!" exclaimed Miss Minchin.

"I don't know how I dare," Miss Amelia answered, with a kind of reckless courage; "but now I've begun I may as well finish, whatever happens to me. The child was a clever child and a good child—and she would have paid you for any kindness you had shown her. But you didn't show her any. The fact was, she was too clever for you, and you always disliked her for that reason. She used to see through us both—"

"Amelia!" gasped her infuriated elder, looking as if she would box her ears and knock her cap off, as she had often done to Becky.

But Miss Amelia's disappointment had made her hysterical enough not to care what occurred next.

"She did! She did!" she cried. "She saw through us both. She saw that you were a hard-hearted, worldly woman, and that I was a weak fool, and that we were both of us vulgar and mean enough to grovel on our knees before her money, and behave ill to her because it was taken from her—though she behaved herself like a little princess even when she was a beggar. She did—she did—like a little princess!" and her hysterics got the better of the poor woman, and she began to laugh and cry both at once, and rock herself backward and forward in such a way as made Miss Minchin stare aghast.

"And now you've lost her," she cried wildly; "and some other school will get her and her money; and if she were like any other child she'd tell how she's been treated, and all our pupils would be taken away and we should be ruined. And it serves us right; but it serves you right more than it does me, for you are a hard woman, Maria Minchin—you're a hard, selfish, worldly woman!"

And she was in danger of making so much noise with her hysterical chokes and gurgles that her sister was obliged to go to her and apply salts and sal volatile to quiet her, instead of pouring forth her indignation at her audacity.

And from that time forward, it may be mentioned, the elder Miss Minchin actually began to stand a little in awe of a sister who, while she looked so foolish, was evidently not quite so foolish as she looked, and might, consequently, break out and speak truths people did not want to hear.

That evening, when the pupils were gathered together before the fire in the school-room, as was their custom before going to bed, Ermengarde came in with a letter in her hand and a queer expression on her round face. It was queer because, while it was an expression of delighted excitement, it was combined with such amazement as seemed to belong to a kind of shock just received.

"What *is* the matter?" cried two or three voices at once.

"Is it anything to do with the row that has been going on?" said Lavinia, eagerly. "There has been such a row in Miss Minchin's room, Miss Amelia has had something like hysterics and has had to go to bed."

Ermengarde answered them slowly as if she were half stunned.

"I have just had this letter from Sara," she said, holding it out to let them see what a long letter it was.

"From Sara!" Every voice joined in that exclamation.

"Where is she?" almost shrieked Jessie.

"Next door," said Ermengarde, still slowly; "with the Indian gentleman."

"Where? Where? Has she been sent away? Does Miss Minchin know? Was the row about that? Why did she write? Tell us! Tell us!"

There was a perfect babel, and Lottie began to cry plaintively.

Ermengarde answered them slowly as if she were half plunged out into what, at the moment, seemed the most important and self-explaining thing.

"There *were* diamond-mines," she said stoutly; "there *were!*"

Open mouths and open eyes confronted her.

"They were real," she hurried on. "It was all a mistake about them. Something happened for a time, and Mr. Carrisford thought they were ruined—"

"Who is Mr. Carrisford?" shouted Jessie.

"The Indian gentleman. And Captain Crewe thought so, too—and he died; and Mr. Carrisford had brain-fever and ran away, and *he* almost died. And he did not know where Sara was. And it turned out that there were millions and millions of diamonds in the mines; and half of them belong to Sara; and they belonged to her when she was living in the attic with no one but Melchisedec for a friend, and the cook ordering her about. And Mr. Carrisford found her this afternoon, and he has got her in his home—and she will never come back—and she will be more a princess than she ever was—a hundred and fifty thousand times more. And I am going to see her to-morrow afternoon. There!"

Even Miss Minchin herself could scarcely have controlled the uproar after this; and though she heard the noise, she did not try. She was not in the mood to face anything more than she was facing in her room, while Miss Amelia was weeping in bed. She knew that the news had penetrated the walls in some mysterious manner, and that every servant and every child would go to bed talking about it.

So until almost midnight the entire seminary, realizing somehow that all rules were laid aside, crowded around Ermengarde in the school-room and heard read and re-read the letter containing a story which was quite as wonderful as any Sara herself had ever invented, and which had the amazing charm of having happened to Sara herself and the mystic Indian gentleman in the very next house.

Becky, who had heard it also, managed to creep up-stairs earlier than usual. She wanted to get away from people and go and look at the little magic room once more. She did not know what would happen to it. It was not likely that it would be left to Miss Minchin. It would be taken away, and the attic would be bare and empty again. Glad as she was for Sara's sake, she went up the last flight of stairs with a lump in her throat and tears blurring her sight. There would be no fire to-night, and no rosy lamp; no supper; and no princess sitting in the glow reading or telling stories—no princess!

She choked down a sob as she pushed the attic door open, and then she broke into a low cry.

The lamp was flushing the room, the fire was blazing, the supper was waiting; and Ram Dass was standing smiling into her startled face.

"Missee sahib remembered," he said. "She told the sahib all. She wished you to know the good fortune which has befallen her. Behold a letter on the tray. She has written. She did not wish that you should go to sleep unhappy. The sahib commands you to come to him to-morrow. You are to be the attendant of missee sahib. To-night I take these things back over the roof."

And having said this with a beaming face, he made a little salaam and slipped through the skylight with an agile silentness of movement which showed Becky how easily he had done it before.

Though soon Chidori she was her wards when she went up the last
flight of stairs. With a lamp in her hand and tears filling her
eyes. They would have to try to sleep until the rest jump up
surprise, getting refreshed so sure in the glory feeding or telling
house, no time, yes.

She looked down and was sleeping deep in a chair upon and
then she broke into a cry.

The lamp was flooding the room, the fire was blazing down,
now was waiting and Gran Dave was smoking smiling into her
startled face.

"Meena really remembered," he said, "she was in the wild all."

She wished you'd know them and told us which I'd remained a
month to learn on its bay. She was written. She told her well, that
you should go to sleep perhaps. The scale continued, you'll
come in just to inform we told me look. The sublime quiet mess so
safe. To-night to take these three thing back off the road.

"I'd just up," said this with a beaming face. He made a little
reform and stopped through the system with an aged shuffle of
entertainment above. Luckily before he had done a letter.

CHAPTER 19
"ANNE"

Never had such joy reigned in the nursery of the Large Family. Never had they dreamed of such delights as resulted from an intimate acquaintance with the little-girl-who-was-not-a-beggar. The mere fact of her sufferings and adventures made her a priceless possession. Everybody wanted to be told over and over again the things which had happened to her. When one was sitting by a warm fire in a big, glowing room, it was quite delightful to hear how cold it could be in an attic. It must be admitted that the attic was rather delighted in, and that its coldness and bareness quite sank into insignificance when Melchisedec was remembered, and one heard about the sparrows and things one could see if one climbed on the table and stuck one's head and shoulder's out of the skylight.

Of course the thing loved best was the story of the banquet and the dream which was true. Sara told it for the first time the day after she had been found. Several members of the Large Family came to take tea with her, and as they sat or curled up on the hearth-rug she told the story in her own way, and the Indian gentleman listened and watched her. When she had finished she looked up at him and put her hand on his knee.

"That is my part," she said. "Now won't you tell your part of it, Uncle Tom?" He had asked her to call him always "Uncle Tom." "I don't know your part yet, and it must be beautiful."

So he told them how, when he sat alone, ill and dull and irritable, Ram Dass had tried to distract him by describing the passers by, and there was one child who passed oftener than any one else; he had begun to be interested in her—partly perhaps because he was thinking a great deal of a little girl, and partly because Ram Dass had been able to relate the incident of his visit to the attic in chase of the monkey. He had described its cheerless look, and the bearing of the child, who seemed as if she was not of the class of those who were treated as drudges and servants. Bit by bit, Ram Dass had made discoveries concerning the wretchedness of her life. He had found out how easy a matter it was to climb across the few yards of roof to the skylight, and this fact had been the beginning of all that followed.

"Sahib," he had said one day, "I could cross the slates and make the child a fire when she is out on some errand. When she returned, wet and cold, to find it blazing, she would think a magician had done it."

The idea had been so fanciful that Mr. Carrisford's sad face had lighted with a smile, and Ram Dass had been so filled with rapture that he had enlarged upon it and explained to his master how simple it would be to accomplish numbers of other things. He had shown a childlike pleasure and invention, and the preparations for the carrying out of the plan had filled many a day with interest which would otherwise have dragged wearily. On the night of the frustrated banquet Ram Dass had kept watch, all his packages being in readiness in the attic which was his own; and the person who was to help him had waited with him, as interested as himself in the odd adventure. Ram Dass had been lying flat upon the slates, looking in at the skylight, when the banquet had come to its disastrous conclusion; he had been sure of the profoundness of Sara's wearied sleep; and then, with a dark lantern, he had crept into the room, while his companion had remained outside and handed the things to him. When Sara had stirred ever so faintly, Ram Dass had closed the lantern-slide and lain flat upon the floor. These and many other exciting things the children found out by asking a thousand questions.

"I am so glad," Sara said. "I am so *glad* it was you who were my friend!"

There never were such friends as these two became. Somehow,

they seemed to suit each other in a wonderful way. The Indian gentleman had never had a companion he liked quite as much as he liked Sara. In a month's time he was, as Mr. Carmichael had prophesied he would be, a new man. He was always amused and interested, and he began to find an actual pleasure in the possession of the wealth he had imagined that he loathed the burden of. There were so many charming things to plan for Sara. There was a little joke between them that he was a magician, and it was one of his pleasures to invent things to surprise her. She found beautiful new flowers growing in her room, whimsical little gifts tucked under pillows, and once, as they sat together in the evening, they heard the scratch of a heavy paw on the door, and when Sara went to find out what it was, there stood a great dog—a splendid Russian boarhound—with a grand silver and gold collar bearing an inscription in raised letters. "I am Boris," it read; "I serve the Princess Sara."

There was nothing the Indian gentleman loved more than the recollection of the little princess in rags and tatters. The afternoons in which the Large Family, or Ermengarde and Lottie, gathered to rejoice together were very delightful. But the hours when Sara and the Indian gentleman sat alone and read or talked had a special charm of their own. During their passing many interesting things occurred.

One evening, Mr. Carrisford, looking up from his book, noticed that his companion had not stirred for some time, but sat gazing into the fire.

"What are you 'supposing,' Sara?" he asked.

Sara looked up, with a bright color on her cheek.

"I was supposing," she said; "I was remembering that hungry day, and a child I saw."

"But there were a great many hungry days," said the Indian gentleman, with rather a sad tone in his voice. "Which hungry day was it?"

"I forgot you didn't know," said Sara. "It was the day the dream came true."

Then she told him the story of the bun-shop, and the fourpence she picked up out of the sloppy mud, and the child who was hungrier than herself. She told it quite simply, and in as few words as possible; but somehow the Indian gentleman found it necessary to shade his eyes with his hand and look down at the carpet.

"And I was supposing a kind of plan," she said, when she had finished. "I was thinking I should like to do something."

"What was it?" said Mr. Carrisford, in a low tone. "You may do anything you like to do, princess."

"I was wondering," rather hesitated Sara—"you know, you say I have so much money—I was wondering if I could go to see the bun-woman, and tell her that if, when hungry children—particularly on those dreadful days—come and sit on the steps, or look in at the window, she would just call them in and give them something to eat, she might send the bills to me. Could I do that?"

"You shall do it to-morrow morning," said the Indian gentleman.

"Thank you," said Sara. "You see, I know what it is to be hungry, and it is very hard when one cannot even *pretend* it away."

"Yes, yes, my dear," said the Indian gentleman. "Yes, yes, it must be. Try to forget it. Come and sit on this footstool near my knee, and only remember you are a princess."

"Yes," said Sara, smiling; "and I can give buns and bread to the populace." And she went and sat on the stool, and the Indian gentleman (he used to like her to call him that, too, sometimes) drew her small dark head down upon his knee and stroked her hair.

The next morning, Miss Minchin, in looking out of her window, saw the thing she perhaps least enjoyed seeing. The Indian gentleman's carriage, with tall horses, drew up before the door of the next house, and its owner and a little figure, warm with soft, rich furs, descended the steps to get into it. The little figure was a familiar one, and reminded Miss Minchin of days in the past. It was followed by another as familiar—the sight of which she found very irritating. It was Becky, who, in the character of delighted attendant, always accompanied her young mistress to her carriage, carrying wraps and belongings. Already Becky had a pink, round face.

A little later the carriage drew up before the door of the baker's shop, and its occupants got out, oddly enough, just as the bun-woman was putting a tray of smoking-hot buns into the window.

When Sara entered the shop the woman turned and looked at her, and, leaving the buns, came and stood behind the counter. For a moment she looked at Sara very hard indeed, and then her good-natured face lighted up.

"I'm sure that I remember you, miss," she said. "And yet—"

"Yes," said Sara; "once you gave me six buns for fourpence, and—"

"And you gave five of 'em to a beggar child," the woman broke in on her. "I've always remembered it. I couldn't make it out at first." She turned round to the Indian gentleman and spoke her next words to him. "I beg your pardon, sir, but there's not many young people that notices a hungry face in that way; and I've thought of it many a time. Excuse the liberty, miss"—to Sara,— "but you look rosier and—well, better than you did that—that—"

"I am better, thank you," said Sara. "And—I am much happier—and I have come to ask you to do something for me."

"Me, miss!" exclaimed the bun-woman, smiling cheerfully. "Why, bless you! yes, miss. What can I do?"

And then Sara, leaning on the counter, made her little proposal concerning the dreadful days and the hungry waifs and the hot buns.

The woman watched her, and listened with an astonished face.

"Why, bless me!" she said again when she had heard it all; "it'll be a pleasure for me to do it. I am a working-woman myself and cannot afford to do much on my own account, and there's sights of trouble on every side; but, if you'll excuse me, I'm bound to say I've given away many a bit of bread since that wet afternoon, just along o' thinking of you—an' how wet an' cold you was, an' how hungry you looked; an' yet you gave away your hot buns as if you were a princess."

The Indian gentleman smiled involuntarily at this, and Sara smiled a little, too, remembering what she had said to herself when she put the buns down on the ravenous child's ragged lap.

"She looked so hungry," she said. "She was even hungrier than I was."

"She was starving," said the woman. "Many's the time she's told me of it since—how she sat there in the wet, and felt as if a wolf was a-tearing at her poor young insides."

"Oh, have you seen her since then?" exclaimed Sara. "Do you know where she is?"

"Yes, I do," answered the woman, smiling more good-naturedly than ever. "Why, she's in that there back room, miss, an' has been for a month; an' a decent well-meanin' girl she's goin' to turn out, an' such a help to me in the shop an' in the kitchen as you'd scarce believe, knowin' how she's lived."

She stepped to the door of the little back parlor and spoke; and the next minute a girl came out and followed her behind the counter. And actually it was the beggar-child, clean and neatly clothed, and looking as if she had not been hungry for a long time. She looked shy, but she had a nice face, now that she was no longer a savage, and the wild look had gone from her eyes. She knew Sara in an instant, and stood and looked at her as if she could never look enough.

"You see," said the woman, "I told her to come when she was hungry, and when she'd come I'd give her odd jobs to do; an' I found she was willing, and somehow I got to like her; and the end of it was, I've given her a place an' a home, and she helps me, an' behaves well, an' is as thankful as a girl can be. Her name's Anne. She has no other."

The children stood and looked at each other for a few minutes; and then Sara took her hand out of her muff and held it out across the counter, and Anne took it, and they looked straight into each other's eyes.

"I am so glad," Sara said. "And I have just thought of something. Perhaps Mrs. Brown will let you be the one to give the buns and bread to the children. Perhaps you would like to do it because you know what it is to be hungry, too."

"Yes, miss," said the girl.

And, somehow, Sara felt as if she understood her, though she said so little, and only stood still and looked and looked after her as she went out of the shop with the Indian gentleman, and they got into the carriage and drove away.

THE SECRET GARDEN

CHAPTER 1
THERE IS NO ONE LEFT

When Mary Lennox was sent to Misselthwaite Manor to live with her uncle everybody said she was the most disagreeable-looking child ever seen. It was true, too. She had a little thin face and a little thin body, thin light hair and a sour expression. Her hair was yellow, and her face was yellow because she had been born in India and had always been ill in one way or another. Her father had held a position under the English government and had always been busy and ill himself, and her mother had been a great beauty who cared only to go to parties and amuse herself with gay people. She had not wanted a little girl at all, and when Mary was born she handed her over to the care of an Ayah, who was made to understand that if she wished to please the Mem Sahib she must keep the child out of sight as much as possible. So when she was a sickly, fretful, ugly little baby she was kept out of the way, and when she became a sickly, fretful, toddling thing she was kept out of the way also. She never remembered seeing familiarly anything but the dark faces of her Ayah and the other native servants, and as they always obeyed her and gave her her own way in everything, because the Mem Sahib would be angry if she was disturbed by her crying, by the time she was six years old she was as tyrannical and selfish a little pig as ever lived. The young English governess who came to teach her to read and write disliked her so much that she gave up her place in three months, and when other governesses came to try to fill it they always went away in a shorter time than the first one. So if Mary had not chosen to really want to know how to read books she would never have learned her letters at all.

One frightfully hot morning, when she was about nine years old, she awakened feeling very cross, and she became crosser still when she saw that the servant who stood by her bedside was not her Ayah.

"Why did you come?" she said to the strange woman. "I will not let you stay. Send my Ayah to me."

The woman looked frightened, but she only stammered that the Ayah could not come and when Mary threw herself into a passion and beat and kicked her, she looked only more frightened and repeated that it was not possible for the Ayah to come to Missie Sahib.

There was something mysterious in the air that morning. Nothing was done in its regular order and several of the native servants seemed missing, while those whom Mary saw slunk or hurried about with ashy and scared faces. But no one would tell her anything and her Ayah did not come. She was actually left alone as the morning went on, and at last she wandered out into the garden and began to play by herself under a tree near the veranda. She pretended that she was making a flower-bed, and she stuck big scarlet hibiscus blossoms into little heaps of earth, all the time growing more and more angry and muttering to herself the things she would say and the names she would call Saidie when she returned.

"Pig! Pig! Daughter of Pigs!" she said, because to call a native a pig is the worst insult of all.

She was grinding her teeth and saying this over and over again when she heard her mother come out on the veranda with some one. She was with a fair young man and they stood talking together in low strange voices. Mary knew the fair young man who looked like a boy. She had heard that he was a very young officer who had just come from England. The child stared at him, but she stared most at her mother. She always did this when she had a chance to see her, because the Mem Sahib—Mary used to call her that oftener than anything else—was such a tall, slim, pretty person and wore such lovely clothes. Her hair was like curly silk and she had a delicate little nose which seemed to be disdaining things, and she had large laughing eyes. All her clothes were thin and floating, and Mary said they were "full of lace." They looked fuller of lace than ever this morning, but her eyes were not laughing at all. They were large and scared and lifted imploringly to the fair boy officer's face.

"Is it so very bad? Oh, is it?" Mary heard her say.

"Awfully," the young man answered in a trembling voice. "Awfully, Mrs. Lennox. You ought to have gone to the hills two weeks ago."

The Mem Sahib wrung her hands.

"Oh, I know I ought!" she cried. "I only stayed to go to that silly dinner party. What a fool I was!"

At that very moment such a loud sound of wailing broke out from the servants' quarters that she clutched the young man's arm, and Mary stood shivering from head to foot. The wailing grew wilder and wilder.

"What is it? What is it?" Mrs. Lennox gasped.

"Some one has died," answered the boy officer. "You did not say it had broken out among your servants."

"I did not know!" the Mem Sahib cried. "Come with me! Come with me!" and she turned and ran into the house.

After that appalling things happened, and the mysteriousness of the morning was explained to Mary. The cholera had broken out in its most fatal form and people were dying like flies. The Ayah had taken ill in the night, and it was because she had just died that the servants had wailed in the huts. Before the next day three other servants were dead and others had run away in terror. There was panic on every side, and dying people in all the bungalows.

During the confusion and bewilderment of the second day Mary hid herself in the nursery and was forgotten by every one. Nobody thought of her, nobody wanted her, and strange things happened of which she knew nothing. Mary alternately cried and slept through the hours. She only knew that people were ill and that she heard mysterious and frightening sounds. Once she crept into the dining-room and found it empty, though a partly finished meal was on the table and chairs and plates looked as if they had been hastily pushed back when the diners rose suddenly for some reason. The child ate some fruit and biscuits, and being thirsty she drank a glass of wine which stood nearly filled. It was sweet, and she did not know how strong it was. Very soon it made her intensely drowsy, and she went back to her nursery and shut herself in again, frightened by cries she heard in the huts and by the hurrying sound of feet. The wine made her so sleepy that she could scarcely keep her eyes open and she lay down on her bed and knew nothing more for a long time.

Many things happened during the hours in which she slept so heavily, but she was not disturbed by the wails and the sound of things being carried in and out of the bungalow.

When she awakened she lay and stared at the wall. The house was perfectly still. She had never known it to be so silent before. She heard neither voices nor footsteps, and wondered if everybody had got well of the cholera and all the trouble was over. She wondered also who would take care of her now her Ayah was dead. There would be a new Ayah, and perhaps she would know some new stories. Mary had been rather tired of the old ones. She did not cry because her nurse had died. She was not an affectionate child and had never cared much for any one. The noise and hurrying about and wailing over the cholera had frightened her, and she had been angry because no one seemed to remember that she was alive. Every one was too panic-stricken to think of a little girl no one was fond of. When people had the cholera it seemed that they remembered nothing but themselves. But if every one had got well again, surely some one would remember and come to look for her.

But no one came, and as she lay waiting the house seemed to grow more and more silent. She heard something rustling on the matting and when she looked down she saw a little snake gliding along and watching her with eyes like jewels. She was not frightened, because he was a harmless little thing who would not hurt her and he seemed in a hurry to get out of the room. He slipped under the door as she watched him.

"How queer and quiet it is," she said. "It sounds as if there was no one in the bungalow but me and the snake."

Almost the next minute she heard footsteps in the compound, and then on the veranda. They were men's footsteps, and the men entered the bungalow and talked in low voices. No one went to meet or speak to them and they seemed to open doors and look into rooms.

"What desolation!" she heard one voice say. "That pretty, pretty woman! I suppose the child, too. I heard there was a child, though no one ever saw her."

Mary was standing in the middle of the nursery when they opened the door a few minutes later. She looked an ugly, cross little thing and was frowning because she was beginning to be hungry and feel disgracefully neglected. The first man who came in was a large officer she had once seen talking to her father. He looked tired and troubled, but when he saw her he was so startled that he almost jumped back.

"Barney!" he cried out. "There is a child here! A child alone! In a place like this! Mercy on us, who is she!"

"I am Mary Lennox," the little girl said, drawing herself up stiffly. She thought the man was very rude to call her father's bungalow "A place like this!" "I fell asleep when every one had the cholera and I have only just wakened up. Why does nobody come?"

"It is the child no one ever saw!" exclaimed the man, turning to his companions. "She has actually been forgotten!"

"Why was I forgotten?" Mary said, stamping her foot. "Why does nobody come?"

The young man whose name was Barney looked at her very sadly. Mary even thought she saw him wink his eyes as if to wink tears away.

"Poor little kid!" he said. "There is nobody left to come."

It was in that strange and sudden way that Mary found out

that she had neither father nor mother left; that they had died and been carried away in the night, and that the few native servants who had not died also had left the house as quickly as they could get out of it, none of them even remembering that there was a Missie Sahib. That was why the place was so quiet. It was true that there was no one in the bungalow but herself and the little rustling snake.

CHAPTER 2
MISTRESS MARY QUITE CONTRARY

Mary had liked to look at her mother from a distance and she had thought her very pretty, but as she knew very little of her she could scarcely have been expected to love her or to miss her very much when she was gone. She did not miss her at all, in fact, and as she was a self-absorbed child she gave her entire thought to herself, as she had always done. If she had been older she would no doubt have been very anxious at being left alone in the world, but she was very young, and as she had always been taken care of, she supposed she always would be. What she thought was that she would like to know if she was going to nice people, who would be polite to her and give her her own way as her Ayah and the other native servants had done.

She knew that she was not going to stay at the English clergyman's house where she was taken at first. She did not want to stay. The English clergyman was poor and he had five children nearly all the same age and they wore shabby clothes and were always quarreling and snatching toys from each other. Mary hated their untidy bungalow and was so disagreeable to them that after the first day or two nobody would play with her. By the second day they had given her a nickname which made her furious.

It was Basil who thought of it first. Basil was a little boy with impudent blue eyes and a turned-up nose and Mary hated him. She was playing by herself under a tree, just as she had been playing the day the cholera broke out. She was making heaps of earth and paths for a garden and Basil came and stood near to watch her. Presently he got rather interested and suddenly made a suggestion.

"Why don't you put a heap of stones there and pretend it is a rockery?" he said. "There in the middle," and he leaned over her to point.

"Go away!" cried Mary. "I don't want boys. Go away!"

For a moment Basil looked angry, and then he began to tease. He was always teasing his sisters. He danced round and round her and made faces and sang and laughed.

> "Mistress Mary, quite contrary,
>   How does your garden grow?
> With silver bells, and cockle shells,
>   And marigolds all in a row."

He sang it until the other children heard and laughed, too; and the crosser Mary got, the more they sang "Mistress Mary, quite contrary"; and after that as long as she stayed with them they called her "Mistress Mary Quite Contrary" when they spoke of her to each other, and often when they spoke to her.

"You are going to be sent home," Basil said to her, "at the end of the week. And we're glad of it."

"I am glad of it, too," answered Mary. "Where is home?"

"She doesn't know where home is!" said Basil, with seven-year-old scorn. "It's England, of course. Our grandmama lives there and our sister Mabel was sent to her last year. You are not going to your grandmama. You have none. You are going to your uncle. His name is Mr. Archibald Craven."

"I don't know anything about him," snapped Mary.

"I know you don't," Basil answered. "You don't know anything. Girls never do. I heard father and mother talking about him. He lives in a great, big, desolate old house in the country and no one goes near him. He's so cross he won't let them, and they wouldn't come if he would let them. He's a hunchback, and he's horrid."

"I don't believe you," said Mary; and she turned her back and stuck her fingers in her ears, because she would not listen any more.

But she thought over it a great deal afterward; and when Mrs. Crawford told her that night that she was going to sail away to England in a few days and go to her uncle, Mr. Archibald Craven, who lived at Misselthwaite Manor, she looked so stony and stubbornly uninterested that they did not know what to think about her. They tried to be kind to her, but she only turned her face away when Mrs. Crawford attempted to kiss her, and held herself stiffly when Mr. Crawford patted her shoulder.

"She is such a plain child," Mrs. Crawford said pityingly, afterward. "And her mother was such a pretty creature. She had a very pretty manner, too, and Mary has the most unattractive ways I ever saw in a child. The children call her 'Mistress Mary Quite Contrary,' and though it's naughty of them, one can't help understanding it."

"Perhaps if her mother had carried her pretty face and her pretty manners oftener into the nursery Mary might have learned some pretty ways too. It is very sad, now the poor beautiful thing is gone, to remember that many people never even knew that she had a child at all."

"I believe she scarcely ever looked at her," sighed Mrs. Crawford. "When her Ayah was dead there was no one to give a thought to the little thing. Think of the servants running away and leaving her all alone in that deserted bungalow. Colonel McGrew said he nearly jumped out of his skin when he opened the door and found her standing by herself in the middle of the room."

Mary made the long voyage to England under the care of an officer's wife, who was taking her children to leave them in a boarding-school. She was very much absorbed in her own little boy and girl, and was rather glad to hand the child over to the woman Mr. Archibald Craven sent to meet her, in London. The woman was his housekeeper at Misselthwaite Manor, and her name was Mrs. Medlock. She was a stout woman, with very red cheeks and sharp black eyes. She wore a very purple dress, a black silk mantle with jet fringe on it and a black bonnet with purple velvet flowers which stuck up and trembled when she moved her head. Mary did not like her at all, but as she very seldom liked people there was nothing remarkable in that; besides which it was very evident Mrs. Medlock did not think much of her.

"My word! she's a plain little piece of goods!" she said. "And we'd heard that her mother was a beauty. She hasn't handed much of it down, has she, ma'am?"

"Perhaps she will improve as she grows older," the officer's wife said good-naturedly. "If she were not so sallow and had a nicer expression, her features are rather good. Children alter so much."

"She'll have to alter a good deal," answered Mrs. Medlock. "And there's nothing likely to improve children at Misselthwaite —if you ask me!"

They thought Mary was not listening because she was standing a little apart from them at the window of the private hotel they had gone to. She was watching the passing buses and cabs, and people, but she heard quite well and was made very curious about her uncle and the place he lived in. What sort of a place was it, and what would he be like? What was a hunchback? She had never seen one. Perhaps there were none in India.

Since she had been living in other people's houses and had had no Ayah, she had begun to feel lonely and to think queer thoughts which were new to her. She had begun to wonder why she had never seemed to belong to any one even when her father and mother had been alive. Other children seemed to belong to their fathers and mothers, but she had never seemed to really be any one's little girl. She had had servants, and food and clothes, but no one had taken any notice of her. She did not know that this was because she was a disagreeable child; but then, of course, she did not know she was disagreeable. She often thought that other people were, but she did not know that she was so herself.

She thought Mrs. Medlock the most disagreeable person she had ever seen, with her common, highly colored face and her common fine bonnet. When the next day they set out on their journey to Yorkshire, she walked through the station to the railway carriage with her head up and trying to keep as far away from her as she could, because she did not want to seem to belong to her. It would have made her very angry to think people imagined she was her little girl.

But Mrs. Medlock was not in the least disturbed by her and her thoughts. She was the kind of woman who would "stand no nonsense from young ones." At least, that is what she would have said if she had been asked. She had not wanted to go to London just when her sister Maria's daughter was going to be married, but she had a comfortable, well paid place as housekeeper at Misselthwaite Manor and the only way in which she could keep it was to do at once what Mr. Archibald Craven told her to do. She never dared even to ask a question.

"Captain Lennox and his wife died of the cholera," Mr. Craven had said in his short, cold way. "Captain Lennox was my wife's brother and I am their daughter's guardian. The child is to be brought here. You must go to London and bring her yourself."

So she packed her small trunk and made the journey.

Mary sat in her corner of the railway carriage and looked plain and fretful. She had nothing to read or to look at, and she had folded her thin little black-gloved hands in her lap. Her black dress made her look yellower than ever, and her limp light hair straggled from under her black crêpe hat.

"A more marred-looking young one I never saw in my life," Mrs. Medlock thought. (Marred is a Yorkshire word and means spoiled and pettish.) She had never seen a child who sat so still without doing anything; and at last she got tired of watching her and began to talk in a brisk, hard voice.

"I suppose I may as well tell you something about where you are going to," she said. "Do you know anything about your uncle?"

"No," said Mary.

"Never heard your father and mother talk about him?"

"No," said Mary frowning. She frowned because she remembered that her father and mother had never talked to her about anything in particular. Certainly they had never told her things.

"Humph," muttered Mrs. Medlock, staring at her queer, unresponsive little face. She did not say any more for a few moments and then she began again.

"I suppose you might as well be told something—to prepare you. You are going to a queer place."

Mary said nothing at all, and Mrs. Medlock looked rather discomfited by her apparent indifference, but, after taking a breath, she went on.

"Not but that it's a grand big place in a gloomy way, and Mr. Craven's proud of it in his way—and that's gloomy enough, too. The house is six hundred years old and it's on the edge of the moor, and there's near a hundred rooms in it, though most of them's shut up and locked. And there's pictures and fine old furniture and things that's been there for ages, and there's a big park round it and gardens and trees with branches trailing to the ground—some of them." She paused and took another breath. "But there's nothing else," she ended suddenly.

Mary had begun to listen in spite of herself. It all sounded so unlike India, and anything new rather attracted her. But she did not intend to look as if she were interested. That was one of her unhappy, disagreeable ways. So she sat still.

"Well," said Mrs. Medlock. "What do you think of it?"

"Nothing," she answered. "I know nothing about such places."

That made Mrs. Medlock laugh a short sort of laugh.

"Eh!" she said, "but you are like an old woman. Don't you care?"

"It doesn't matter," said Mary, "whether I care or not."

"You are right enough there," said Mrs. Medlock. "It doesn't. What you're to be kept at Misselthwaite Manor for I don't know, unless because it's the easiest way. *He's* not going to trouble himself about you, that's sure and certain. He never troubles himself about no one."

She stopped herself as if she had just remembered something in time.

"He's got a crooked back," she said. "That set him wrong. He was a sour young man and got no good of all his money and big place till he was married."

Mary's eyes turned toward her in spite of her intention not to seem to care. She had never thought of the hunchback's being married and she was a trifle surprised. Mrs. Medlock saw this, and as she was a talkative woman she continued with more interest. This was one way of passing some of the time, at any rate.

"She was a sweet, pretty thing and he'd have walked the world over to get her a blade o' grass she wanted. Nobody thought she'd marry him, but she did, and people said she married him for his money. But she didn't—she didn't," positively. "When she died—"

Mary gave a little involuntary jump.

"Oh! did she die!" she exclaimed, quite without meaning to. She had just remembered a French fairy story she had once read called "Riquet à la Houppe." It had been about a poor hunchback and a beautiful princess and it had made her suddenly sorry for Mr. Archibald Craven.

"Yes, she died," Mrs. Medlock answered. "And it made him queerer than ever. He cares about nobody. He won't see people. Most of the time he goes away, and when he is at Misselthwaite he shuts himself up in the West Wing and won't let any one but Pitcher see him. Pitcher's an old fellow, but he took care of him when he was a child and he knows his ways."

It sounded like something in a book and it did not make Mary feel cheerful. A house with a hundred rooms, nearly all shut up and with their doors locked—a house on the edge of a moor— whatsoever a moor was—sounded dreary. A man with a crooked back who shut himself up also! She stared out of the window with her lips pinched together, and it seemed quite natural that the rain should have begun to pour down in gray slanting lines and splash and stream down the window-panes. If the pretty wife had been alive she might have made things cheerful by being something like her own mother and by running in and out and going to parties as she had done in frocks "full of lace." But she was not there any more.

"You needn't expect to see him, because ten to one you won't," said Mrs. Medlock. "And you mustn't expect that there will be people to talk to you. You'll have to play about and look after yourself. You'll be told what rooms you can go into and what rooms you're to keep out of. There's gardens enough. But when you're in the house don't go wandering and poking about. Mr. Craven won't have it."

"I shall not want to go poking about," said sour little Mary; and just as suddenly as she had begun to be rather sorry for Mr. Archibald Craven she began to cease to be sorry and to think he was unpleasant enough to deserve all that had happened to him.

And she turned her face toward the streaming panes of the window of the railway carriage and gazed out at the gray rainstorm which looked as if it would go on forever and ever. She watched it so long and steadily that the grayness grew heavier and heavier before her eyes and she fell asleep.

CHAPTER 3
ACROSS THE MOOR

She slept a long time, and when she awakened Mrs. Medlock had bought a lunchbasket at one of the stations and they had some chicken and cold beef and bread and butter and some hot tea. The rain seemed to be streaming down more heavily than ever and everybody in the station wore wet and glistening waterproofs. The guard lighted the lamps in the carriage, and Mrs. Medlock cheered up very much over her tea and chicken and beef. She ate a great deal and afterward fell asleep herself, and Mary sat and stared at her and watched her fine bonnet slip on one side until she herself fell asleep once more in the corner of the carriage, lulled by the splashing of the rain against the windows. It was quite dark when she awakened again. The train had stopped at a station and Mrs. Medlock was shaking her.

"You have had a sleep!" she said. "It's time to open your eyes! We're at Thwaite Station and we've got a long drive before us."

Mary stood up and tried to keep her eyes open while Mrs. Medlock collected her parcels. The little girl did not offer to help her, because in India native servants always picked up or carried things and it seemed quite proper that other people should wait on one.

The station was a small one and nobody but themselves seemed to be getting out of the train. The station-master spoke to Mrs. Medlock in a rough, good-natured way, pronouncing his words in a queer broad fashion which Mary found out afterward was Yorkshire.

"I see tha's got back," he said. "An' tha's browt th' young 'un with thee."

"Aye, that's her," answered Mrs. Medlock, speaking with a Yorkshire accent herself and jerking her head over her shoulder toward Mary. "How's thy Missus?"

"Well enow. Th' carriage is waitin' outside for thee."

A brougham stood on the road before the little outside platform. Mary saw that it was a smart carriage and that it was a smart footman who helped her in. His long waterproof coat and the waterproof covering of his hat were shining and dripping with rain as everything was, the burly station-master included.

When he shut the door, mounted the box with the coachman, and they drove off, the little girl found herself seated in a comfortably cushioned corner, but she was not inclined to go to sleep again. She sat and looked out of the window, curious to see something of the road over which she was being driven to the queer place Mrs. Medlock had spoken of. She was not at all a timid child and she was not exactly frightened, but she felt that there was no knowing what might happen in a house with a hundred rooms nearly all shut up—a house standing on the edge of a moor.

"What is a moor?" she said suddenly to Mrs. Medlock.

"Look out of the window in about ten minutes and you'll see," the woman answered. "We've got to drive five miles across Missel Moor before we get to the Manor. You won't see much because it's a dark night, but you can see something."

Mary asked no more questions but waited in the darkness of her corner, keeping her eyes on the window. The carriage lamps cast rays of light a little distance ahead of them and she caught glimpses of the things they passed. After they had left the station they had driven through a tiny village and she had seen whitewashed cottages and the lights of a public house. Then they had passed a church and a vicarage and a little shop-window or so in a cottage with toys and sweets and odd things set out for sale. Then they were on the highroad and she saw hedges and trees. After that there seemed nothing different for a long time—or at least it seemed a long time to her.

At last the horses began to go more slowly, as if they were climbing up-hill, and presently there seemed to be no more hedges and no more trees. She could see nothing, in fact, but a dense darkness on either side. She leaned forward and pressed her face against the window just as the carriage gave a big jolt.

"Eh! We're on the moor now sure enough," said Mrs. Medlock.

The carriage lamps shed a yellow light on a rough-looking road which seemed to be cut through bushes and low growing things which ended in the great expanse of dark apparently spread out before and around them. A wind was rising and making a singular, wild, low, rushing sound.

"It's—it's not the sea, is it?" said Mary, looking round at her companion.

"No, not it," answered Mrs. Medlock. "Nor it isn't fields nor mountains, it's just miles and miles and miles of wild land that nothing grows on but heather and gorse and broom, and nothing lives on but wild ponies and sheep."

"I feel as if it might be the sea, if there were water on it," said Mary. "It sounds like the sea just now."

"That's the wind blowing through the bushes," Mrs. Medlock said. "It's a wild, dreary enough place to my mind, though there's plenty that likes it—particularly when the heather's in bloom."

On and on they drove through the darkness, and though the rain stopped, the wind rushed by and whistled and made strange sounds. The road went up and down, and several times the carriage passed over a little bridge beneath which water rushed very fast with a great deal of noise. Mary felt as if the drive would never come to an end and that the wide, bleak moor was a wide expanse of black ocean through which she was passing on a strip of dry land.

"I don't like it," she said to herself. "I don't like it," and she pinched her thin lips more tightly together.

The horses were climbing up a hilly piece of road when she first caught sight of a light. Mrs. Medlock saw it as soon as she did and drew a long sigh of relief.

"Eh, I am glad to see that bit o' light twinkling," she exclaimed. "It's the light in the lodge window. We shall get a good cup of tea after a bit, at all events."

It was "after a bit," as she said, for when the carriage passed through the park gates there was still two miles of avenue to drive through and the trees (which nearly met overhead) made it seem as if they were driving through a long dark vault.

They drove out of the vault into a clear space and stopped before an immensely long but low-built house which seemed to ramble round a stone court. At first Mary thought that there were no lights at all in the windows, but as she got out of the carriage she saw that one room in a corner up-stairs showed a dull glow.

The entrance door was a huge one made of massive, curiously shaped panels of oak studded with big iron nails and bound with great iron bars. It opened into an enormous hall, which was so dimly lighted that the faces in the portraits on the walls and the figures in the suits of armor made Mary feel that she did not want to look at them. As she stood on the stone floor she looked a very small, odd little black figure, and she felt as small and lost and odd as she looked.

A neat, thin old man stood near the manservant who opened the door for them.

"You are to take her to her room," he said in a husky voice. "He doesn't want to see her. He's going to London in the morning."

"Very well, Mr. Pitcher," Mrs. Medlock answered. "So long as I know what's expected of me, I can manage."

"'What's expected of you, Mrs. Medlock," Mr. Pitcher said, "is that you make sure that he's not disturbed and that he doesn't see what he doesn't want to see."

And then Mary Lennox was led up a broad staircase and down a long corridor and up a short flight of steps and through another corridor and another, until a door opened in a wall and she found herself in a room with a fire in it and a supper on a table.

Mrs. Medlock said unceremoniously:

"Well, here you are! This room and the next are where you'll live—and you must keep to them. Don't you forget that!"

It was in this way Mistress Mary arrived at Misselthwaite Manor and she had perhaps never felt quite so contrary in all her life.

CHAPTER 4
MARTHA

When she opened her eyes in the morning it was because a young housemaid had come into her room to light the fire and was kneeling on the hearth-rug raking out the cinders noisily. Mary lay and watched her for a few moments and then began to look about the room. She had never seen a room at all like it and thought it curious and gloomy. The walls were covered with tapestry with a forest scene embroidered on it. There were fantastically dressed people under the trees and in the distance there was a glimpse of the turrets of a castle. There were hunters and horses and dogs and ladies. Mary felt as if she were in the forest with them. Out of a deep window she could see a great climbing stretch of land which seemed to have no trees on it, and to look rather like an endless, dull, purplish sea.

"What is that?" she said, pointing out of the window.

Martha, the young housemaid, who had just risen to her feet, looked and pointed also.

"That there?" she said.

"Yes."

"That's th' moor," with a good-natured grin. "Does tha' like it?"

"No," answered Mary. "I hate it."

"That's because tha'rt not used to it," Martha said, going back to her hearth. "Tha' thinks it's too big an' bare now. But tha' will like it."

"Do you?" inquired Mary.

"Aye, that I do," answered Martha, cheerfully polishing away at the grate. "I just love it. It's none bare. It's covered wi' growin' things as smells sweet. It's fair lovely in spring an' summer when

th' gorse an' broom an' heather's in flower. It smells o' honey an'
there's such a lot o' fresh air—an' th' sky looks so high an' th' bees
an' skylarks makes such a nice noise hummin' an' singin'. Eh! I
wouldn't live away from th' moor for anythin'.".

Mary listened to her with a grave, puzzled expression. The
native servants she had been used to in India were not in the least
like this. They were obsequious and servile and did not presume
to talk to their masters as if they were their equals. They made
salaams and called them "protector of the poor" and names of
that sort. Indian servants were commanded to do things, not
asked. It was not the custom to say "please" and "thank you" and
Mary had always slapped her Ayah in the face when she was
angry. She wondered a little what this girl would do if one slapped
her in the face. She was a round, rosy, good-natured looking creature, but she had a sturdy way which made Mistress Mary wonder
if she might not even slap back—if the person who slapped her
was only a little girl.

"You are a strange servant," she said from her pillows, rather
haughtily.

Martha sat up on her heels, with her blacking-brush in her
hand, and laughed, without seeming the least out of temper.

"Eh! I know that," she said. "If there was a grand Missus at
Misselthwaite I should never have been even one of th' under
housemaids. I might have been let to be scullery-maid but I'd
never have been let up-stairs. I'm too common an' I talk too much
Yorkshire. But this is a funny house for all it's so grand. Seems like
there's neither Master nor Mistress except Mr. Pitcher an' Mrs.
Medlock. Mr. Craven, he won't be troubled about anythin' when
he's here, an' he's nearly always away. Mrs. Medlock gave me th'
place out o' kindness. She told me she could never have done it if
Misselthwaite had been like other big houses."

"Are you going to be my servant?" Mary asked, still in her
imperious little Indian way.

Martha began to rub her grate again.

"I'm Mrs. Medlock's servant," she said stoutly. "An' she's Mr.

Craven's—but I'm to do the housemaid's work up here an' wait on you a bit. But you won't need much waitin' on."

"Who is going to dress me?" demanded Mary.

Martha sat up on her heels again and stared. She spoke in broad Yorkshire in her amazement.

"Canna' tha' dress thysen!" she said.

"What do you mean? I don't understand your language," said Mary.

"Eh! I forgot," Martha said. "Mrs. Medlock told me I'd have to be careful or you wouldn't know what I was sayin'. I mean can't you put on your own clothes?"

"No," answered Mary, quite indignantly. "I never did in my life. My Ayah dressed me, of course."

"Well," said Martha, evidently not in the least aware that she was impudent, "it's time tha' should learn. Tha' cannot begin younger. It'll do thee good to wait on thysen a bit. My mother always said she couldn't see why grand people's children didn't turn out fair fools—what with nurses an' bein' washed an' dressed an' took out to walk as if they was puppies!"

"It is different in India," said Mistress Mary disdainfully. She could scarcely stand this.

But Martha was not at all crushed.

"Eh! I can see it's different," she answered almost sympathetically. "I dare say it's because there's such a lot o' blacks there instead o' respectable white people. When I heard you was comin' from India I thought you was a black too."

Mary sat up in bed furious.

"What!" she said. "What! You thought I was a native. You—you daughter of a pig!"

Martha stared and looked hot.

"Who are you callin' names?" she said. "You needn't be so vexed. That's not th' way for a young lady to talk. I've nothin' against th' blacks. When you read about 'em in tracts they're always very religious. You always read as a black's a man an' a brother. I've never seen a black an' I was fair pleased to think I was goin' to see one close. When I come in to light your fire this mornin' I crep' up to your bed an' pulled th' cover back careful to look at you. An' there you was," disappointedly, "no more black than me—for all you're so yeller."

Mary did not even try to control her rage and humiliation.

"You thought I was a native! You dared! You don't know anything about natives! They are not people—they're servants who must salaam to you. You know nothing about India. You know nothing about anything!"

She was in such a rage and felt so helpless before the girl's simple stare, and somehow she suddenly felt so horribly lonely and far away from everything she understood and which understood her, that she threw herself face downward on the pillows and burst into passionate sobbing. She sobbed so unrestrainedly that good-natured Yorkshire Martha was a little frightened and quite sorry for her. She went to the bed and bent over her.

"Eh! you mustn't cry like that there!" she begged. "You mustn't for sure. I didn't know you'd be vexed. I don't know anythin' about anythin'—just like you said. I beg your pardon, Miss. Do stop cryin'."

There was something comforting and really friendly in her queer Yorkshire speech and sturdy way which had a good effect on Mary. She gradually ceased crying and became quiet. Martha looked relieved.

"It's time for thee to get up now," she said. "Mrs. Medlock said I was to carry tha' breakfast an' tea an' dinner into th' room next to this. It's been made into a nursery for thee. I'll help thee on with thy clothes if tha'll get out o' bed. If th' buttons are at th' back tha' cannot button them up tha'self."

When Mary at last decided to get up, the clothes Martha took from the wardrobe were not the ones she had worn when she arrived the night before with Mrs. Medlock.

"Those are not mine," she said. "Mine are black."

She looked the thick white wool coat and dress over, and added with cool approval:

"Those are nicer than mine."

"These are th' ones tha' must put on," Martha answered.
"Mr. Craven ordered Mrs. Medlock to get 'em in London. He
said 'I won't have a child dressed in black wanderin' about like
a lost soul,' he said. 'It'd make the place sadder than it is. Put
color on her.' Mother she said she knew what he meant.
Mother always knows what a body means. She doesn't hold with
black hersel'.''

"I hate black things," said Mary.

The dressing process was one which taught them both something. Martha had "buttoned up" her little sisters and brothers
but she had never seen a child who stood still and waited for
another person to do things for her as if she had neither hands
nor feet of her own.

"Why doesn't tha' put on tha' own shoes?" she said when
Mary quietly held out her foot.

"My Ayah did it," answered Mary, staring. "It was the custom."

She said that very often—"It was the custom." The native servants were always saying it. If one told them to do a thing their
ancestors had not done for a thousand years they gazed at one
mildly and said, "It is not the custom" and one knew that was the
end of the matter.

It had not been the custom that Mistress Mary should do anything but stand and allow herself to be dressed like a doll, but
before she was ready for breakfast she began to suspect that her
life at Misselthwaite Manor would end by teaching her a number
of things quite new to her—things such as putting on her own
shoes and stockings, and picking up things she let fall. If Martha
had been a well-trained fine young lady's maid she would have
been more subservient and respectful and would have known that
it was her business to brush hair, and button boots, and pick
things up and lay them away. She was, however, only an un-
trained Yorkshire rustic who had been brought up in a moorland
cottage with a swarm of little brothers and sisters who had never
dreamed of doing anything but waiting on themselves and on the

younger ones who were either babies in arms or just learning to totter about and tumble over things.

If Mary Lennox had been a child who was ready to be amused she would perhaps have laughed at Martha's readiness to talk, but Mary only listened to her coldly and wondered at her freedom of manner. At first she was not at all interested, but gradually, as the girl rattled on in her good-tempered, homely way, Mary began to notice what she was saying.

"Eh! you should see 'em all," she said. "There's twelve of us an' my father only gets sixteen shilling a week. I can tell you my mother's put to it to get porridge for 'em all. They tumble about on th' moor an' play there all day an' mother says th' air of th' moor fattens 'em. She says she believes they eat th' grass same as th' wild ponies do. Our Dickon, he's twelve years old and he's got a young pony he calls his own."

"Where did he get it?" asked Mary.

"He found it on th' moor with its mother when it was a little one an' he began to make friends with it an' give it bits o' bread an' pluck young grass for it. And it got to like him so it follows him about an' it lets him get on its back. Dickon's a kind lad an' animals likes him."

Mary had never possessed an animal pet of her own and had always thought she should like one. So she began to feel a slight interest in Dickon, and as she had never before been interested in any one but herself, it was the dawning of a healthy sentiment. When she went into the room which had been made into a nursery for her, she found that it was rather like the one she had slept in. It was not a child's room, but a grown-up person's room, with gloomy old pictures on the walls and heavy old oak chairs. A table in the center was set with a good substantial breakfast. But she had always had a very small appetite, and she looked with something more than indifference at the first plate Martha set before her.

"I don't want it," she said.

"Tha' doesn't want thy porridge!" Martha exclaimed incredulously.

"No."

"Tha' doesn't know how good it is. Put a bit o' treacle on it or a bit o' sugar."

"I don't want it," repeated Mary.

"Eh!" said Martha. "I can't abide to see good victuals go to waste. If our children was at this table they'd clean it bare in five minutes."

"Why?" said Mary coldly.

"Why!" echoed Martha. "Because they scarce ever had their stomachs full in their lives. They're as hungry as young hawks an' foxes."

"I don't know what it is to be hungry," said Mary, with the indifference of ignorance.

Martha looked indignant.

"Well, it would do thee good to try it. I can see that plain enough," she said outspokenly. "I've no patience with folk as sits an' just stares at good bread an' meat. My word! don't I wish Dickon and Phil an' Jane an' th' rest of 'em had what's here under their pinafores."

"Why don't you take it to them?" suggested Mary.

"It's not mine," answered Martha stoutly. "An' this isn't my day out. I get my day out once a month same as th' rest. Then I go home an' clean up for mother an' give her a day's rest."

Mary drank some tea and ate a little toast and some marmalade.

"You wrap up warm an' run out an' play you," said Martha. "It'll do you good and give you some stomach for your meat."

Mary went to the window. There were gardens and paths and big trees, but everything looked dull and wintry.

"Out? Why should I go out on a day like this?"

"Well, if tha' doesn't go out tha'lt have to stay in, an' what has tha' got to do?"

Mary glanced about her. There was nothing to do. When Mrs. Medlock had prepared the nursery she had not thought of amusement. Perhaps it would be better to go and see what the gardens were like.

"Who will go with me?" she inquired.

Martha stared.

"You'll go by yourself," she answered. "You'll have to learn to play like other children does when they haven't got sisters and brothers. Our Dickon goes off on th' moor by himself an' plays for hours. That's how he made friends with th' pony. He's got sheep on th' moor that knows him, an' birds as comes an' eats out of his hand. However little there is to eat, he always saves a bit o' his bread to coax his pets."

It was really this mention of Dickon which made Mary decide to go out, though she was not aware of it. There would be birds outside though there would not be ponies or sheep. They would be different from the birds in India and it might amuse her to look at them.

Martha found her coat and hat for her and a pair of stout little boots and she showed her her way down-stairs.

"If tha' goes round that way tha'll come to th' gardens," she said, pointing to a gate in a wall of shrubbery. "There's lots o' flowers in summer-time, but there's nothin' bloomin' now." She seemed to hesitate a second before she added, "One of th' gardens is locked up. No one has been in it for ten years."

"Why?" asked Mary in spite of herself. Here was another locked door added to the hundred in the strange house.

"Mr. Craven had it shut when his wife died so sudden. He won't let no one go inside. It was her garden. He locked th' door an' dug a hole and buried th' key. There's Mrs. Medlock's bell ring-ing—I must run."

After she was gone Mary turned down the walk which led to the door in the shrubbery. She could not help thinking about the garden which no one had been into for ten years. She wondered what it would look like and whether there were any flowers still alive in it. When she had passed through the shrubbery gate she found herself in great gardens, with wide lawns and winding walks with clipped borders. There were trees, and flower-beds, and evergreens clipped into strange shapes, and a large pool with an old gray fountain in its midst. But the flower-beds were bare and wintry and the fountain was not playing. This was not the garden which was shut up. How could a garden be shut up? You could always walk into a garden.

She was just thinking this when she saw that, at the end of the path she was following, there seemed to be a long wall, with ivy growing over it. She was not familiar enough with England to know that she was coming upon the kitchen-gardens where the vegetables and fruit were growing. She went toward the wall and found that there was a green door in the ivy, and that it stood open. This was not the closed garden, evidently, and she could go into it.

She went through the door and found that it was a garden with walls all round it and that it was only one of several walled gardens which seemed to open into one another. She saw another open green door, revealing bushes and pathways between beds containing winter vegetables. Fruit-trees were trained flat against the wall, and over some of the beds there were glass frames. The place was bare and ugly enough, Mary thought, as she stood and stared about her. It might be nicer in summer when things were green, but there was nothing pretty about it now.

Presently an old man with a spade over his shoulder walked through the door leading from the second garden. He looked startled when he saw Mary, and then touched his cap. He had a surly old face, and did not seem at all pleased to see her—but then she was displeased with his garden and wore her "quite contrary" expression, and certainly did not seem at all pleased to see him.

"What is this place?" she asked.

"One o' th' kitchen-gardens," he answered.

"What is that?" said Mary, pointing through the other green door.

"Another of 'em," shortly. "There's another on t'other side o' th' wall an' there's th' orchard t'other side o' that."

"Can I go in them?" asked Mary.

"If tha' likes. But there's nowt to see."

Mary made no response. She went down the path and through the second green door. There she found more walls and winter vegetables and glass frames, but in the second wall there was another green door and it was not open. Perhaps it led into the garden which no one had seen for ten years. As she was not at all a timid child and always did what she wanted to do, Mary went to the green door and turned the handle. She hoped the door would not open because she wanted to be sure she had found the mysterious garden—but it did open quite easily and she walked through it and found herself in an orchard. There were walls all round it also and trees trained against them, and there were bare fruit-trees growing in the winter-browned grass—but there was no green door to be seen anywhere. Mary looked for it, and yet when she had entered the upper end of the garden she had noticed that the wall did not seem to end with the orchard but to extend beyond it as if it enclosed a place at the other side. She could see the tops of trees above the wall, and when she stood still she saw a bird with a bright red breast sitting on the topmost branch of one of them, and suddenly he burst into his winter song—almost as if he had caught sight of her and was calling to her.

She stopped and listened to him and somehow his cheerful, friendly little whistle gave her a pleased feeling—even a disagreeable little girl may be lonely, and the big closed house and big bare moor and big bare gardens had made this one feel as if there was no one left in the world but herself. If she had been an affectionate child, who had been used to being loved, she would have broken her heart, but even though she was "Mistress Mary Quite Contrary" she was desolate, and the bright-breasted little bird brought a look into her sour little face which was almost a smile. She listened to him until he flew away. He was not like an Indian bird and she liked him and wondered if she should ever see him again. Perhaps he lived in the mysterious garden and knew all about it.

Perhaps it was because she had nothing whatever to do that she thought so much of the deserted garden. She was curious about it and wanted to see what it was like. Why had Mr. Archibald Craven buried the key? If he had liked his wife so much why did he hate her garden? She wondered if she should ever see him, but she knew that if she did she should not like him, and he would not like her, and that she should only stand and stare at him and say nothing, though she should be wanting dreadfully to ask him why he had done such a queer thing.

"People never like me and I never like people," she thought. "And I never can talk as the Crawford children could. They were always talking and laughing and making noises."

She thought of the robin and of the way he seemed to sing his song at her, and as she remembered the tree-top he perched on she stopped rather suddenly on the path.

"I believe that tree was in the secret garden—I feel sure it was," she said. "There was a wall round the place and there was no door."

She walked back into the first kitchen-garden she had entered and found the old man digging there. She went and stood beside him and watched him a few moments in her cold little way. He took no notice of her and so at last she spoke to him.

"I have been into the other gardens," she said.

"There was nothin' to prevent thee," he answered crustily.

"I went into the orchard."

"There was no dog at th' door to bite thee," he answered.

"There was no door there into the other garden," said Mary.

"What garden?" he said in a rough voice, stopping his digging for a moment.

"The one on the other side of the wall," answered Mistress Mary. "There are trees there—I saw the tops of them. A bird with a red breast was sitting on one of them and he sang."

To her surprise the surly old weather-beaten face actually changed its expression. A slow smile spread over it and the gardener looked quite different. It made her think that it was curious how much nicer a person looked when he smiled. She had not thought of it before.

He turned about to the orchard side of his garden and began to whistle—a low soft whistle. She could not understand how such a surly man could make such a coaxing sound.

Almost the next moment a wonderful thing happened. She heard a soft little rushing flight through the air—and it was the bird with the red breast flying to them, and he actually alighted on the big clod of earth quite near to the gardener's foot.

"Here he is," chuckled the old man, and then he spoke to the bird as if he were speaking to a child.

"Where has tha' been, tha' cheeky little beggar?" he said. "I've not seen thee before today. Has tha' begun tha' courtin' this early in th' season? Tha'rt too forrad."

The bird put his tiny head on one side and looked up at him with his soft bright eye which was like a black dewdrop. He seemed quite familiar and not the least afraid. He hopped about and pecked the earth briskly, looking for seeds and insects. It actually gave Mary a queer feeling in her heart, because he was so pretty and cheerful and seemed so like a person. He had a plump body and a delicate beak, and slender delicate legs.

"Will he always come when you call him?" she asked almost in a whisper.

"Aye, that he will. I've knowed him ever since he was a fledgling. He come out of th' nest in th' other garden an' when first he flew over th' wall he was too weak to fly back for a few days an' we got friendly. When he went over th' wall again th' rest of th' brood was gone an' he was lonely an' he come back to me."

"What kind of a bird is he?" Mary asked.

"Doesn't tha' know? He's a robin redbreast an' they're th' friendliest, curiousest birds alive. They're almost as friendly as dogs—if you know how to get on with 'em. Watch him peckin' about there an' lookin' round at us now an' again. He knows we're talkin' about him."

It was the queerest thing in the world to see the old fellow. He looked at the plump little scarlet-waistcoated bird as if he were both proud and fond of him.

"He's a conceited one," he chuckled. "He likes to hear folk talk about him. An' curious—bless me, there never was his like for curiosity an' meddlin'. He's always comin' to see what I'm plantin'. He knows all th' things Mester Craven never troubles hissel' to find out. He's th' head gardener, he is."

The robin hopped about busily pecking the soil and now and then stopped and looked at them a little. Mary thought his black dewdrop eyes gazed at her with great curiosity. It really seemed as if he were finding out all about her. The queer feeling in her heart increased.

"Where did the rest of the brood fly to?" she asked.

"There's no knowin'. The old ones turn 'em out o' their nest an' make 'em fly an' they're scattered before you know it. This one was a knowin' one an' he knew he was lonely."

Mistress Mary went a step nearer to the robin and looked at him very hard.

"I'm lonely," she said.

She had not known before that this was one of the things which made her feel sour and cross. She seemed to find it out when the robin looked at her and she looked at the robin.

The old gardener pushed his cap back on his bald head and stared at her a minute.

"Art tha' th' little wench from India?" he asked.

Mary nodded.

"Then no wonder tha'rt lonely. Tha'lt be lonelier before tha's done," he said.

He began to dig again, driving his spade deep into the rich black garden soil while the robin hopped about very busily employed.

"What is your name?" Mary inquired.

He stood up to answer her.

"Ben Weatherstaff," he answered, and then he added with a surly chuckle, "I'm lonely mysel' except when he's with me," and he jerked his thumb toward the robin. "He's th' only friend I've got."

"I have no friends at all," said Mary. "I never had. My Ayah didn't like me and I never played with any one."

It is a Yorkshire habit to say what you think with blunt frankness, and old Ben Weatherstaff was a Yorkshire moor man.

"Tha' an' me are a good bit alike," he said. "We was wove out of th' same cloth. We're neither of us good lookin' an' we're both of us as sour as we look. We've got the same nasty tempers, both of us, I'll warrant."

This was plain speaking, and Mary Lennox had never heard the truth about herself in her life. Native servants always salaamed and submitted to you, whatever you did. She had never thought much about her looks, but she wondered if she was as unattractive as Ben Weatherstaff and she also wondered if she looked as sour as he had looked before the robin came. She actually began to wonder also if she was "nasty tempered." She felt uncomfortable.

Suddenly a clear rippling little sound broke out near her and she turned round. She was standing a few feet from a young apple-tree and the robin had flown on to one of its branches and had burst out into a scrap of a song. Ben Weatherstaff laughed outright.

"What did he do that for?" asked Mary.

"He's made up his mind to make friends with thee," replied Ben. "Dang me if he hasn't took a fancy to thee."

"To me?" said Mary, and she moved toward the little tree softly and looked up.

"Would you make friends with me?" she said to the robin just as if she was speaking to a person. "Would you?" And she did not say it either in her hard little voice or in her imperious Indian voice, but in a tone so soft and eager and coaxing that Ben Weatherstaff was as surprised as she had been when she heard him whistle.

"Why," he cried out, "tha' said that as nice an' human as if tha' was a real child instead of a sharp old woman. Tha' said it almost like Dickon talks to his wild things on th' moor."

"Do you know Dickon?" Mary asked, turning round rather in a hurry.

"Everybody knows him. Dickon's wanderin' about everywhere. Th' very blackberries an' heather-bells knows him. I warrant th' foxes shows him where their cubs lies an' th' skylarks doesn't hide their nests from him."

Mary would have liked to ask some more questions. She was almost as curious about Dickon as she was about the deserted garden. But just that moment the robin, who had ended his song, gave a little shake of his wings, spread them and flew away. He had made his visit and had other things to do.

"He has flown over the wall!" Mary cried out, watching him. "He has flown into the orchard—he has flown across the other wall—into the garden where there is no door!"

"He lives there," said old Ben. "He came out o' th' egg there. If he's courtin', he's makin' up to some young madam of a robin that lives among th' old rose-trees there."

"Rose-trees," said Mary. "Are there rose-trees?"

Ben Weatherstaff took up his spade again and began to dig.

"There was ten year' ago," he mumbled.

"I should like to see them," said Mary. "Where is the green door? There must be a door somewhere."

Ben drove his spade deep and looked as uncompanionable as he had looked when she first saw him.

"There was ten year' ago, but there isn't now," he said.

"No door!" cried Mary. "There must be."

"None as any one can find, an' none as is any one's business. Don't you be a meddlesome wench an' poke your nose where it's no cause to go. Here, I must go on with my work. Get you gone an' play you. I've no more time."

And he actually stopped digging, threw his spade over his shoulder and walked off, without even glancing at her or saying good-by.

CHAPTER 5
THE CRY IN THE CORRIDOR

At first each day which passed by for Mary Lennox was exactly like the others. Every morning she awoke in her tapestried room and found Martha kneeling upon the hearth building her fire; every morning she ate her breakfast in the nursery which had nothing amusing in it; and after each breakfast she gazed out of the window across to the huge moor which seemed to spread out on all sides and climb up to the sky, and after she had stared for a while she realized that if she did not go out she would have to stay in and do nothing—and so she went out. She did not know that this was the best thing she could have done, and she did not know that, when she began to walk quickly or even run along the paths and down the avenue, she was stirring her slow blood and making herself stronger by fighting with the wind which swept down from the moor. She ran only to make herself warm, and she hated the wind which rushed at her face and roared and held her back as if it were some giant she could not see. But the big breaths of rough fresh air blown over the heather filled her lungs with something which was good for her whole thin body and whipped some red color into her cheeks and brightened her dull eyes when she did not know anything about it.

But after a few days spent almost entirely out of doors she wakened one morning knowing what it was to be hungry, and when she sat down to her breakfast she did not glance disdainfully at her porridge and push it away, but took up her spoon and began to eat it and went on eating it until her bowl was empty.

"Tha' got on well enough with that this mornin', didn't tha'?" said Martha.

"It tastes nice to-day," said Mary, feeling a little surprised herself.

"It's th' air of th' moor that's givin' thee stomach for tha' vict-uals," answered Martha. "It's lucky for thee that tha's got victuals as well as appetite. There's been twelve in our cottage as had th' stomach an' nothin' to put in it. You go on playin' you out o' doors every day an' you'll get some flesh on your bones an' you won't be so yeller."

"I don't play," said Mary. "I have nothing to play with."

"Nothin' to play with!" exclaimed Martha. "Our children plays with sticks and stones. They just runs about an' shouts an' looks at things."

Mary did not shout, but she looked at things. There was noth-ing else to do. She walked round and round the gardens and wandered about the paths in the park. Sometimes she looked for Ben Weatherstaff, but though several times she saw him at work he was too busy to look at her or was too surly. Once when she was walking toward him he picked up his spade and turned away as if he did it on purpose.

One place she went to oftener than to any other. It was the long walk outside the gardens with the walls round them. There were bare flower-beds on either side of it and against the walls ivy grew thickly. There was one part of the wall where the creeping dark green leaves were more bushy than elsewhere. It seemed as if for a long time that part had been neglected. The rest of it had been clipped and made to look neat, but at this lower end of the walk it had not been trimmed at all.

A few days after she had talked to Ben Weatherstaff Mary stopped to notice this and wondered why it was so. She had just paused and was looking up at a long spray of ivy swinging in the wind when she saw a gleam of scarlet and heard a brilliant chirp, and there, on the top of the wall, perched Ben Weatherstaff's robin redbreast, tilting forward to look at her with his small head on one side.

"Oh!" she cried out, "is it you—is it you?" And it did not seem at all queer to her that she spoke to him as if she was sure that he would understand and answer her.

He did answer. He twittered and chirped and hopped along the wall as if he were telling her all sorts of things. It seemed to Mistress Mary as if she understood him, too, though he was not speaking in words. It was as if he said:

"Good morning! Isn't the wind nice? Isn't the sun nice? Isn't everything nice? Let us both chirp and hop and twitter. Come on! Come on!"

Mary began to laugh, and as he hopped and took little flights along the wall she ran after him. Poor little thin, sallow, ugly Mary—she actually looked almost pretty for a moment.

"I like you! I like you!" she cried out, pattering down the walk; and she chirped and tried to whistle, which last she did not know how to do in the least. But the robin seemed to be quite satisfied and chirped and whistled back at her. At last he spread his wings and made a darting flight to the top of a tree, where he perched and sang loudly.

That reminded Mary of the first time she had seen him. He had been swinging on a tree-top then and she had been standing in the orchard. Now she was on the other side of the orchard and standing in the path outside a wall—much lower down—and there was the same tree inside.

"It's in the garden no one can go into," she said to herself. "It's the garden without a door. He lives in there. How I wish I could see what it is like!"

She ran up the walk to the green door she had entered the first morning. Then she ran down the path through the other door and then into the orchard, and when she stood and looked up there was the tree on the other side of the wall, and there was the robin just finishing his song and beginning to preen his feathers with his beak.

"It is the garden," she said. "I am sure it is."

She walked round and looked closely at that side of the orchard wall, but she only found what she had found before—that there was no door in it. Then she ran through the kitchen-gardens again and out into the walk outside the long ivy-covered wall, and she walked to the end of it and looked at it, but there was no door; and then she walked to the other end, looking again, but there was no door.

"It's very queer," she said. "Ben Weatherstaff said there was no door and there is no door. But there must have been one ten years ago, because Mr. Craven buried the key."

This gave her so much to think of that she began to be quite interested and feel that she was not sorry that she had come to Misselthwaite Manor. In India she had always felt hot and too languid to care much about anything. The fact was that the fresh wind from the moor had begun to blow the cobwebs out of her young brain and to waken her up a little.

She stayed out of doors nearly all day, and when she sat down to her supper at night she felt hungry and drowsy and comfortable. She did not feel cross when Martha chattered away. She felt as if she rather liked to hear her, and at last she thought she would ask her a question. She asked it after she had finished her supper and had sat down on the hearth-rug before the fire.

"Why did Mr. Craven hate the garden?" she said.

She had made Martha stay with her and Martha had not objected at all. She was very young, and used to a crowded cottage full of brothers and sisters, and she found it dull in the great servants' hall down-stairs where the footman and upper-housemaids made fun of her Yorkshire speech and looked upon her as a common little thing, and sat and whispered among themselves. Martha liked to talk, and the strange child who had lived in India, and been waited upon by "blacks," was novelty enough to attract her.

She sat down on the hearth herself without waiting to be asked.

"Art tha' thinkin' about that garden yet?" she said. "I knew tha' would. That was just the way with me when I first heard about it."

"Why did he hate it?" Mary persisted.

Martha tucked her feet under her and made herself quite comfortable.

"Listen to th' wind wutherin' round the house," she said. "You could bare stand up on the moor if you was out on it to-night."

Mary did not know what "wutherin'" meant until she listened, and then she understood. It must mean that hollow shuddering sort of roar which rushed round and round the house as if the giant no one could see were buffeting it and beating at the walls and windows to try to break in. But one knew he could not get in, and somehow it made one feel very safe and warm inside a room with a red coal fire.

"But why did he hate it so?" she asked, after she had listened. She intended to know if Martha did.

Then Martha gave up her store of knowledge.

"Mind," she said, "Mrs. Medlock said it's not to be talked about. There's lots o' things in this place that's not to be talked over. That's Mr. Craven's orders. His troubles are none servants' business, he says. But for th' garden he wouldn't be like he is. It was Mrs. Craven's garden that she had made when first they were married an' she just loved it, an' they used to 'tend the flowers themselves. An' none o' th' gardeners was ever let to go in. Him an' her used to go in an' shut th' door an' stay there hours an' hours, readin' and talkin'. An' she was just a bit of a girl an' there was an old tree with a branch bent like a seat on it. An' she made roses grow over it an' she used to sit there. But one day when she was sittin' there th' branch broke an' she fell on th' ground an' was hurt so bad that next day she died. Th' doctors thought he'd go out o' his mind an' die, too. That's why he hates it. No one's never gone in since, an' he won't let any one talk about it."

Mary did not ask any more questions. She looked at the red fire and listened to the wind "wutherin'." It seemed to be "wutherin'" louder than ever.

At that moment a very good thing was happening to her. Four good things had happened to her, in fact, since she came to Misselthwaite Manor. She had felt as if she had understood a robin and that he had understood her; she had run in the wind until her blood had grown warm; she had been healthily hungry for the first time in her life; and she had found out what it was to be sorry for some one. She was getting on.

But as she was listening to the wind she began to listen to something else. She did not know what it was, because at first she could scarcely distinguish it from the wind itself. It was a curious sound—it seemed almost as if a child were crying somewhere. Sometimes the wind sounded rather like a child crying, but presently Mistress Mary felt quite sure that this sound was inside the house, not outside it. It was far away, but it was inside. She turned round and looked at Martha.

"Do you hear any one crying?" she said.

Martha suddenly looked confused.

"No," she answered. "It's th' wind. Sometimes it sounds like as if some one was lost on th' moor an' wailin'. It's got all sorts o' sounds."

"But listen," said Mary. "It's in the house—down one of those long corridors."

And at that very moment a door must have been opened somewhere down-stairs; for a great rushing draft blew along the passage and the door of the room they sat in was blown open with a crash, and as they both jumped to their feet the light was blown out and the crying sound was swept down the far corridor so that it was to be heard more plainly than ever.

"There!" said Mary. "I told you so! It is some one crying—and it isn't a grown-up person."

Martha ran and shut the door and turned the key, but before she did it they both heard the sound of a door in some far passage shutting with a bang, and then everything was quiet, for even the wind ceased "wutherin'" for a few moments.

"It was th' wind," said Martha stubbornly. "An' if it wasn't, it was little Betty Butterworth, th' scullery-maid. She's had th' toothache all day."

But something troubled and awkward in her manner made Mistress Mary stare very hard at her. She did not believe she was speaking the truth.

CHAPTER 6
"THERE WAS SOME ONE CRYING—THERE WAS!"

The next day the rain poured down in torrents again, and when Mary looked out of her window the moor was almost hidden by gray mist and cloud. There could be no going out to-day.

"What do you do in your cottage when it rains like this?" she asked Martha.

"Try to keep from under each other's feet mostly," Martha answered. "Eh! there does seem a lot of us then. Mother's a good-tempered woman but she gets fair moithered. The biggest ones goes out in th' cow-shed and plays there. Dickon he doesn't mind th' wet. He goes out just th' same as if th' sun was shinin'. He says he sees things on rainy days as doesn't show when it's fair weather. He once found a little fox cub half drowned in its hole and he brought it home in th' bosom of his shirt to keep it warm. Its mother had been killed nearby an' th' hole was swum out an' th' rest o' th' litter was dead. He's got it at home now. He found a half-drowned young crow another time an' he brought it home, too, an' tamed it. It's named Soot because it's so black, an' it hops an' flies about with him everywhere."

The time had come when Mary had forgotten to resent Martha's familiar talk. She had even begun to find it interesting and to be sorry when she stopped or went away. The stories she had been told by her Ayah when she lived in India had been quite unlike those Martha had to tell about the moorland cottage which held fourteen people who lived in four little rooms and never had quite enough to eat. The children seemed to tumble about and amuse themselves like a litter of rough, good-natured collie puppies. Mary was most attracted by the mother and Dickon. When

Martha told stories of what "mother" said or did they always sounded comfortable.

"If I had a raven or a fox cub I could play with it," said Mary. "But I have nothing."

Martha looked perplexed.

"Can tha' knit?" she asked.

"No," answered Mary.

"Can tha' sew?"

"No."

"Can tha' read?"

"Yes."

"Then why doesn't tha' read somethin', or learn a bit o' spellin'? Tha'st old enough to be learnin' thy book a good bit now."

"I haven't any books," said Mary. "Those I had were left in India."

"That's a pity," said Martha. "If Mrs. Medlock'd let thee go to th' library, there's thousands o' books there."

Mary did not ask where the library was, because she was suddenly inspired by a new idea. She made up her mind to go and find it herself. She was not troubled about Mrs. Medlock. Mrs. Medlock seemed always to be in her comfortable housekeeper's sitting-room down-stairs. In this queer place one scarcely ever saw any one at all. In fact, there was no one to see but the servants, and when their master was away they lived a luxurious life below stairs, where there was a huge kitchen hung about with shining brass and pewter, and a large servants' hall where there were four or five abundant meals eaten every day, and where a great deal of lively romping went on when Mrs. Medlock was out of the way.

Mary's meals were served regularly, and Martha waited on her, but no one troubled themselves about her in the least. Mrs. Medlock came and looked at her every day or two, but no one inquired what she did or told her what to do. She supposed that perhaps this was the English way of treating children. In India she had always been attended by her Ayah, who had followed her about and waited on her, hand and foot. She had often been tired of her company. Now she was followed by nobody and was learning to dress herself because Martha looked as though she thought she was silly and stupid when she wanted to have things handed to her and put on.

"Hasn't tha' got good sense?" she said once, when Mary had stood waiting for her to put on her gloves for her. "Our Susan Ann is twice as sharp as thee an' she's only four year' old. Sometimes tha' looks fair soft in th' head."

Mary had worn her contrary scowl for an hour after that, but it made her think several entirely new things.

She stood at the window for about ten minutes this morning after Martha had swept up the hearth for the last time and gone down-stairs. She was thinking over the new idea which had come to her when she heard of the library. She did not care very much about the library itself, because she had read very few books; but to hear of it brought back to her mind the hundred rooms with closed doors. She wondered if they were all really locked and what she would find if she could get into any of them. Were there a hundred really? Why shouldn't she go and see how many doors she could count? It would be something to do on this morning when she could not go out. She had never been taught to ask permission to do things, and she knew nothing at all about authority, so she would not have thought it necessary to ask Mrs. Medlock if she might walk about the house, even if she had seen her.

She opened the door of the room and went into the corridor, and then she began her wanderings. It was a long corridor and it branched into other corridors and it led her up short flights of steps which mounted to others again. There were doors and doors, and there were pictures on the walls. Sometimes they were pictures of dark, curious landscapes, but oftenest they were portraits of men and women in queer, grand costumes made of satin and velvet. She found herself in one long gallery whose walls were covered with these portraits. She had never thought there could be so many in any house. She walked slowly down this place and stared at the faces which also seemed to stare at her. She felt as if they were wondering what a little girl from India was doing in their house. Some were pictures of children—little girls in thick satin frocks which reached to their feet and stood out about them, and boys with puffed sleeves and lace collars and long hair, or with big ruffs around their necks. She always stopped to look at the children, and wonder what their names were, and where they had gone, and why they wore such odd clothes. There was a stiff, plain little girl rather like herself. She wore a green brocade dress and held a green parrot on her finger. Her eyes had a sharp, curious look.

"Where do you live now?" said Mary aloud to her. "I wish you were here."

Surely no other little girl ever spent such a queer morning. It seemed as if there was no one in all the huge rambling house but her own small self, wandering about up-stairs and down, through narrow passages and wide ones, where it seemed to her that no one but herself had ever walked. Since so many rooms had been built, people must have lived in them, but it all seemed so empty that she could not quite believe it true.

It was not until she climbed to the second floor that she thought of turning the handle of a door. All the doors were shut, as Mrs. Medlock had said they were, but at last she put her hand on the handle of one of them and turned it. She was almost frightened for a moment when she felt that it turned without difficulty and that when she pushed upon the door itself it slowly and heavily opened. It was a massive door and opened into a big bedroom. There were embroidered hangings on the wall, and inlaid furniture such as she had seen in India stood about the room. A broad window with leaded panes looked out upon the moor; and over the mantel was another portrait of the stiff, plain little girl who seemed to stare at her more curiously than ever.

"Perhaps she slept here once," said Mary. "She stares at me so that she makes me feel queer."

After that she opened more doors and more. She saw so many

rooms that she became quite tired and began to think that there must be a hundred, though she had not counted them. In all of them there were old pictures or old tapestries with strange scenes worked on them. There were curious pieces of furniture and curious ornaments in nearly all of them.

In one room, which looked like a lady's sitting-room, the hangings were all embroidered velvet, and in a cabinet were about a hundred little elephants made of ivory. They were of different sizes, and some had their mahouts or palanquins on their backs. Some were much bigger than the others and some were so tiny that they seemed only babies. Mary had seen carved ivory in India and she knew all about elephants. She opened the door of the cabinet and stood on a footstool and played with these for quite a long time. When she got tired she set the elephants in order and shut the door of the cabinet.

In all her wanderings through the long corridors and the empty rooms, she had seen nothing alive; but in this room she saw something. Just after she had closed the cabinet door she heard a tiny rustling sound. It made her jump and look around at the sofa by the fireplace, from which it seemed to come. In the corner of the sofa there was a cushion, and in the velvet which covered it there was a hole, and out of the hole peeped a tiny head with a pair of frightened eyes in it.

Mary crept softly across the room to look. The bright eyes belonged to a little gray mouse, and the mouse had eaten a hole into the cushion and made a comfortable nest there. Six baby mice were cuddled up asleep near her. If there was no one else alive in the hundred rooms there were seven mice who did not look lonely at all.

"If they wouldn't be so frightened I would take them back with me," said Mary.

She had wandered about long enough to feel too tired to wander any farther, and she turned back. Two or three times she lost her way by turning down the wrong corridor and was obliged to ramble up and down until she found the right one; but at last she reached her own floor again, though she was some distance from her own room and did not know exactly where she was.

"I believe I have taken a wrong turning again," she said, standing still at what seemed the end of a short passage with tapestry on the wall. "I don't know which way to go. How still everything is!"

It was while she was standing here and just after she had said this that the stillness was broken by a sound. It was another cry, but not quite like the one she had heard last night; it was only a short one, a fretful, childish whine muffled by passing through walls.

"It's nearer than it was," said Mary, her heart beating rather faster. "And it *is* crying."

She put her hand accidentally upon the tapestry near her, and then sprang back, feeling quite startled. The tapestry was the covering of a door which fell open and showed her that there was another part of the corridor behind it, and Mrs. Medlock was coming up it with her bunch of keys in her hand and a very cross look on her face.

"What are you doing here?" she said, and she took Mary by the arm and pulled her away. "What did I tell you?"

"I turned round the wrong corner," explained Mary. "I didn't know which way to go and I heard some one crying."

She quite hated Mrs. Medlock at the moment, but she hated her more the next.

"You didn't hear anything of the sort," said the housekeeper. "You come along back to your own nursery or I'll box your ears."

And she took her by the arm and half pushed, half pulled her up one passage and down another until she pushed her in at the door of her own room.

"Now," she said, "you stay where you're told to stay or you'll find yourself locked up. The master had better get you a governess, same as he said he would. You're one that needs some one to look sharp after you. I've got enough to do."

She went out of the room and slammed the door after her, and Mary went and sat on the hearth-rug, pale with rage. She did not cry, but ground her teeth.

"There *was* some one crying—there *was*—there *was*!" she said to herself.

She had heard it twice now, and sometime she would find out. She had found out a great deal this morning. She felt as if she had been on a long journey, and at any rate she had had something to amuse her all the time, and she had played with the ivory elephants and had seen the gray mouse and its babies in their nest in the velvet cushion.

CHAPTER 7
THE KEY OF THE GARDEN

Two days after this, when Mary opened her eyes she sat upright in bed immediately, and called to Martha.

"Look at the moor! Look at the moor!"

The rain-storm had ended and the gray mist and clouds had been swept away in the night by the wind. The wind itself had ceased and a brilliant, deep blue sky arched high over the moorland. Never, never had Mary dreamed of a sky so blue. In India skies were hot and blazing; this was of a deep cool blue which almost seemed to sparkle like the waters of some lovely bottomless lake, and here and there, high, high in the arched blueness floated small clouds of snow-white fleece. The far-reaching world of the moor itself looked softly blue instead of gloomy purple-black or awful dreary gray.

"Aye," said Martha with a cheerful grin. "Th' storm's over for a bit. It does like this at this time o' th' year. It goes off in a night like it was pretendin' it had never been here an' never meant to come again. That's because th' spring-time's on its way. It's a long way off yet, but it's comin'."

"I thought perhaps it always rained or looked dark in England," Mary said.

"Eh! No!" said Martha, sitting up on her heels among her black lead brushes. "Nowt o' th' soart!"

"What does that mean?" asked Mary seriously. In India the natives spoke different dialects which only a few people understood, so she was not surprised when Martha used words she did not know.

Martha laughed as she had done the first morning.

"There now," she said. "I've talked broad Yorkshire again like Mrs. Medlock said I mustn't. 'Nowt o' th' soart' means 'nothin'-of-the-sort,'" slowly and carefully, "but it takes so long to say it. Yorkshire's th' sunniest place on earth when it is sunny. I told thee tha'd like th' moor after a bit. Just you wait till you see th' gold colored gorse blossoms an' th' blossoms o' th' broom, an' th' heather flowerin', all purple bells, an' hundreds o' butterflies flutterin' an' bees hummin' an' skylarks soarin' up an' singin'. You'll want to get out on it at sunrise an' live out on it all day like Dickon does."

"Could I ever get there?" asked Mary wistfully, looking through her window at the far-off blue. It was so new and big and wonderful and such a heavenly color.

"I don't know," answered Martha. "Tha's never used tha' legs since tha' was born, it seems to me. Tha' couldn't walk five mile. It's five mile to our cottage."

"I should like to see your cottage."

Martha stared at her a moment curiously before she took up her polishing brush and began to rub the grate again. She was thinking that the small plain face did not look quite as sour at this moment as it had done the first morning she saw it. It looked just a trifle like little Susan Ann's when she wanted something very much.

"I'll ask my mother about it," she said. "She's one o' them that nearly always sees a way to do things. It's my day out to-day an' I'm goin' home. Eh! I am glad. Mrs. Medlock thinks a lot o' mother. Perhaps she could talk to her."

"I like your mother," said Mary.

"I should think tha' did," agreed Martha, polishing away.

"I've never seen her," said Mary.

"No, tha' hasn't," replied Martha.

She sat up on her heels again and rubbed the end of her nose with the back of her hand as if puzzled for a moment, but she ended quite positively.

"Well, she's that sensible an' hard workin' an' good-natured an' clean that no one could help likin' her whether they'd seen her or not. When I'm goin' home to her on my day out I just jump for joy when I'm crossin' th' moor."

"I like Dickon," added Mary. "And I've never seen him."

"Well," said Martha stoutly, "I've told thee that th' very birds likes him an' th' rabbits an' wild sheep an' ponies, an' th' foxes themselves. I wonder," staring at her reflectively, "what Dickon would think of thee?"

"He wouldn't like me," said Mary in her stiff, cold little way. "No one does."

Martha looked reflective again.

"How does tha' like thysel'?" she inquired, really quite as if she were curious to know.

Mary hesitated a moment and thought it over.

"Not at all—really," she answered. "But I never thought of that before."

Martha grinned a little as if at some homely recollection.

"Mother said that to me once," she said. "She was at her washtub an' I was in a bad temper an' talkin' ill of folk, an' she turns round on me an' says: 'Tha' young vixon, tha'! There tha' stands sayin' tha' doesn't like this one an' tha' doesn't like that one. How does tha' like thysel'?' It made me laugh an' it brought me to my senses in a minute."

She went away in high spirits as soon as she had given Mary her breakfast. She was going to walk five miles across the moor to the cottage, and she was going to help her mother with the washing and do the week's baking and enjoy herself thoroughly.

Mary felt lonelier than ever when she knew she was no longer in the house. She went out into the garden as quickly as possible, and the first thing she did was to run round and round the fountain flower garden ten times. She counted the times carefully and when she had finished she felt in better spirits. The sunshine made the whole place look different. The high, deep, blue sky arched over Misselthwaite as well as over the moor, and she kept lifting her face and looking up into it, trying to imagine what it would be like to lie down on one of the little snow-white clouds and float about. She went into the first kitchen-garden and found Ben Weatherstaff working there with two other gardeners. The change in the weather seemed to have done him good. He spoke to her of his own accord.

"Springtime's comin'," he said. "Cannot tha' smell it?"

Mary sniffed and thought she could.

"I smell something nice and fresh and damp," she said.

"That's th' good rich earth," he answered, digging away. "It's in a good humor makin' ready to grow things. It's glad when plantin' time comes. It's dull in th' winter when it's got nowt to do. In th' flower gardens out there things will be stirrin' down below in th' dark. Th' sun's warmin' 'em. You'll see bits o' green spikes stickin' out o' th' black earth after a bit."

"What will they be?" asked Mary.

"Crocuses an' snowdrops an' daffydowndillys. Has tha' never seen them?"

"No. Everything is hot, and wet, and green after the rains in India," said Mary. "And I think things grow up in a night."

"These won't grow up in a night," said Weatherstaff. "Tha'll have to wait for 'em. They'll poke up a bit higher here, an' push out a spike more there, an' uncurl a leaf this day an' another that. You watch 'em."

"I am going to," answered Mary.

Very soon she heard the soft rustling flight of wings again and she knew at once that the robin had come again. He was very pert and lively, and hopped about so close to her feet, and put his head on one side and looked at her so slyly that she asked Ben Weatherstaff a question.

"Do you think he remembers me?" she said.

"Remembers thee!" said Weatherstaff indignantly. "He knows every cabbage stump in th' gardens, let alone th' people. He's never seen a little wench here before, an' he's bent on findin' out all about thee. Tha's no need to try to hide anything from *him*."

"Are things stirring down below in the dark in that garden where he lives?" Mary inquired.

"What garden?" grunted Weatherstaff, becoming surly again.

"The one where the old rose-trees are." She could not help asking, because she wanted so much to know. "Are all the flowers dead, or do some of them come again in the summer? Are there ever any roses?"

"Ask him," said Ben Weatherstaff, hunching his shoulders toward the robin. "He's the only one as knows. No one else has seen inside it for ten year'."

Ten years was a long time, Mary thought. She had been born ten years ago.

She walked away, slowly thinking. She had begun to like the garden just as she had begun to like the robin and Dickon and Martha's mother. She was beginning to like Martha, too. That seemed a good many people to like—when you were not used to liking. She thought of the robin as one of the people. She went to her walk outside the long, ivy-covered wall over which she could see the tree-tops; and the second time she walked up and down the most interesting and exciting thing happened to her, and it was all through Ben Weatherstaff's robin.

She heard a chirp and a twitter, and when she looked at the bare flower-bed at her left side there he was hopping about and pretending to peck things out of the earth to persuade her that he had not followed her. But she knew he had followed her and the surprise so filled her with delight that she almost trembled a little.

"You do remember me!" she cried out. "You do! You are prettier than anything else in the world!"

She chirped, and talked, and coaxed and he hopped, and flirted his tail and twittered. It was as if he were talking. His red waistcoat was like satin and he puffed his tiny breast out and was so fine and so grand and so pretty that it was really as if he were showing her how important and like a human person a robin could be. Mistress Mary forgot that she had ever been contrary in her life when he allowed her to draw closer and closer to him, and bend down and talk and try to make something like robin sounds.

Oh! to think that he should actually let her come as near to him as that! He knew nothing in the world would make her put out her hand toward him or startle him in the least tiniest way. He knew it because he was a real person—only nicer than any other person in the world. She was so happy that she scarcely dared to breathe.

The flower-bed was not quite bare. It was bare of flowers because the perennial plants had been cut down for their winter rest, but there were tall shrubs and low ones which grew together at the back of the bed, and as the robin hopped about under them she saw him hop over a small pile of freshly turned up earth. He stopped on it to look for a worm. The earth had been turned up because a dog had been trying to dig up a mole and he had scratched quite a deep hole.

Mary looked at it, not really knowing why the hole was there, and as she looked she saw something almost buried in the newly turned soil. It was something like a ring of rusty iron or brass and when the robin flew up into a tree nearby she put out her hand and picked the ring up. It was more than a ring, however; it was an old key which looked as if it had been buried a long time.

Mistress Mary stood up and looked at it with an almost frightened face as it hung from her finger.

"Perhaps it has been buried for ten years," she said in a whisper. "Perhaps it is the key to the garden!"

CHAPTER 8
THE ROBIN WHO SHOWED THE WAY

She looked at the key quite a long time. She turned it over and over, and thought about it. As I have said before, she was not a child who had been trained to ask permission or consult her elders about things. All she thought about the key was that if it was the key to the closed garden, and she could find out where the door was, she could perhaps open it and see what was inside the walls, and what had happened to the old rose-trees. It was because it had been shut up so long that she wanted to see it. It seemed as if it must be different from other places and that something strange must have happened to it during ten years. Besides that, if she liked it she could go into it every day and shut the door behind her, and she could make up some play of her own and play it quite alone, because nobody would ever know where she was, but would think the door was still locked and the key buried in the earth. The thought of that pleased her very much.

Living as it were, all by herself in a house with a hundred mysteriously closed rooms and having nothing whatever to do to amuse herself, had set her inactive brain to working and was actually awakening her imagination. There is no doubt that the fresh, strong, pure air from the moor had a great deal to do with it. Just as it had given her an appetite, and fighting with the wind had stirred her blood, so the same things had stirred her mind. In India she had always been too hot and languid and weak to care much about anything, but in this place she was beginning to care and to want to do new things. Already she felt less "contrary," though she did not know why.

She put the key in her pocket and walked up and down her

walk. No one but herself ever seemed to come there, so she could walk slowly and look at the wall, or, rather, at the ivy growing on it. The ivy was the baffling thing. Howsoever carefully she looked she could see nothing but thickly-growing, glossy, dark green leaves. She was very much disappointed. Something of her contrariness came back to her as she paced the walk and looked over it at the tree-tops inside. It seemed so silly, she said to herself, to be near it and not be able to get in. She took the key in her pocket when she went back to the house, and she made up her mind that she would always carry it with her when she went out, so that if she ever should find the hidden door she would be ready.

Mrs. Medlock had allowed Martha to sleep all night at the cottage, but she was back at her work in the morning with cheeks redder than ever and in the best of spirits.

"I got up at four o'clock," she said. "Eh! it was pretty on th' moor with th' birds gettin' up an' th' rabbits scamperin' about an' th' sun risin'. I didn't walk all th' way. A man gave me a ride in his cart an' I can tell you I did enjoy myself."

She was full of stories of the delights of her day out. Her mother had been glad to see her and they had got the baking and washing all out of the way. She had even made each of the children a dough-cake with a bit of brown sugar in it.

"I had 'em all pipin' hot when they came in from playin' on th' moor. An' th' cottage all smelt o' nice, clean hot bakin' an' there was a good fire, an' they just shouted for joy. Our Dickon he said our cottage was good enough for a king to live in."

In the evening they had all sat round the fire, and Martha and her mother had sewed patches on torn clothes and mended stockings and Martha had told them about the little girl who had come from India and who had been waited on all her life by what Martha called "blacks" until she didn't know how to put on her own stockings.

"Eh! they did like to hear about you," said Martha. "They wanted to know all about th' blacks an' about th' ship you came in. I couldn't tell 'em enough."

Mary reflected a little.

"I'll tell you a great deal more before your next day out," she said, "so that you will have more to talk about. I dare say they would like to hear about riding on elephants and camels, and about the officers going to hunt tigers."

"My word!" cried delighted Martha. "It would set 'em clean off their heads. Would tha' really do that, Miss? It would be same as a wild beast show like we heard they had in York once."

"India is quite different from Yorkshire," Mary said slowly, as she thought the matter over. "I never thought of that. Did Dickon and your mother like to hear you talk about me?"

"Why, our Dickon's eyes nearly started out o' his head, they got that round," answered Martha. "But mother, she was put out about your seemin' to be all by yourself like. She said, 'Hasn't Mr. Craven got no governess for her, nor no nurse?' and I said, 'No, he hasn't, though Mrs. Medlock says he will when he thinks of it, but she says he mayn't think of it for two or three years.'"

"I don't want a governess," said Mary sharply.

"But mother says you ought to be learnin' your book by this time an' you ought to have a woman to look after you, an' she says: 'Now, Martha, you just think how you'd feel yourself, in a big place like that, wanderin' about all alone, an' no mother. You do your best to cheer her up,' she says, an' I said I would."

Mary gave her a long, steady look.

"You do cheer me up," she said. "I like to hear you talk."

Presently Martha went out of the room and came back with something held in her hands under her apron.

"What does tha' think," she said, with a cheerful grin. "I've brought thee a present."

"A present!" exclaimed Mistress Mary. How could a cottage full of fourteen hungry people give any one a present!

"A man was drivin' across the moor peddlin'," Martha explained. "An' he stopped his cart at our door. He had pots an' pans an' odds an' ends, but mother had no money to buy anythin'. Just as he was goin' away our 'Lizabeth Ellen called out,

'Mother, he's got skippin'-ropes with red an' blue handles.' An' mother she calls out quite sudden, 'Here, stop, mister! How much are they?' An' he says 'Tuppence,' an' mother she began fumblin' in her pocket an' she says to me, 'Martha, tha's brought me thy wages like a good lass, an' I've got four places to put every penny, but I'm just goin' to take tuppence out of it to buy that child a skippin'-rope,' an' she bought one an' here it is."

She brought it out from under her apron and exhibited it quite proudly. It was a strong, slender rope with a striped red and blue handle at each end, but Mary Lennox had never seen a skipping-rope before. She gazed at it with a mystified expression.

"What is it for?" she asked curiously.

"For!" cried out Martha. "Does tha' mean that they've not got skippin'-ropes in India, for all they've got elephants and tigers and camels! No wonder most of 'em's black. This is what it's for; just watch me."

And she ran into the middle of the room and, taking a handle in each hand, began to skip, and skip, and skip, while Mary turned in her chair to stare at her, and the queer faces in the old portraits seemed to stare at her, too, and wonder what on earth this common little cottager had the impudence to be doing under their very noses. But Martha did not even see them. The interest and curiosity in Mistress Mary's face delighted her, and she went on skipping and counted as she skipped until she had reached a hundred.

"I could skip longer than that," she said when she stopped. "I've skipped as much as five hundred when I was twelve, but I wasn't as fat then as I am now, an' I was in practice."

Mary got up from her chair beginning to feel excited herself.

"It looks nice," she said. "Your mother is a kind woman. Do you think I could ever skip like that?"

"You just try it," urged Martha, handing her the skipping-rope. "You can't skip a hundred at first, but if you practise you'll mount up. That's what mother said. She says, 'Nothin' will do her more good than skippin' rope. It's th' sensiblest toy a child can have. Let her play out in th' fresh air skippin' an' it'll stretch her legs an' arms an' give her some strength in 'em.' "

It was plain that there was not a great deal of strength in Mistress Mary's arms and legs when she first began to skip. She was not very clever at it, but she liked it so much that she did not want to stop.

"Put on tha' things and run an' skip out o' doors," said Martha. "Mother said I must tell you to keep out o' doors as much as you could, even when it rains a bit, so as tha' wrap up warm."

Mary put on her coat and hat and took her skipping-rope over her arm. She opened the door to go out, and then suddenly thought of something and turned back rather slowly.

"Martha," she said, "they were your wages. It was your two-pence really. Thank you." She said it stiffly because she was not used to thanking people or noticing that they did things for her. "Thank you," she said, and held out her hand because she did not know what else to do.

Martha gave her hand a clumsy little shake, as if she was not accustomed to this sort of thing either. Then she laughed.

"Eh! tha' art a queer, old-womanish thing," she said. "If tha'd been our 'Lizabeth Ellen tha'd have give me a kiss."

Mary looked stiffer then ever.

"Do you want me to kiss you?"

Martha laughed again.

"Nay, not me," she answered. "If tha' was different, p'raps tha'd want to thysel'. But tha' isn't. Run off outside an' play with thy rope."

Mistress Mary felt a little awkward as she went out of the room. Yorkshire people seemed strange, and Martha was always rather a puzzle to her. At first she had disliked her very much, but now she did not.

The skipping-rope was a wonderful thing. She counted and skipped, and skipped and counted, until her cheeks were quite red, and she was more interested than she had ever been since she was born. The sun was shining and a little wind was blowing—not a rough wind, but one which came in delightful little gusts and brought a fresh scent of newly turned earth with it. She skipped round the fountain garden, and up one walk and down another. She skipped at last into the kitchen-garden and saw Ben Weatherstaff digging and talking to his robin, which was hopping about him. She skipped down the walk toward him and he lifted his head and looked at her with a curious expression. She had wondered if he would notice her. She really wanted him to see her skip.

"Well!" he exclaimed. "Upon my word! P'raps tha' art a young 'un, after all, an' p'raps tha's got child's blood in thy veins instead of sour buttermilk. Tha's skipped red into thy cheeks as sure as my name's Ben Weatherstaff. I wouldn't have believed tha' could do it."

"I never skipped before," Mary said. "I'm just beginning. I can only go up to twenty."

"Tha' keep on," said Ben. "Tha' shapes well enough at it for a young 'un that's lived with heathen. Just see how he's watchin' thee," jerking his head toward the robin. "He followed after thee yesterday. He'll be at it again to-day. He'll be bound to find out what th' skippin'-rope is. He's never seen one. Eh!" shaking his head at the bird, "tha' curiosity will be th' death of thee sometime if tha' doesn't look sharp."

Mary skipped round all the gardens and round the orchard, resting every few minutes. At length she went to her own special walk and made up her mind to try if she could skip the whole length of it. It was a good long skip and she began slowly, but before she had gone half-way down the path she was so hot and breathless that she was obliged to stop. She did not mind much, because she had already counted up to thirty. She stopped with a little laugh of pleasure, and there, lo and behold, was the robin swaying on a long branch of ivy. He had followed her and he greeted her with a chirp. As Mary had skipped toward him she felt something heavy in her pocket strike against her at each jump, and when she saw the robin she laughed again.

"You showed me where the key was yesterday," she said. "You ought to show me the door to-day; but I don't believe you know!"

The robin flew from his swinging spray of ivy on to the top of the wall and he opened his beak and sang a loud, lovely trill, merely to show off. Nothing in the world is quite as adorably lovely as a robin when he shows off—and they are nearly always doing it.

Mary Lennox had heard a great deal about Magic in her Ayah's stories, and she always said that what happened almost at that moment was Magic.

One of the nice little gusts of wind rushed down the walk, and it was a stronger one than the rest. It was strong enough to wave the branches of the trees, and it was more than strong enough to sway the trailing sprays of untrimmed ivy hanging from the wall. Mary had stepped close to the robin, and suddenly the gust of wind swung aside some loose ivy trails, and more suddenly still she jumped toward it and caught it in her hand. This she did because she had seen something under it—a round knob which had been covered by the leaves hanging over it. It was the knob of a door.

She put her hands under the leaves and began to pull and push them aside. Thick as the ivy hung, it nearly all was a loose and swinging curtain, though some had crept over wood and iron. Mary's heart began to thump and her hands to shake a little in her delight and excitement. The robin kept singing and twittering away and tilting his head on one side, as if he were as excited as she was. What was this under her hands which was square and made of iron and which her fingers found a hole in?

It was the lock of the door which had been closed ten years and she put her hand in her pocket, drew out the key and found it fitted the keyhole. She put the key in and turned it. It took two hands to do it, but it did turn.

And then she took a long breath and looked behind her up the long walk to see if any one was coming. No one was coming. No one ever did come, it seemed, and she took another long breath,

because she could not help it, and she held back the swinging curtain of ivy and pushed back the door which opened
slowly—slowly.

Then she slipped through it, and shut it behind her, and stood
with her back against it, looking about her and breathing quite
fast with excitement, and wonder, and delight.

She was standing *inside* the secret garden.

CHAPTER 9
THE STRANGEST HOUSE ANY ONE EVER LIVED IN

It was the sweetest, most mysterious-looking place any one could imagine. The high walls which shut it in were covered with the leafless stems of climbing roses which were so thick that they were matted together. Mary Lennox knew they were roses because she had seen a great many roses in India. All the ground was covered with grass of a wintry brown and out of it grew clumps of bushes which were surely rose-bushes if they were alive. There were numbers of standard roses which had so spread their branches that they were like little trees. There were other trees in the garden, and one of the things which made the place look strangest and loveliest was that climbing roses had run all over them and swung down long tendrils which made light sway-ing curtains, and here and there they had caught at each other or at a far-reaching branch and had crept from one tree to another and made lovely bridges of themselves. There were neither leaves nor roses on them now and Mary did not know whether they were dead or alive, but their thin gray or brown branches and sprays looked like a sort of hazy mantle spreading over every-thing, walls, and trees, and even brown grass, where they had fallen from their fastenings and run along the ground. It was this hazy tangle from tree to tree which made it all look so mysterious. Mary had thought it must be different from other gardens which had not been left all by themselves so long; and indeed it was dif-ferent from any other place she had ever seen in her life.

"How still it is!" she whispered. "How still!"

Then she waited a moment and listened at the stillness. The robin, who had flown to his tree-top, was still as all the rest. He did not even flutter his wings; he sat without stirring, and looked at Mary.

"No wonder it is still," she whispered again. "I am the first person who has spoken in here for ten years."

She moved away from the door, stepping as softly as if she were afraid of awakening some one. She was glad that there was grass under her feet and that her steps made no sounds. She walked under one of the fairy-like gray arches between the trees and looked up at the sprays and tendrils which formed them.

"I wonder if they are all quite dead," she said. "Is it all a quite dead garden? I wish it wasn't."

If she had been Ben Weatherstaff she could have told whether the wood was alive by looking at it, but she could only see that there were only gray or brown sprays and branches and none showed any signs of even a tiny leaf-bud anywhere.

But she was *inside* the wonderful garden and she could come through the door under the ivy any time and she felt as if she had found a world all her own.

The sun was shining inside the four walls and the high arch of blue sky over this particular piece of Misselthwaite seemed even more brilliant and soft than it was over the moor. The robin flew down from his tree-top and hopped about or flew after her from one bush to another. He chirped a good deal and had a very busy air, as if he were showing her things. Everything was strange and silent and she seemed to be hundreds of miles away from any one, but somehow she did not feel lonely at all. All that troubled her was her wish that she knew whether all the roses were dead, or if perhaps some of them had lived and might put out leaves and buds as the weather got warmer. She did not want it to be a quite dead garden. If it were a quite alive garden, how wonderful it would be, and what thousands of roses would grow on every side!

Her skipping-rope had hung over her arm when she came in and after she had walked about for a while she thought she would skip round the whole garden, stopping when she wanted to look at things. There seemed to have been grass paths here and there, and in one or two corners there were alcoves of evergreen with stone seats or tall moss-covered flower urns in them.

As she came near the second of these alcoves she stopped skipping. There had once been a flower-bed in it, and she thought she saw something sticking out of the black earth—some sharp little pale green points. She remembered what Ben Weatherstaff had said and she knelt down to look at them.

"Yes, they are tiny growing things and they *might* be crocuses or snowdrops or daffodils," she whispered.

She bent very close to them and sniffed the fresh scent of the damp earth. She liked it very much.

"Perhaps there are some other ones coming up in other places," she said. "I will go all over the garden and look."

She did not skip, but walked. She went slowly and kept her eyes on the ground. She looked in the old border beds and among the grass, and after she had gone round, trying to miss nothing, she had found ever so many more sharp, pale green points, and she had become quite excited again.

"It isn't a quite dead garden," she cried out softly to herself. "Even if the roses are dead, there are other things alive."

She did not know anything about gardening, but the grass seemed so thick in some of the places where the green points were pushing their way through that she thought they did not seem to have room enough to grow. She searched about until she found a rather sharp piece of wood and knelt down and dug and weeded out the weeds and grass until she made nice little clear places around them.

"Now they look as if they could breathe," she said, after she had finished with the first ones. "I am going to do ever so many more. I'll do all I can see. If I haven't time to-day I can come to-morrow."

She went from place to place, and dug and weeded, and enjoyed herself so immensely that she was led on from bed to bed and into the grass under the trees. The exercise made her so warm that she first threw her coat off, and then her hat, and without knowing it she was smiling down on to the grass and the pale green points all the time.

The robin was tremendously busy. He was very much pleased to see gardening begun on his own estate. He had often wondered at Ben Weatherstaff. Where gardening is done all sorts of delightful things to eat are turned up with the soil. Now here was this new kind of creature who was not half Ben's size and yet had had the sense to come into his garden and begin at once.

Mistress Mary worked in her garden until it was time to go to her midday dinner. In fact, she was rather late in remembering, and when she put on her coat and hat, and picked up her skipping-rope, she could not believe that she had been working two or three hours. She had been actually happy all the time; and dozens and dozens of the tiny, pale green points were to be seen in cleared places, looking twice as cheerful as they had looked before when the grass and weeds had been smothering them.

"I shall come back this afternoon," she said, looking all round at her new kingdom, and speaking to the trees and the rose-bushes as if they heard her.

Then she ran lightly across the grass, pushed open the slow old door and slipped through it under the ivy. She had such red cheeks and such bright eyes and ate such a dinner that Martha was delighted.

"Two pieces o' meat an' two helps o' rice puddin'!" she said. "Eh! mother will be pleased when I tell her what th' skippin'-rope's done for thee."

In the course of her digging with her pointed stick Mistress Mary had found herself digging up a sort of white root rather like an onion. She had put it back in its place and patted the earth carefully down on it and just now she wondered if Martha could tell her what it was.

"Martha," she said, "what are those white roots that look like onions?"

"They're bulbs," answered Martha. "Lots o' spring flowers grow from 'em. Th' very little ones are snowdrops an' crocuses an' th' big ones are narcissusis an' jonquils an' daffydowndillys. Th' biggest of all is lilies an' purple flags. Eh! they are nice. Dickon's got a whole lot of 'em planted in our bit o' garden."

"Does Dickon know all about them?" asked Mary, a new idea taking possession of her.

"Our Dickon can make a flower grow out of a brick walk. Mother says he just whispers things out o' th' ground."

"Do bulbs live a long time? Would they live years and years if no one helped them?" inquired Mary anxiously.

"They're things as helps themselves," said Martha. "That's why poor folk can afford to have 'em. If you don't trouble 'em, most of 'em'll work away underground for a lifetime an' spread out an' have little 'uns. There's a place in th' park woods here where there's snow-drops by thousands. They're the prettiest sight in Yorkshire when th' spring comes. No one knows when they was first planted."

"I wish the spring was here now," said Mary. "I want to see all the things that grow in England."

She had finished her dinner and gone to her favorite seat on the hearth-rug.

"I wish—I wish I had a little spade," she said.

"Whatever does tha' want a spade for?" asked Martha, laughing. "Art tha' goin' to take to diggin'? I must tell mother that, too."

Mary looked at the fire and pondered a little. She must be careful if she meant to keep her secret kingdom. She wasn't doing any harm, but if Mr. Craven found out about the open door he would be fearfully angry and get a new key and lock it up forever-more. She really could not bear that.

"This is such a big lonely place," she said slowly, as if she were turning matters over in her mind. "The house is lonely, and the park is lonely, and the gardens are lonely. So many places seem shut up. I never did many things in India, but there were more people to look at—natives and soldiers marching by—and some-times bands playing, and my Ayah told me stories. There is no one to talk to here except you and Ben Weatherstaff. And you have to do your work and Ben Weatherstaff won't speak to me often. I thought if I had a little spade I could dig somewhere as he does, and I might make a little garden if he would give me some seeds."

Martha's face quite lighted up.

"There now!" she exclaimed, "if that wasn't one of th' things mother said. She says, 'There's such a lot o' room in that big place, why don't they give her a bit for herself, even if she doesn't plant nothin' but parsley an' radishes? She'd dig an' rake away an' be right down happy over it.' Them was the very words she said."

"Were they?" said Mary. "How many things she knows, doesn't she?"

"Eh!" said Martha. "It's like she says: 'A woman as brings up twelve children learns something besides her A B C. Children's as good as 'rithmetic to set you findin' out things.'"

"How much would a spade cost—a little one?" Mary asked.

"Well," was Martha's reflective answer, "at Thwaite village there's a shop or so an' I saw little garden sets with a spade an' a rake an' a fork all tied together for two shillings. An' they was stout enough to work with, too."

"I've got more than that in my purse," said Mary. "Mrs. Morrison gave me five shillings and Mrs. Medlock gave me some money from Mr. Craven."

"Did he remember thee that much?" exclaimed Martha.

"Mrs. Medlock said I was to have a shilling a week to spend. She gives me one every Saturday. I didn't know what to spend it on."

"My word! that's riches," said Martha. "Tha' can buy anything in th' world tha' wants. Th' rent of our cottage is only one an' threepence an' it's like pullin' eye-teeth to get it. Now I've just thought of somethin'," putting her hands on her hips.

"What?" said Mary eagerly.

"In the shop at Thwaite they sell packages o' flower-seeds for a penny each, and our Dickon he knows which is th' prettiest ones an' how to make 'em grow. He walks over to Thwaite many a day just for th' fun of it. Does tha' know how to print letters?" suddenly.

"I know how to write," Mary answered.

Martha shook her head.

"Our Dickon can only read printin'. If tha' could print we could write a letter to him an' ask him to go an' buy th' garden tools an' th' seeds at th' same time."

"Oh! you're a good girl!" Mary cried. "You are, really! I didn't know you were so nice. I know I can print letters if I try. Let's ask Mrs. Medlock for a pen and ink and some paper."

"I've got some of my own," said Martha. "I bought 'em so I could print a bit of a letter to mother of a Sunday. I'll go and get it."

She ran out of the room, and Mary stood by the fire and twisted her thin little hands together with sheer pleasure.

"If I have a spade," she whispered, "I can make the earth nice and soft and dig up weeds. If I have seeds and can make flowers grow the garden won't be dead at all—it will come alive."

She did not go out again that afternoon because when Martha returned with her pen and ink and paper she was obliged to clear the table and carry the plates and dishes down-stairs and when she got into the kitchen Mrs. Medlock was there and told her to do something, so Mary waited for what seemed to her a long time before she came back. Then it was a serious piece of work to write to Dickon. Mary had been taught very little because her governesses had disliked her too much to stay with her. She could not spell particularly well but she found that she could print letters when she tried. This was the letter Martha dictated to her:

"*My Dear Dickon:*

This comes hoping to find you well as it leaves me at present. Miss Mary has plenty of money and will you go to Thwaite and buy her some flower seeds and a set of garden tools to make a flower-bed. Pick the prettiest ones and easy to grow because she has never done it before and lived in India which is different. Give my love to mother and every one of you. Miss Mary is going to tell me a lot more so that on my next day out you can hear about elephants and camels and gentlemen going hunting lions and tigers.

"Your loving sister,

"MARTHA PHŒBE SOWERBY."

"We'll put the money in th' envelope an' I'll get th' butcher's boy to take it in his cart. He's a great friend o' Dickon's," said Martha.

"How shall I get the things when Dickon buys them?" asked Mary.

"He'll bring 'em to you himself. He'll like to walk over this way."

"Oh!" exclaimed Mary, "then I shall see him! I never thought I should see Dickon."

"Does tha' want to see him?" asked Martha suddenly, she looked so pleased.

"Yes, I do. I never saw a boy foxes and crows loved. I want to see him very much."

Martha gave a little start, as if she suddenly remembered something.

"Now to think," she broke out, "to think o' me forgettin' that there; an' I thought I was goin' to tell you first thing this mornin'. I asked mother—and she said she'd ask Mrs. Medlock her own self."

"Do you mean—" Mary began.

"What I said Tuesday. Ask her if you might be driven over to our cottage some day and have a bit o' mother's hot oat cake, an' butter, an' a glass o' milk."

It seemed as if all the interesting things were happening in one day. To think of going over the moor in the daylight and when the sky was blue! To think of going into the cottage which held twelve children!

"Does she think Mrs. Medlock would let me go?" she asked, quite anxiously.

"Aye, she thinks she would. She knows what a tidy woman mother is and how clean she keeps the cottage."

"If I went I should see your mother as well as Dickon," said Mary, thinking it over and liking the idea very much. "She doesn't seem to be like the mothers in India."

Her work in the garden and the excitement of the afternoon ended by making her feel quiet and thoughtful. Martha stayed with her until tea-time, but they sat in comfortable quiet and talked very little. But just before Martha went down-stairs for the tea-tray, Mary asked a question.

"Martha," she said, "has the scullery-maid had the toothache again to-day?"

Martha certainly started slightly.

"What makes thee ask that?" she said.

"Because when I waited so long for you to come back I opened the door and walked down the corridor to see if you were coming. And I heard that far-off crying again, just as we heard it the other night. There isn't a wind to-day, so you see it couldn't have been the wind."

"Eh!" said Martha restlessly. "Tha' mustn't go walkin' about in corridors an' listenin'. Mr. Craven would be that there angry there's no knowin' what he'd do."

"I wasn't listening," said Mary. "I was just waiting for you— and I heard it. That's three times."

"My word! There's Mrs. Medlock's bell," said Martha, and she almost ran out of the room.

"It's the strangest house any one ever lived in," said Mary drowsily, as she dropped her head on the cushioned seat of the armchair near her. Fresh air, and digging, and skipping-rope had made her feel so comfortably tired that she fell asleep.

CHAPTER 10
DICKON

The sun shone down for nearly a week on the secret garden. The Secret Garden was what Mary called it when she was thinking of it. She liked the name, and she liked still more the feeling that when its beautiful old walls shut her in no one knew where she was. It seemed almost like being shut out of the world in some fairy place. The few books she had read and liked had been fairy-story books, and she had read of secret gardens in some of the stories. Sometimes people went to sleep in them for a hundred years, which she had thought must be rather stupid. She had no intention of going to sleep, and, in fact, she was becoming wider awake every day which passed at Misselthwaite. She was beginning to like to be out of doors; she no longer hated the wind, but enjoyed it. She could run faster, and longer, and she could skip up to a hundred. The bulbs in the secret garden must have been much astonished. Such nice clear places were made round them that they had all the breathing space they wanted, and really, if Mistress Mary had known it, they began to cheer up under the dark earth and work tremendously. The sun could get at them and warm them, and when the rain came down it could reach them at once, so they began to feel very much alive.

Mary was an odd, determined little person, and now she had something interesting to be determined about, she was very much absorbed, indeed. She worked and dug and pulled up weeds steadily, only becoming more pleased with her work every hour instead of tiring of it. It seemed to her like a fascinating sort of play. She found many more of the sprouting pale green points than she had ever hoped to find. They seemed to be starting up everywhere and each day she was sure she found tiny new ones, some so tiny that they barely peeped above the earth. There were so many that she remembered what Martha had said about the "snowdrops by the thousands," and about bulbs spreading and making new ones. These had been left to themselves for ten years and perhaps they had spread, like the snowdrops, into thousands. She wondered how long it would be before they showed that they were flowers. Sometimes she stopped digging to look at the garden and try to imagine what it would be like when it was covered with thousands of lovely things in bloom.

During that week of sunshine, she became more intimate with Ben Weatherstaff. She surprised him several times by seeming to start up beside him as if she sprang out of the earth. The truth was that she was afraid that he would pick up his tools and go away if he saw her coming, so she always walked toward him as silently as possible. But, in fact, he did not object to her as strongly as he had at first. Perhaps he was secretly rather flattered by her evident desire for his elderly company. Then, also, she was more civil than she had been. He did not know that when she first saw him she spoke to him as she would have spoken to a native, and had not known that a cross, sturdy old Yorkshire man was not accustomed to salaam to his masters, and be merely commanded by them to do things.

"Tha'rt like th' robin," he said to her one morning when he lifted his head and saw her standing by him. "I never knows when I shall see thee or which side tha'll come from."

"He's friends with me now," said Mary.

"That's like him," snapped Ben Weatherstaff. "Makin' up to th' women folk just for vanity an' flightiness. There's nothin' he wouldn't do for th' sake o' showin' off an' flirtin' his tail-feathers. He's as full o' pride as an egg's full o' meat."

He very seldom talked much and sometimes did not even answer Mary's questions except by a grunt, but this morning he said more than usual. He stood up and rested one hobnailed boot on the top of his spade while he looked her over.

"How long has tha' been here?" he jerked out.

"I think it's about a month," she answered.

"Tha's beginnin' to do Misselthwaite credit," he said. "Tha's a bit fatter than tha' was an' tha's not quite so yeller. Tha' looked like a young plucked crow when tha' first came into this garden. Thinks I to myself I never set eyes on an uglier, sourer faced young 'un."

Mary was not vain and as she had never thought much of her looks she was not greatly disturbed.

"I know I'm fatter," she said. "My stockings are getting tighter. They used to make wrinkles. There's the robin, Ben Weatherstaff."

There, indeed, was the robin, and she thought he looked nicer than ever. His red waistcoat was as glossy as satin and he flirted his wings and tail and tilted his head and hopped about with all sorts of lively graces. He seemed determined to make Ben Weatherstaff admire him. But Ben was sarcastic.

"Aye, there tha' art!" he said. "Tha' can put up with me for a bit sometimes when tha's got no one better. Tha's been reddinin' up thy waistcoat an' polishin' thy feathers this two weeks. I know what tha's up to. Tha's courtin' some bold young madam somewhere, tellin' thy lies to her about bein' th' finest cock robin on Missel Moor an' ready to fight all th' rest of 'em."

"Oh! look at him!" exclaimed Mary.

The robin was evidently in a fascinating, bold mood. He hopped closer and closer and looked at Ben Weatherstaff more and more engagingly. He flew on to the nearest currant bush and tilted his head and sang a little song right at him.

"Tha' thinks tha'll get over me by doin' that," said Ben, wrinkling his face up in such a way that Mary felt sure he was trying not to look pleased. "Tha' thinks no one can stand out against thee—that's what tha' thinks."

The robin spread his wings—Mary could scarcely believe her eyes. He flew right up to the handle of Ben Weatherstaff's spade and alighted on the top of it. Then the old man's face wrinkled itself slowly into a new expression. He stood still as if he were afraid to breathe—as if he would not have stirred for the world, lest his robin should start away. He spoke quite in a whisper.

"Well, I'm danged!" he said as softly as if he were saying something quite different. "Tha' does know how to get at a chap—tha' does! Tha's fair unearthly, tha's so knowin'."

And he stood without stirring—almost without drawing his breath—until the robin gave another flirt to his wings and flew away. Then he stood looking at the handle of the spade as if there might be Magic in it, and then he began to dig again and said nothing for several minutes.

But because he kept breaking into a slow grin now and then, Mary was not afraid to talk to him.

"Have you a garden of your own?" she asked.

"No. I'm bachelder an' lodge with Martin at th' gate."

"If you had one," said Mary, "what would you plant?"

"Cabbages an' 'taters an' onions."

"But if you wanted to make a flower garden," persisted Mary, "what would you plant?"

"Bulbs an' sweet-smellin' things—but mostly roses."

Mary's face lighted up.

"Do you like roses?" she said.

Ben Weatherstaff rooted up a weed and threw it aside before he answered.

"Well, yes, I do. I was learned that by a young lady I was gardener to. She had a lot in a place she was fond of, an' she loved 'em like they was children—or robins. I've seen her bend over an' kiss 'em." He dragged out another weed and scowled at it. "That were as much as ten year' ago."

"Where is she now?" asked Mary, much interested.

"Heaven," he answered, and drove his spade deep into the soil, "'cording to what parson says."

"What happened to the roses?" Mary asked again, more interested than ever.

"They was left to themselves."

Mary was becoming quite excited.

"Did they quite die? Do roses quite die when they are left to themselves?" she ventured.

"Well, I'd got to like 'em—an' I liked her—an' she liked 'em," Ben Weatherstaff admitted reluctantly. "Once or twice a year I'd go an' work at 'em a bit—prune 'em an' dig about th' roots. They run wild, but they was in rich soil, so some of 'em lived."

"When they have no leaves and look gray and brown and dry, how can you tell whether they are dead or alive?" inquired Mary.

"Wait till th' spring gets at 'em—wait till th' sun shines on th' rain an' th' rain falls on th' sunshine an' then tha'll find out."

"How—how?" cried Mary, forgetting to be careful.

"Look along th' twigs an' branches an' if tha' sees a bit of a brown lump swelling here an' there, watch it after th' warm rain an' see what happens." He stopped suddenly and looked curiously at her eager face. "Why does tha' care so much about roses an' such, all of a sudden?" he demanded.

Mistress Mary felt her face grow red. She was almost afraid to answer.

"I—I want to play that—that I have a garden of my own," she stammered. "I—there is nothing for me to do. I have nothing—and no one."

"Well," said Ben Weatherstaff slowly, as he watched her, "that's true. Tha' hasn't."

He said it in such an odd way that Mary wondered if he was actually a little sorry for her. She had never felt sorry for herself; she had only felt tired and cross, because she disliked people and things so much. But now the world seemed to be changing and getting nicer. If no one found out about the secret garden, she should enjoy herself always.

She stayed with him for ten or fifteen minutes longer and asked him as many questions as she dared. He answered every one of them in his queer grunting way and he did not seem really cross and did not pick up his spade and leave her. He said something about roses just as she was going away and it reminded her of the ones he had said he had been fond of.

"Do you go and see those other roses now?" she asked.

"Not been this year. My rheumatics has made me too stiff in th' joints."

He said it in his grumbling voice, and then quite suddenly he seemed to get angry with her, though she did not see why he should.

"Now look here!" he said sharply. "Don't tha' ask so many questions. Tha'rt th' worst wench for askin' questions I've ever come across. Get thee gone an' play thee. I've done talkin' for to-day."

And he said it so crossly that she knew there was not the least use in staying another minute. She went skipping slowly down the outside walk, thinking him over and saying to herself that, queer as it was, here was another person whom she liked in spite of his crossness. She liked old Ben Weatherstaff. Yes, she did like him. She always wanted to try to make him talk to her. Also she began to believe that he knew everything in the world about flowers.

There was a laurel-hedged walk which curved round the secret garden and ended at a gate which opened into a wood, in the park. She thought she would skip round this walk and look into the wood and see if there were any rabbits hopping about. She enjoyed the skipping very much and when she reached the little gate she opened it and went through because she heard a low, peculiar whistling sound and wanted to find out what it was.

It was a very strange thing indeed. She quite caught her breath as she stopped to look at it. A boy was sitting under a tree, with his back against it, playing on a rough wooden pipe. He was a funny looking boy about twelve. He looked very clean and his nose turned up and his cheeks were as red as poppies and never had Mistress Mary seen such round and such blue eyes in any boy's face. And on the trunk of the tree he leaned against, a brown squirrel was clinging and watching him, and from behind a bush nearby a cock pheasant was delicately stretching his neck to peep out, and quite near him were two rabbits sitting up and sniffing with tremulous noses—and actually it appeared as if they were all drawing near to watch him and listen to the strange low little call his pipe seemed to make.

When he saw Mary he held up his hand and spoke to her in a voice almost as low as and rather like his piping.

"Don't tha' move," he said. "It'd flight 'em."

Mary remained motionless. He stopped playing his pipe and began to rise from the ground. He moved so slowly that it scarcely seemed as though he were moving at all, but at last he stood on his feet and then the squirrel scampered back up into the branches of his tree, the pheasant withdrew his head and the rabbits dropped on all fours and began to hop away, though not at all as if they were frightened.

"I'm Dickon," the boy said. "I know tha'rt Miss Mary."

Then Mary realized that somehow she had known at first that he was Dickon. Who else could have been charming rabbits and pheasants as the natives charm snakes in India? He had a wide, red, curving mouth and his smile spread all over his face.

"I got up slow," he explained, "because if tha' makes a quick move it startles 'em. A body 'as to move gentle an' speak low when wild things is about."

He did not speak to her as if they had never seen each other before but as if he knew her quite well. Mary knew nothing about boys and she spoke to him a little stiffly because she felt rather shy.

"Did you get Martha's letter?" she asked.

He nodded his curly, rust-colored head.

"That's why I come."

He stooped to pick up something which had been lying on the ground beside him when he piped.

"I've got th' garden tools. There's a little spade an' rake an' a fork an' hoe. Eh! they are good 'uns. There's a trowel, too. An' th' woman in th' shop threw in a packet o' white poppy an' one o' blue larkspur when I bought th' other seeds."

"Will you show the seeds to me?" Mary said.

She wished she could talk as he did. His speech was so quick and easy. It sounded as if he liked her and was not the least afraid she would not like him, though he was only a common moor boy, in patched clothes and with a funny face and a rough, rusty-red head. As she came closer to him she noticed that there was a fresh scent of heather and grass and leaves about him, almost as if he were made of them. She liked it very much and when she looked into his funny face with the red cheeks and round blue eyes she forgot that she had felt shy.

"Let us sit down on this log and look at them," she said.

They sat down and he took a clumsy little brown paper package out of his coat pocket. He untied the string and inside there were ever so many neater and smaller packages with a picture of a flower on each one.

"There's a lot o' mignonette an' poppies," he said. "Mignonette's th' sweetest smellin' thing as grows, an' it'll grow wherever you cast it, same as poppies will. Them as'll come up an' bloom if you just whistle to 'em, them's th' nicest of all."

He stopped and turned his head quickly, his poppy-cheeked face lighting up.

"Where's that robin as is callin' us?" he said.

The chirp came from a thick holly bush, bright with scarlet berries, and Mary thought she knew whose it was.

"Is it really calling us?" she asked.

"Aye," said Dickon, as if it was the most natural thing in the world, "he's callin' some one he's friends with. That's same as sayin' 'Here I am. Look at me. I wants a bit of a chat.' There he is in the bush. Whose is he?"

"He's Ben Weatherstaff's, but I think he knows me a little," answered Mary.

"Aye, he knows thee," said Dickon in his low voice again. "An' he likes thee. He's took thee on. He'll tell me all about thee in a minute."

He moved quite close to the bush with the slow movement Mary had noticed before, and then he made a sound almost like the robin's own twitter. The robin listened a few seconds, intently, and then answered quite as if he were replying to a question.

"Aye, he's a friend o' yours," chuckled Dickon.

"Do you think he is?" cried Mary eagerly. She did so want to know. "Do you think he really likes me?"

"He wouldn't come near thee if he didn't," answered Dickon. "Birds is rare choosers an' a robin can flout a body worse than a man. See, he's making up to thee now. 'Cannot tha' see a chap?' he's sayin'."

And it really seemed as if it must be true. He so sidled and twittered and tilted as he hopped on his bush.

"Do you understand everything birds say?" said Mary.

Dickon's grin spread until he seemed all wide, red, curving mouth, and he rubbed his rough head.

"I think I do, and they think I do," he said. "I've lived on th' moor with 'em so long. I've watched 'em break shell an' come out an' fledge an' learn to fly an' begin to sing, till I think I'm one of 'em. Sometimes I think 'praps I'm a bird, or a fox, or a rabbit, or a squirrel, or even a beetle, an' I don't know it."

He laughed and came back to the log and began to talk about the flower seeds again. He told her what they looked like when they were flowers; he told her how to plant them, and watch them, and feed and water them.

"See here," he said suddenly, turning round to look at her. "I'll plant them for thee myself. Where is tha' garden?"

Mary's thin hands clutched each other as they lay on her lap. She did not know what to say, so for a whole minute she said nothing. She had never thought of this. She felt miserable. And she felt as if she went red and then pale.

"Tha's got a bit o' garden, hasn't tha'?" Dickon said.

It was true that she had turned red and then pale. Dickon saw her do it, and as she still said nothing, he began to be puzzled.

"Wouldn't they give thee a bit?" he asked. "Hasn't tha' got any yet?"

She held her hands even tighter and turned her eyes toward him.

"I don't know anything about boys," she said slowly. "Could

you keep a secret, if I told you one? It's a great secret. I don't know what I should do if any one found it out. I believe I should die!" She said the last sentence quite fiercely.

Dickon looked more puzzled than ever and even rubbed his hand over his rough head again, but answered quite good-humoredly.

"I'm keepin' secrets all th' time," he said. "If I couldn't keep secrets from th' other lads, secrets about foxes' cubs, an' birds' nests, an' wild things' holes, there'd be naught safe on th' moor. Aye, I can keep secrets."

Mistress Mary did not mean to put out her hand and clutch his sleeve but she did it.

"I've stolen a garden," she said very fast. "It isn't mine. It isn't anybody's. Nobody wants it, nobody cares for it, nobody ever goes into it. Perhaps everything is dead in it already; I don't know."

She began to feel hot and as contrary as she had ever felt in her life.

"I don't care, I don't care! Nobody has any right to take it from me when I care about it and they don't. They're letting it die, all shut in by itself," she ended passionately, and she threw her arms over her face and burst out crying—poor little Mistress Mary.

Dickon's curious blue eyes grew rounder and rounder.

"Eh-h-h!" he said, drawing his exclamation out slowly, and the way he did it meant both wonder and sympathy.

"I've nothing to do," said Mary. "Nothing belongs to me. I found it myself and I got into it myself. I was only just like the robin, and they wouldn't take it from the robin."

"Where is it?" asked Dickon in a dropped voice.

Mistress Mary got up from the log at once. She knew she felt contrary again, and obstinate, and she did not care at all. She was imperious and Indian, and at the same time hot and sorrowful.

"Come with me and I'll show you," she said.

She led him round the laurel path and to the walk where the ivy grew so thickly. Dickon followed her with a queer, almost pitying, look on his face. He felt as if he were being led to look at some strange bird's nest and must move softly. When she stepped to the wall and lifted the hanging ivy he started. There was a door and Mary pushed it slowly open and they passed in together, and then Mary stood and waved her hand round defiantly.

"It's this," she said. "It's a secret garden, and I'm the only one in the world who wants it to be alive."

Dickon looked round and round about it, and round and round again.

"Eh!" he almost whispered, "it is a queer, pretty place! It's like as if a body was in a dream."

CHAPTER 11
THE NEST OF THE MISSEL THRUSH

For two or three minutes he stood looking round him, while Mary watched him, and then he began to walk about softly, even more lightly than Mary had walked the first time she had found herself inside the four walls. His eyes seemed to be taking in everything—the gray trees with the gray creepers climbing over them and hanging from their branches, the tangle on the walls and among the grass, the evergreen alcoves with the stone seats and tall flower urns standing in them.

"I never thought I'd see this place," he said at last, in a whisper.

"Did you know about it?" asked Mary.

She had spoken aloud and he made a sign to her.

"We must talk low," he said, "or some one'll hear us an' wonder what's to do in here."

"Oh! I forgot!" said Mary, feeling frightened and putting her hand quickly against her mouth. "Did you know about the garden?" she asked again when she had recovered herself.

Dickon nodded.

"Martha told me there was one as no one ever went inside," he answered. "Us used to wonder what it was like."

He stopped and looked round at the lovely gray tangle about him, and his round eyes looked queerly happy.

"Eh! the nests as'll be here come springtime," he said. "It'd be th' safest nestin' place in England. No one never comin' near an' tangles o' trees an' roses to build in. I wonder all th' birds on th' moor don't build here."

Mistress Mary put her hand on his arm again without knowing it.

"Will there be roses?" she whispered. "Can you tell? I thought perhaps they were all dead."

"Eh! No! Not them—not all of 'em!" he answered. "Look here!"

He stepped over to the nearest tree—an old, old one with gray lichen all over its bark, but upholding a curtain of tangled sprays and branches. He took a thick knife out of his pocket and opened one of its blades.

"There's lots o' dead wood as ought to be cut out," he said. "An' there's a lot o' old wood, but it made some new last year. This here's a new bit," and he touched a shoot which looked brownish green instead of hard, dry gray.

Mary touched it herself in an eager, reverent way.

"That one?" she said. "Is that one quite alive—quite?"

Dickon curved his wide smiling mouth.

"It's as wick as you or me," he said; and Mary remembered that Martha had told her that "wick" meant "alive" or "lively."

"I'm glad it's wick!" she cried out in her whisper. "I want them all to be wick. Let us go round the garden and count how many wick ones there are."

She quite panted with eagerness, and Dickon was as eager as she was. They went from tree to tree and from bush to bush. Dickon carried his knife in his hand and showed her things which she thought wonderful.

"They've run wild," he said, "but th' strongest ones has fair thrived on it. The delicatest ones has died out, but th' others has growed an' growed, an' spread an' spread, till they's a wonder. See here!" and he pulled down a thick gray, dry-looking branch. "A body might think this was dead wood, but I don't believe it is—down to th' root. I'll cut it low down an' see."

He knelt and with his knife cut the lifeless-looking branch through, not far above the earth.

"There!" he said exultantly. "I told thee so. There's green in that wood yet. Look at it."

Mary was down on her knees before he spoke, gazing with all her might.

"When it looks a bit greenish an' juicy like that, it's wick," he explained. "When th' inside is dry an' breaks easy, like this here piece I've cut off, it's done for. There's a big root here as all this live wood sprung out of, an' if th' old wood's cut off an' it's dug round, an' took care of there'll be—" he stopped and lifted his face to look up at the climbing and hanging sprays above him—"there'll be a fountain o' roses here this summer."

They went from bush to bush and from tree to tree. He was very strong and clever with his knife and knew how to cut the dry and dead wood away, and could tell when an unpromising bough or twig had still green life in it. In the course of half an hour Mary thought she could tell too, and when he cut through a lifeless-looking branch she would cry out joyfully under her breath when she caught sight of the least shade of moist green. The spade, and hoe, and fork were very useful. He showed her how to use the fork while he dug about roots with the spade and stirred the earth and let the air in.

They were working industriously round one of the biggest standard roses when he caught sight of something which made him utter an exclamation of surprise.

"Why!" he cried, pointing to the grass a few feet away. "Who did that there?"

It was one of Mary's own little clearings round the pale green points.

"I did it," said Mary.

"Why, I thought tha' didn't know nothin' about gardenin'," he exclaimed.

"I don't," she answered, "but they were so little, and the grass was so thick and strong, and they looked as if they had no room to breathe. So I made a place for them. I don't even know what they are."

Dickon went and knelt down by them, smiling his wide smile.

"Tha' was right," he said. "A gardener couldn't have told thee better. They'll grow now like Jack's bean-stalk. They're crocuses an' snowdrops, an' these here is narcissuses," turning to another patch, "an' here's daffydowndillys. Eh! they will be a sight."

He ran from one clearing to another.

"Tha' has done a lot o' work for such a little wench," he said, looking her over.

"I'm growing fatter," said Mary, "and I'm growing stronger. I used always to be tired. When I dig I'm not tired at all. I like to smell the earth when it's turned up."

"It's rare good for thee," he said, nodding his head wisely. "There's naught as nice as th' smell o' good clean earth, except th' smell o' fresh growin' things when th' rain falls on 'em. I get out on th' moor many a day when it's rainin' an' I lie under a bush an' listen to th' soft swish o' drops on th' heather an' I just sniff an' sniff. My nose end fair quivers like a rabbit's, mother says."

"Do you never catch cold?" inquired Mary, gazing at him wonderingly. She had never seen such a funny boy, or such a nice one.

"Not me," he said, grinning. "I never ketched cold since I was born. I wasn't brought up nesh enough. I've chased about th' moor in all weathers same as th' rabbits does. Mother says I've sniffed up too much fresh air for twelve year' to ever get to sniffin' with cold. I'm as tough as a white-thorn knobstick."

He was working all the time he was talking and Mary was following him and helping him with her fork or the trowel.

"There's a lot of work to do here!" he said once, looking about quite exultantly.

"Will you come again and help me to do it?" Mary begged. "I'm sure I can help, too. I can dig and pull up weeds, and do whatever you tell me. Oh! do come, Dickon!"

"I'll come every day if tha' wants me, rain or shine," he answered stoutly. "It's the best fun I ever had in my life—shut in here an' wakenin' up a garden."

"If you will come," said Mary, "if you will help me to make it alive I'll—I don't know what I'll do," she ended helplessly. What could you do for a boy like that?

"I'll tell thee what tha'll do," said Dickon, with his happy grin.

"Tha'll get fat an' tha'll get as hungry as a young fox an' tha'll learn how to talk to th' robin same as I do. Eh! we'll have a lot o' fun."

He began to walk about, looking up in the trees and at the walls and bushes with a thoughtful expression.

"I wouldn't want to make it look like a gardener's garden, all clipped an' spick an' span, would you?" he said. "It's nicer like this with things runnin' wild, an' swingin' an' catchin' hold of each other."

"Don't let us make it tidy," said Mary anxiously. "It wouldn't seem like a secret garden if it was tidy."

Dickon stood rubbing his rusty-red head with a rather puzzled look.

"It's a secret garden sure enough," he said, "but seems like some one besides th' robin must have been in it since it was shut up ten year' ago."

"But the door was locked and the key was buried," said Mary. "No one could get in."

"That's true," he answered. "It's a queer place. Seems to me as if there'd been a bit o' prunin' done here an' there, later than ten year' ago."

"But how could it have been done?" said Mary.

He was examining a branch of a standard rose and he shook his head.

"Aye! how could it!" he murmured. "With the door locked an' th' key buried."

Mistress Mary always felt that however many years she lived she should never forget that first morning when her garden began to grow. Of course, it did seem to begin to grow for her that morning. When Dickon began to clear places to plant seeds, she remembered what Basil had sung at her when he wanted to tease her.

"Are there any flowers that look like bells?" she inquired.

"Lilies o' th' valley does," he answered, digging away with the trowel, "an' there's Canterbury bells, an' campanulas."

"Let us plant some," said Mary.

"There's lilies o' th' valley here already; I saw 'em. They'll have growed too close an' we'll have to separate 'em, but there's plenty. Th' other ones takes two years to bloom from seed, but I can bring you some bits o' plants from our cottage garden. Why does tha' want 'em?"

Then Mary told him about Basil and his brothers and sisters in India and of how she had hated them and of their calling her "Mistress Mary Quite Contrary."

"They used to dance round and sing at me. They sang—

> 'Mistress Mary, quite contrary,
>   How does your garden grow?
> With silver bells, and cockle shells,
>   And marigolds all in a row.'

I just remembered it and it made me wonder if there were really flowers like silver bells."

She frowned a little and gave her trowel a rather spiteful dig into the earth.

"I wasn't as contrary as they were."

But Dickon laughed.

"Eh!" he said, and as he crumbled the rich black soil she saw he was sniffing up the scent of it, "there doesn't seem to be no need for no one to be contrary when there's flowers an' such like, an' such lots o' friendly wild things runnin' about makin' homes for themselves, or buildin' nests an' singin' an' whistlin', does there?"

Mary, kneeling by him holding the seeds, looked at him and stopped frowning.

"Dickon," she said. "You are as nice as Martha said you were. I like you, and you make the fifth person. I never thought I should like five people."

Dickon sat up on his heels as Martha did when she was polishing the grate. He did look funny and delightful, Mary thought, with his round blue eyes and red cheeks and happy looking turned-up nose.

"Only five folk as tha' likes?" he said. "Who is th' other four?"

"Your mother and Martha," Mary checked them off on her fingers, "and the robin and Ben Weatherstaff."

Dickon laughed so that he was obliged to stifle the sound by putting his arm over his mouth.

"I know tha' thinks I'm a queer lad," he said, "but I think tha' art th' queerest little lass I ever saw."

Then Mary did a strange thing. She leaned forward and asked him a question she had never dreamed of asking any one before. And she tried to ask it in Yorkshire because that was his language, and in India a native was always pleased if you knew his speech.

"Does tha' like me?" she said.

"Eh!" he answered heartily, "that I does. I likes thee wonderful, an' so does th' robin, I do believe!"

"That's two, then," said Mary. "That's two for me."

And then they began to work harder than ever and more joyfully. Mary was startled and sorry when she heard the big clock in the courtyard strike the hour of her midday dinner.

"I shall have to go," she said mournfully. "And you will have to go too, won't you?"

Dickon grinned.

"My dinner's easy to carry about with me," he said. "Mother always lets me put a bit o' somethin' in my pocket."

He picked up his coat from the grass and brought out of a pocket a lumpy little bundle tied up in a quite clean, coarse, blue and white handkerchief. It held two thick pieces of bread with a slice of something laid between them.

"It's oftenest naught but bread," he said, "but I've got a fine slice o' fat bacon with it to-day."

Mary thought it looked a queer dinner, but he seemed ready to enjoy it.

"Run on an' get thy victuals," he said. "I'll be done with mine first. I'll get some more work done before I start back home."

He sat down with his back against a tree.

"I'll call th' robin up," he said, "and give him th' rind o' th' bacon to peck at. They likes a bit o' fat wonderful."

Mary could scarcely bear to leave him. Suddenly it seemed as if he might be a sort of wood fairy who might be gone when she came into the garden again. He seemed too good to be true. She went slowly half-way to the door in the wall and then she stopped and went back.

"Whatever happens, you—you never would tell?" she said.

His poppy-colored cheeks were distended with his first big bite of bread and bacon, but he managed to smile encouragingly.

"If tha' was a missel thrush an' showed me where thy nest was, does tha' think I'd tell any one? Not me," he said. "Tha' art as safe as a missel thrush."

And she was quite sure she was.

CHAPTER 12
"MIGHT I HAVE A BIT OF EARTH?"

Mary ran so fast that she was rather out of breath when she reached her room. Her hair was ruffled on her forehead and her cheeks were bright pink. Her dinner was waiting on the table, and Martha was waiting near it.

"Tha's a bit late," she said. "Where has tha' been?"

"I've seen Dickon!" said Mary. "I've seen Dickon!"

"I knew he'd come," said Martha exultantly. "How does tha' like him?"

"I think—I think he's beautiful!" said Mary in a determined voice.

Martha looked rather taken aback but she looked pleased, too.

"Well," she said, "he's th' best lad as ever was born, but us never thought he was handsome. His nose turns up too much."

"I like it to turn up," said Mary.

"An' his eyes is so round," said Martha, a trifle doubtful. "Though they're a nice color."

"I like them round," said Mary. "And they are exactly the color of the sky over the moor."

Martha beamed with satisfaction.

"Mother says he made 'em that color with always lookin' up at th' birds an' th' clouds. But he has got a big mouth, hasn't he, now?"

"I love his big mouth," said Mary obstinately. "I wish mine were just like it."

Martha chuckled delightedly.

"It'd look rare an' funny in thy bit of a face," she said. "But I knowed it would be that way when tha' saw him. How did tha' like th' seeds an' th' garden tools?"

"How did you know he brought them?" asked Mary.

"Eh! I never thought of him not bringin' 'em. He'd be sure to bring 'em if they was in Yorkshire. He's such a trusty lad."

Mary was afraid that she might begin to ask difficult questions, but she did not. She was very much interested in the seeds and gardening tools, and there was only one moment when Mary was frightened. This was when she began to ask where the flowers were to be planted.

"Who did tha' ask about it?" she inquired.

"I haven't asked anybody yet," said Mary, hesitating.

"Well, I wouldn't ask th' head gardener. He's too grand, Mr. Roach is."

"I've never seen him," said Mary. "I've only seen under-gardeners and Ben Weatherstaff."

"If I was you, I'd ask Ben Weatherstaff," advised Martha. "He's not half as bad as he looks, for all he's so crabbed. Mr. Craven lets him do what he likes because he was here when Mrs. Craven was alive, an' he used to make her laugh. She liked him. Perhaps he'd find you a corner somewhere out o' the way."

"If it was out of the way and no one wanted it, no one *could* mind my having it, could they?" Mary said anxiously.

"There wouldn't be no reason," answered Martha. "You wouldn't do no harm."

Mary ate her dinner as quickly as she could and when she rose from the table she was going to run to her room to put on her hat again, but Martha stopped her.

"I've got somethin' to tell you," she said. "I thought I'd let you eat your dinner first. Mr. Craven came back this mornin' and I think he wants to see you."

Mary turned quite pale.

"Oh!" she said. "Why! Why! He didn't want to see me when I came. I heard Pitcher say he didn't."

"Well," explained Martha, "Mrs. Medlock says it's because o' mother. She was walkin' to Thwaite village an' she met him. She'd never spoke to him before, but Mrs. Craven had been to our cottage two or three times. He'd forgot, but mother hadn't an' she made bold to stop him. I don't know what she said to him about you but she said somethin' as put him in th' mind to see you before he goes away again, to-morrow."

"Oh!" cried Mary, "is he going away to-morrow? I am so glad!"

"He's goin' for a long time. He mayn't come back till autumn or winter. He's goin' to travel in foreign places. He's always doin' it."

"Oh! I'm so glad—so glad!" said Mary thankfully.

If he did not come back until winter, or even autumn, there would be time to watch the secret garden come alive. Even if he found out then and took it away from her she would have had that much at least.

"When do you think he will want to see—"

She did not finish the sentence, because the door opened, and Mrs. Medlock walked in. She had on her best black dress and cap, and her collar was fastened with a large brooch with a picture of a man's face on it. It was a colored photograph of Mr. Medlock who had died years ago, and she always wore it when she was dressed up. She looked nervous and excited.

"Your hair's rough," she said quickly. "Go and brush it. Martha, help her slip on her best dress. Mr. Craven sent me to bring her to him in his study."

All the pink left Mary's cheeks. Her heart began to thump and she felt herself changing into a stiff, plain, silent child again. She did not even answer Mrs. Medlock, but turned and walked into her bedroom, followed by Martha. She said nothing while her dress was changed, and her hair brushed, and after she was quite tidy she followed Mrs. Medlock down the corridors, in silence. What was there for her to say? She was obliged to go and see Mr. Craven and he would not like her, and she would not like him. She knew what he would think of her.

She was taken to a part of the house she had not been into before. At last Mrs. Medlock knocked at a door, and when some one said, "Come in," they entered the room together. A man was sitting in an armchair before the fire, and Mrs. Medlock spoke to him.

"This is Miss Mary, sir," she said.

"You can go and leave her here. I will ring for you when I want you to take her away," said Mr. Craven.

When she went out and closed the door, Mary could only stand waiting, a plain little thing, twisting her thin hands together. She could see that the man in the chair was not so much a hunchback as a man with high, rather crooked shoulders, and he had black hair streaked with white. He turned his head over his high shoulders and spoke to her.

"Come here!" he said.

Mary went to him.

He was not ugly. His face would have been handsome if it had not been so miserable. He looked as if the sight of her worried and fretted him and as if he did not know what in the world to do with her.

"Are you well?" he asked.

"Yes," answered Mary.

"Do they take good care of you?"

"Yes."

He rubbed his forehead fretfully as he looked her over.

"You are very thin," he said.

"I am getting fatter," Mary answered in what she knew was her stiffest way.

What an unhappy face he had! His black eyes seemed as if they scarcely saw her, as if they were seeing something else, and he could hardly keep his thoughts upon her.

"I forgot you," he said. "How could I remember you? I intended to send you a governess or a nurse, or some one of that sort, but I forgot."

"Please," began Mary. "Please—" and then the lump in her throat choked her.

"What do you want to say?" he inquired.

"I am—I am too big for a nurse," said Mary. "And please—please don't make me have a governess yet."

He rubbed his forehead again and stared at her.

"That was what the Sowerby woman said," he muttered absent-mindedly.

Then Mary gathered a scrap of courage.

"Is she—is she Martha's mother?" she stammered.

"Yes, I think so," he replied.

"She knows about children," said Mary. "She has twelve. She knows."

He seemed to rouse himself.

"What do you want to do?"

"I want to play out of doors," Mary answered, hoping that her voice did not tremble. "I never liked it in India. It makes me hungry here, and I am getting fatter."

He was watching her.

"Mrs. Sowerby said it would do you good. Perhaps it will," he said. "She thought you had better get stronger before you had a governess."

"It makes me feel strong when I play and the wind comes over the moor," argued Mary.

"Where do you play?" he asked next.

"Everywhere," gasped Mary. "Martha's mother sent me a skipping-rope. I skip and run—and I look about to see if things are beginning to stick up out of the earth. I don't do any harm."

"Don't look so frightened," he said in a worried voice. "You could not do any harm, a child like you! You may do what you like."

Mary put her hand up to her throat because she was afraid he might see the excited lump which she felt jump into it. She came a step nearer to him.

"May I?" she said tremulously.

Her anxious little face seemed to worry him more than ever.

"Don't look so frightened," he exclaimed. "Of course you may. I am your guardian, though I am a poor one for any child. I cannot give you time or attention. I am too ill, and wretched and distracted; but I wish you to be happy and comfortable. I don't know anything about children, but Mrs. Medlock is to see that you have all you need. I sent for you to-day because Mrs. Sowerby said I ought to see you. Her daughter had talked about you. She thought you needed fresh air and freedom and running about."

"She knows all about children," Mary said again in spite of herself.

"She ought to," said Mr. Craven. "I thought her rather bold to stop me on the moor, but she said—Mrs. Craven had been kind to her." It seemed hard for him to speak his dead wife's name. "She is a respectable woman. Now I have seen you I think she said sensible things. Play out of doors as much as you like. It's a big place and you may go where you like and amuse yourself as you like. Is there anything you want?" as if a sudden thought had struck him. "Do you want toys, books, dolls?"

"Might I," quavered Mary, "might I have a bit of earth?"

In her eagerness she did not realize how queer the words would sound and that they were not the ones she had meant to say. Mr. Craven looked quite startled.

"Earth!" he repeated. "What do you mean?"

"To plant seeds in—to make things grow—to see them come alive," Mary faltered.

He gazed at her a moment and then passed his hand quickly over his eyes.

"Do you—care about gardens so much," he said slowly.

"I didn't know about them in India," said Mary. "I was always ill and tired and it was too hot. I sometimes made little beds in the sand and stuck flowers in them. But here it is different."

Mr. Craven got up and began to walk slowly across the room.

"A bit of earth," he said to himself, and Mary thought that somehow she must have reminded him of something. When he stopped and spoke to her his dark eyes looked almost soft and kind.

"You can have as much earth as you want," he said. "You remind me of some one else who loved the earth and things that grow. When you see a bit of earth you want," with something like a smile, "take it, child, and make it come alive."

"May I take it from anywhere—if it's not wanted?"

"Anywhere," he answered. "There! You must go now, I am tired." He touched the bell to call Mrs. Medlock. "Good-by. I shall be away all summer."

Mrs. Medlock came so quickly that Mary thought she must have been waiting in the corridor.

"Mrs. Medlock," Mr. Craven said to her, "now I have seen the child I understand what Mrs. Sowerby meant. She must be less delicate before she begins lessons. Give her simple, healthy food. Let her run wild in the garden. Don't look after her too much. She needs liberty and fresh air and romping about. Mrs. Sowerby is to come and see her now and then and she may sometimes go to the cottage."

Mrs. Medlock looked pleased. She was relieved to hear that she need not "look after" Mary too much. She had felt her a tiresome charge and had indeed seen as little of her as she dared. In addition to this she was fond of Martha's mother.

"Thank you, sir," she said. "Susan Sowerby and me went to school together and she's as sensible and good-hearted a woman as you'd find in a day's walk. I never had any children myself and she's had twelve, and there never was healthier or better ones. Miss Mary can get no harm from them. I'd always take Susan Sowerby's advice about children myself. She's what you might call healthy-minded—if you understand me."

"I understand," Mr. Craven answered. "Take Miss Mary away now and send Pitcher to me."

When Mrs. Medlock left her at the end of her own corridor Mary flew back to her room. She found Martha waiting there. Martha had, in fact, hurried back after she had removed the dinner service.

"I can have my garden!" cried Mary. "I may have it where I like! I am not going to have a governess for a long time! Your mother is coming to see me and I may go to your cottage! He says a little girl like me could not do any harm and I may do what I like—anywhere!"

"Eh!" said Martha delightedly, "that was nice of him wasn't it?"

"Martha," said Mary solemnly, "he is really a nice man, only his face is so miserable and his forehead is all drawn together."

She ran as quickly as she could to the garden. She had been away so much longer than she had thought she should and she knew Dickon would have to set out early on his five-mile walk. When she slipped through the door under the ivy, she saw he was not working where she had left him. The gardening tools were laid together under a tree. She ran to them, looking all round the place, but there was no Dickon to be seen. He had gone away and the secret garden was empty—except for the robin who had just flown across the wall and sat on a standard rose-bush watching her.

"He's gone," she said wofully. "Oh! was he—was he—was he only a wood fairy?"

Something white fastened to the standard rose-bush caught her eye. It was a piece of paper—in fact, it was a piece of the letter she had printed for Martha to send to Dickon. It was fastened on the bush with a long thorn, and in a minute she knew Dickon had left it there. There were some roughly printed letters on it and a sort of picture. At first she could not tell what it was. Then she saw it was meant for a nest with a bird sitting on it. Underneath were the printed letters and they said:

"I will cum bak."

CHAPTER 13
"I AM COLIN"

Mary took the picture back to the house when she went to her supper and she showed it to Martha.

"Eh!" said Martha with great pride. "I never knew our Dickon was as clever as that. That there's a picture of a missel thrush on her nest, as large as life an' twice as natural."

Then Mary knew Dickon had meant the picture to be a message. He had meant that she might be sure he would keep her secret. Her garden was her nest and she was like a missel thrush. Oh, how she did like that queer, common boy!

She hoped he would come back the very next day and she fell asleep looking forward to the morning.

But you never know what the weather will do in Yorkshire, particularly in the springtime. She was awakened in the night by the sound of rain beating with heavy drops against her window. It was pouring down in torrents and the wind was "wuthering" round the corners and in the chimneys of the huge old house. Mary sat up in bed and felt miserable and angry.

"The rain is as contrary as I ever was," she said. "It came because it knew I did not want it."

She threw herself back on her pillow and buried her face. She did not cry, but she lay and hated the sound of the heavily beating rain, she hated the wind and its "wuthering." She could not go to sleep again. The mournful sound kept her awake because she felt mournful herself. If she had felt happy it would probably have lulled her to sleep. How it "wuthered" and how the big rain-drops poured down and beat against the pane!

"It sounds just like a person lost on the moor and wandering on and on crying," she said.

She had been lying awake turning from side to side for about an hour, when suddenly something made her sit up in bed and turn her head toward the door listening. She listened and she listened.

"It isn't the wind now," she said in a loud whisper. "That isn't the wind. It is different. It is that crying I heard before."

The door of her room was ajar and the sound came down the corridor, a far-off faint sound of fretful crying. She listened for a few minutes and each minute she became more and more sure. She felt as if she must find out what it was. It seemed even stranger than the secret garden and the buried key. Perhaps the fact that she was in a rebellious mood made her bold. She put her foot out of bed and stood on the floor.

"I am going to find out what it is," she said. "Everybody is in bed and I don't care about Mrs. Medlock—I don't care!"

There was a candle by her bedside and she took it up and went softly out of the room. The corridor looked very long and dark, but she was too excited to mind that. She thought she remembered the corners she must turn to find the short corridor with the door covered with tapestry—the one Mrs. Medlock had come through the day she lost herself. The sound had come up that passage. So she went on with her dim light, almost feeling her way, her heart beating so loud that she fancied she could hear it. The far-off faint crying went on and led her. Sometimes it stopped for a moment or so and then began again. Was this the right corner to turn? She stopped and thought. Yes it was. Down this passage and then to the left, and then up two broad steps, and then to the right again. Yes, there was the tapestry door.

She pushed it open very gently and closed it behind her, and she stood in the corridor and could hear the crying quite plainly, though it was not loud. It was on the other side of the wall at her left and a few yards farther on there was a door. She could see a glimmer of light coming from beneath it. The Someone was crying in that room, and it was quite a young Someone.

So she walked to the door and pushed it open, and there she was standing in the room!

It was a big room with ancient, handsome furniture in it. There was a low fire glowing faintly on the hearth and a night light burning by the side of a carved four-posted bed hung with brocade, and on the bed was lying a boy, crying fretfully.

Mary wondered if she was in a real place or if she had fallen asleep again and was dreaming without knowing it.

The boy had a sharp, delicate face the color of ivory and he seemed to have eyes too big for it. He had also a lot of hair which tumbled over his forehead in heavy locks and made his thin face seem smaller. He looked like a boy who had been ill, but he was crying more as if he were tired and cross than as if he were in pain.

Mary stood near the door with her candle in her hand, holding her breath. Then she crept across the room, and as she drew nearer the light attracted the boy's attention and he turned his head on his pillow and stared at her, his gray eyes opening so wide that they seemed immense.

"Who are you?" he said at last in a half-frightened whisper. "Are you a ghost?"

"No, I am not," Mary answered, her own whisper sounding half frightened. "Are you one?"

He stared and stared and stared. Mary could not help noticing what strange eyes he had. They were agate gray and they looked too big for his face because they had black lashes all round them.

"No," he replied after waiting a moment or so. "I am Colin."

"Who is Colin?" she faltered.

"I am Colin Craven. Who are you?"

"I am Mary Lennox. Mr. Craven is my uncle."

"He is my father," said the boy.

"Your father!" gasped Mary. "No one ever told me he had a boy! Why didn't they?"

"Come here," he said, still keeping his strange eyes fixed on her with an anxious expression.

She came close to the bed and he put out his hand and touched her.

"You are real, aren't you?" he said. "I have such real dreams very often. You might be one of them."

Mary had slipped on a woolen wrapper before she left her room and she put a piece of it between his fingers.

"Rub that and see how thick and warm it is," she said. "I will pinch you a little if you like, to show you how real I am. For a minute I thought you might be a dream too."

"Where did you come from?" he asked.

"From my own room. The wind wuthered so I couldn't go to sleep and I heard some one crying and wanted to find out who it was. What were you crying for?"

"Because I couldn't go to sleep either and my head ached. Tell me your name again."

"Mary Lennox. Did no one ever tell you I had come to live here?"

He was still fingering the fold of her wrapper, but he began to look a little more as if he believed in her reality.

"No," he answered. "They daren't."

"Why?" asked Mary.

"Because I should have been afraid you would see me. I won't let people see me and talk me over."

"Why?" Mary asked again, feeling more mystified every moment.

"Because I am like this always, ill and having to lie down. My father won't let people talk me over either. The servants are not allowed to speak about me. If I live I may be a hunchback, but I shan't live. My father hates to think I may be like him."

"Oh, what a queer house this is!" Mary said. "What a queer house! Everything is a kind of secret. Rooms are locked up and gardens are locked up—and you! Have you been locked up?"

"No. I stay in this room because I don't want to be moved out of it. It tires me too much."

"Does your father come and see you?" Mary ventured.

"Sometimes. Generally when I am asleep. He doesn't want to see me."

"Why?" Mary could not help asking again.

A sort of angry shadow passed over the boy's face.

"My mother died when I was born and it makes him wretched to look at me. He thinks I don't know, but I've heard people talking. He almost hates me."

"He hates the garden, because she died," said Mary half speaking to herself.

"What garden?" the boy asked.

"Oh! just—just a garden she used to like," Mary stammered. "Have you been here always?"

"Nearly always. Sometimes I have been taken to places at the seaside, but I won't stay because people stare at me. I used to wear an iron thing to keep my back straight, but a grand doctor came from London to see me and said it was stupid. He told them to take it off and keep me out in the fresh air. I hate fresh air and I don't want to go out."

"I didn't when first I came here," said Mary. "Why do you keep looking at me like that?"

"Because of the dreams that are so real," he answered rather fretfully. "Sometimes when I open my eyes I don't believe I'm awake."

"We're both awake," said Mary. She glanced round the room with its high ceiling and shadowy corners and dim firelight. "It looks quite like a dream, and it's the middle of the night, and everybody in the house is asleep—everybody but us. We are wide awake."

"I don't want it to be a dream," the boy said restlessly.

Mary thought of something all at once.

"If you don't like people to see you," she began, "do you want me to go away?"

He still held the fold of her wrapper and he gave it a little pull.

"No," he said. "I should be sure you were a dream if you went.

If you are real, sit down on that big footstool and talk. I want to hear about you."

Mary put down her candle on the table near the bed and sat down on the cushioned stool. She did not want to go away at all. She wanted to stay in the mysterious hidden-away room and talk to the mysterious boy.

"What do you want me to tell you?" she said.

He wanted to know how long she had been at Misselthwaite; he wanted to know which corridor her room was on; he wanted to know what she had been doing; if she disliked the moor as he disliked it; where she had lived before she came to Yorkshire. She answered all these questions and many more and he lay back on his pillow and listened. He made her tell him a great deal about India and about her voyage across the ocean. She found out that because he had been an invalid he had not learned things as other children had. One of his nurses had taught him to read when he was quite little and he was always reading and looking at pictures in splendid books.

Though his father rarely saw him when he was awake, he was given all sorts of wonderful things to amuse himself with. He never seemed to have been amused, however. He could have anything he asked for and was never made to do anything he did not like to do.

"Every one is obliged to do what pleases me," he said indifferently. "It makes me ill to be angry. No one believes I shall live to grow up."

He said it as if he was so accustomed to the idea that it had ceased to matter to him at all. He seemed to like the sound of Mary's voice. As she went on talking he listened in a drowsy, interested way. Once or twice she wondered if he were not gradually falling into a doze. But at last he asked a question which opened up a new subject.

"How old are you?" he asked.

"I am ten," answered Mary, forgetting herself for the moment, "and so are you."

"How do you know that?" he demanded in a surprised voice.

"Because when you were born the garden door was locked and the key was buried. And it has been locked for ten years."

Colin half sat up, turning toward her, leaning on his elbows.

"What garden door was locked? Who did it? Where was the key buried?" he exclaimed as if he were suddenly very much interested.

"It—it was the garden Mr. Craven hates," said Mary nervously. "He locked the door. No one—no one knew where he buried the key."

"What sort of a garden is it?" Colin persisted eagerly.

"No one has been allowed to go into it for ten years," was Mary's careful answer.

But it was too late to be careful. He was too much like herself. He too had had nothing to think about and the idea of a hidden garden attracted him as it had attracted her. He asked question after question. Where was it? Had she never looked for the door? Had she never asked the gardeners?

"They won't talk about it," said Mary. "I think they have been told not to answer questions."

"I would make them," said Colin.

"Could you?" Mary faltered, beginning to feel frightened. If he could make people answer questions, who knew what might happen!

"Every one is obliged to please me. I told you that," he said. "If I were to live, this place would sometime belong to me. They all know that. I would make them tell me."

Mary had not known that she herself had been spoiled, but she could see quite plainly that this mysterious boy had been. He thought that the whole world belonged to him. How peculiar he was and how coolly he spoke of not living.

"Do you think you won't live?" she asked, partly because she was curious and partly in hope of making him forget the garden.

"I don't suppose I shall," he answered as indifferently as he had spoken before. "Ever since I remember anything I have heard

people say I shan't. At first they thought I was too little to understand and now they think I don't hear. But I do. My doctor is my
father's cousin. He is quite poor and if I die he will have all Misselthwaite when my father is dead. I should think he wouldn't
want me to live."

"Do you want to live?" inquired Mary.

"No," he answered, in a cross, tired fashion. "But I don't
want to die. When I feel ill I lie here and think about it until I cry
and cry."

"I have heard you crying three times," Mary said, "but I did
not know who it was. Were you crying about that?" She did so
want him to forget the garden.

"I dare say," he answered. "Let us talk about something else.
Talk about that garden. Don't you want to see it?"

"Yes," answered Mary, in quite a low voice.

"I do," he went on persistently. "I don't think I ever really
wanted to see anything before, but I want to see that garden. I
want the key dug up. I want the door unlocked. I would let them
take me there in my chair. That would be getting fresh air. I am
going to make them open the door."

He had become quite excited and his strange eyes began to
shine like stars and looked more immense than ever.

"They have to please me," he said. "I will make them take me
there and I will let you go, too."

Mary's hands clutched each other. Everything would be
spoiled—everything! Dickon would never come back. She would
never again feel like a missel thrush with a safe-hidden nest.

"Oh, don't—don't—don't—don't do that!" she cried out.

He stared as if he thought she had gone crazy!

"Why?" he exclaimed. "You said you wanted to see it."

"I do," she answered almost with a sob in her throat, "but if
you make them open the door and take you in like that it will
never be a secret again."

He leaned still farther forward.

"A secret," he said. "What do you mean? Tell me."

Mary's words almost tumbled over one another.

"You see—you see," she panted, "if no one knows but our-selves—if there was a door, hidden somewhere under the ivy—if there was—and we could find it; and if we could slip through it together and shut it behind us, and no one knew any one was in-side and we called it our garden and pretended that—that we were missel thrushes and it was our nest, and if we played there almost every day and dug and planted seeds and made it all come alive—"

"Is it dead?" he interrupted her.

"It soon will be if no one cares for it," she went on. "The bulbs will live but the roses—"

He stopped her again as excited as she was herself.

"What are bulbs?" he put in quickly.

"They are daffodils and lilies and snowdrops. They are work-ing in the earth now—pushing up pale green points because the spring is coming."

"Is the spring coming?" he said. "What is it like? You don't see it in rooms if you are ill."

"It is the sun shining on the rain and the rain falling on the sunshine, and things pushing up and working under the earth," said Mary. "If the garden was a secret and we could get into it we could watch the things grow bigger every day, and see how many roses are alive. Don't you see? Oh, don't you see how much nicer it would be if it was a secret?"

He dropped back on his pillow and lay there with an odd expression on his face.

"I never had a secret," he said, "except that one about not liv-ing to grow up. They don't know I know that, so it is a sort of secret. But I like this kind better."

"If you won't make them take you to the garden," pleaded Mary, "perhaps—I feel almost sure I can find out how to get in sometime. And then—if the doctor wants you to go out in your chair, and if you can always do what you want to do, perhaps—perhaps we might find some boy who would push you, and we could go alone and it would always be a secret garden."

Mary began to recover her breath and feel safer because the idea of keeping the secret seemed to please him. She felt almost sure that if she kept on talking and could make him see the garden in his mind as she had seen it he would like it so much that he could not bear to think that everybody might tramp into it when they chose.

"I'll tell you what I *think* it would be like, if we could go into it," she said. "It has been shut up so long things have grown into a tangle perhaps."

He lay quite still and listened while she went on talking about the roses which *might* have clambered from tree to tree and hung down—about the many birds which *might* have built their nests there because it was so safe. And then she told him about the robin and Ben Weatherstaff, and there was so much to tell about the robin and it was so easy and safe to talk about it that she ceased to feel afraid. The robin pleased him so much that he smiled until he looked almost beautiful, and at first Mary had thought that he was even plainer than herself, with his big eyes and heavy locks of hair.

"I did not know birds could be like that," he said. "But if you stay in a room you never see things. What a lot of things you know. I feel as if you had been inside that garden."

She did not know what to say, so she did not say anything. He evidently did not expect an answer and the next moment he gave her a surprise.

"I am going to let you look at something," he said. "Do you see that rose-colored silk curtain hanging on the wall over the mantel-piece?"

Mary had not noticed it before, but she looked up and saw it. It was a curtain of soft silk hanging over what seemed to be some picture.

"Yes," she answered.

"There is a cord hanging from it," said Colin. "Go and pull it."

Mary got up, much mystified, and found the cord. When she pulled it the silk curtain ran back on rings and when it ran back it uncovered a picture. It was the picture of a girl with a laughing face. She had bright hair tied up with a blue ribbon and her gay, lovely eyes were exactly like Colin's unhappy ones, agate gray and looking twice as big as they really were because of the black lashes all round them.

"She is my mother," said Colin complainingly. "I don't see why she died. Sometimes I hate her for doing it."

"How queer!" said Mary.

"If she had lived I believe I should not have been ill always," he grumbled. "I dare say I should have lived, too. And my father would not have hated to look at me. I dare say I should have had a strong back. Draw the curtain again."

Mary did as she was told and returned to her footstool.

"She is much prettier than you," she said, "but her eyes are just like yours—at least they are the same shape and color. Why is the curtain drawn over her?"

He moved uncomfortably.

"I made them do it," he said. "Sometimes I don't like to see her looking at me. She smiles too much when I am ill and miserable. Besides, she is mine and I don't want every one to see her."

There were a few moments of silence and then Mary spoke.

"What would Mrs. Medlock do if she found out that I had been here?" she inquired.

"She would do as I told her to do," he answered. "And I should tell her that I wanted you to come here and talk to me every day. I am glad you came."

"So am I," said Mary. "I will come as often as I can, but"—she hesitated—"I shall have to look every day for the garden door."

"Yes, you must," said Colin, "and you can tell me about it afterward."

He lay thinking a few minutes, as he had done before, and then he spoke again.

"I think you shall be a secret, too," he said. "I will not tell them until they find out. I can always send the nurse out of the room and say that I want to be by myself. Do you know Martha?"

"Yes, I know her very well," said Mary. "She waits on me."

He nodded his head toward the outer corridor.

"She is the one who is asleep in the other room. The nurse went away yesterday to stay all night with her sister and she always makes Martha attend to me when she wants to go out. Martha shall tell you when to come here."

Then Mary understood Martha's troubled look when she had asked questions about the crying.

"Martha knew about you all the time?" she said.

"Yes; she often attends to me. The nurse likes to get away from me and then Martha comes."

"I have been here a long time," said Mary. "Shall I go away now? Your eyes look sleepy."

"I wish I could go to sleep before you leave me," he said rather shyly.

"Shut your eyes," said Mary, drawing her footstool closer, "and I will do what my Ayah used to do in India. I will pat your hand and stroke it and sing something quite low."

"I should like that perhaps," he said drowsily.

Somehow she was sorry for him and did not want him to lie awake, so she leaned against the bed and began to stroke and pat his hand and sing a very low little chanting song in Hindustani.

"That is nice," he said more drowsily still, and she went on chanting and stroking, but when she looked at him again his black lashes were lying close against his cheeks, for his eyes were shut and he was fast asleep. So she got up softly, took her candle and crept away without making a sound.

CHAPTER 14
A YOUNG RAJAH

The moor was hidden in mist when the morning came and the rain had not stopped pouring down. There could be no going out of doors. Martha was so busy that Mary had no opportunity of talking to her, but in the afternoon she asked her to come and sit with her in the nursery. She came bringing the stocking she was always knitting when she was doing nothing else.

"What's the matter with thee?" she asked as soon as they sat down. "Tha' looks as if tha'd somethin' to say."

"I have. I have found out what the crying was," said Mary.

Martha let her knitting drop on her knee and gazed at her with startled eyes.

"Tha' hasn't!" she exclaimed. "Never!"

"I heard it in the night," Mary went on. "And I got up and went to see where it came from. It was Colin. I found him."

Martha's face became red with fright.

"Eh! Miss Mary!" she said half crying. "Tha' shouldn't have done it—tha' shouldn't! Tha'll get me in trouble. I never told thee nothin' about him—but tha'll get me in trouble. I shall lose my place and what'll mother do!"

"You won't lose your place," said Mary. "He was glad I came. We talked and talked and he said he was glad I came."

"Was he?" cried Martha. "Art tha' sure? Tha' doesn't know what he's like when anything vexes him. He's a big lad to cry like a baby, but when he's in a passion he'll fair scream just to frighten us. He knows us daren't call our souls our own."

"He wasn't vexed," said Mary. "I asked him if I should go away and he made me stay. He asked me questions and I sat on a big

footstool and talked to him about India and about the robin and
gardens. He wouldn't let me go. He let me see his mother's picture. Before I left him I sang him to sleep."

Martha fairly gasped with amazement.

"I can scarcely believe thee!" she protested. "It's as if tha'd
walked straight into a lion's den. If he'd been like he is most times
he'd have throwed himself into one of his tantrums and roused th'
house. He won't let strangers look at him."

"He let me look at him. I looked at him all the time and he
looked at me. We stared!" said Mary.

"I don't know what to do!" cried agitated Martha. "If Mrs.
Medlock finds out, she'll think I broke orders and told thee and I
shall be packed back to mother."

"He is not going to tell Mrs. Medlock anything about it yet. It's
to be a sort of secret just at first," said Mary firmly. "And he says
everybody is obliged to do as he pleases."

"Aye, that's true enough—th' bad lad!" sighed Martha, wiping
her forehead with her apron.

"He says Mrs. Medlock must. And he wants me to come
and talk to him every day. And you are to tell me when he wants
me."

"Me!" said Martha; "I shall lose my place—I shall for sure!"

"You can't if you are doing what he wants you to do and everybody is ordered to obey him," Mary argued.

"Does tha' mean to say," cried Martha with wide open eyes,
"that he was nice to thee!"

"I think he almost liked me," Mary answered.

"Then tha' must have bewitched him!" decided Martha, drawing a long breath.

"Do you mean Magic?" inquired Mary. "I've heard about Magic
in India, but I can't make it. I just went into his room and I was so
surprised to see him I stood and stared. And then he turned
round and stared at me. And he thought I was a ghost or a dream
and I thought perhaps he was. And it was so queer being there
alone together in the middle of the night and not knowing about

each other. And we began to ask each other questions. And when I asked him if I must go away he said I must not."

"Th' world's comin' to a end!" gasped Martha.

"What is the matter with him?" asked Mary.

"Nobody knows for sure and certain," said Martha. "Mr. Craven went off his head like when he was born. Th' doctors thought he'd have to be put in a 'sylum. It was because Mrs. Craven died like I told you. He wouldn't set eyes on th' baby. He just raved and said it'd be another hunchback like him and it'd better die."

"Is Colin a hunchback?" Mary asked. "He didn't look like one."

"He isn't yet," said Martha. "But he began all wrong. Mother said that there was enough trouble and raging in th' house to set any child wrong. They was afraid his back was weak an' they've always been takin' care of it—keepin' him lyin' down and not lettin' him walk. Once they made him wear a brace but he fretted so he was downright ill. Then a big doctor came to see him an' made them take it off. He talked to th' other doctor quite rough—in a polite way. He said there'd been too much medicine and too much lettin' him have his own way."

"I think he's a very spoiled boy," said Mary.

"He's th' worst young nowt as ever was!" said Martha. "I won't say as he hasn't been ill a good bit. He's had coughs an' colds that's nearly killed him two or three times. Once he had rheumatic fever an' once he had typhoid. Eh! Mrs. Medlock did get a fright then. He'd been out of his head an' she was talkin' to th' nurse, thinkin' he didn't know nothin', an' she said, 'He'll die this time sure enough, an' best thing for him an' for everybody.' An' she looked at him an' there he was with his big eyes open, starin' at her as sensible as she was herself. She didn't know what'd happen but he just stared at her an' says, 'You give me some water an' stop talkin'.'"

"Do you think he will die?" asked Mary.

"Mother says there's no reason why any child should live that gets no fresh air an' doesn't do nothin' but lie on his back an' read

picture-books an' take medicine. He's weak and hates th' trouble
o' bein' taken out o' doors, an' he gets cold so easy he says it
makes him ill."

Mary sat and looked at the fire.

"I wonder," she said slowly, "if it would not do him good to go
out into a garden and watch things growing. It did me good."

"One of th' worst fits he ever had," said Martha, "was one tine
they took him out where the roses is by the fountain. He'd been
readin' in a paper about people gettin' somethin' he called 'rose
cold' an' he began to sneeze an' said he'd got it an' then a new gardener as didn't know th' rules passed by an' looked at him
curious. He threw himself into a passion an' he said he'd looked at
him because he was going to be a hunchback. He cried himself
into a fever an' was ill all night."

"If he ever gets angry at me, I'll never go and see him again,"
said Mary.

"He'll have thee if he wants thee," said Martha. "Tha' may as
well know that at th' start."

Very soon afterward a bell rang and she rolled up her knitting.

"I dare say th' nurse wants me to stay with him a bit," she said.
"I hope he's in a good temper."

She was out of the room about ten minutes and then she came
back with a puzzled expression.

"Well, tha' has bewitched him," she said. "He's up on his sofa
with his picture-books. He's told the nurse to stay away until six
o'clock. I'm to wait in the next room. Th' minute she was gone he
called me to him an' says, 'I want Mary Lennox to come and talk
to me, and remember you're not to tell any one.' You'd better go
as quick as you can."

Mary was quite willing to go quickly. She did not want to see
Colin as much as she wanted to see Dickon, but she wanted to
see him very much.

There was a bright fire on the hearth when she entered his
room, and in the daylight she saw it was a very beautiful room
indeed. There were rich colors in the rugs and hangings and

pictures and books on the walls which made it look glowing and comfortable even in spite of the gray sky and falling rain. Colin looked rather like a picture himself. He was wrapped in a velvet dressing-gown and sat against a big brocaded cushion. He had a red spot on each cheek.

"Come in," he said. "I've been thinking about you all morning."

"I've been thinking about you, too," answered Mary. "You don't know how frightened Martha is. She says Mrs. Medlock will think she told me about you and then she will be sent away."

He frowned.

"Go and tell her to come here," he said. "She is in the next room."

Mary went and brought her back. Poor Martha was shaking in her shoes. Colin was still frowning.

"Have you to do what I please or have you not?" he demanded.

"I have to do what you please, sir," Martha faltered, turning quite red.

"Has Medlock to do what I please?"

"Everybody has, sir," said Martha.

"Well, then, if I order you to bring Miss Mary to me, how can Medlock send you away if she finds it out?"

"Please don't let her, sir," pleaded Martha.

"I'll send *her* away if she dares to say a word about such a thing," said Master Craven grandly. "She wouldn't like that, I can tell you."

"Thank you, sir," bobbing a curtsy, "I want to do my duty, sir."

"What I want is your duty," said Colin more grandly still. "I'll take care of you. Now go away."

When the door closed behind Martha, Colin found Mistress Mary gazing at him as if he had set her wondering.

"Why do you look at me like that?" he asked her. "What are you thinking about?"

"I am thinking about two things."

"What are they? Sit down and tell me."

"This is the first one," said Mary, seating herself on the big stool. "Once in India I saw a boy who was a Rajah. He had rubies and emeralds and diamonds stuck all over him. He spoke to his people just as you spoke to Martha. Everybody had to do everything he told them—in a minute. I think they would have been killed if they hadn't."

"I shall make you tell me about Rajahs presently," he said, "but first tell me what the second thing was."

"I was thinking," said Mary, "how different you are from Dickon."

"Who is Dickon?" he said. "What a queer name!"

She might as well tell him, she thought. She could talk about Dickon without mentioning the secret garden. She had liked to hear Martha talk about him. Besides, she longed to talk about him. It would seem to bring him nearer.

"He is Martha's brother. He is twelve years old," she explained. "He is not like any one else in the world. He can charm foxes and squirrels and birds just as the natives in India charm snakes. He plays a very soft tune on a pipe and they come and listen."

There were some big books on a table at his side and he dragged one suddenly toward him.

"There is a picture of a snake-charmer in this," he exclaimed. "Come and look at it."

The book was a beautiful one with superb colored illustrations and he turned to one of them.

"Can he do that?" he asked eagerly.

"He played on his pipe and they listened," Mary explained. "But he doesn't call it Magic. He says it's because he lives on the moor so much and he knows their ways. He says he feels sometimes as if he was a bird or a rabbit himself, he likes them so. I think he asked the robin questions. It seemed as if they talked to each other in soft chirps."

Colin lay back on his cushion and his eyes grew larger and larger and the spots on his cheeks burned.

"Tell me some more about him," he said.

"He knows all about eggs and nests," Mary went on. "And he

knows where foxes and badgers and otters live. He keeps them secret so that other boys won't find their holes and frighten them. He knows about everything that grows or lives on the moor."

"Does he like the moor?" said Colin. "How can he when it's such a great, bare, dreary place?"

"It's the most beautiful place," protested Mary. "Thousands of lovely things grow on it and there are thousands of little creatures all busy building nests and making holes and burrows and chippering or singing or squeaking to each other. They are so busy and having such fun under the earth or in the trees or heather. It's their world."

"How do you know all that?" said Colin, turning on his elbow to look at her.

"I have never been there once, really," said Mary suddenly remembering. "I only drove over it in the dark. I thought it was hideous. Martha told me about it first and then Dickon. When Dickon talks about it you feel as if you saw things and heard them and as if you were standing in the heather with the sun shining and the gorse smelling like honey—and all full of bees and butterflies."

"You never see anything if you are ill," said Colin restlessly. He looked like a person listening to a new sound in the distance and wondering what it was.

"You can't if you stay in a room," said Mary.

"I couldn't go on the moor," he said in a resentful tone.

Mary was silent for a minute and then she said something bold.

"You might—sometime."

He moved as if he were startled.

"Go on the moor! How could I? I am going to die."

"How do you know?" said Mary unsympathetically. She didn't like the way he had of talking about dying. She did not feel very sympathetic. She felt rather as if he almost boasted about it.

"Oh, I've heard it ever since I remember," he answered crossly. "They are always whispering about it and thinking I don't notice. They wish I would, too."

Mistress Mary felt quite contrary. She pinched her lips together.

"If they wished I would," she said, "I wouldn't. Who wishes you would?"

"The servants—and of course Dr. Craven because he would get Misselthwaite and be rich instead of poor. He daren't say so, but he always looks cheerful when I am worse. When I had typhoid fever his face got quite fat. I think my father wishes it, too."

"I don't believe he does," said Mary quite obstinately.

That made Colin turn and look at her again.

"Don't you?" he said.

And then he lay back on his cushion and was quite still, as if he were thinking. And there was quite a long silence. Perhaps they were both of them thinking strange things children do not usually think of.

"I like the grand doctor from London, because he made them take the iron thing off," said Mary at last. "Did he say you were going to die?"

"No."

"What did he say?"

"He didn't whisper," Colin answered. "Perhaps he knew I hated whispering. I heard him say one thing quite aloud. He said, 'The lad might live if he would make up his mind to it. Put him in the humor.' It sounded as if he was in a temper."

"I'll tell you who would put you in the humor, perhaps," said Mary reflecting. She felt as if she would like this thing to be settled one way or the other. "I believe Dickon would. He's always talking about live things. He never talks about dead things or things that are ill. He's always looking up in the sky to watch birds flying—or looking down at the earth to see something growing. He has such round blue eyes and they are so wide open with looking about. And he laughs such a big laugh with his wide mouth—and his cheeks are as red—as red as cherries."

She pulled her stool nearer to the sofa and her expression quite changed at the remembrance of the wide curving mouth and wide open eyes.

"See here," she said. "Don't let us talk about dying; I don't like it. Let us talk about living. Let us talk and talk about Dickon. And then we will look at your pictures."

It was the best thing she could have said. To talk about Dickon meant to talk about the moor and about the cottage and the fourteen people who lived in it on sixteen shillings a week—and the children who got fat on the moor grass like the wild ponies. And about Dickon's mother—and the skipping-rope—and the moor with the sun on it—and about pale green points sticking up out of the black sod. And it was all so alive that Mary talked more than she had ever talked before—and Colin both talked and listened as he had never done either before. And they both began to laugh over nothings as children will when they are happy together. And they laughed so that in the end they were making as much noise as if they had been two ordinary healthy natural ten-year-old creatures—instead of a hard, little, unloving girl and a sickly boy who believed that he was going to die.

They enjoyed themselves so much that they forgot the pictures and they forgot about the time. They had been laughing quite loudly over Ben Weatherstaff and his robin and Colin was actually sitting up as if he had forgotten about his weak back when he suddenly remembered something.

"Do you know there is one thing we have never once thought of," he said. "We are cousins."

It seemed so queer that they had talked so much and never remembered this simple thing that they laughed more than ever, because they had got into the humor to laugh at anything. And in the midst of the fun the door opened and in walked Dr. Craven and Mrs. Medlock.

Dr. Craven started in actual alarm and Mrs. Medlock almost fell back because he had accidentally bumped against her.

"Good Lord!" exclaimed poor Mrs. Medlock, with her eyes almost starting out of her head. "Good Lord!"

"What is this?" said Dr. Craven, coming forward. "What does it mean?"

Then Mary was reminded of the boy Rajah again. Colin answered as if neither the doctor's alarm nor Mrs. Medlock's terror were of the slightest consequence. He was as little disturbed or frightened as if an elderly cat and dog had walked into the room.

"This is my cousin, Mary Lennox," he said. "I asked her to come and talk to me. I like her. She must come and talk to me whenever I send for her."

Dr. Craven turned reproachfully to Mrs. Medlock.

"Oh, sir," she panted. "I don't know how it's happened. There's not a servant on the place that'd dare to talk—they all have their orders."

"Nobody told her anything," said Colin. "She heard me crying and found me herself. I am glad she came. Don't be silly, Medlock."

Mary saw that Dr. Craven did not look pleased, but it was quite plain that he dare not oppose his patient. He sat down by Colin and felt his pulse.

"I am afraid there has been too much excitement. Excitement is not good for you, my boy," he said.

"I should be excited if she kept away," answered Colin, his eyes beginning to look dangerously sparkling. "I am better. She makes me better. The nurse must bring up her tea with mine. We will have tea together."

Mrs. Medlock and Dr. Craven looked at each other in a troubled way, but there was evidently nothing to be done.

"He does look rather better, sir," ventured Mrs. Medlock. "But"—thinking the matter over—"he looked better this morning before she came into the room."

"She came into the room last night. She stayed with me a long time. She sang a Hindustani song to me and it made me go to sleep," said Colin. "I was better when I wakened up. I wanted my breakfast. I want my tea now. Tell nurse, Medlock."

Dr. Craven did not stay very long. He talked to the nurse for a few minutes when she came into the room and said a few words of warning to Colin. He must not talk too much; he must not forget that he was ill; he must not forget that he was very easily tired. Mary thought that there seemed to be a number of uncomfortable things he was not to forget.

Colin looked fretful and kept his strange black-lashed eyes fixed on Dr. Craven's face.

"I *want* to forget it," he said at last. "She makes me forget it. That is why I want her."

Dr. Craven did not look happy when he left the room. He gave a puzzled glance at the little girl sitting on the large stool. She had become a stiff, silent child again as soon as he entered and he could not see what the attraction was. The boy actually did look brighter, however—and he sighed rather heavily as he went down the corridor.

"They are always wanting me to eat things when I don't want to," said Colin, as the nurse brought in the tea and put it on the table by the sofa. "Now, if you'll eat I will. Those muffins look so nice and hot. Tell me about Rajahs."

CHAPTER 15
NEST BUILDING

After another week of rain the high arch of blue sky appeared again and the sun which poured down was quite hot. Though there had been no chance to see either the secret garden or Dickon, Mistress Mary had enjoyed herself very much. The week had not seemed long. She had spent hours of every day with Colin in his room, talking about Rajahs or gardens or Dickon and the cottage on the moor. They had looked at the splendid books and pictures and sometimes Mary had read things to Colin, and sometimes he had read a little to her. What he was amused and interested she thought he scarcely looked like an invalid at all, except that his face was so colorless and he was always on the sofa.

"You are a sly young one to listen and get out of your bed to go following things up like you did that night," Mrs. Medlock said once. "But there's no saying it's not been a sort of blessing to the lot of us. He's not had a tantrum or a whining fit since you made friends. The nurse was just going to give up the case because she was so sick of him, but she says she doesn't mind staying now you've gone on duty with her," laughing a little.

In her talks with Colin, Mary had tried to be very cautious about the secret garden. There were certain things she wanted to find out from him, but she felt that she must find them out without asking him direct questions. In the first place, as she began to like to be with him, she wanted to discover whether he was the kind of boy you could tell a secret to. He was not in the least like Dickon, but he was evidently so pleased with the idea of a garden no one knew anything about that she thought perhaps he could be trusted. But she had not known him long enough to be sure.

The second thing she wanted to find out was this: If he could be trusted—if he really could—wouldn't it be possible to take him to the garden without having any one find it out? The grand doctor had said that he must have fresh air and Colin had said that he would not mind fresh air in a secret garden. Perhaps if he had a great deal of fresh air and knew Dickon and the robin and saw things growing he might not think so much about dying. Mary had seen herself in the glass sometimes lately when she had realized that she looked quite a different creature from the child she had seen when she arrived from India. This child looked nicer. Even Martha had seen a change in her.

"Th' air from th' moor has done thee good already," she had said. "Tha'rt not nigh so yeller and tha'rt not nigh so scrawny. Even tha' hair doesn't slamp down on tha' head so flat. It's got some life in it so as it sticks out a bit."

"It's like me," said Mary. "It's growing stronger and fatter. I'm sure there's more of it."

"It looks it, for sure," said Martha, ruffling it up a little round her face. "Tha'rt not half so ugly when it's that way an' there's a bit o' red in tha' cheeks."

If gardens and fresh air had been good for her perhaps they would be good for Colin. But then, if he hated people to look at him, perhaps he would not like to see Dickon.

"Why does it make you angry when you are looked at?" she inquired one day.

"I always hated it," he answered, "even when I was very little. Then when they took me to the seaside and I used to lie in my carriage everybody used to stare and ladies would stop and talk to my nurse and then they would begin to whisper and I knew then they were saying I shouldn't live to grow up. Then sometimes the ladies would pat my cheeks and say 'Poor child!' Once when a lady did that I screamed out loud and bit her hand. She was so frightened she ran away."

"She thought you had gone mad like a dog," said Mary, not at all admiringly.

"I don't care what she thought," said Colin, frowning.

"I wonder why you didn't scream and bite me when I came into your room?" said Mary. Then she began to smile slowly.

"I thought you were a ghost or a dream," he said. "You can't bite a ghost or a dream, and if you scream they don't care."

"Would you hate it if—if a boy looked at you?" Mary asked uncertainly.

He lay back on his cushion and paused thoughtfully.

"There's one boy," he said quite slowly, as if he were thinking over every word, "there's one boy I believe I shouldn't mind. It's that boy who knows where the foxes live—Dickon."

"I'm sure you wouldn't mind him," said Mary.

"The birds don't and other animals," he said, still thinking it over, "perhaps that's why I shouldn't. He's a sort of animal charmer and I am a boy animal."

Then he laughed and she laughed too; in fact it ended in their both laughing a great deal and finding the idea of a boy animal hiding in his hole very funny indeed.

What Mary felt afterward was that she need not fear about Dickon.

On that first morning when the sky was blue again Mary wakened very early. The sun was pouring in slanting rays through the blinds and there was something so joyous in the sight of it that she jumped out of bed and ran to the window. She drew up the blinds and opened the window itself and a great waft of fresh, scented air blew in upon her. The moor was blue and the whole world looked as if something Magic had happened to it. There were tender little fluting sounds here and there and everywhere, as if scores of birds were beginning to tune up for a concert. Mary put her hand out of the window and held it in the sun.

"It's warm—warm!" she said. "It will make the green points push up and up and up, and it will make the bulbs and roots work and struggle with all their might under the earth."

She kneeled down and leaned out of the window as far as she

could, breathing big breaths and sniffing the air until she laughed
because she remembered what Dickon's mother had said about
the end of his nose quivering like a rabbit's.

"It must be very early," she said. "The little clouds are all pink
and I've never seen the sky look like this. No one is up. I don't
even hear the stable boys."

A sudden thought made her scramble to her feet.

"I can't wait! I am going to see the garden!"

She had learned to dress herself by this time and she put on
her clothes in five minutes. She knew a small side door which she
could unbolt herself and she flew down-stairs in her stocking feet
and put on her shoes in the hall. She unchained and unbolted and
unlocked and when the door was open she sprang across the step
with one bound, and there she was standing on the grass, which
seemed to have turned green, and with the sun pouring down on
her and warm sweet wafts about her and the fluting and twittering and singing coming from every bush and tree. She clasped her
hands for pure joy and looked up in the sky and it was so blue
and pink and pearly and white and flooded with springtime light
that she felt as if she must flute and sing aloud herself and knew
that thrushes and robins and skylarks could not possibly help it.
She ran around the shrubs and paths toward the secret garden.

"It is all different already," she said. "The grass is greener and
things are sticking up everywhere and things are uncurling and
green buds of leaves are showing. This afternoon I am sure Dickon will come."

The long warm rain had done strange things to the herbaceous
beds which bordered the walk by the lower wall. There were
things sprouting and pushing out from the roots of clumps of
plants and there were actually here and there glimpses of royal
purple and yellow unfurling among the stems of crocuses. Six
months before Mistress Mary would not have seen how the world
was waking up, but now she missed nothing.

When she had reached the place where the door hid itself
under the ivy, she was startled by a curious loud sound. It was the

caw—caw of a crow and it came from the top of the wall, and when she looked up, there sat a big glossy-plumaged blue-black bird, looking down at her very wisely indeed. She had never seen a crow so close before and he made her a little nervous, but the next moment he spread his wings and flapped away across the garden. She hoped he was not going to stay inside and she pushed the door open wondering if he would. When she got fairly into the garden she saw that he probably did intend to stay because he had alighted on a dwarf apple-tree, and under the apple-tree was lying a little reddish animal with a bushy tail, and both of them were watching the stooping body and rust-red head of Dickon, who was kneeling on the grass working hard.

Mary flew across the grass to him.

"Oh, Dickon! Dickon!" she cried out. "How could you get here so early! How could you! The sun has only just got up!"

He got up himself, laughing and glowing, and tousled; his eyes like a bit of the sky.

"Eh!" he said. "I was up long before him. How could I have stayed abed! Th' world's all fair begun again this mornin', it has. An' it's workin' an' hummin' an' scratchin' an' pipin' an' nest buildin' an' breathin' out scents, till you've got to be out on it 'stead o' lyin' on your back. When th' sun did jump up, th' moor went mad for joy, an' I was in the midst of th' heather, an' I run like mad myself, shoutin' an' singin'. An' I come straight here. I couldn't have stayed away. Why, th' garden was lyin' here waitin'!"

Mary put her hands on her chest, panting, as if she had been running herself.

"Oh, Dickon! Dickon!" she said. "I'm so happy I can scarcely breathe!"

Seeing him talking to a stranger, the little bushy-tailed animal rose from its place under the tree and came to him, and the rook, cawing once, flew down from its branch and settled quietly on his shoulder.

"This is th' little fox cub," he said, rubbing the little reddish animal's head. "It's named Captain. An' this here's Soot. Soot he flew across th' moor with me an' Captain he run same as if th' hounds had been after him. They both felt same as I did."

Neither of the creatures looked as if he were the least afraid of Mary. When Dickon began to walk about, Soot stayed on his shoulder and Captain trotted quietly close to his side.

"See here!" said Dickon. "See how these has pushed up, an' these an' these! An' Eh! look at these here!"

He threw himself upon his knees and Mary went down beside him. They had come upon a whole clump of crocuses burst into purple and orange and gold. Mary bent her face down and kissed and kissed them.

"You never kiss a person in that way," she said when she lifted her head. "Flowers are so different."

He looked puzzled but smiled.

"Eh!" he said, "I've kissed mother many a time that way when I come in from th' moor after a day's roamin' an' she stood there at th' door in th' sun, lookin' so glad an' comfortable."

They ran from one part of the garden to another and found so many wonders that they were obliged to remind themselves that they must whisper or speak low. He showed her swelling leaf-buds on rose branches which had seemed dead. He showed her ten thousand new green points pushing through the mould. They put their eager young noses close to the earth and sniffed its warmed springtime breathing; they dug and pulled and laughed low with rapture until Mistress Mary's hair was as tumbled as Dickon's and her cheeks were almost as poppy red as his.

There was every joy on earth in the secret garden that morning, and in the midst of them came a delight more delightful than all, because it was more wonderful. Swiftly something flew across the wall and darted through the trees to a close grown corner, a little flare of red-breasted bird with something hanging from its beak. Dickon stood quite still and put his hand on Mary almost as if they had suddenly found themselves laughing in a church.

"We munnot stir," he whispered in broad Yorkshire. "We munnot scarce breathe. I knowed he was mate-huntin' when I seed him last. It's Ben Weatherstaff's robin. He's buildin' his nest. He'll stay here if us don't flight him."

They settled down softly upon the grass and sat there without moving.

"Us mustn't seem as if us was watchin' him too close," said Dickon. "He'd be out with us for good if he got th' notion us was interferin' now. He'll be a good bit different till all this is over. He's settin' up housekeepin'. He'll be shyer an' readier to take things ill. He's got no time for visitin' an' gossipin'. Us must keep still a bit an' try to look as if us was grass an' trees an' bushes. Then when he's got used to seein' us I'll chirp a bit an' he'll know us'll not be in his way."

Mistress Mary was not at all sure that she knew, as Dickon seemed to, how to try to look like grass and trees and bushes. But he had said the queer thing as if it were the simplest and most natural thing in the world, and she felt it must be quite easy to him, and indeed she watched him for a few minutes carefully, wondering if it was possible for him to quietly turn green and put out branches and leaves. But he only sat wonderfully still, and when he spoke dropped his voice to such a softness that it was curious that she could hear him, but she could.

"It's part o' th' springtime, this nest buildin' is," he said. "I warrant it's been goin' on in th' same way every year since th' world was begun. They've got their way o' thinkin' and doin' things an' a body had better not meddle. You can lose a friend in springtime easier than any other season if you're too curious."

"If we talk about him I can't help looking at him," Mary said as softly as possible. "We must talk of something else. There is something I want to tell you."

"He'll like it better if us talks o' somethin' else," said Dickon. "What is it tha's got to tell me?"

"Well—do you know about Colin?" she whispered.

He turned his head to look at her.

"What does tha' know about him?" he asked.

"I've seen him. I have been to talk to him every day this week.

He wants me to come. He says I'm making him forget about being ill and dying," answered Mary.

Dickon looked actually relieved as soon as the surprise died away from his round face.

"I am glad o' that," he exclaimed. "I'm right down glad. It makes me easier. I knowed I must say nothin' about him an' I don't like havin' to hide things."

"Don't you like hiding the garden?" said Mary.

"I'll never tell about it," he answered. "But I says to mother, 'Mother,' I says, 'I got a secret to keep. It's not a bad 'un, tha' knows that. It's no worse than hidin' where a bird's nest is. Tha' doesn't mind it, does tha'?'"

Mary always wanted to hear about mother.

"What did she say?" she asked, not at all afraid to hear.

Dickon grinned sweet-temperedly.

"It was just like her, what she said," he answered. "She give my head a bit of a rub an' laughed an' she says, 'Eh, lad, tha' can have all th' secrets tha' likes. I've knowed thee twelve year'.'"

"How did you know about Colin?" asked Mary.

"Everybody as knowed about Mester Craven knowed there was a little lad as was like to be a cripple, an' they knowed Mester Craven didn't like him to be talked about. Folks is sorry for Mester Craven because Mrs. Craven was such a pretty young lady an' they was so fond of each other. Mrs. Medlock stops in our cottage whenever she goes to Thwaite an' she doesn't mind talkin' to mother before us children, because she knows us has been brought up to be trusty. How did tha' find out about him? Martha was in fine trouble th' last time she came home. She said tha'd heard him frettin' an' tha' was askin' questions an' she didn't know what to say."

Mary told him her story about the midnight wuthering of the wind which had wakened her and about the faint far-off sounds of the complaining voice which had led her down the dark corridors with her candle and had ended with her opening of the door of the dimly lighted room with the carven four-posted bed in the corner. When she described the small ivory-white face and the strange black-rimmed eyes Dickon shook his head.

"Them's just like his mother's eyes, only hers was always laughin', they say," he said. "They say as Mr. Craven can't bear to see him when he's awake an' it's because his eyes is so like his mother's an' yet looks so different in his miserable bit of a face."

"Do you think he wants him to die?" whispered Mary.

"No, but he wishes he'd never been born. Mother she says that's th' worst thing on earth for a child. Them as is not wanted scarce ever thrives. Mester Craven he'd buy anythin' as money could buy for th' poor lad but he'd like to forget as he's on earth. For one thing, he's afraid he'll look at him some day and find he's growed hunchback."

"Colin's so afraid of it himself that he won't sit up," said Mary. "He says he's always thinking that if he should feel a lump coming he should go crazy and scream himself to death."

"Eh! he oughtn't to lie there thinkin' things like that," said Dickon. "No lad could get well as thought them sort o' things."

The fox was lying on the grass close by him looking up to ask for a pat now and then, and Dickon bent down and rubbed his neck softly and thought a few minutes in silence. Presently he lifted his head and looked round the garden.

"When first we got in here," he said, "it seemed like everything was gray. Look round now and tell me if tha' doesn't see a difference."

Mary looked and caught her breath a little.

"Why!" she cried, "the gray wall is changing. It is as if a green mist were creeping over it. It's almost like a green gauze veil."

"Aye," said Dickon. "An' it'll be greener and greener till th' gray's all gone. Can tha' guess what I was thinkin'?"

"I know it was something nice," said Mary eagerly. "I believe it was something about Colin."

"I was thinkin' that if he was out here he wouldn't be watchin' for lumps to grow on his back; he'd be watchin' for buds to break on th' rose-bushes, an' he'd likely be healthier," explained Dickon.

"I was wonderin' if us could ever get him in th' humor to come out here an' lie under th' trees in his carriage."

"I've been wondering that myself. I've thought of it almost every time I've talked to him," said Mary. "I've wondered if he could keep a secret and I've wondered if we could bring him here without any one seeing us. I thought perhaps you could push his carriage. The doctor said he must have fresh air and if he wants us to take him out no one dare disobey him. He won't go out for other people and perhaps they will be glad if he will go out with us. He could order the gardeners to keep away so they wouldn't find out."

Dickon was thinking very hard as he scratched Captain's back.

"It'd be good for him, I'll warrant," he said. "Us'd not be thinkin' he'd better never been born. Us'd be just two children watchin' a garden grow, an' he'd be another. Two lads an' a little lass just lookin' on at th' springtime. I warrant it'd be better than doctor's stuff."

"He's been lying in his room so long and he's always been so afraid of his back that it has made him queer," said Mary. "He knows a good many things out of books but he doesn't know anything else. He says he has been too ill to notice things and he hates going out of doors and hates gardens and gardeners. But he likes to hear about this garden because it is a secret. I daren't tell him much but he said he wanted to see it."

"Us'll have him out here sometime for sure," said Dickon. "I could push his carriage well enough. Has tha' noticed how th' robin an' his mate has been workin' while we've been sittin' here? Look at him perched on that branch wonderin' where it'd be best to put that twig he's got in his beak."

He made one of his low whistling calls and the robin turned his head and looked at him inquiringly, still holding his twig. Dickon spoke to him as Ben Weatherstaff did, but Dickon's tone was one of friendly advice.

"Wheres'ever tha' puts it," he said, "it'll be all right. Tha' knew how to build tha' nest before tha' came out o' th' egg. Get on with thee, lad. Tha'st got no time to lose."

"Oh, I do like to hear you talk to him!" Mary said, laughing delightedly. "Ben Weatherstaff scolds him and makes fun of him, and he hops about and looks as if he understood every word, and I know he likes it. Ben Weatherstaff says he is so conceited he would rather have stones thrown at him than not be noticed."

Dickon laughed too and went on talking.

"Tha' knows us won't trouble thee," he said to the robin. "Us is near bein' wild things ourselves. Us is nest buildin' too, bless thee. Look out tha' doesn't tell on us."

And though the robin did not answer, because his beak was occupied, Mary knew that when he flew away with his twig to his own corner of the garden the darkness of his dew-bright eye meant that he would not tell their secret for the world.

to do life to each word within him," Mary said, laughing
delightedly. Then "really I told scold him and makes fun of him
and . . hope about his looks . . . I'd understand every word, and
I . . . nice as he is at then we all understand . . . so expected to
even I rather have smiled once . . . that him than me be more . . .
and on myself to endless . . . up falling.

"I do know his worst quality there," he said trust trouble at all
near one . . . will things ourselves. "at is best holding face bless these . . .
I said of all I'd gained to me at . . .

And though she felt, she did not answer, because his eyes were
mer had Mary . . . new that when he flew away with his love to his
dispose and . . . of the arms and the abandons . . . of life, she, the his . . .
meant that he would not yet until . . . rest to the world.

CHAPTER 16
"I WON'T!" SAID MARY

They found a great deal to do that morning and Mary was late in returning to the house and was also in such a hurry to get back to her work that she quite forgot Colin until the last moment.

"Tell Colin that I can't come and see him yet," she said to Martha. "I'm very busy in the garden."

Martha looked rather frightened.

"Eh! Miss Mary," she said, "it may put him all out of humor when I tell him that."

But Mary was not as afraid of him as other people were and she was not a self-sacrificing person.

"I can't stay," she answered. "Dickon's waiting for me;" and she ran away.

The afternoon was even lovelier and busier than the morning had been. Already nearly all the weeds were cleared out of the garden and most of the roses and trees had been pruned or dug about. Dickon had brought a spade of his own and he had taught Mary to use all her tools, so that by this time it was plain that though the lovely wild place was not likely to become a "gardener's garden" it would be a wilderness of growing things before the springtime was over.

"There'll be apple blossoms an' cherry blossoms overhead," Dickon said, working away with all his might. "An' there'll be peach an' plum trees in bloom against th' walls, an' th' grass'll be a carpet o' flowers."

The little fox and the rook were as happy and busy as they were, and the robin and his mate flew backward and forward like tiny streaks of lightning. Sometimes the rook flapped his black

wings and soared away over the tree-tops in the park. Each time
he came back and perched near Dickon and cawed several times as
if he were relating his adventures, and Dickon talked to him just as
he had talked to the robin. Once when Dickon was so busy that he
did not answer him at first, Soot flew on to his shoulders and gently tweaked his ear with his large beak. When Mary wanted to rest
a little Dickon sat down with her under a tree and once he took
his pipe out of his pocket and played the soft strange little notes
and two squirrels appeared on the wall and looked and listened.

"Tha's a good bit stronger than tha' was," Dickon said, looking at her as she was digging. "Tha's beginning to look different,
for sure."

Mary was glowing with exercise and good spirits.

"I'm getting fatter and fatter every day," she said quite exultantly. "Mrs. Medlock will have to get me some bigger dresses.
Martha says my hair is growing thicker. It isn't so flat and stringy."

The sun was beginning to set and sending deep gold-colored
rays slanting under the trees when they parted.

"It'll be fine to-morrow," said Dickon. "I'll be at work by
sunrise."

"So will I," said Mary.

She ran back to the house as quickly as her feet would carry
her. She wanted to tell Colin about Dickon's fox cub and the rook
and about what the springtime had been doing. She felt sure he
would like to hear. So it was not very pleasant when she opened
the door of her room, to see Martha standing waiting for her with
a doleful face.

"What is the matter?" she asked. "What did Colin say when
you told him I couldn't come?"

"Eh!" said Martha, "I wish tha'd gone. He was nigh goin' into
one o' his tantrums. There's been a nice to do all afternoon to
keep him quiet. He would watch the clock all th' time."

Mary's lips pinched themselves together. She was no more
used to considering other people than Colin was and she saw no

reason why an ill-tempered boy should interfere with the thing she liked best. She knew nothing about the pitifulness of people who had been ill and nervous and who did not know that they could control their tempers and need not make other people ill and nervous, too. When she had had a headache in India she had done her best to see that everybody else also had a headache or something quite as bad. And she felt she was quite right; but of course now she felt that Colin was quite wrong.

He was not on his sofa when she went into his room. He was lying flat on his back in bed and he did not turn his head toward her as she came in. This was a bad beginning and Mary marched up to him with her stiff manner.

"Why didn't you get up?" she said.

"I did get up this morning when I thought you were coming," he answered, without looking at her. "I made them put me back in bed this afternoon. My back ached and my head ached and I was tired. Why didn't you come?"

"I was working in the garden with Dickon," said Mary.

Colin frowned and condescended to look at her.

"I won't let that boy come here if you go and stay with him instead of coming to talk to me," he said.

Mary flew into a fine passion. She could fly into a passion without making a noise. She just grew sour and obstinate and did not care what happened.

"If you send Dickon away, I'll never come into this room again!" she retorted.

"You'll have to if I want you," said Colin.

"I won't!" said Mary.

"I'll make you," said Colin. "They shall drag you in."

"Shall they, Mr. Rajah!" said Mary fiercely. "They may drag me in but they can't make me talk when they get me here. I'll sit and clench my teeth and never tell you one thing. I won't even look at you. I'll stare at the floor!"

They were a nice agreeable pair as they glared at each other. If they had been two little street boys they would have sprung at each other and had a rough-and-tumble fight. As it was, they did the next thing to it.

"You are a selfish thing!" cried Colin.

"What are you?" said Mary. "Selfish people always say that. Any one is selfish who doesn't do what they want. You're more selfish than I am. You're the most selfish boy I ever saw."

"I'm not!" snapped Colin. "I'm not as selfish as your fine Dickon is! He keeps you playing in the dirt when he knows I am all by myself. He's selfish, if you like!"

Mary's eyes flashed fire.

"He's nicer than any other boy that ever lived!" she said. "He's—he's like an angel!" It might sound rather silly to say that but she did not care.

"A nice angel!" Colin sneered ferociously. "He's a common cottage boy off the moor!"

"He's better than a common Rajah!" retorted Mary. "He's a thousand times better!"

Because she was the stronger of the two she was beginning to get the better of him. The truth was that he had never had a fight with any one like himself in his life and, upon the whole, it was rather good for him, though neither he nor Mary knew anything about that. He turned his head on his pillow and shut his eyes and a big tear was squeezed out and ran down his cheek. He was beginning to feel pathetic and sorry for himself—not for any one else.

"I'm not as selfish as you, because I'm always ill, and I'm sure there is a lump coming on my back," he said. "And I am going to die besides."

"You're not!" contradicted Mary unsympathetically.

He opened his eyes quite wide with indignation. He had never heard such a thing said before. He was at once furious and slightly pleased, if a person could be both at the same time.

"I'm not?" he cried. "I am! You know I am! Everybody says so."

"I don't believe it!" said Mary sourly. "You just say that to make people sorry. I believe you're proud of it. I don't believe it! If you were a nice boy it might be true—but you're too nasty!"

In spite of his invalid back Colin sat up in bed in quite a healthy rage.

"Get out of the room!" he shouted and he caught hold of his pillow and threw it at her. He was not strong enough to throw it far and it only fell at her feet, but Mary's face looked as pinched as a nutcracker.

"I'm going," she said. "And I won't come back!"

She walked to the door and when she reached it she turned round and spoke again.

"I was going to tell you all sorts of nice things," she said. "Dickon brought his fox and his rook and I was going to tell you all about them. Now I won't tell you a single thing!"

She marched out of the door and closed it behind her, and there to her great astonishment she found the trained nurse standing as if she had been listening and, amazing still—she was laughing. She was a big handsome young woman who ought not to have been a trained nurse at all, as she could not bear invalids and she was always making excuses to leave Colin to Martha or any one else who would take her place. Mary had never liked her, and she simply stood and gazed up at her as she stood giggling into her handkerchief.

"What are you laughing at?" she asked her.

"At you two young ones," said the nurse. "It's the best thing that could happen to the sickly pampered thing to have some one to stand up to him that's as spoiled as himself;" and she laughed into her handkerchief again. "If he'd had a young vixen of a sister to fight with it would have been the saving of him."

"Is he going to die?"

"I don't know and I don't care," said the nurse. "Hysterics and temper are half what ails him."

"What are hysterics?" asked Mary.

"You'll find out if you work him into a tantrum after this—but at any rate you've given him something to have hysterics about, and I'm glad of it."

Mary went back to her room not feeling at all as she had felt when she had come in from the garden. She was cross and disappointed but not at all sorry for Colin. She had looked forward to telling him a great many things and she had meant to try to make up her mind whether it would be safe to trust him with the great secret. She had been beginning to think it would be, but now she had changed her mind entirely. She would never tell him and he could stay in his room and never get any fresh air and die if he liked! It would serve him right! She felt so sour and unrelenting that for a few minutes she almost forgot about Dickon and the green veil creeping over the world and the soft wind blowing down from the moor.

Martha was waiting for her and the trouble in her face had been temporarily replaced by interest and curiosity. There was a wooden box on the table and its cover had been removed and revealed that it was full of neat packages.

"Mr. Craven sent it to you," said Martha. "It looks as if it had picture-books in it."

Mary remembered what he had asked her the day she had gone to his room. "Do you want anything—dolls—toys—books?" She opened the package wondering if he had sent a doll, and also wondering what she should do with it if he had. But he had not sent one. There were several beautiful books such as Colin had, and two of them were about gardens and were full of pictures. There were two or three games and there was a beautiful little writing-case with a gold monogram on it and a gold pen and inkstand.

Everything was so nice that her pleasure began to crowd her anger out of her mind. She had not expected him to remember her at all and her hard little heart grew quite warm.

"I can write better than I can print," she said, "and the first thing I shall write with that pen will be a letter to tell him I am much obliged."

If she had been friends with Colin she would have run to show him her presents at once, and they would have looked at the pictures and read some of the gardening books and perhaps tried playing the games, and he would have enjoyed himself so much he would never once have thought he was going to die or have put his hand on his spine to see if there was a lump coming. He had a way of doing that which she could not bear. It gave her an uncomfortable frightened feeling because he always looked so frightened himself. He said that if he felt even quite a little lump some day he should know his hunch had begun to grow. Something he had heard Mrs. Medlock whispering to the nurse had given him the idea and he had thought over it in secret until it was quite firmly fixed in his mind. Mrs. Medlock had said his father's back had begun to show its crookedness in that way when he was a child. He had never told any one but Mary that most of his "tantrums" as they called them grew out of his hysterical hidden fear. Mary had been sorry for him when he had told her.

"He always began to think about it when he was cross or tired," she said to herself. "And he has been cross to-day. Perhaps—perhaps he has been thinking about it all afternoon."

She stood still, looking down at the carpet and thinking.

"I said I would never go back again—" she hesitated, knitting her brows—"but perhaps, just perhaps, I will go and see—if he wants me—in the morning. Perhaps he'll try to throw his pillow at me again, but—I think—I'll go."

CHAPTER 17
A TANTRUM

She had got up very early in the morning and had worked hard in the garden and she was tired and sleepy, so as soon as Martha had brought her supper and she had eaten it, she was glad to go to bed. As she laid her head on the pillow she murmured to herself:

"I'll go out before breakfast and work with Dickon and then afterward—I believe—I'll go to see him."

She thought it was the middle of the night when she was wakened by such dreadful sounds that she jumped out of bed in an instant. What was it—what was it? The next minute she felt quite sure she knew. Doors were opened and shut and there were hurrying feet in the corridors and some one was crying and screaming at the same time, screaming and crying in a horrible way.

"It's Colin," she said. "He's having one of those tantrums the nurse called hysterics. How awful it sounds."

As she listened to the sobbing screams she did not wonder that people were so frightened that they gave him his own way in everything rather than hear them. She put her hands over her ears and felt sick and shivering.

"I don't know what to do. I don't know what to do," she kept saying. "I can't bear it."

Once she wondered if he would stop if she dared go to him and then she remembered how he had driven her out of the room and thought that perhaps the sight of her might make him worse. Even when she pressed her hands more tightly over her ears she could not keep the awful sounds out. She hated them so and was

so terrified by them that suddenly they began to make her angry
and she felt as if she should like to fly into a tantrum herself and
frighten him as he was frightening her. She was not used to any
one's tempers but her own. She took her hands from her ears and
sprang up and stamped her foot.

"He ought to be stopped! Somebody ought to make him stop!
Somebody ought to beat him!" she cried out.

Just then she heard feet almost running down the corridor and
her door opened and the nurse came in. She was not laughing
now by any means. She even looked rather pale.

"He's worked himself into hysterics," she said in a great hurry.
"He'll do himself harm. No one can do anything with him. You
come and try, like a good child. He likes you."

"He turned me out of the room this morning," said Mary,
stamping her foot with excitement.

The stamp rather pleased the nurse. The truth was that she
had been afraid she might find Mary crying and hiding her head
under the bedclothes.

"That's right," she said. "You're in the right humor. You go and
scold him. Give him something new to think of. Do go, child, as
quick as ever you can."

It was not until afterward that Mary realized that the thing had
been funny as well as dreadful—that it was funny that all the
grown-up people were so frightened that they came to a little girl
just because they guessed she was almost as bad as Colin himself.

She flew along the corridor and the nearer she got to the
screams the higher her temper mounted. She felt quite wicked by
the time she reached the door. She slapped it open with her hand
and ran across the room to the four-posted bed.

"You stop!" she almost shouted. "You stop! I hate you! Everybody hates you! I wish everybody would run out of the house
and let you scream yourself to death! You *will* scream yourself to
death in a minute, and I wish you would!"

A nice sympathetic child could neither have thought nor said
such things, but it just happened that the shock of hearing them

was the best possible thing for this hysterical boy whom no one had ever dared to restrain or contradict.

He had been lying on his face beating his pillow with his hands and he actually almost jumped around, he turned so quickly at the sound of the furious little voice. His face looked dreadful, white and red and swollen, and he was gasping and choking; but savage little Mary did not care an atom.

"If you scream another scream," she said, "I'll scream too—and I can scream louder than you can and I'll frighten you, I'll frighten you!"

He actually had stopped screaming because she had startled him so. The scream which had been coming almost choked him. The tears were streaming down his face and he shook all over.

"I can't stop!" he gasped and sobbed. "I can't—I can't!"

"You can!" shouted Mary. "Half that ails you is hysterics and temper—just hysterics—hysterics—hysterics!" and she stamped each time she said it.

"I felt the lump—I felt it," choked out Colin. "I knew I should. I shall have a hunch on my back and then I shall die," and he began to writhe again and turned on his face and sobbed and wailed but he didn't scream.

"You didn't feel a lump!" contradicted Mary fiercely. "If you did it was only a hysterical lump. Hysterics makes lumps. There's nothing the matter with your horrid back—nothing but hysterics! Turn over and let me look at it!"

She liked the word "hysterics" and felt somehow as if it had an effect on him. He was probably like herself and had never heard it before.

"Nurse," she commanded, "come here and show me his back this minute!"

The nurse, Mrs. Medlock and Martha had been standing huddled together near the door staring at her, their mouths half open. All three had gasped with fright more than once. The nurse came forward as if she were half afraid. Colin was heaving with great breathless sobs.

"Perhaps he—he won't let me," she hesitated in a low voice.

Colin heard her, however, and he gasped out between two sobs: "Sh-show her! She-she'll see then!"

It was a poor thin back to look at when it was bared. Every rib could be counted and every joint of the spine, though Mistress Mary did not count them as she bent over and examined them with a solemn savage little face. She looked so sour and old-fashioned that the nurse turned her head aside to hide the twitching of her mouth. There was just a minute's silence, for even Colin tried to hold his breath while Mary looked up and down his spine, and down and up, as intently as if she had been the great doctor from London.

"There's not a single lump there!" she said at last. "There's not a lump as big as a pin—except backbone lumps, and you can only feel them because you're thin. I've got backbone lumps myself, and they used to stick out as much as yours do, until I began to get fatter, and I am not fat enough yet to hide them. There's not a lump as big as a pin! If you ever say there is again, I shall laugh!"

No one but Colin himself knew what effect those crossly spoken childish words had on him. If he had ever had any one to talk to about his secret terrors—if he had ever dared to let himself ask questions—if he had had childish companions and had not lain on his back in the huge closed house, breathing an atmosphere heavy with the fears of people who were most of them ignorant and tired of him, he would have found out that most of his fright and illness was created by himself. But he had lain and thought of himself and his aches and weariness for hours and days and months and years. And now that an angry unsympathetic little girl insisted obstinately that he was not as ill as he thought he was he actually felt as if she might be speaking the truth.

"I didn't know," ventured the nurse, "that he thought he had a lump on his spine. His back is weak because he won't try to sit up. I could have told him there was no lump there."

Colin gulped and turned his face a little to look at her.

"C-could you?" he said pathetically.

"Yes, sir."

"There!" said Mary, and she gulped too.

Colin turned on his face again and but for his long-drawn broken breaths, which were the dying down of his storm of sobbing, he lay still for a minute, though great tears streamed down his face and wet the pillow. Actually the tears meant that a curious great relief had come to him. Presently he turned and looked at the nurse again and strangely enough he was not like a Rajah at all as he spoke to her.

"Do you think—I could—live to grow up?" he said.

The nurse was neither clever nor soft-hearted but she could repeat some of the London doctor's words.

"You probably will if you will do what you are told to do and not give way to your temper, and stay out a great deal in the fresh air."

Colin's tantrum had passed and he was weak and worn out with crying and this perhaps made him feel gentle. He put out his hand a little toward Mary, and I am glad to say that, her own tantrum having passed, she was softened too and met him halfway with her hand, so that it was a sort of making up.

"I'll—I'll go out with you, Mary," he said. "I shan't hate fresh air if we can find—" He remembered just in time to stop himself from saying "if we can find the secret garden" and he ended, "I shall like to go out with you if Dickon will come and push my chair. I do so want to see Dickon and the fox and the crow."

The nurse remade the tumbled bed and shook and straightened the pillows. Then she made Colin a cup of beef tea and gave a cup to Mary, who really was very glad to get it after her excitement. Mrs. Medlock and Martha gladly slipped away, and after everything was neat and calm and in order the nurse looked as if she would very gladly slip away also. She was a healthy young woman who resented being robbed of her sleep and she yawned quite openly as she looked at Mary, who had pushed her big footstool close to the four-posted bed and was holding Colin's hand.

"You must go back and get your sleep out," she said. "He'll drop off after a while—if he's not too upset. Then I'll lie down myself in the next room."

"Would you like me to sing you that song I learned from my Ayah?" Mary whispered to Colin.

His hand pulled hers gently and he turned his tired eyes on her appealingly.

"Oh, yes!" he answered. "It's such a soft song. I shall go to sleep in a minute."

"I will put him to sleep," Mary said to the yawning nurse. "You can go if you like."

"Well," said the nurse, with an attempt at reluctance. "If he doesn't go to sleep in half an hour you must call me."

"Very well," answered Mary.

The nurse was out of the room in a minute and as soon as she was gone Colin pulled Mary's hand again.

"I almost told," he said; "but I stopped myself in time. I won't talk and I'll go to sleep, but you said you had a whole lot of nice things to tell me. Have you—do you think you have found out anything at all about the way into the secret garden?"

Mary looked at his poor little tired face and swollen eyes and her heart relented.

"Ye-es," she answered, "I think I have. And if you will go to sleep I will tell you to-morrow."

His hand quite trembled.

"Oh, Mary!" he said. "Oh, Mary! If I could get into it I think I should live to grow up! Do you suppose that instead of singing the Ayah song—you could just tell me softly as you did that first day what you imagine it looks like inside? I am sure it will make me go to sleep."

"Yes," answered Mary. "Shut your eyes."

He closed his eyes and lay quite still and she held his hand and began to speak very slowly and in a very low voice.

"I think it has been left alone so long—that it has grown all into a lovely tangle. I think the roses have climbed and climbed and climbed until they hang from the branches and walls and creep over the ground—almost like a strange gray mist. Some of them have died but many—are alive and when the summer comes there will be curtains and fountains of roses. I think the ground is full of daffodils and snowdrops and lilies and iris working their way out of the dark. Now the spring has begun—perhaps—perhaps—"

The soft drone of her voice was making him stiller and stiller and she saw it and went on.

"Perhaps they are coming up through the grass—perhaps there are clusters of purple crocuses and gold ones—even now. Perhaps the leaves are beginning to break out and uncurl—and perhaps—the gray is changing and a green gauze veil is creeping—and creeping over—everything. And the birds are coming to look at it—because it is—so safe and still. And perhaps—perhaps—perhaps—" very softly and slowly indeed, "the robin has found a mate—and is building a nest."

And Colin was asleep.

and climbed until they rang it, made the echoes and well, and
keep on the mound—then—like a charge and made some of
them have died, but night ... like that who ... the sunlight
some dear, ... but increase, and remains ... all gone, I think, to
ground ... full of orchids, and snowdrops ... and lilies, and his
... and the farewell out of the trees. Now it's all but begun—
perhaps ... this year.

The soft drone of her voice was gentle but soft ... and still,
and she saw it and went on.

"Twilight, they are coming up, though the other ... perhaps
there are chances of purple ... and cold wide—. Go now.
Perhaps the roses are beginning to break out, and the tree, but
perhaps ... they've clinging and a green ... look like it, then
too—and creeping over ... wording. And the birds in soft low ...
chook in ... distance. It ... sad and still, At first maybe up
may ... of up ... very soft and slowly upward, the mist has
rounded mist ... and a ... a nest—

And ... the water was clear ..."

CHAPTER 18
"THA' MUNNOT WASTE NO TIME"

Of course Mary did not waken early the next morning. She slept late because she was tired, and when Martha brought her breakfast she told her that though Colin was quite quiet he was ill and feverish as he always was after he had worn himself out with a fit of crying. Mary ate her breakfast slowly as she listened.

"He says he wishes tha' would please go and see him as soon as tha' can," Martha said. "It's queer what a fancy he's took to thee. Tha' did give it him last night for sure—didn't tha'? Nobody else would have dared to do it. Eh! poor lad! He's been spoiled till salt won't save him. Mother says as th' two worst things as can happen to a child is never to have his own way—or always to have it. She doesn't know which is th' worst. Tha' was in a fine temper tha'self, too. But he says to me when I went into his room, 'Please ask Miss Mary if she'll please come an' talk to me?' Think o' him saying please! Will you go, Miss?"

"I'll run and see Dickon first," said Mary. "No, I'll go and see Colin first and tell him—I know what I'll tell him," with a sudden inspiration.

She had her hat on when she appeared in Colin's room and for a second he looked disappointed. He was in bed and his face was pitifully white and there were dark circles round his eyes.

"I'm glad you came," he said. "My head aches and I ache all over because I'm so tired. Are you going somewhere?"

Mary went and leaned against his bed.

"I won't be long," she said. "I'm going to Dickon, but I'll come back. Colin, it's—it's something about the secret garden."

His whole face brightened and a little color came into it.

"Oh! is it!" he cried out. "I dreamed about it all night. I heard you say something about gray changing into green, and I dreamed I was standing in a place all filled with trembling little green leaves—and there were birds on nests everywhere and they looked so soft and still. I'll lie and think about it until you come back."

In five minutes Mary was with Dickon in their garden. The fox and the crow were with him again and this time he had brought two tame squirrels.

"I came over on the pony this mornin'," he said. "Eh! he is a good little chap—Jump is! I brought these two in my pockets. This here one he's called Nut an' this here other one's called Shell."

When he said "Nut" one squirrel leaped on to his right shoulder and when he said "Shell" the other one leaped on to his left shoulder.

When they sat down on the grass with Captain curled at their feet, Soot solemnly listening on a tree and Nut and Shell nosing about close to them, it seemed to Mary that it would be scarcely bearable to leave such delightfulness, but when she began to tell her story somehow the look in Dickon's funny face gradually changed her mind. She could see he felt sorrier for Colin than she did. He looked up at the sky and all about him.

"Just listen to them birds—th' world seems full of 'em—all whistlin' an' pipin'," he said. "Look at 'em dartin' about, an' hearken at 'em callin' to each other. Come springtime seems like as if all th' world's callin'. The leaves is uncurlin' so you can see 'em—an', my word, th' nice smells there is about!" sniffing with his happy turned-up nose. "An' that poor lad lyin' shut up an' seein' so little that he gets to thinkin' o' things as sets him screamin'. Eh! my! we mun get him out here—we mun get him watchin' an' listenin' an' sniffin' up th' air an' get him just soaked through wi' sunshine. An' we munnot lose no time about it."

When he was very much interested he often spoke quite broad Yorkshire though at other times he tried to modify his dialect so that Mary could better understand. But she loved his broad

Yorkshire and had in fact been trying to learn to speak it herself. So she spoke a little now.

"Aye, that we mun," she said (which meant "Yes, indeed, we must"). "I'll tell thee what us'll do first," she proceeded, and Dickon grinned, because when the little wench tried to twist her tongue into speaking Yorkshire it amused him very much. "He's took a graidely fancy to thee. He wants to see thee and he wants to see Soot an' Captain. When I go back to the house to talk to him I'll ax him if tha' canna' come an' see him tomorrow mornin'—an' bring tha' creatures wi' thee—an' then—in a bit, when there's more leaves out, an' happen a bud or two, we'll get him in his chair an' we'll bring him here an' show him everything."

When she stopped she was quite proud of herself. She had never made a long speech in Yorkshire before and she had remembered very well.

"Tha' mun talk a bit o' Yorkshire like that to Mester Colin," Dickon chuckled. "Tha'll make him laugh an' there's nowt as good for ill folk as laughin' is. Mother says she believes as half a hour's good laugh every mornin' 'ud cure a chap as was makin' ready for typhus fever."

"I'm going to talk Yorkshire to him this very day," said Mary, chuckling herself.

The garden had reached the time when every day and every night it seemed as if Magicians were passing through it drawing loveliness out of the earth and the boughs with wands. It was hard to go away and leave it all, particularly as Nut had actually crept on to her dress and Shell had scrambled down the trunk of the apple-tree they sat under and stayed there looking at her with inquiring eyes. But she went back to the house and when she sat down close to Colin's bed he began to sniff as Dickon did though not in such an experienced way.

"You smell like flowers and—and fresh things," he cried out quite joyously. "What is it you smell of? It's cool and warm and sweet all at the same time."

"It's th' wind from th' moor," said Mary. "It comes o' sittin' on th' grass under a tree wi' Dickon an' wi' Captain an' Soot an' Nut an' Shell. It's th' springtime an' out o' doors an' sunshine as smells so graidely."

She said it as broadly as she could, and you do not know how broadly Yorkshire sounds until you have heard some one speak it. Colin began to laugh.

"What are you doing?" he said. "I never heard you talk like that before. How funny it sounds."

"I'm givin' thee a bit o' Yorkshire," answered Mary triumphantly. "I canna' talk as graidely as Dickon an' Martha can but tha' sees I can shape a bit. Doesn't tha' understand a bit o' Yorkshire when tha' hears it? An' tha' a Yorkshire lad thysel' bred an' born! Eh! I wonder tha'rt not ashamed o' thy face."

And then she began to laugh too and they both laughed until they could not stop themselves and they laughed until the room echoed and Mrs. Medlock opening the door to come in drew back into the corridor and stood listening amazed.

"Well, upon my word!" she said, speaking rather broad Yorkshire herself because there was no one to hear her and she was so astonished. "Whoever heard th' like! Whoever on earth would ha' thought it!"

There was so much to talk about. It seemed as if Colin could never hear enough of Dickon and Captain and Soot and Nut and Shell and the pony whose name was Jump. Mary had run round into the wood with Dickon to see Jump. He was a tiny little shaggy moor pony with thick locks hanging over his eyes and with a pretty face and a nuzzling velvet nose. He was rather thin with living on moor grass but he was as tough and wiry as if the muscle in his little legs had been made of steel springs. He had lifted his head and whinnied softly the moment he saw Dickon and he had trotted up to him and put his head across his shoulder and then Dickon had talked into his ear and Jump had talked back in odd little whinnies and puffs and snorts. Dickon had made him give Mary his small front hoof and kiss her on her cheek with his velvet muzzle.

"Does he really understand everything Dickon says?" Colin asked.

"It seems as if he does," answered Mary. "Dickon says anything will understand if you're friends with it for sure, but you have to be friends for sure."

Colin lay quiet a little while and his strange gray eyes seemed to be staring at the wall, but Mary saw he was thinking.

"I wish I was friends with things," he said at last, "but I'm not. I never had anything to be friends with, and I can't bear people."

"Can't you bear me?" asked Mary.

"Yes, I can," he answered. "It's very funny but I even like you."

"Ben Weatherstaff said I was like him," said Mary. "He said he'd warrant we'd both got the same nasty tempers. I think you are like him too. We are all three alike—you and I and Ben Weatherstaff. He said we were neither of us much to look at and we were as sour as we looked. But I don't feel as sour as I used to before I knew the robin and Dickon."

"Did you feel as if you hated people?"

"Yes," answered Mary without any affectation. "I should have detested you if I had seen you before I saw the robin and Dickon."

Colin put out his thin hand and touched her.

"Mary," he said, "I wish I hadn't said what I did about sending Dickon away. I hated you when you said he was like an angel and I laughed at you but—but perhaps he is."

"Well, it was rather funny to say it," she admitted frankly, "because his nose does turn up and he has a big mouth and his clothes have patches all over them and he talks broad Yorkshire, but—but if an angel did come to Yorkshire and live on the moor—if there was a Yorkshire angel—I believe he'd understand the green things and know how to make them grow and he would know how to talk to the wild creatures as Dickon does and they'd know he was friends for sure."

"I shouldn't mind Dickon looking at me," said Colin; "I want to see him."

"I'm glad you said that," answered Mary, "because—because—"

Quite suddenly it came into her mind that this was the minute to tell him. Colin knew something new was coming.

"Because what?" he cried eagerly.

Mary was so anxious that she got up from her stool and came to him and caught hold of both his hands.

"Can I trust you? I trusted Dickon because birds trusted him. Can I trust you—for sure—*for sure*?" she implored.

Her face was so solemn that he almost whispered his answer.

"Yes—yes!"

"Well, Dickon will come to see you to-morrow morning, and he'll bring his creatures with him."

"Oh! Oh!" Colin cried out in delight.

"But that's not all," Mary went on, almost pale with solemn excitement. "The rest is better. There is a door into the garden. I found it. It is under the ivy on the wall."

If he had been a strong healthy boy Colin would probably have shouted "Hooray! Hooray! Hooray!" but he was weak and rather hysterical; his eyes grew bigger and bigger and he gasped for breath.

"Oh! Mary!" he cried out with a half sob. "Shall I see it? Shall I get into it? Shall I *live* to get into it?" and he clutched her hands and dragged her toward him.

"Of course you'll see it!" snapped Mary indignantly. "Of course you'll live to get into it! Don't be silly!"

And she was so un-hysterical and natural and childish that she brought him to his senses and he began to laugh at himself and a few minutes afterward she was sitting on her stool again telling him not what she imagined the secret garden to be like but what it really was, and Colin's aches and tiredness were forgotten and he was listening enraptured.

"It is just what you thought it would be," he said at last. "It sounds just as if you had really seen it. You know I said that when you told me first."

Mary hesitated about two minutes and then boldly spoke the truth.

"I had seen it—and I had been in," she said. "I found the key and got in weeks ago. But I daren't tell you—I daren't because I was so afraid I couldn't trust you—*for sure!*"

CHAPTER 19
"IT HAS COME!"

Of course Dr. Craven had been sent for the morning after Colin had had his tantrum. He was always sent for at once when such a thing occurred and he always found, when he arrived, a white shaken boy lying on his bed, sulky and still so hysterical that he was ready to break into fresh sobbing at the least word. In fact, Dr. Craven dreaded and detested the difficulties of these visits. On this occasion he was away from Misselthwaite Manor until afternoon.

"How is he?" he asked Mrs. Medlock rather irritably when he arrived. "He will break a blood-vessel in one of those fits some day. The boy is half insane with hysteria and self-indulgence."

"Well, sir," answered Mrs. Medlock, "you'll scarcely believe your eyes when you see him. That plain sour-faced child that's almost as bad as himself has just bewitched him. How she's done it there's no telling. The Lord knows she's nothing to look at and you scarcely ever hear her speak, but she did what none of us dare do. She just flew at him like a little cat last night, and stamped her feet and ordered him to stop screaming, and somehow she startled him so that he actually did stop, and this afternoon—well just come up and see, sir. It's past crediting."

The scene which Dr. Craven beheld when he entered his patient's room was indeed rather astonishing to him. As Mrs. Medlock opened the door he heard laughing and chattering. Colin was on his sofa in his dressing-gown and he was sitting up quite straight looking at a picture in one of the garden books and talking to the plain child who at the moment could scarcely be called plain at all because her face was glowing with enjoyment.

"Those long spires of blue ones—we'll have a lot of those," Colin was announcing. "They're called Del-phin-iums."

"Dickon says they're larkspurs made big and grand," cried Mistress Mary. There are clumps there already."

Then they saw Dr. Craven and stopped. Mary became quite still and Colin looked fretful.

"I am sorry to hear you were ill last night, my boy," Dr. Craven said a trifle nervously. He was rather a nervous man.

"I'm better now—much better," Colin answered, rather like a Rajah. "I'm going out in my chair in a day or two if it is fine. I want some fresh air."

Dr. Craven sat down by him and felt his pulse and looked at him curiously.

"It must be a very fine day," he said, "and you must be very careful not to tire yourself."

"Fresh air won't tire me," said the young Rajah.

As there had been occasions when this same young gentleman had shrieked aloud with rage and had insisted that fresh air would give him cold and kill him, it is not to be wondered at that his doctor felt somewhat startled.

"I thought you did not like fresh air," he said.

"I don't when I am by myself," replied the Rajah; "but my cousin is going out with me."

"And the nurse, of course?" suggested Dr. Craven.

"No, I will not have the nurse," so magnificently that Mary could not help remembering how the young native Prince had looked with his diamonds and emeralds and pearls stuck all over him and the great rubies on the small dark hand he had waved to command his servants to approach with salaams and receive his orders.

"My cousin knows how to take care of me. I am always better when she is with me. She made me better last night. A very strong boy I know will push my carriage."

Dr. Craven felt rather alarmed. If this tiresome hysterical boy should chance to get well he himself would lose all chance of inheriting Misselthwaite; but he was not an unscrupulous man, though he was a weak one, and he did not intend to let him run into actual danger.

"He must be a strong boy and a steady boy," he said. "And I must know something about him. Who is he? What is his name?"

"It's Dickon," Mary spoke up suddenly. She felt somehow that everybody who knew the moor must know Dickon. And she was right, too. She saw that in a moment Dr. Craven's serious face relaxed into a relieved smile.

"Oh, Dickon," he said. "If it is Dickon you will be safe enough. He's as strong as a moor pony, is Dickon."

"And he's trusty," said Mary. "He's th' trustiest lad i' Yorkshire." She had been talking Yorkshire to Colin and she forgot herself.

"Did Dickon teach you that?" asked Dr. Craven, laughing outright.

"I'm learning it as if it was French," said Mary rather coldly. "It's like a native dialect in India. Very clever people try to learn them. I like it and so does Colin."

"Well, well," he said. "If it amuses you perhaps it won't do you any harm. Did you take your bromide last night, Colin?"

"No," Colin answered. "I wouldn't take it at first and after Mary made me quiet she talked me to sleep—in a low voice—about the spring creeping into a garden."

"That sounds soothing," said Dr. Craven, more perplexed than ever and glancing sideways at Mistress Mary sitting on her stool and looking down silently at the carpet. "You are evidently better, but you must remember—"

"I don't want to remember," interrupted the Rajah, appearing again. "When I lie by myself and remember I begin to have pains everywhere and I think of things that make me begin to scream because I hate them so. If there was a doctor anywhere who could make you forget you were ill instead of remembering it I would have him brought here." And he waved a thin hand which ought really to have been covered with royal signet rings made of rubies. "It is because my cousin makes me forget that she makes me better."

Dr. Craven had never made such a short stay after a "tantrum"; usually he was obliged to remain a very long time and do a great many things. This afternoon he did not give any medicine or leave any new orders and he was spared any disagreeable scenes. When he went downstairs he looked very thoughtful and when he talked to Mrs. Medlock in the library she felt that he was a much puzzled man.

"Well, sir," she ventured, "could you have believed it?"

"It is certainly a new state of affairs," said the doctor. "And there's no denying it is better than the old one."

"I believe Susan Sowerby's right—I do that," said Mrs. Medlock. "I stopped in her cottage on my way to Thwaite yesterday and had a bit of talk with her. And she says to me, 'Well, Sarah Ann, she mayn't be a good child, an' she mayn't be a pretty one, but she's a child, an' children needs children.' We went to school together, Susan Sowerby and me."

"She's the best sick nurse I know," said Dr. Craven. "When I find her in a cottage I know the chances are that I shall save my patient."

Mrs. Medlock smiled. She was fond of Susan Sowerby.

"She's got a way with her, has Susan," she went on quite volubly. "I've been thinking all morning of one thing she said yesterday. She says, 'Once when I was givin' th' children a bit of a preach after they'd been fightin' I ses to 'em all, "When I was at school my jography told as th' world was shaped like a orange an' I found out before I was ten that th' whole orange doesn't belong to nobody. No one owns more than his bit of a quarter an' there's times it seems like there's not enow quarters to go round. But don't you—none o' you—think as you own th' whole orange or you'll find out you're mistaken, an' you won't find it out without hard knocks." What children learns from children,' she says, 'is that there's no sense in grabbin' at th' whole orange—peel an' all. If you do you'll likely not get even th' pips, an' them's too bitter to eat.'"

"She's a shrewd woman," said Dr. Craven, putting on his coat.

"Well, she's got a way of saying things," ended Mrs. Medlock, much pleased. "Sometimes I've said to her, 'Eh! Susan, if you was a different woman an' didn't talk such broad Yorkshire I've seen the times when I should have said you was clever.'"

That night Colin slept without once awakening and when he opened his eyes in the morning he lay still and smiled without knowing it—smiled because he felt so curiously comfortable. It was actually nice to be awake, and he turned over and stretched his limbs luxuriously. He felt as if tight strings which had held him had loosened themselves and let him go. He did not know that Dr. Craven would have said that his nerves had relaxed and rested themselves. Instead of lying and staring at the wall and wishing he had not awakened, his mind was full of the plans he and Mary had made yesterday, of pictures of the garden and of Dickon and his wild creatures. It was so nice to have things to think about. And he had not been awake more than ten minutes when he heard feet running along the corridor and Mary was at the door. The next minute she was in the room and had run across to his bed, bringing with her a waft of fresh air full of the scent of the morning.

"You've been out! You've been out! There's that nice smell of leaves!" he cried.

She had been running and her hair was loose and blown and she was bright with the air and pink-cheeked, though he could not see it.

"It's so beautiful!" she said, a little breathless with her speed. "You never saw anything so beautiful! It has *come*! I thought it had come that other morning, but it was only coming. It is here now! It has come, the Spring! Dickon says so!"

"Has it?" cried Colin, and though he really knew nothing about it he felt his heart beat. He actually sat up in bed.

"Open the window!" he added, laughing half with joyful excitement and half at his own fancy. "Perhaps we may hear golden trumpets!"

And though he laughed, Mary was at the window in a moment and in a moment more it was opened wide and freshness and softness and scents and birds' songs were pouring through.

"That's fresh air," she said. "Lie on your back and draw in long breaths of it. That's what Dickon does when he's lying on the moor. He says he feels it in his veins and it makes him strong and he feels as if he could live forever and ever. Breathe it and breathe it!"

She was only repeating what Dickon had told her, but she caught Colin's fancy.

"'Forever and ever'! Does it make him feel like that?" he said, and he did as she told him, drawing in long deep breaths over and over again until he felt that something quite new and delightful was happening to him.

Mary was at his bedside again.

"Things are crowding up out of the earth," she ran on in a hurry. "And there are flowers uncurling and buds on everything and the green veil has covered nearly all the gray and the birds are in such a hurry about their nests for fear they may be too late that some of them are even fighting for places in the secret garden. And the rose-bushes look as wick as wick can be, and there are primroses in the lanes and woods, and the seeds we planted are up, and Dickon has brought the fox and the crow and the squirrels and a new-born lamb."

And then she paused for breath. The new-born lamb Dickon had found three days before lying by its dead mother among the gorse bushes on the moor. It was not the first motherless lamb he had found and he knew what to do with it. He had taken it to the cottage wrapped in his jacket and he had let it lie near the fire and had fed it with warm milk. It was a soft thing with a darling silly baby face and legs rather long for its body. Dickon had carried it over the moor in his arms and its feeding bottle was in his pocket with a squirrel, and when Mary had sat under a tree with its limp warmness huddled on her lap she had felt as if she were too full of strange joy to speak. A lamb—a lamb! A living lamb who lay on your lap like a baby!

She was describing it with great joy and Colin was listening and drawing in long breaths of air when the nurse entered. She started a little at the sight of the open window. She had sat stifling in the room many a warm day because her patient was sure that open windows gave people cold.

"Are you sure you are not chilly, Master Colin?" she inquired.

"No," was the answer. "I am breathing long breaths of fresh air. It makes you strong. I am going to get up to the sofa for breakfast and my cousin will have breakfast with me."

The nurse went away, concealing a smile, to give the order for two breakfasts. She found the servants' hall a more amusing place than the invalid's chamber and just now everybody wanted to hear the news from up-stairs. There was a great deal of joking about the unpopular young recluse who, as the cook said, "had found his master, and good for him." The servants' hall had been very tired of the tantrums, and the butler, who was a man with a family, had more than once expressed his opinion that the invalid would be all the better "for a good hiding."

When Colin was on his sofa and the breakfast for two was put upon the table he made an announcement to the nurse in his most Rajah-like manner.

"A boy, and a fox, and a crow, and two squirrels, and a new-born lamb, are coming to see me this morning. I want them brought up-stairs as soon as they come," he said. "You are not to begin playing with the animals in the servants' hall and keep them there. I want them here."

The nurse gave a slight gasp and tried to conceal it with a cough.

"Yes, sir," she answered.

"I'll tell you what you can do," added Colin, waving his hand. "You can tell Martha to bring them here. The boy is Martha's brother. His name is Dickon and he is an animal charmer."

"I hope the animals won't bite, Master Colin," said the nurse.

"I told you he was a charmer," said Colin austerely. "Charmers' animals never bite."

"There are snake-charmers in India," said Mary; "and they can put their snakes' heads in their mouths."

"Goodness!" shuddered the nurse.

They ate their breakfast with the morning air pouring in upon them. Colin's breakfast was a very good one and Mary watched him with serious interest.

"You will begin to get fatter just as I did," she said. "I never wanted my breakfast when I was in India and now I always want it."

"I wanted mine this morning," said Colin. "Perhaps it was the fresh air. When do you think Dickon will come?"

He was not long in coming. In about ten minutes Mary held up her hand.

"Listen!" she said. "Did you hear a caw?"

Colin listened and heard it, the oddest sound in the world to hear inside a house, a hoarse "caw-caw."

"Yes," he answered.

"That's Soot," said Mary. "Listen again! Do you hear a bleat—a tiny one?"

"Oh, yes!" cried Colin, quite flushing.

"That's the new-born lamb," said Mary. "He's coming."

Dickon's moorland boots were thick and clumsy and though he tried to walk quietly they made a clumping sound as he walked through the long corridors. Mary and Colin heard him marching—marching, until he passed through the tapestry door on to the soft carpet of Colin's own passage.

"If you please, sir," announced Martha, opening the door, "if you please, sir, here's Dickon an' his creatures."

Dickon came in smiling his nicest wide smile. The new-born lamb was in his arms and the little red fox trotted by his side. Nut sat on his left shoulder and Soot on his right and Shell's head and paws peeped out of his coat pocket.

Colin slowly sat up and stared and stared—as he had stared when he first saw Mary; but this was a stare of wonder and delight. The truth was that in spite of all he had heard he had not in the least understood what this boy would be like and that his fox and his crow and his squirrels and his lamb were so near to him and his friendliness that they seemed almost to be part of himself. Colin had never talked to a boy in his life and he was so overwhelmed by his own pleasure and curiosity that he did not even think of speaking.

But Dickon did not feel the least shy or awkward. He had not felt embarrassed because the crow had not known his language and had only stared and had not spoken to him the first time they met. Creatures were always like that until they found out about you. He walked over to Colin's sofa and put the new-born lamb quietly on his lap, and immediately the little creature turned to the warm velvet dressing-gown and began to nuzzle and nuzzle into its folds and butt its tight-curled head with soft impatience against his side. Of course no boy could have helped speaking then.

"What is it doing?" cried Colin. "What does it want?"

"It wants its mother," said Dickon, smiling more and more. "I brought it to thee a bit hungry because I knowed tha'd like to see it feed."

He knelt down by the sofa and took a feeding-bottle from his pocket.

"Come on, little 'un," he said, turning the small woolly white head with a gentle brown hand. "This is what tha's after. Tha'll get more out o' this than tha' will out o' silk velvet coats. There now," and he pushed the rubber tip of the bottle into the nuzzling mouth and the lamb began to suck it with ravenous ecstasy.

After that there was no wondering what to say. By the time the lamb fell asleep questions poured forth and Dickon answered them all. He told them how he had found the lamb just as the sun was rising three mornings ago. He had been standing on the moor listening to a skylark and watching him swing higher and higher into the sky until he was only a speck in the heights of blue.

"I'd almost lost him but for his song an' I was wonderin' how a chap could hear it when it seemed as if he'd get out o' th' world in a minute—an' just then I heard somethin' else far off among th' gorse bushes. It was a weak bleatin' an' I knowed it was a new lamb as was hungry an' I knowed it wouldn't be hungry if it hadn't lost its mother somehow, so I set off searchin'. Eh! I did have a look for it. I went in an' out among th' gorse bushes an' round an' round an' I always seemed to take th' wrong turnin'. But at last I seed a bit o' white by a rock on top o' th' moor an' I climbed up an' found th' little 'un half dead wi' cold an' clemmin'."

While he talked, Soot flew solemnly in and out of the open window and cawed remarks about the scenery while Nut and Shell made excursions into the big trees outside and ran up and down trunks and explored branches. Captain curled up near Dickon, who sat on the hearth-rug from preference.

They looked at the pictures in the gardening books and Dickon knew all the flowers by their country names and knew exactly which ones were already growing in the secret garden.

"I couldna' say that there name," he said, pointing to one under which was written "Aquilegia," "but us calls that a columbine, an' that there one it's a snapdragon and they both grow wild in hedges, but these is garden ones an' they're bigger an' grander. There's some big clumps o' columbine in th' garden. They'll look like a bed o' blue an' white butterflies flutterin' when they're out."

"I'm going to see them," cried Colin. "I am going to see them!"

"Aye, that tha' mun," said Mary quite seriously. "An tha' munnot lose no time about it."

CHAPTER 20
"I SHALL LIVE FOREVER—AND EVER—AND EVER!"

But they were obliged to wait more than a week because first there came some very windy days and then Colin was threatened with a cold, which two things happening one after the other would no doubt have thrown him into a rage but that there was so much careful and mysterious planning to do and almost every day Dickon came in, if only for a few minutes, to talk about what was happening on the moor and in the lanes and hedges and on the borders of streams. The things he had to tell about otters' and badgers' and water-rats' houses, not to mention birds' nests and field-mice and their burrows, were enough to make you almost tremble with excitement when you heard all the intimate details from an animal charmer and realized with what thrilling eagerness and anxiety the whole busy underworld was working.

"They're same as us," said Dickon, "only they have to build their homes every year. An' it keeps 'em so busy they fair scuffle to get 'em done."

The most absorbing thing, however, was the preparations to be made before Colin could be transported with sufficient secrecy to the garden. No one must see the chair-carriage and Dickon and Mary after they turned a certain corner of the shrubbery and entered upon the walk outside the ivied walls. As each day passed, Colin had become more and more fixed in his feeling that the mystery surrounding the garden was one of its greatest charms. Nothing must spoil that. No one must ever suspect that they had a secret. People must think that he was simply going out with Mary and Dickon because he liked them and did not object to their looking at him. They had long and quite delightful talks about their route. They would go up this path and down that one and cross the other and go round among the fountain flower-beds as if they were looking at the "bedding-out plants" the head gardener, Mr. Roach, had been having arranged. That would seem such a rational thing to do that no one would think it at all mysterious. They would turn into the shrubbery walks and lose themselves until they came to the long walls. It was almost as serious and elaborately thought out as the plans of march made by great generals in time of war.

Rumors of the new and curious things which were occurring in the invalid's apartments had of course filtered through the servants' hall into the stable yards and out among the gardeners, but notwithstanding this, Mr. Roach was startled one day when he received orders from Master Colin's room to the effect that he must report himself in the apartment no outsider had ever seen, as the invalid himself desired to speak to him.

"Well, well," he said to himself as he hurriedly changed his coat, "what's to do now? His Royal Highness that wasn't to be looked at calling up a man he's never set eyes on."

Mr. Roach was not without curiosity. He had never caught even a glimpse of the boy and had heard a dozen exaggerated stories about his uncanny looks and ways and his insane tempers. The thing he had heard oftenest was that he might die at any moment and there had been numerous fanciful descriptions of a humped back and helpless limbs, given by people who had never seen him.

"Things are changing in this house, Mr. Roach," said Mrs. Medlock, as she led him up the back staircase to the corridor on to which opened the hitherto mysterious chamber.

"Let's hope they're changing for the better, Mrs. Medlock," he answered.

"They couldn't well change for the worse," she continued; "and queer as it all is there's them as finds their duties made a lot easier to stand up under. Don't you be surprised, Mr. Roach, if you find yourself in the middle of a menagerie and Martha Sowerby's Dickon more at home than you or me could ever be."

There really was a sort of Magic about Dickon, as Mary always privately believed. When Mr. Roach heard his name he smiled quite leniently.

"He'd be at home in Buckingham Palace or at the bottom of a coal mine," he said. "And yet it's not impudence, either. He's just fine, is that lad."

It was perhaps well he had been prepared or he might have been startled. When the bedroom door was opened a large crow, which seemed quite at home perched on the high back of a carven chair, announced the entrance of a visitor by saying "Caw —Caw" quite loudly. In spite of Mrs. Medlock's warning, Mr. Roach only just escaped being sufficiently undignified to jump backward.

The young Rajah was neither in bed nor on his sofa. He was sitting in an armchair and a young lamb was standing by him shaking its tail in feeding-lamb fashion as Dickon knelt giving it milk from its bottle. A squirrel was perched on Dickon's bent back attentively nibbling a nut. The little girl from India was sitting on a big footstool looking on.

"Here is Mr. Roach, Master Colin," said Mrs. Medlock.

The young Rajah turned and looked his servitor over—at least that was what the head gardener felt happened.

"Oh, you are Roach, are you?" he said. "I sent for you to give you some very important orders."

"Very good, sir," answered Roach, wondering if he was to receive instructions to fell all the oaks in the park or to transform the orchards into water-gardens.

"I am going out in my chair this afternoon," said Colin. "If the fresh air agrees with me I may go out every day. When I go, none of the gardeners are to be anywhere near the Long Walk by the garden walls. No one is to be there. I shall go out about two o'clock and every one must keep away until I send word that they may go back to their work."

"Very good, sir," replied Mr. Roach, much relieved to hear that the oaks might remain and that the orchards were safe.

"Mary," said Colin, turning to her, "what is that thing you say in India when you have finished talking and want people to go?"

"You say, 'You have my permission to go,'" answered Mary.

The Rajah waved his hand.

"You have my permission to go, Roach," he said. "But, remember, this is very important."

"Caw—Caw!" remarked the crow hoarsely but not impolitely.

"Very good, sir. Thank you, sir," said Mr. Roach, and Mrs. Medlock took him out of the room.

Outside in the corridor, being a rather good-natured man, he smiled until he almost laughed.

"My word!" he said, "he's got a fine lordly way with him, hasn't he? You'd think he was a whole Royal Family rolled into one—Prince Consort and all."

"Eh!" protested Mrs. Medlock, "we've had to let him trample all over every one of us ever since he had feet and he thinks that's what folks was born for."

"Perhaps he'll grow out of it, if he lives," suggested Mr. Roach.

"Well, there's one thing pretty sure," said Mrs. Medlock. "If he does live and that Indian child stays here I'll warrant she teaches him that the whole orange does not belong to him, as Susan Sowerby says. And he'll be likely to find out the size of his own quarter."

Inside the room Colin was leaning back on his cushions.

"It's all safe now," he said. "And this afternoon I shall see it—this afternoon I shall be in it!"

Dickon went back to the garden with his creatures and Mary stayed with Colin. She did not think he looked tired but he was very quiet before their lunch came and he was quiet while they were eating it. She wondered why and asked him about it.

"What big eyes you've got, Colin," she said. "When you are thinking they get as big as saucers. What are you thinking about now?"

"I can't help thinking about what it will look like," he answered.

"The garden?" asked Mary.

"The springtime," he said. "I was thinking that I've really never seen it before. I scarcely ever went out and when I did go I never looked at it. I didn't even think about it."

"I never saw it in India because there wasn't any," said Mary.

Shut in and morbid as his life had been, Colin had more imagination than she had and at least he had spent a good deal of time looking at wonderful books and pictures.

"That morning when you ran in and said 'It's come! It's come!' you made me feel quite queer. It sounded as if things were coming with a great procession and big bursts and wafts of music. I've a picture like it in one of my books—crowds of lovely people and children with garlands and branches with blossoms on them, every one laughing and dancing and crowding and playing on pipes. That was why I said, 'Perhaps we shall hear golden trumpets' and told you to throw open the window."

"How funny!" said Mary. "That's really just what it feels like. And if all the flowers and leaves and green things and birds and wild creatures danced past at once, what a crowd it would be! I'm sure they'd dance and sing and flute and that would be the wafts of music."

They both laughed but it was not because the idea was laughable but because they both so liked it.

A little later the nurse made Colin ready. She noticed that instead of lying like a log while his clothes were put on he sat up and made some efforts to help himself, and he talked and laughed with Mary all the time.

"This is one of his good days, sir," she said to Dr. Craven, who dropped in to inspect him. "He's in such good spirits that it makes him stronger."

"I'll call in again later in the afternoon, after he has come in," said Dr. Craven. "I must see how the going out agrees with him. I wish," in a very low voice, "that he would let you go with him."

"I'd rather give up the case this moment, sir, than even stay here while it's suggested," answered the nurse with sudden firmness.

"I hadn't really decided to suggest it," said the doctor, with his slight nervousness. "We'll try the experiment. Dickon's a lad I'd trust with a new-born child."

The strongest footman in the house carried Colin down-stairs and put him in his wheeled chair near which Dickon waited outside. After the manservant had arranged his rugs and cushions the Rajah waved his hand to him and to the nurse.

"You have my permission to go," he said, and they both disappeared quickly and it must be confessed giggled when they were safely inside the house.

Dickon began to push the wheeled chair slowly and steadily. Mistress Mary walked beside it and Colin leaned back and lifted his face to the sky. The arch of it looked very high and the small snowy clouds seemed like white birds floating on outspread wings below its crystal blueness. The wind swept in soft big breaths down from the moor and was strange with a wild clear scented sweetness. Colin kept lifting his thin chest to draw it in, and his big eyes looked as if it were they which were listening—listening, instead of his ears.

"There are so many sounds of singing and humming and calling out," he said. "What is that scent the puffs of wind bring?"

"It's gorse on th' moor that's openin' out," answered Dickon. "Eh! th' bees are at it wonderful to-day."

Not a human creature was to be caught sight of in the paths they took. In fact every gardener or gardener's lad had been witched away. But they wound in and out among the shrubbery and out and round the fountain beds, following their carefully planned route for the mere mysterious pleasure of it. But when at last they turned into the Long Walk by the ivied walls the excited sense of an approaching thrill made them, for some curious reason they could not have explained, begin to speak in whispers.

"This is it," breathed Mary. "This is where I used to walk up and down and wonder and wonder."

"Is it?" cried Colin, and his eyes began to search the ivy with eager curiousness. "But I can see nothing," he whispered. "There is no door."

"That's what I thought," said Mary.

Then there was a lovely breathless silence and the chair wheeled on.

"That is the garden where Ben Weatherstaff works," said Mary.

"Is it?" said Colin.

A few yards more and Mary whispered again.

"This is where the robin flew over the wall," she said.

"Is it?" cried Colin. "Oh! I wish he'd come again!"

"And that," said Mary with solemn delight, pointing under a big lilac bush, "is where he perched on the little heap of earth and showed me the key."

Then Colin sat up.

"Where? Where? There?" he cried, and his eyes were as big as the wolf's in Red Riding-Hood, when Red Riding-Hood felt called upon to remark on them. Dickon stood still and the wheeled chair stopped.

"And this," said Mary, stepping on to the bed close to the ivy, "is where I went to talk to him when he chirped at me from the top of the wall. And this is the ivy the wind blew back," and she took hold of the hanging green curtain.

"Oh! is it—is it!" gasped Colin.

"And here is the handle, and here is the door. Dickon push him in—push him in quickly!"

And Dickon did it with one strong, steady, splendid push.

But Colin had actually dropped back against his cushions, even though he gasped with delight, and he had covered his eyes with his hands and held them there shutting out everything until they were inside and the chair stopped as if by magic and the door was closed. Not till then did he take them away and look round and round and round as Dickon and Mary had done. And over walls and earth and trees and swinging sprays and tendrils the fair green veil of tender little leaves had crept, and in the grass under the trees and the gray urns in the alcoves and here and there everywhere were touches or splashes of gold and purple and white and the trees were showing pink and snow above his head and there were fluttering of wings and faint sweet pipes and humming and scents and scents. And the sun fell warm upon his face like a hand with a lovely touch. And in wonder Mary and Dickon stood and stared at him. He looked so strange and different because a pink glow of color had actually crept all over him—ivory face and neck and hands and all.

"I shall get well! I shall get well!" he cried out. "Mary! Dickon! I shall get well! And I shall live forever and ever and ever!"

CHAPTER 21
BEN WEATHERSTAFF

One of the strange things about living in the world is that it is only now and then one is quite sure one is going to live forever and ever and ever. One knows it sometimes when one gets up at the tender solemn dawn-time and goes out and stands alone and throws one's head far back and looks up and up and watches the pale sky slowly changing and flushing and marvelous unknown things happening until the East almost makes one cry out and one's heart stands still at the strange unchanging majesty of the rising of the sun—which has been happening every morning for thousands and thousands and thousands of years. One knows it then for a moment or so. And one knows it sometimes when one stands by oneself in a wood at sunset and the mysterious deep gold stillness slanting through and under the branches seems to be saying slowly again and again something one cannot quite hear, however much one tries. Then sometimes the immense quiet of the dark blue at night with millions of stars waiting and watching makes one sure; and sometimes a sound of far-off music makes it true; and sometimes a look in some one's eyes.

And it was like that with Colin when he first saw and heard and felt the Springtime inside the four high walls of a hidden garden. That afternoon the whole world seemed to devote itself to being perfect and radiantly beautiful and kind to one boy. Perhaps out of pure heavenly goodness the spring came and crowded everything it possibly could into that one place. More than once Dickon paused in what he was doing and stood still with a sort of growing wonder in his eyes, shaking his head softly.

"Eh! it is graidely," he said. "I'm twelve goin' on thirteen an' there's a lot o' afternoons in thirteen years, but seems to me like I never seed one as graidely as this 'ere."

"Aye, it is a graidely one," said Mary, and she sighed for mere joy. "I'll warrant it's th' graidelest one as ever was in this world."

"Does tha' think," said Colin with dreamy carefulness, "as happen it was made loike this 'ere all o' purpose for me?"

"My word!" cried Mary admiringly, "that there is a bit o' good Yorkshire. Tha'rt shapin' first-rate—that tha' art."

And delight reigned.

They drew the chair under the plum-tree, which was snow-white with blossoms and musical with bees. It was like a king's canopy, a fairy king's. There were flowering cherry-trees near and apple-trees whose buds were pink and white, and here and there one had burst open wide. Between the blossoming branches of the canopy bits of blue sky looked down like wonderful eyes.

Mary and Dickon worked a little here and there and Colin watched them. They brought him things to look at—buds which were opening, buds which were tight closed, bits of twig whose leaves were just showing green, the feather of a woodpecker which had dropped on the grass, the empty shell of some bird early hatched. Dickon pushed the chair slowly round and round the garden, stopping every other moment to let him look at wonders springing out of the earth or trailing down from trees. It was like being taken in state round the country of a magic king and queen and shown all the mysterious riches it contained.

"I wonder if we shall see the robin?" said Colin.

"Tha'll see him often enow after a bit," answered Dickon. "When th' eggs hatches out th' little chap he'll be kep' so busy it'll make his head swim. Tha'll see him flyin' backward an' for'ard carryin' worms nigh as big as himsel' an' that much noise goin' on in th' nest when he gets there as fair flusters him so as he scarce knows which big mouth to drop th' first piece in. An' gapin' beaks an' squawks on every side. Mother says as when she sees th' work a robin has to keep them gapin' beaks filled, she feels like she was a lady with nothin' to do. She says she's seen th' little chaps when it seemed like th' sweat must be droppin' off 'em, though folk can't see it."

This made them giggle so delightedly that they were obliged to cover their mouths with their hands, remembering that they must not be heard. Colin had been instructed as to the law of whispers and low voices several days before. He liked the mysteriousness of it and did his best, but in the midst of excited enjoyment it is rather difficult never to laugh above a whisper.

Every moment of the afternoon was full of new things and every hour the sunshine grew more golden. The wheeled chair had been drawn back under the canopy and Dickon had sat down on the grass and had just drawn out his pipe when Colin saw something he had not had time to notice before.

"That's a very old tree over there, isn't it?" he said.

Dickon looked across the grass at the tree and Mary looked and there was a brief moment of stillness.

"Yes," answered Dickon, after it, and his low voice had a very gentle sound.

Mary gazed at the tree and thought.

"The branches are quite gray and there's not a single leaf anywhere," Colin went on. "It's quite dead, isn't it?"

"Aye," admitted Dickon. "But them roses as has climbed all over it will near hide every bit o' th' dead wood when they're full o' leaves an' flowers. It won't look dead then. It'll be th' prettiest of all."

Mary still gazed at the tree and thought.

"It looks as if a big branch had been broken off," said Colin. "I wonder how it was done."

"It's been done many a year," answered Dickon. "Eh!" with a sudden relieved start and laying his hand on Colin. "Look at that robin! There he is! He's been foragin' for his mate."

Colin was almost too late but he just caught sight of him, the flash of red-breasted bird with something in his beak. He darted through the greenness and into the close-grown corner and was out of sight. Colin leaned back on his cushion again, laughing a little.

"He's taking her tea to her. Perhaps it's five o'clock. I think I'd like some tea myself."

And so they were safe.

"It was Magic which sent the robin," said Mary, secretly to Dickon afterward. "I know it was Magic." For both she and Dickon had been afraid Colin might ask something about the tree whose branch had broken off ten years ago and they had talked it over together and Dickon had stood and rubbed his head in a troubled way.

"We mun look as if it wasn't no different from th' other trees," he had said. "We couldn't never tell him how it broke, poor lad. If he says anything about it we mun—we mun try to look cheerful."

"Aye, that we mun," had answered Mary.

But she had not felt as if she looked cheerful when she gazed at the tree. She wondered and wondered in those few moments if there was any reality in that other thing Dickon had said. He had gone on rubbing his rust-red hair in a puzzled way, but a nice comforted look had begun to grow in his blue eyes.

"Mrs. Craven was a very lovely young lady," he had gone on rather hesitatingly. "An' mother she thinks maybe she's about Misselthwaite many a time lookin' after Mester Colin, same as all mothers do when they're took out o' th' world. They have to come back, tha' sees. Happen she's been in the garden an' happen it was her set us to work, an' told us to bring him here."

Mary had thought he meant something about Magic. She was a great believer in Magic. Secretly she quite believed that Dickon worked Magic, of course good Magic, on everything near him and that was why people liked him so much and wild creatures knew he was their friend. She wondered, indeed, if it were not possible that his gift had brought the robin just at the right moment when Colin asked that dangerous question. She felt that his Magic was working all the afternoon and making Colin look like an entirely different boy. It did not seem possible that he could be the crazy creature who had screamed and beaten and bitten his pillow. Even his ivory whiteness seemed to change. The faint glow of color which had shown on his face and neck and hands when he first got inside the garden really never quite died away. He looked as if he were made of flesh instead of ivory or wax.

They saw the robin carry food to his mate two or three times, and it was so suggestive of afternoon tea that Colin felt they must have some.

"Go and make one of the men servants bring some in a basket to the rhododendron walk," he said. "And then you and Dickon can bring it here."

It was an agreeable idea, easily carried out, and when the white cloth was spread upon the grass, with hot tea and buttered toast and crumpets, a delightfully hungry meal was eaten, and several birds on domestic errands paused to inquire what was going on and were led into investigating crumbs with great activity. Nut and Shell whisked up trees with pieces of cake and Soot took the entire half of a buttered crumpet into a corner and pecked at and examined and turned it over and made hoarse remarks about it until he decided to swallow it all joyfully in one gulp.

The afternoon was dragging toward its mellow hour. The sun was deepening the gold of its lances, the bees were going home and the birds were flying past less often. Dickon and Mary were sitting on the grass, the tea-basket was repacked ready to be taken back to the house, and Colin was lying against his cushions with his heavy locks pushed back from his forehead and his face looking quite a natural color.

"I don't want this afternoon to go," he said; "but I shall come back to-morrow, and the day after, and the day after, and the day after."

"You'll get plenty of fresh air, won't you?" said Mary.

"I'm going to get nothing else," he answered. "I've seen the spring now and I'm going to see the summer. I'm going to see everything grow here. I'm going to grow here myself."

"That tha' will," said Dickon. "Us'll have thee walkin' about here an' diggin' same as other folk afore long."

Colin flushed tremendously.

"Walk!" he said. "Dig! Shall I?"

Dickon's glance at him was delicately cautious. Neither he nor Mary had ever asked if anything was the matter with his legs.

"For sure tha' will," he said stoutly. "Tha'—tha's got legs o' thine own, same as other folks!"

Mary was rather frightened until she heard Colin's answer.

"Nothing really ails them," he said, "but they are so thin and weak. They shake so that I'm afraid to try to stand on them."

Both Mary and Dickon drew a relieved breath.

"When tha' stops bein' afraid tha'lt stand on 'em," Dickon said with renewed cheer. "An' tha'lt stop bein' afraid in a bit."

"I shall?" said Colin, and he lay still as if he were wondering about things.

They were really very quiet for a little while. The sun was dropping lower. It was that hour when everything stills itself, and they really had had a busy and exciting afternoon. Colin looked as if he were resting luxuriously. Even the creatures had ceased moving about and had drawn together and were resting near them. Soot had perched on a low branch and drawn up one leg and dropped the gray film drowsily over his eyes. Mary privately thought he looked as if he might snore in a minute.

In the midst of this stillness it was rather startling when Colin half lifted his head and exclaimed in a loud suddenly alarmed whisper:

"Who is that man?"

Dickon and Mary scrambled to their feet.

"Man!" they both cried in low quick voices.

Colin pointed to the high wall.

"Look!" he whispered excitedly. "Just look!"

Mary and Dickon wheeled about and looked. There was Ben Weatherstaff's indignant face glaring at them over the wall from the top of a ladder! He actually shook his fist at Mary.

"If I wasn't a bachelder, an' tha' was a wench o' mine," he cried, "I'd give thee a hidin'!"

He mounted another step threateningly as if it were his

energetic intention to jump down and deal with her; but as she came toward him he evidently thought better of it and stood on the top step of his ladder shaking his fist down at her.

"I never thowt much o' thee!" he harangued. "I couldna' abide thee th' first time I set eyes on thee. A scrawny buttermilk-faced young besom, allus askin' questions an' pokin' tha' nose where it wasna' wanted. I never knowed how tha' got so thick wi' me. If it hadna' been for th' robin—Drat him—"

"Ben Weatherstaff," called out Mary, finding her breath. She stood below him and called up to him with a sort of gasp. "Ben Weatherstaff, it was the robin who showed me the way!"

Then it did seem as if Ben really would scramble down on her side of the wall, he was so outraged.

"Tha' young bad 'un!" he called down at her. "Layin' tha' badness on a robin,—not but what he's impidint enow for anythin'. Him showin' thee th' way! Him! Eh! tha' young nowt,"—she could see his next words burst out because he was overpowered by curiosity—"however i' this world did tha' get in?"

"It was the robin who showed me the way," she protested obstinately. "He didn't know he was doing it but he did. And I can't tell you from here while you're shaking your fist at me."

He stopped shaking his fist very suddenly at that very moment and his jaw actually dropped as he stared over her head at something he saw coming over the grass toward him.

At the first sound of his torrent of words Colin had been so surprised that he had only sat up and listened as if he were spellbound. But in the midst of it he had recovered himself and beckoned imperiously to Dickon.

"Wheel me over there!" he commanded. "Wheel me quite close and stop right in front of him!"

And this, if you please, this is what Ben Weatherstaff beheld and which made his jaw drop. A wheeled chair with luxurious cushions and robes which came toward him looking rather like some sort of State Coach because a young Rajah leaned back in it with royal command in his great black-rimmed eyes and a thin white hand extended haughtily toward him. And it stopped right under Ben Weatherstaff's nose. It was really no wonder his mouth dropped open.

"Do you know who I am?" demanded the Rajah.

How Ben Weatherstaff stared! His red old eyes fixed themselves on what was before him as if he were seeing a ghost. He gazed and gazed and gulped a lump down his throat and did not say a word.

"Do you know who I am?" demanded Colin still more imperiously. "Answer!"

Ben Weatherstaff put his gnarled hand up and passed it over his eyes and over his forehead and then he did answer in a queer shaky voice.

"Who tha' art?" he said. "Aye, that I do—wi' tha' mother's eyes starin' at me out o' tha' face. Lord knows how tha' come here. But tha'rt th' poor cripple."

Colin forgot that he had ever had a back. His face flushed scarlet and he sat bolt upright.

"I'm not a cripple!" he cried out furiously. "I'm not!"

"He's not!" cried Mary, almost shouting up the wall in her fierce indignation. "He's not got a lump as big as a pin! I looked and there was none there—not one!"

Ben Weatherstaff passed his hand over his forehead again and gazed as if he could never gaze enough. His hand shook and his mouth shook and his voice shook. He was an ignorant old man and a tactless old man and he could only remember the things he had heard.

"Tha'—tha' hasn't got a crooked back?" he said hoarsely.

"No!" shouted Colin.

"Tha'—tha' hasn't got crooked legs?" quavered Ben more hoarsely yet.

It was too much. The strength which Colin usually threw into his tantrums rushed through him now in a new way. Never yet had he been accused of crooked legs—even in whispers—and the perfectly simple belief in their existence which was revealed by

Ben Weatherstaff's voice was more than Rajah flesh and blood could endure. His anger and insulted pride made him forget everything but this one moment and filled him with a power he had never known before, an almost unnatural strength.

"Come here!" he shouted to Dickon, and he actually began to tear the coverings off his lower limbs and disentangle himself. "Come here! Come here! This minute!"

Dickon was by his side in a second. Mary caught her breath in a short gasp and felt herself turn pale.

"He can do it! He can do it! He can do it! He can!" she gabbled over to herself under her breath as fast as ever she could.

There was a brief fierce scramble, the rugs were tossed on to the ground, Dickon held Colin's arm, the thin legs were out, the thin feet were on the grass. Colin was standing upright—upright—as straight as an arrow and looking strangely tall—his head thrown back and his strange eyes flashing lightning.

"Look at me!" he flung up at Ben Weatherstaff. "Just look at me—you! Just look at me!"

"He's as straight as I am!" cried Dickon. "He's as straight as any lad i' Yorkshire!"

What Ben Weatherstaff did Mary thought queer beyond measure. He choked and gulped and suddenly tears ran down his weather-wrinkled cheeks as he struck his old hands together.

"Eh!" he burst forth, "th' lies folk tells! Tha'rt as thin as a lath an' as white as a wraith, but there's not a knob on thee. Tha'lt make a mon yet. God bless thee!"

Dickon held Colin's arm strongly but the boy had not begun to falter. He stood straighter and straighter and looked Ben Weatherstaff in the face.

"I'm your master," he said, "when my father is away. And you are to obey me. This is my garden. Don't dare to say a word about it! You get down from that ladder and go out the Long Walk and Miss Mary will meet you and bring you here. I want to talk to you. We did not want you, but now you will have to be in the secret. Be quick!"

Ben Weatherstaff's crabbed old face was still wet with that one queer rush of tears. It seemed as if he could not take his eyes from thin straight Colin standing on his feet with his head thrown back.

"Eh! lad," he almost whispered. "Eh! my lad!" And then remembering himself he suddenly touched his hat gardener fashion and said, "Yes, sir! Yes, sir!" and obediently disappeared as he descended the ladder.

CHAPTER 22
WHEN THE SUN WENT DOWN

When his head was out of sight Colin turned to Mary.

"Go and meet him," he said; and Mary flew across the grass to the door under the ivy.

Dickon was watching him with sharp eyes. There were scarlet spots on his cheeks and he looked amazing, but he showed no signs of falling.

"I can stand," he said, and his head was still held up and he said it quite grandly.

"I told thee tha' could as soon as tha' stopped bein' afraid," answered Dickon. "An tha's stopped."

"Yes, I've stopped," said Colin.

Then suddenly he remembered something Mary had said.

"Are you making Magic?" he asked sharply.

Dickon's curly mouth spread in a cheerful grin.

"Tha's doin' Magic thysel'," he said. "It's the same Magic as made these 'ere work out o' th' earth," and he touched with his thick boot a clump of crocuses in the grass.

Colin looked down at them.

"Aye," he said slowly, "there couldna' be bigger Magic then that there—there couldna' be."

He drew himself up straighter than ever.

"I'm going to walk to that tree," he said, pointing to one a few feet away from him. "I'm going to be standing when Weatherstaff comes here. I can rest against the tree if I like. When I want to sit down I will sit down, but not before. Bring a rug from the chair."

He walked to the tree and though Dickon held his arm he was wonderfully steady. When he stood against the tree trunk it was not too plain that he supported himself against it, and he still held himself so straight that he looked tall.

"When Ben Weatherstaff came through the door in the wall he saw him standing there and he heard Mary muttering something under her breath.

"What art sayin'?" he asked rather testily because he did not want his attention distracted from the long thin straight boy figure and proud face.

But she did not tell him. What she was saying was this:

"You can do it! You can do it! I told you you could! You can do it! You can do it! You *can*!"

She was saying it to Colin because she wanted to make Magic and keep him on his feet looking like that. She could not bear that he should give in before Ben Weatherstaff. He did not give in. She was uplifted by a sudden feeling that he looked quite beautiful in spite of his thinness. He fixed his eyes on Ben Weatherstaff in his funny imperious way.

"Look at me!" he commanded. "Look at me all over! Am I a hunchback? Have I got crooked legs?"

Ben Weatherstaff had not quite got over his emotion, but he had recovered a little and answered almost in his usual way.

"Not tha'," he said. "Nowt o' th' sort. What's tha' been doin' with thysel'—hidin' out o' sight an' lettin' folk think tha' was cripple an' half-witted?"

"Half-witted!" said Colin angrily. "Who thought that?"

"Lots o' fools," said Ben. "Th' world's full o' jackasses brayin' an' they never bray nowt but lies. What did tha' shut thysel' up for?"

"Every one thought I was going to die," said Colin shortly. "I'm not!"

And he said it with such decision Ben Weatherstaff looked him over, up and down, down and up.

"Tha' die!" he said with dry exultation. "Nowt o' th' sort! Tha's got too much pluck in thee. When I seed thee put tha' legs on th' ground in such a hurry I knowed tha' was all right. Sit thee down on th' rug a bit young Mester an' give me thy orders."

There was a queer mixture of crabbed tenderness and shrewd understanding in his manner. Mary had poured out speech as rapidly as she could as they had come down the Long Walk. The chief thing to be remembered, she had told him, was that Colin was getting well—getting well. The garden was doing it. No one must let him remember about having humps and dying.

The Rajah condescended to seat himself on a rug under the tree.

"What work do you do in the gardens, Weatherstaff?" he inquired.

"Anythin' I'm told to do," answered old Ben. "I'm kep' on by favor—because she liked me."

"She?" said Colin.

"Tha' mother," answered Ben Weatherstaff.

"My mother?" said Colin, and he looked about him quietly. "This was her garden, wasn't it?"

"Aye, it was that!" and Ben Weatherstaff looked about him too. "She were main fond of it."

"It is my garden now. I am fond of it. I shall come here every day," announced Colin. "But it is to be a secret. My orders are that no one is to know that we come here. Dickon and my cousin have worked and made it come alive. I shall send for you sometimes to help—but you must come when no one can see you."

Ben Weatherstaff's face twisted itself in a dry old smile.

"I've come here before when no one saw me," he said.

"What!" exclaimed Colin. "When?"

"Th' last time I was here," rubbing his chin and looking round, "was about two year' ago."

"But no one has been in it for ten years!" cried Colin. "There was no door!"

"I'm no one," said old Ben dryly. "An' I didn't come through th' door. I come over th' wall. Th' rheumatics held me back th' last two year'."

"Tha' come an' did a bit o' prunin'!" cried Dickon. "I couldn't make out how it had been done."

"She was so fond of it—she was!" said Ben Weatherstaff slowly. "An' she was such a pretty young thing. She says to me once, 'Ben,' says she laughin', 'if ever I'm ill or if I go away you must take care of my roses.' When she did go away th' orders was no one was ever to come nigh. But I come," with grumpy obstinacy. "Over th' wall I come—until the rheumatics stopped me—an' I did a bit o' work once a year. She'd gave her order first."

"It wouldn't have been as wick as it is if tha' hadn't done it," said Dickon. "I did wonder."

"I'm glad you did it, Weatherstaff," said Colin. "You'll know how to keep the secret."

"Aye, I'll know, sir," answered Ben. "An' it'll be easier for a man wi' rheumatics to come in at th' door."

On the grass near the tree Mary had dropped her trowel. Colin stretched out his hand and took it up. An odd expression came into his face and he began to scratch at the earth. His thin hand was weak enough but presently as they watched him—Mary with quite breathless interest—he drove the end of the trowel into the soil and turned some over.

"You can do it! You can do it!" said Mary to herself. "I tell you, you can!"

Dickon's round eyes were full of eager curiousness but he said not a word. Ben Weatherstaff looked on with interested face.

Colin persevered. After he had turned a few trowelfuls of soil he spoke exultantly to Dickon in his best Yorkshire.

"Tha' said as tha'd have me walkin' about here same as other folk—an' tha' said tha'd have me diggin'. I thowt tha' was just leein' to please me. This is only th' first day an' I've walked—an' here I am diggin'."

Ben Weatherstaff's mouth fell open again when he heard him, but he ended by chuckling.

"Eh!" he said, "that sounds as if tha'd got wits enow. Tha'rt a Yorkshire lad for sure. An' tha'rt diggin', too. How'd tha' like to plant a bit o' somethin'? I can get thee a rose in a pot."

"Go and get it!" said Colin, digging excitedly. "Quick! Quick!"

It was done quickly enough indeed. Ben Weatherstaff went his way forgetting rheumatics. Dickon took his spade and dug the hole deeper and wider than a new digger with thin white hands could make it. Mary slipped out to run and bring back a watering-can. When Dickon had deepened the hole Colin went on turning the soft earth over and over. He looked up at the sky, flushed and glowing with the strangely new exercise, slight as it was.

"I want to do it before the sun goes quite—quite down," he said.

Mary thought that perhaps the sun held back a few minutes just on purpose. Ben Weatherstaff brought the rose in its pot from the greenhouse. He hobbled over the grass as fast as he could. He had begun to be excited, too. He knelt down by the hole and broke the pot from the mould.

"Here, lad," he said, handing the plant to Colin. "Set it in the earth thysel' same as th' king does when he goes to a new place."

The thin white hands shook a little and Colin's flush grew deeper as he set the rose in the mould and held it while old Ben made firm the earth. It was filled in and pressed down and made steady. Mary was leaning forward on her hands and knees. Soot had flown down and marched forward to see what was being done. Nut and Shell chattered about it from a cherry-tree.

"It's planted!" said Colin at last. "And the sun is only slipping over the edge. Help me up, Dickon. I want to be standing when it goes. That's part of the Magic."

And Dickon helped him, and the Magic—or whatever it was—so gave him strength that when the sun did slip over the edge and end the strange lovely afternoon for them there he actually stood on his two feet—laughing.

CHAPTER 23
MAGIC

Dr. Craven had been waiting some time at the house when they returned to it. He had indeed begun to wonder if it might not be wise to send some one out to explore the garden paths. When Colin was brought back to his room the poor man looked him over seriously.

"You should not have stayed so long," he said. "You must not overexert yourself."

"I am not tired at all," said Colin. "It has made me well. To-morrow I am going out in the morning as well as in the afternoon."

"I am not sure that I can allow it," answered Dr. Craven. "I am afraid it would not be wise."

"It would not be wise to try to stop me," said Colin quite seriously. "I am going."

Even Mary had found out that one of Colin's chief peculiarities was that he did not know in the least what a rude little brute he was with his way of ordering people about. He had lived on a sort of desert island all his life and as he had been the king of it he had made his own manners and had had no one to compare himself with. Mary had indeed been rather like him herself and since she had been at Misselthwaite had gradually discovered that her own manners had not been of the kind which is usual or popular. Having made this discovery she naturally thought it of enough interest to communicate to Colin. So she sat and looked at him curiously for a few minutes after Dr. Craven had gone. She wanted to make him ask her why she was doing it and of course she did.

"What are you looking at me for?" he said.

"I'm thinking that I am rather sorry for Dr. Craven."

"So am I," said Colin calmly, but not without an air of some satisfaction. "He won't get Misselthwaite at all now I'm not going to die."

"I'm sorry for him because of that, of course," said Mary, "but I was thinking just then that it must have been very horrid to have had to be polite for ten years to a boy who was always rude. I would never have done it."

"Am I rude?" Colin inquired undisturbedly.

"If you had been his own boy and he had been a slapping sort of man," said Mary, "he would have slapped you."

"But he daren't," said Colin.

"No, he daren't," answered Mistress Mary, thinking the thing out quite without prejudice. "Nobody ever dared to do anything you didn't like—because you were going to die and things like that. You were such a poor thing."

"But," announced Colin stubbornly, "I am not going to be a poor thing. I won't let people think I'm one. I stood on my feet this afternoon."

"It is always having your own way that has made you so queer," Mary went on, thinking aloud.

Colin turned his head, frowning.

"Am I queer?" he demanded.

"Yes," answered Mary, "very. But you needn't be cross," she added impartially, "because so am I queer—and so is Ben Weatherstaff. But I am not as queer as I was before I began to like people and before I found the garden."

"I don't want to be queer," said Colin. "I am not going to be," and he frowned again with determination.

He was a very proud boy. He lay thinking for a while and then Mary saw his beautiful smile begin and gradually change his whole face.

"I shall stop being queer," he said, "if I go every day to the garden. There is Magic in there—good Magic, you know, Mary. I am sure there is."

"So am I," said Mary.

"Even if it isn't real Magic," Colin said, "we can pretend it is. *Something* is there—*something*!"

"It's Magic," said Mary, "but not black. It's as white as snow."

They always called it Magic and indeed it seemed like it in the months that followed—the wonderful months—the radiant months—the amazing ones. Oh! the things which happened in that garden! If you have never had a garden, you cannot understand, and if you have had a garden you will know that it would take a whole book to describe all that came to pass there. At first it seemed that green things would never cease pushing their way through the earth, in the grass, in the beds, even in the crevices of the walls. Then the green things began to show buds and the buds began to unfurl and show color, every shade of blue, every shade of purple, every tint and hue of crimson. In its happy days flowers had been tucked away into every inch and hole and corner. Ben Weatherstaff had seen it done and had himself scraped out mortar from between the bricks of the wall and made pockets of earth for lovely clinging things to grow on. Iris and white lilies rose out of the grass in sheaves, and the green alcoves filled themselves with amazing armies of the blue and white flower lances of tall delphiniums or columbines or campanulas.

"She was main fond o' them—she was," Ben Weatherstaff said. "She liked them things as was allus pointin' up to th' blue sky, she used to tell. Not as she was one o' them as looked down on th' earth—not her. She just loved it but she said as th' blue sky allus looked so joyful."

The seeds Dickon and Mary had planted grew as if fairies had tended them. Satiny poppies of all tints danced in the breeze by the score, gaily defying flowers which had lived in the garden for years and which it might be confessed seemed rather to wonder how such new people had got there. And the roses—the roses! Rising out of the grass, tangled round the sun-dial, wreathing the tree trunks and hanging from their branches, climbing up the walls and spreading over them with long garlands falling in cascades—they

came alive day by day, hour by hour. Fair fresh leaves, and buds—
and buds—tiny at first but swelling and working Magic until they
burst and uncurled into cups of scent delicately spilling themselves
over their brims and filling the garden air.

Colin saw it all, watching each change as it took place. Every
morning he was brought out and every hour of each day when it
didn't rain he spent in the garden. Even gray days pleased him. He
would lie on the grass "watching things growing," he said. If you
watched long enough, he declared, you could see buds unsheath
themselves. Also you could make the acquaintance of strange
busy insect things running about on various unknown but evidently serious errands, sometimes carrying tiny scraps of straw or
feather or food, or climbing blades of grass as if they were trees
from whose tops one could look out to explore the country. A
mole throwing up its mound at the end of its burrow and making
its way out at last with the long-nailed paws which looked so like
elfish hands, had absorbed him one whole morning. Ants' ways,
beetles' ways, bees' ways, frogs' ways, birds' ways, plants' ways,
gave him a new world to explore and when Dickon revealed them
all and added foxes' ways, otters' ways, ferrets' ways, squirrels'
ways, and trout's and water-rats' and badgers' ways, there was no
end to the things to talk about and think over.

And this was not the half of the Magic. The fact that he had
really once stood on his feet had set Colin thinking tremendously
and when Mary told him of the spell she had worked he was
excited and approved of it greatly. He talked of it constantly.

"Of course there must be lots of Magic in the world," he said
wisely one day, "but people don't know what it is like or how to
make it. Perhaps the beginning is just to say nice things are going
to happen until you make them happen. I am going to try and
experiment."

The next morning when they went to the secret garden he sent
at once for Ben Weatherstaff. Ben came as quickly as he could and
found the Rajah standing on his feet under a tree and looking
very grand but also very beautifully smiling.

"Good morning, Ben Weatherstaff," he said. "I want you and Dickon and Miss Mary to stand in a row and listen to me because I am going to tell you something very important."

"Aye, aye, sir!" answered Ben Weatherstaff, touching his forehead. (One of the long concealed charms of Ben Weatherstaff was that in his boyhood he had once run away to sea and had made voyages. So he could reply like a sailor.)

"I am going to try a scientific experiment," explained the Rajah. "When I grow up I am going to make great scientific discoveries and I am going to begin now with this experiment."

"Aye, aye, sir!" said Ben Weatherstaff promptly, though this was the first time he had heard of great scientific discoveries.

It was the first time Mary had heard of them, either, but even at this stage she had begun to realize that, queer as he was, Colin had read about a great many singular things and was somehow a very convincing sort of boy. When he held up his head and fixed his strange eyes on you it seemed as if you believed him almost in spite of yourself though he was only ten years old—going on eleven. At this moment he was especially convincing because he suddenly felt the fascination of actually making a sort of speech like a grown-up person.

"The great scientific discoveries I am going to make," he went on, "will be about Magic. Magic is a great thing and scarcely any one knows anything about it except a few people in old books—and Mary a little, because she was born in India where there are fakirs. I believe Dickon knows some Magic, but perhaps he doesn't know he knows it. He charms animals and people. I would never have let him come to see me if he had not been an animal charmer—which is a boy charmer, too, because a boy is an animal. I am sure there is Magic in everything, only we have not sense enough to get hold of it and make it do things for us—like electricity and horses and steam."

This sounded so imposing that Ben Weatherstaff became quite excited and really could not keep still.

"Aye, aye, sir," he said and he began to stand up quite straight.

"When Mary found this garden it looked quite dead," the orator proceeded. "Then something began pushing things up out of the soil and making things out of nothing. One day things weren't there and another they were. I had never watched things before and it made me feel very curious. Scientific people are always curious and I am going to be scientific. I keep saying to myself 'What is it? What is it?' It's something. It can't be nothing! I don't know its name so I call it Magic. I have never seen the sun rise but Mary and Dickon have and from what they tell me I am sure that is Magic too. Something pushes it up and draws it. Sometimes since I've been in the garden I've looked up through the trees at the sky and I have had a strange feeling of being happy as if something were pushing and drawing in my chest and making me breathe fast. Magic is always pushing and drawing and making things out of nothing. Everything is made out of Magic, leaves and trees, flowers and birds, badgers and foxes and squirrels and people. So it must be all around us. In this garden—in all the places. The Magic in this garden has made me stand up and know I am going to live to be a man. I am going to make the scientific experiment of trying to get some and put it in myself and make it push and draw me and make me strong. I don't know how to do it but I think that if you keep thinking about it and calling it perhaps it will come. Perhaps that is the first baby way to get it. When I was going to try to stand that first time Mary kept saying to herself as fast as she could, 'You can do it! You can do it!' and I did. I had to try myself at the same time, of course, but her Magic helped me—and so did Dickon's. Every morning and evening and as often in the daytime as I can remember I am going to say, 'Magic is in me! Magic is making me well! I am going to be as strong as Dickon, as strong as Dickon!' And you must all do it, too. That is my experiment. Will you help, Ben Weatherstaff?"

"Aye, aye, sir!" said Ben Weatherstaff. "Aye, aye!"

"If you keep doing it every day as regularly as soldiers go through drill we shall see what will happen and find out if the experiment succeeds. You learn things by saying them over and over and thinking about them until they stay in your mind forever and I think it will be the same with Magic. If you keep calling it to come to you and help you it will get to be part of you and it will stay and do things."

"I once heard an officer in India tell my mother that there were fakirs who said words over and over thousands of times," said Mary.

"I've heard Jem Fettleworth's wife say th' same thing over thousands o' times—callin' Jem a drunken brute," said Ben Weatherstaff dryly. "Summat allus come o' that, sure enough. He gave her a good hidin' an' went to th' Blue Lion an' got as drunk as a lord."

Colin drew his brows together and thought a few minutes. Then he cheered up.

"Well," he said, "you see something did come of it. She used the wrong Magic until she made him beat her. If she'd used the right Magic and had said something nice perhaps he wouldn't have got as drunk as a lord and perhaps—perhaps he might have bought her a new bonnet."

Ben Weatherstaff chuckled and there was shrewd admiration in his little old eyes.

"Tha'rt a clever lad as well as a straight-legged one, Mester Colin," he said. "Next time I see Bess Fettleworth I'll give her a bit of a hint o' what Magic will do for her. She'd be rare an' pleased if th' sinetifik 'speriment worked—an' so 'ud Jem."

Dickon had stood listening to the lecture, his round eyes shining with curious delight. Nut and Shell were on his shoulders and he held a long-eared white rabbit in his arm and stroked and stroked it softly while it laid its ears along its back and enjoyed itself.

"Do you think the experiment will work?" Colin asked him, wondering what he was thinking. He so often wondered what Dickon was thinking when he saw him looking at him or at one of his "creatures" with his happy wide smile.

He smiled now and his smile was wider than usual.

"Aye," he answered, "that I do. It'll work same as th' seeds do when th' sun shines on 'em. It'll work for sure. Shall us begin it now?"

Colin was delighted and so was Mary. Fired by recollections of fakirs and devotees in illustrations Colin suggested that they should all sit cross-legged under the tree which made a canopy.

"It will be like sitting in a sort of temple," said Colin. "I'm rather tired and I want to sit down."

"Eh!" said Dickon, "tha' musn't begin by sayin' tha'rt tired. Tha' might spoil th' Magic."

Colin turned and looked at him—into his innocent round eyes.

"That's true," he said slowly. "I must only think of the Magic."

It all seemed most majestic and mysterious when they sat down in their circle. Ben Weatherstaff felt as if he had somehow been led into appearing at a prayer-meeting. Ordinarily he was very fixed in being what he called "agen' prayer-meetin's" but this being the Rajah's affair he did not resent it and was indeed inclined to be gratified at being called upon to assist. Mistress Mary felt solemnly enraptured. Dickon held his rabbit in his arm, and perhaps he made some charmer's signal no one heard, for when he sat down, cross-legged like the rest, the crow, the fox, the squirrels and the lamb slowly drew near and made part of the circle, settling each into a place of rest as if of their own desire.

"The 'creatures' have come," said Colin gravely. "They want to help us."

Colin really looked quite beautiful, Mary thought. He held his head high as if he felt like a sort of priest and his strange eyes had a wonderful look in them. The light shone on him through the tree canopy.

"Now we will begin," he said. "Shall we sway backward and forward, Mary, as if we were dervishes?"

"I canna' do no swayin' back'ard and for'ard," said Ben Weatherstaff. "I've got th' rheumatics."

"The Magic will take them away," said Colin in a High Priest tone. "But we won't sway until it has done it. We will only chant."

"I canna do no chantin'," said Ben Weatherstaff a trifle testily. "They turned me out o' th' church choir th' only time I ever tried it."

No one smiled. They were all too much in earnest. Colin's face was not even crossed by a shadow. He was thinking only of the Magic.

"Then I will chant," he said. And he began, looking like a strange boy spirit. "The sun is shining—the sun is shining. That is the Magic. The flowers are growing—the roots are stirring. That is the Magic. Being alive is the Magic—being strong is the Magic. The Magic is in me—the Magic is in me. It is in me—it is in me. It's in every one of us. It's in Ben Weatherstaff's back. Magic! Magic! Come and help!"

He said it a great many times—not a thousand times but quite a goodly number. Mary listened entranced. She felt as if it were at once queer and beautiful and she wanted him to go on and on. Ben Weatherstaff began to feel soothed into a sort of dream which was quite agreeable. The humming of the bees in the blossoms mingled with the chanting voice and drowsily melted into a doze. Dickon sat cross-legged with his rabbit asleep on his arm and a hand resting on the lamb's back. Soot had pushed away a squirrel and huddled close to him on his shoulder, the gray film dropped over his eyes. At last Colin stopped.

"Now I am going to walk round the garden," he announced.

Ben Weatherstaff's head had just dropped forward and he lifted it with a jerk.

"You have been asleep," said Colin.

"Nowt o' th' sort," mumbled Ben. "Th' sermon was good enow—but I'm bound to get out afore th' collection."

He was not quite awake yet.

"You're not in church," said Colin.

"Not me," said Ben, straightening himself. "Who said I were? I heard every bit of it. You said th' Magic was in my back. Th' doctor calls it rheumatics."

The Rajah waved his hand.

"That was the wrong Magic," he said. "You will get better. You have my permission to go to your work. But come back to-morrow."

"I'd like to see thee walk round the garden," grunted Ben.

It was not an unfriendly grunt, but it was a grunt. In fact, being a stubborn old party and not having entire faith in Magic he had made up his mind that if he were sent away he would climb his ladder and look over the wall so that he might be ready to hobble back if there were any stumbling.

The Rajah did not object to his staying and so the procession was formed. It really did look like a procession. Colin was at its head with Dickon on one side and Mary on the other. Ben Weath-erstaff walked behind, and the "creatures" trailed after them, the lamb and the fox cub keeping close to Dickon, the white rabbit hopping along or stopping to nibble and Soot following with the solemnity of a person who felt himself in charge.

It was a procession which moved slowly but with dignity. Every few yards it stopped to rest. Colin leaned on Dickon's arm and privately Ben Weatherstaff kept a sharp lookout, but now and then Colin took his hand from its support and walked a few steps alone. His head was held up all the time and he looked very grand.

"The Magic is in me!" he kept saying. "The Magic is making me strong! I can feel it! I can feel it!"

It seemed very certain that something was upholding and up-lifting him. He sat on the seats in the alcoves, and once or twice he sat down on the grass and several times he paused in the path and leaned on Dickon, but he would not give up until he had gone all round the garden. When he returned to the canopy tree his cheeks were flushed and he looked triumphant.

"I did it! The Magic worked!" he cried. "That is my first scien-tific discovery."

"What will Dr. Craven say?" broke out Mary.

"He won't say anything," Colin answered, "because he will not be told. This is to be the biggest secret of all. No one is to know anything about it until I have grown so strong that I can walk and run like any other boy. I shall come here every day in my chair and I shall be taken back in it. I won't have people whispering and asking questions and I won't let my father hear about it until the experiment has quite succeeded. Then sometime when he comes back to Misselthwaite I shall just walk into his study and say 'Here I am; I am like any other boy. I am quite well and I shall live to be a man. It has been done by a scientific experiment.'"

"He will think he is in a dream," cried Mary. "He won't believe his eyes."

Colin flushed triumphantly. He had made himself believe that he was going to get well, which was really more than half the battle, if he had been aware of it. And the thought which stimulated him more than any other was this imagining what his father would look like when he saw that he had a son who was as straight and strong as other fathers' sons. One of his darkest miseries in the unhealthy morbid past days had been his hatred of being a sickly weak-backed boy whose father was afraid to look at him.

"He'll be obliged to believe them," he said. "One of the things I am going to do, after the Magic works and before I begin to make scientific discoveries is to be an athlete."

"We shall have thee takin' to boxin' in a week or so," said Ben Weatherstaff. "Tha'lt end wi' winnin', th' Belt an' bein' champion prize-fighter of all England."

Colin fixed his eyes on him sternly.

"Weatherstaff," he said, "that is disrespectful. You must not take liberties because you are in the secret. However much the Magic works I shall not be a prize-fighter. I shall be a Scientific Discoverer."

"Ax pardon—ax pardon, sir," answered Ben, touching his forehead in salute. "I ought to have seed it wasn't a jokin' matter," but his eyes twinkled and secretly he was immensely pleased. He really did not mind being snubbed since the snubbing meant that the lad was gaining strength and spirit.

CHAPTER 24
"LET THEM LAUGH"

The secret garden was not the only one Dickon worked in. Round the cottage on the moor there was a piece of ground enclosed by a low wall of rough stones. Early in the morning and late in the fading twilight and on all the days Colin and Mary did not see him, Dickon worked there planting or tending potatoes and cabbages, turnips and carrots and herbs for his mother. In the company of his "creatures" he did wonders there and was never tired of doing them, it seemed. While he dug or weeded he whistled or sang bits of Yorkshire moor songs or talked to Soot or Captain or the brothers and sisters he had taught to help him.

"We'd never get on as comfortable as we do," Mrs. Sowerby said, "if it wasn't for Dickon's garden. Anything 'll grow for him. His 'taters and cabbages is twice th' size of any one else's an' they've got a flavor with 'em as nobody's has."

When she found a moment to spare she liked to go out and talk to him. After supper there was still a long clear twilight to work in and that was her quiet time. She could sit upon the low rough wall and look on and hear stories of the day. She loved this time. There were not only vegetables in this garden. Dickon had bought penny packages of flower seeds now and then and sown bright sweet-scented things among the gooseberry bushes and even cabbages and he grew borders of mignonette and pinks and pansies and things whose seeds he could save year after year or whose roots would bloom each spring and spread in time into fine clumps. The low wall was one of the prettiest things in York-shire because he had tucked moorland foxglove and ferns and

rockcress and hedgerow flowers into every crevice until only here
and there glimpses of the stones were to be seen.

"All a chap's got to do to make 'em thrive, mother," he would say,
"is to be friends with 'em for sure. They're just like th' 'creatures.' If
they're thirsty give 'em a drink and if they're hungry give 'em a bit o'
food. They want to live same as we do. If they died I should feel as if
I'd been a bad lad and somehow treated them heartless."

It was in these twilight hours that Mrs. Sowerby heard of all
that happened at Misselthwaite Manor. At first she was only told
that "Mester Colin" had taken a fancy to going out into the
grounds with Miss Mary and that it was doing him good. But it
was not long before it was agreed between the two children that
Dickon's mother might "come into the secret." Somehow it was
not doubted that she was "safe for sure."

So one beautiful still evening Dickon told the whole story,
with all the thrilling details of the buried key and the robin and
the gray haze which had seemed like deadness and the secret Mistress Mary had planned never to reveal. The coming of Dickon
and how it had been told to him, the doubt of Mester Colin and
the final drama of his introduction to the hidden domain, combined with the incident of Ben Weatherstaff's angry face peering
over the wall and Mester Colin's sudden indignant strength, made
Mrs. Sowerby's nice-looking face quite change color several times.

"My word!" she said. "It was a good thing that little lass came
to th' Manor. It's been th' makin' o' her an' th' savin' o' him.
Standin' on his feet! An' us all thinkin' he was a poor half-witted
lad with not a straight bone in him."

She asked a great many questions and her blue eyes were full
of deep thinking.

"What do they make of it at th' Manor—him being so well an'
cheerful an' never complainin'?" she inquired.

"They don't know what to make of it," answered Dickon.
"Every day as comes round his face looks different. It's fillin' out
and doesn't look so sharp an' th' waxy color is goin'. But he has to
do his bit o' complainin'," with a highly entertained grin.

"What for, i' Mercy's name?" asked Mrs. Sowerby.

Dickon chuckled.

"He does it to keep them from guessin' what's happened. If the doctor knew he'd found out he could stand on his feet he'd likely write and tell Mester Craven. Mester Colin's savin' th' secret to tell himself. He's goin' to practise his Magic on his legs every day till his father comes back an' then he's goin' to march into his room an' show him he's as straight as other lads. But him an' Miss Mary thinks it's best plan to do a bit o' groanin' an' frettin' now an' then to throw folk off th' scent."

Mrs. Sowerby was laughing a low comfortable laugh long before he had finished his last sentence.

"Eh!" she said, "that pair's enjoyin' theirselves, I'll warrant. They'll get a good bit o' play actin' out of it an' there's nothin' children likes as much as play actin'. Let's hear what they do, Dickon lad."

Dickon stopped weeding and sat up on his heels to tell her. His eyes were twinkling with fun.

"Mester Colin is carried down to his chair every time he goes out," he explained. "An' he flies out at John, th' footman, for not carryin' him careful enough. He makes himself as helpless lookin' as he can an' never lifts his head until we're out o' sight o' th' house. An' he grunts an' frets a good bit when he's bein' settled into his chair. Him an' Miss Mary's both got to enjoyin' it an' when he groans an' complains she'll say, 'Poor Colin! Does it hurt you so much? Are you so weak as that, poor Colin?'—but th' trouble is that sometimes they can scarce keep from burstin' out laughin'. When we get safe into the garden they laugh till they've no breath left to laugh with. An' they have to stuff their faces into Mester Colin's cushions to keep the gardeners from hearin', if any of 'em's about."

"Th' more they laugh th' better for 'em!" said Mrs. Sowerby, still laughing herself. "Good healthy child laughin's better than pills any day o' th' year. That pair'll plump up for sure."

"They are plumpin' up," said Dickon. "They're that hungry

they don't know how to get enough to eat without makin' talk. Mester Colin says if he keeps sendin' for more food they won't believe he's an invalid at all. Miss Mary says she'll let him eat her share, but he says that if she goes hungry she'll get thin an' they mun both get fat at once."

Mrs. Sowerby laughed so heartily at the revelation of this difficulty, that she quite rocked backward and forward in her blue cloak, and Dickon laughed with her.

"I'll tell thee what, lad," Mrs. Sowerby said when she could speak. "I've thought of a way to help 'em. When tha' goes to 'em in th' mornin's tha' shall take a pail o' good new milk an' I'll bake 'em a crusty cottage loaf or some buns wi' currants in 'em, same as you children like. Nothin's so good as fresh milk an' bread. Then they could take off th' edge o' their hunger while they were in their garden an' th' fine food they get indoors 'ud polish off th' corners."

"Eh! mother!" said Dickon admiringly, "what a wonder tha' art! Tha' always sees a way out o' things. They was quite in a pother yesterday. They didn't see how they was to manage without orderin' more food—they felt that empty inside."

"They're two young 'uns growin' fast, an' health's comin' back to both of 'em. Children like that feels like young wolves an' food's flesh an' blood to 'em," said Mrs. Sowerby. Then she smiled Dickon's own curving smile. "Eh! but they're enjoyin' theirselves for sure," she said.

She was quite right, the comfortable wonderful mother creature—and she had never been more so than when she said their "play actin'" would be their joy. Colin and Mary found it one of their most thrilling sources of entertainment. The idea of protecting themselves from suspicion had been unconsciously suggested to them first by the puzzled nurse and then by Dr. Craven himself.

"Your appetite is improving very much, Master Colin," the nurse had said one day. "You used to eat nothing, and so many things disagreed with you."

"Nothing disagrees with me now," replied Colin, and then seeing the nurse looking at him curiously he suddenly remembered that perhaps he ought not to appear too well just yet. "At least things don't so often disagree with me. It's the fresh air."

"Perhaps it is," said the nurse, still looking at him with a mystified expression. "But I must talk to Dr. Craven about it."

"How she stared at you!" said Mary when she went away. "As if she thought there must be something to find out."

"I won't have her finding out things," said Colin. "No one must begin to find out yet."

When Dr. Craven came that morning he seemed puzzled, also. He asked a number of questions, to Colin's great annoyance.

"You stay out in the garden a great deal," he suggested. "Where do you go?"

Colin put on his favorite air of dignified indifference to opinion.

"I will not let any one know where I go," he answered. "I go to a place I like. Every one has orders to keep out of the way. I won't be watched and stared at. You know that!"

"You seem to be out all day but I do not think it has done you harm—I do not think so. The nurse says that you eat much more than you have ever done before."

"Perhaps," said Colin, prompted by a sudden inspiration, "perhaps it is an unnatural appetite."

"I do not think so, as your food seems to agree with you," said Dr. Craven. "You are gaining flesh rapidly and your color is better."

"Perhaps—perhaps I am bloated and feverish," said Colin, assuming a discouraging air of gloom. "People who are not going to live are often—different."

Dr. Craven shook his head. He was holding Colin's wrist and he pushed up his sleeve and felt his arm.

"You are not feverish," he said thoughtfully, "and such flesh as you have gained is healthy. If we can keep this up, my boy, we need not talk of dying. Your father will be very happy to hear of this remarkable improvement."

"I won't have him told!" Colin broke forth fiercely. "It will only disappoint him if I get worse again—and I may get worse this very night. I might have a raging fever. I feel as if I might be beginning to have one now. I won't have letters written to my father—I won't—I won't! You are making me angry and you know that is bad for me. I feel hot already. I hate being written about and being talked over as much as I hate being stared at!"

"Hush-h! my boy," Dr. Craven soothed him. "Nothing shall be written without your permission. You are too sensitive about things. You must not undo the good which has been done."

He said no more about writing to Mr. Craven and when he saw the nurse he privately warned her that such a possibility must not be mentioned to the patient.

"The boy is extraordinarily better," he said. "His advance seems almost abnormal. But of course he is doing now of his own free will what we could not make him do before. Still, he excites himself very easily and nothing must be said to irritate him."

Mary and Colin were much alarmed and talked together anxiously. From this time dated their plan of "play actin'."

"I may be obliged to have a tantrum," said Colin regretfully. "I don't want to have one and I'm not miserable enough now to work myself into a big one. Perhaps I couldn't have one at all. That lump doesn't come in my throat now and I keep thinking of nice things instead of horrible ones. But if they talk about writing to my father I shall have to do something."

He made up his mind to eat less, but unfortunately it was not possible to carry out this brilliant idea when he wakened each morning with an amazing appetite and the table near his sofa was set with a breakfast of home-made bread and fresh butter, snow-white eggs, raspberry jam and clotted cream. Mary always breakfasted with him and when they found themselves at the table—particularly if there were delicate slices of sizzling ham sending forth tempting odors from under a hot silver cover—they would look into each other's eyes in desperation.

"I think we shall have to eat it all this morning, Mary," Colin always ended by saying. "We can send away some of the lunch and a great deal of the dinner."

But they never found they could send away anything and the

highly polished condition of the empty plates returned to the pantry awakened much comment.

"I do wish," Colin would say also, "I do wish the slices of ham were thicker, and one muffin each is not enough for any one."

"It's enough for a person who is going to die," answered Mary when first she heard this, "but it's not enough for a person who is going to live. I sometimes feel as if I could eat three when those nice fresh heather and gorse smells from the moor come pouring in at the open window."

The morning that Dickon—after they had been enjoying themselves in the garden for about two hours—went behind a big rose-bush and brought forth two tin pails and revealed that one was full of rich new milk with cream on the top of it, and that the other held cottage-made currant buns folded in a clean blue and white napkin, buns so carefully tucked in that they were still hot, there was a riot of surprised joyfulness. What a wonderful thing for Mrs. Sowerby to think of! What a kind, clever woman she must be! How good the buns were! And what delicious fresh milk!

"Magic is in her just as it is in Dickon," said Colin. "It makes her think of ways to do things—nice things. She is a Magic person. Tell her we are grateful, Dickon—extremely grateful."

He was given to using rather grown-up phrases at times. He enjoyed them. He liked this so much that he improved upon it.

"Tell her she has been most bounteous and our gratitude is extreme."

And then forgetting his grandeur he fell to and stuffed himself with buns and drank milk out of the pail in copious draughts in the manner of any hungry little boy who had been taking unusual exercise and breathing in moorland air and whose breakfast was more than two hours behind him.

This was the beginning of many agreeable incidents of the same kind. They actually awoke to the fact that as Mrs. Sowerby had fourteen people to provide food for she might not have enough to satisfy two extra appetites every day. So they asked her to let them send some of their shillings to buy things.

Dickon made the stimulating discovery that in the wood in the park outside the garden where Mary had first found him piping to the wild creatures there was a deep little hollow where you could build a sort of tiny oven with stones and roast potatoes and eggs in it. Roasted eggs were a previously unknown luxury and very hot potatoes with salt and fresh butter in them were fit for a woodland king—besides being deliciously satisfying. You could buy both potatoes and eggs and eat as many as you liked without feeling as if you were taking food out of the mouths of four-teen people.

Every beautiful morning the Magic was worked by the mystic circle under the plum-tree which provided a canopy of thickening green leaves after its brief blossom-time was ended. After the cere-mony Colin always took his walking exercise and throughout the day he exercised his newly found power at intervals. Each day he grew stronger and could walk more steadily and cover more ground. And each day his belief in the Magic grew stronger—as well it might. He tried one experiment after another as he felt himself gaining strength and it was Dickon who showed him the best things of all.

"Yesterday," he said one morning after an absence, "I went to Thwaite for mother an' near th' Blue Cow Inn I seed Bob Haworth. He's the strongest chap on th' moor. He's the champion wrestler an' he can jump higher than any other chap an' throw th' hammer farther. He's gone all th' way to Scotland for th' sports some years. He's knowed me ever since I was a little 'un an' he's a friendly sort an' I axed him some questions. Th' gentry calls him a athlete and I thought o' thee, Mester Colin, and I says, 'How did tha' make tha' muscles stick out that way, Bob? Did tha' do any-thin' extra to make thysel' so strong?' An' he says 'Well, yes, lad, I did. A strong man in a show that came to Thwaite once showed me how to exercise my arms an' legs an' every muscle in my body.' An' I says, 'Could a delicate chap make himself stronger with 'em, Bob?' an' he laughed an' says, 'Art tha' th' delicate chap?' an' I says, 'No, but I knows a young gentleman that's gettin' well of a long illness an' I wish I knowed some o' them tricks to tell him about.' I didn't say no names an' he didn't ask none. He's friendly same as I said an' he stood up an' showed me good-natured like, an' I imitated what he did till I knowed it by heart."

Colin had been listening excitedly.

"Can you show me?" he cried. "Will you?"

"Aye, to be sure," Dickon answered, getting up. "But he says tha' mun do 'em gentle at first an' be careful not to tire thyself'. Rest in between times an' take deep breaths an' don't overdo."

"I'll be careful," said Colin. "Show me! Show me! Dickon, you are the most Magic boy in the world!"

Dickon stood up on the grass and slowly went through a carefully practical but simple series of muscle exercises. Colin watched them with widening eyes. He could do a few while he was sitting down. Presently he did a few gently while he stood upon his already steadied feet. Mary began to do them also. Soot, who was watching the performance, became much disturbed and left his branch and hopped about restlessly because he could not do them too.

From that time the exercises were part of the day's duties as much as the Magic was. It became possible for both Colin and Mary to do more of them each time they tried, and such appetites were the results that but for the basket Dickon put down behind the bush each morning when he arrived they would have been lost. But the little oven in the hollow and Mrs. Sowerby's bounties were so satisfying that Mrs. Medlock and the nurse and Dr. Craven became mystified again. You can trifle with your breakfast and seem to disdain your dinner if you are full to the brim with roasted eggs and potatoes and richly frothed new milk and oat-cakes and buns and heather honey and clotted cream.

"They are eating next to nothing," said the nurse. "They'll die of starvation if they can't be persuaded to take some nourishment. And yet see how they look."

"Look!" exclaimed Mrs. Medlock indignantly. "Eh! I'm moithered to death with them. They're a pair of young Satans.

Bursting their jackets one day and the next turning up their noses at the best meals Cook can tempt them with. Not a mouthful of that lovely young fowl and bread sauce did they set a fork into yesterday—and the poor woman fair *invented* a pudding for them—and back it's sent. She almost cried. She's afraid she'll be blamed if they starve themselves into their graves."

Dr. Craven came and looked at Colin long and carefully. He wore an extremely worried expression when the nurse talked with him and showed him the almost untouched tray of breakfast she had saved for him to look at—but it was even more worried when he sat down by Colin's sofa and examined him. He had been called to London on business and had not seen the boy for nearly two weeks. When young things begin to gain health they gain it rapidly. The waxen tinge had left Colin's skin and a warm rose showed through it; his beautiful eyes were clear and the hollows under them and in his cheeks and temples had filled out. His once dark, heavy locks had begun to look as if they sprang healthily from his forehead and were soft and warm with life. His lips were fuller and of a normal color. In fact as an imitation of a boy who was a confirmed invalid he was a disgraceful sight. Dr. Craven held his chin in his hand and thought him over.

"I am sorry to hear that you do not eat anything," he said. "That will not do. You will lose all you have gained—and you have gained amazingly. You ate so well a short time ago."

"I told you it was an unnatural appetite," answered Colin.

Mary was sitting on her stool nearby and she suddenly made a very queer sound which she tried so violently to repress that she ended by almost choking.

"What is the matter?" said Dr. Craven, turning to look at her.

Mary became quite severe in her manner.

"It was something between a sneeze and a cough," she replied with reproachful dignity, "and it got into my throat."

"But," she said afterward to Colin, "I couldn't stop myself. It just burst out because all at once I couldn't help remembering that last big potato you ate and the way your mouth stretched when you bit through that thick lovely crust with jam and clotted cream on it."

"Is there any way in which those children can get food secretly?" Dr. Craven inquired of Mrs. Medlock.

"There's no way unless they dig it out of the earth or pick it off the trees," Mrs. Medlock answered. "They stay out in the grounds all day and see no one but each other. And if they want anything different to eat from what's sent up to them they need only ask for it."

"Well," said Dr. Craven, "so long as going without food agrees with them we need not disturb ourselves. The boy is a new creature."

"So is the girl," said Mrs. Medlock. "She's begun to be downright pretty since she's filled out and lost her ugly little sour look. Her hair's grown thick and healthy looking and she's got a bright color. The glummest, ill-natured little thing she used to be and now her and Master Colin laugh together like a pair of crazy young ones. Perhaps they're growing fat on that."

"Perhaps they are," said Dr. Craven. "Let them laugh."

CHAPTER 25
THE CURTAIN

And the secret garden bloomed and bloomed and every morning revealed new miracles. In the robin's nest there were Eggs and the robin's mate sat upon them keeping them warm with her feathery little breast and careful wings. At first she was very nervous and the robin himself was indignantly watchful. Even Dickon did not go near the close-grown corner in those days, but waited until by the quiet working of some mysterious spell he seemed to have conveyed to the soul of the little pair that in the garden there was nothing which was not quite like themselves—nothing which did not understand the wonderfulness of what was happening to them—the immense, tender, terrible, heartbreaking beauty and solemnity of Eggs. If there had been one person in that garden who had not known through all his or her innermost being that if an Egg were taken away or hurt the whole world would whirl round and crash through space and come to an end—if there had been even one who did not feel it and act accordingly there could have been no happiness even in that golden springtime air. But they all knew it and felt it and the robin and his mate knew they knew it.

At first the robin watched Mary and Colin with sharp anxiety. For some mysterious reason he knew he need not watch Dickon. The first moment he set his dew-bright black eye on Dickon he knew he was not a stranger but a sort of robin without beak or feathers. He could speak robin (which is a quite distinct language not to be mistaken for any other). To speak robin to a robin is like speaking French to a Frenchman. Dickon always spoke it to the robin himself, so the queer gibberish he used when he spoke to humans did not matter in the least. The robin thought he spoke this gibberish to them because they were not intelligent enough to understand feathered speech. His movements also were robin. They never startled one by being sudden enough to seem dangerous or threatening. Any robin could understand Dickon, so his presence was not even disturbing.

But at the outset it seemed necessary to be on guard against the other two. In the first place the boy creature did not come into the garden on his legs. He was pushed in on a thing with wheels and the skins of wild animals were thrown over him. That in itself was doubtful. Then when he began to stand up and move about he did it in a queer unaccustomed way and the others seemed to have to help him. The robin used to secrete himself in a bush and watch this anxiously, his head tilted first on one side and then on the other. He thought that the slow movements might mean that he was preparing to pounce, as cats do. When cats are preparing to pounce they creep over the ground very slowly. The robin talked this over with his mate a great deal for a few days but after that he decided not to speak of the subject because her terror was so great that he was afraid it might be injurious to the Eggs.

When the boy began to walk by himself and even to move more quickly it was an immense relief. But for a long time—or it seemed a long time to the robin—he was a source of some anxiety. He did not act as the other humans did. He seemed very fond of walking but he had a way of sitting or lying down for a while and then getting up in a disconcerting manner to begin again.

One day the robin remembered that when he himself had been made to learn to fly by his parents he had done much the same sort of thing. He had taken short flights of a few yards and then had been obliged to rest. So it occurred to him that this boy was learning to fly—or rather to walk. He mentioned this to his mate and when he told her that the Eggs would probably conduct themselves in the same way after they were fledged she was quite comforted and even became eagerly interested and derived great pleasure from watching the boy over the edge of her nest—though she always thought that the Eggs would be much cleverer and learn more quickly. But then she said indulgently that humans were always more clumsy and slow than Eggs and most of them never seemed really to learn to fly at all. You never met them in the air or on tree-tops.

After a while the boy began to move about as the others did, but all three of the children at times did unusual things. They would stand under the trees and move their arms and legs and heads about in a way which was neither walking nor running nor sitting down. They went through these movements at intervals every day and the robin was never able to explain to his mate what they were doing or trying to do. He could only say that he was sure that the Eggs would never flap about in such a manner; but as the boy who could speak robin so fluently was doing the thing with them, birds could be quite sure that the actions were not of a dangerous nature. Of course neither the robin nor his mate had ever heard of the champion wrestler, Bob Haworth, and his exercises for making the muscles stand out like lumps. Robins are not like human beings; their muscles are always exercised from the first and so they develop themselves in a natural manner. If you have to fly about to find every meal you eat, your muscles do not become atrophied (atrophied means wasted away through want of use).

When the boy was walking and running about and digging and weeding like the others, the nest in the corner was brooded over by a great peace and content. Fears for the Eggs became things of the past. Knowing that your Eggs were as safe as if they were locked in a bank vault and the fact that you could watch so many curious things going on made setting a most entertaining occupation. On wet days the Eggs' mother sometimes felt even a little dull because the children did not come into the garden.

But even on wet days it could not be said that Mary and Colin were dull. One morning when the rain streamed down unceasingly and Colin was beginning to feel a little restive, as he was obliged to remain on his sofa because it was not safe to get up and walk about, Mary had an inspiration.

"Now that I am a real boy," Colin had said, "my legs and arms and all my body are so full of Magic that I can't keep them still. They want to be doing things all the time. Do you know that when I waken in the morning, Mary, when it's quite early and the birds are just shouting outside and everything seems just shouting for joy—even the trees and things we can't really hear—I feel as if I must jump out of bed and shout myself. And if I did it, just think what would happen!"

Mary giggled inordinately.

"The nurse would come running and Mrs. Medlock would come running and they would be sure you had gone crazy and they'd send for the doctor," she said.

Colin giggled himself. He could see how they would all look—how horrified by his outbreak and how amazed to see him standing upright.

"I wish my father would come home," he said. "I want to tell him myself. I'm always thinking about it—but we couldn't go on like this much longer. I can't stand lying still and pretending, and besides I look too different. I wish it wasn't raining to-day."

It was then Mistress Mary had her inspiration.

"Colin," she began mysteriously, "do you know how many rooms there are in this house?"

"About a thousand, I suppose," he answered.

"There's about a hundred no one ever goes into," said Mary. "And one rainy day I went and looked into ever so many of them. No one ever knew, though Mrs. Medlock nearly found me out. I lost my way when I was coming back and I stopped at the end of your corridor. That was the second time I heard you crying."

Colin started up on his sofa.

"A hundred rooms no one goes into," he said. "It sounds almost like a secret garden. Suppose we go and look at them. You could wheel me in my chair and nobody would know where we went."

"That's what I was thinking," said Mary. "No one would dare to follow us. There are galleries where you could run. We could do our exercises. There is a little Indian room where there is a cabinet full of ivory elephants. There are all sorts of rooms."

"Ring the bell," said Colin.

When the nurse came in he gave his orders.

"I want my chair," he said. "Miss Mary and I are going to look at the part of the house which is not used. John can push me as far as the picture-gallery because there are some stairs. Then he must go away and leave us alone until I send for him again."

Rainy days lost their terrors that morning. When the footman had wheeled the chair into the picture-gallery and left the two together in obedience to orders, Colin and Mary looked at each other delighted. As soon as Mary had made sure that John was really on his way back to his own quarters below stairs, Colin got out of his chair.

"I am going to run from one end of the gallery to the other," he said, "and then I am going to jump and then we will do Bob Haworth's exercises."

And they did all these things and many others. They looked at the portraits and found the plain little girl dressed in green brocade and holding the parrot on her finger.

"All these," said Colin, "must be my relations. They lived a long time ago. That parrot one, I believe, is one of my great, great, great, great aunts. She looks rather like you, Mary—not as you look now but as you looked when you came here. Now you are a great deal fatter and better looking."

"So are you," said Mary, and they both laughed.

They went to the Indian room and amused themselves with the ivory elephants. They found the rose-colored brocade boudoir and the hole in the cushion the mouse had left but the mice had grown up and run away and the hole was empty. They saw more rooms and made more discoveries than Mary had made on her first pilgrimage. They found new corridors and corners and flights of steps and new old pictures they liked and weird old

things they did not know the use of. It was a curiously entertaining morning and the feeling of wandering about in the same
house with other people but at the same time feeling as if one
were miles away from them was a fascinating thing.

"I'm glad we came," Colin said. "I never knew I lived in such a
big queer old place. I like it. We will ramble about every rainy day.
We shall always be finding new queer corners and things."

That morning they had found among other things such good
appetites that when they returned to Colin's room it was not possible to send the luncheon away untouched.

When the nurse carried the tray down-stairs she slapped it
down on the kitchen dresser so that Mrs. Loomis, the cook, could
see the highly polished dishes and plates.

"Look at that!" she said. "This is a house of mystery, and those
two children are the greatest mysteries in it."

"If they keep that up every day," said the strong young footman John, "there'd be small wonder that he weighs twice as much
to-day as he did a month ago. I should have to give up my place
in time, for fear of doing my muscles an injury."

That afternoon Mary noticed that something new had happened in Colin's room. She had noticed it the day before but had
said nothing because she thought the change might have been
made by chance. She said nothing to-day but she sat and looked
fixedly at the picture over the mantel. She could look at it because the curtain had been drawn aside. That was the change
she noticed.

"I know what you want me to tell you," said Colin, after she
had stared a few minutes. "I always know when you want me to
tell you something. You are wondering why the curtain is drawn
back. I am going to keep it like that."

"Why?" asked Mary.

"Because it doesn't make me angry any more to see her laughing. I wakened when it was bright moonlight two nights ago and
felt as if the Magic was filling the room and making everything so
splendid that I couldn't lie still. I got up and looked out of the

window. The room was quite light and there was a patch of
moonlight on the curtain and somehow that made me go and pull
the cord. She looked right down at me as if she were laughing
because she was glad I was standing there. It made me like to
look at her. I want to see her laughing like that all the time. I
think she must have been a sort of Magic person perhaps."

"You are so like her now," said Mary, "that sometimes I think
perhaps you are her ghost made into a boy."

That idea seemed to impress Colin. He thought it over and
then answered her slowly.

"If I were her ghost—my father would be fond of me," he said.

"Do you want him to be fond of you?" inquired Mary.

"I used to hate it because he was not fond of me. If he grew
fond of me I think I should tell him about the Magic. It might
make him more cheerful."

CHAPTER 26
"IT'S MOTHER!"

Their belief in the Magic was an abiding thing. After the morning's incantations Colin sometimes gave them Magic lectures.

"I like to do it," he explained, "because when I grow up and make great scientific discoveries I shall be obliged to lecture about them and so this is practise. I can only give short lectures now because I am very young, and besides Ben Weatherstaff would feel as if he was in church and he would go to sleep."

"Th' best thing about lecturin'," said Ben, "is that a chap can get up an' say aught he pleases an' no other chap can answer him back. I wouldn't be agen' lecturin' a bit mysel' sometimes."

But when Colin held forth under his tree old Ben fixed devouring eyes on him and kept them there. He looked him over with critical affection. It was not so much the lecture which interested him as the legs which looked straighter and stronger each day, the boyish head which held itself up so well, the once sharp chin and hollow cheeks which had filled and rounded out and the eyes which had begun to hold the light he remembered in another pair. Sometimes when Colin felt Ben's earnest gaze meant that he was much impressed he wondered what he was reflecting on and once when he had seemed quite entranced he questioned him.

"What are you thinking about, Ben Weatherstaff?" he asked.

"I was thinkin'," answered Ben, "as I'd warrant tha's gone up three or four pound this week. I was lookin' at tha' calves an' tha' shoulders. I'd like to get thee on a pair o' scales."

"It's the Magic and—Mrs. Sowerby's buns and milk and things," said Colin. "You see the scientific experiment has succeeded."

That morning Dickon was too late to hear the lecture. When

he came he was ruddy with running and his funny face looked more twinkling than usual. As they had a good deal of weeding to do after the rains they fell to work. They always had plenty to do after a warm deep sinking rain. The moisture which was good for the flowers was also good for the weeds which thrust up tiny blades of grass and points of leaves which must be pulled up before their roots took too firm hold. Colin was as good at weeding as any one in these days and he could lecture while he was doing it.

"The Magic works best when you work yourself," he said this morning. "You can feel it in your bones and muscles. I am going to read books about bones and muscles, but I am going to write a book about Magic. I am making it up now. I keep finding out things."

It was not very long after he had said this that he laid down his trowel and stood up on his feet. He had been silent for several minutes and they had seen that he was thinking out lectures, as he often did. When he dropped his trowel and stood upright it seemed to Mary and Dickon as if a sudden strong thought had made him do it. He stretched himself out to his tallest height and he threw out his arms exultantly. Color glowed in his face and his strange eyes widened with joyfulness. All at once he had realized something to the full.

"Mary! Dickon!" he cried. "Just look at me!"

They stopped their weeding and looked at him.

"Do you remember that first morning you brought me in here?" he demanded.

Dickon was looking at him very hard. Being an animal charmer he could see more things than most people could and many of them were things he never talked about. He saw some of them now in this boy.

"Aye, that we do," he answered.

Mary looked hard too, but she said nothing.

"Just this minute," said Colin, "all at once I remembered it myself—when I looked at my hand digging with the trowel—and

I had to stand up on my feet to see if it was real. And it *is* real! I'm *well*—I'm *well*!"

"Aye, that tha' art!" said Dickon.

"I'm well! I'm well!" said Colin again, and his face went quite red all over.

He had known it before in a way, he had hoped it and felt it and thought about it, but just at that minute something had rushed all through him—a sort of rapturous belief and realization and it had been so strong that he could not help calling out.

"I shall live forever and ever and ever!" he cried grandly. "I shall find out thousands and thousands of things. I shall find out about people and creatures and everything that grows—like Dickon—and I shall never stop making Magic. I'm well! I'm well! I feel—I feel as if I want to shout out something—something thankful, joyful!"

Ben Weatherstaff, who had been working near a rose-bush, glanced round at him.

"Tha' might sing th' Doxology," he suggested in his dryest grunt. He had no opinion of the Doxology and he did not make the suggestion with any particular reverence.

But Colin was of an exploring mind and he knew nothing about the Doxology.

"What is that?" he inquired.

"Dickon can sing it for thee, I'll warrant," replied Ben Weatherstaff.

Dickon answered with his all-perceiving animal charmer's smile.

"They sing it i' church," he said. "Mother says she believes th' skylarks sings it when they gets up i' th' mornin'."

"If she says that, it must be a nice song," Colin answered. "I've never been in a church myself. I was always too ill. Sing it, Dickon. I want to hear it."

Dickon was quite simple and unaffected about it. He understood what Colin felt better than Colin did himself. He understood by a sort of instinct so natural that he did not know it was understanding. He pulled off his cap and looked round still smiling.

"Tha' must take off tha' cap," he said to Colin, "an' so mun tha', Ben—an' tha' mun stand up, tha' knows."

Colin took off his cap and the sun shone on and warmed his thick hair as he watched Dickon intently. Ben Weatherstaff scrambled up from his knees and bared his head too with a sort of puzzled half-resentful look on his old face as if he didn't know exactly why he was doing this remarkable thing.

Dickon stood out among the trees and rose-bushes and began to sing in quite a simple matter-of-fact way and in a nice strong boy voice:

> "Praise God from whom all blessings flow,
> Praise Him all creatures here below,
> Praise Him above ye Heavenly Host,
> Praise Father, Son, and Holy Ghost.
>   Amen."

When he had finished, Ben Weatherstaff was standing quite still with his jaws set obstinately but with a disturbed look in his eyes fixed on Colin. Colin's face was thoughtful and appreciative.

"It is a very nice song," he said. "I like it. Perhaps it means just what I mean when I want to shout out that I am thankful to the Magic." He stopped and thought in a puzzled way. "Perhaps they are both the same thing. How can we know the exact names of everything? Sing it again, Dickon. Let us try, Mary. I want to sing it, too. It's my song. How does it begin? 'Praise God from whom all blessings flow'?"

And they sang it again, and Mary and Colin lifted their voices as musically as they could and Dickon's swelled quite loud and beautiful—and at the second line Ben Weatherstaff raspingly cleared his throat and at the third he joined in with such vigor that it seemed almost savage and when the "Amen" came to an end Mary observed that the very same thing had happened to him which had happened when he found out that Colin was not a cripple—his chin was twitching and he was staring and winking and his leathery old cheeks were wet.

"I never seed no sense in th' Doxology afore," he said hoarsely, "but I may change my mind i' time. I should say tha'd gone up five pound this week, Mester Colin—five on 'em!"

Colin was looking across the garden at something attracting his attention and his expression had become a startled one.

"Who is coming in here?" he said quickly. "Who is it?"

The door in the ivied wall had been pushed gently open and a woman had entered. She had come in with the last line of their song and she had stood still listening and looking at them. With the ivy behind her, the sunlight drifting through the trees and dappling her long blue cloak, and her nice fresh face smiling across the greenery she was rather like a softly colored illustration in one of Colin's books. She had wonderful affectionate eyes which seemed to take everything in—all of them, even Ben Weatherstaff and the "creatures" and every flower that was in bloom. Unexpectedly as she had appeared, not one of them felt that she was an intruder at all. Dickon's eyes lighted like lamps.

"It's Mother—that's who it is!" he cried and he went across the grass at a run.

Colin began to move toward her, too, and Mary went with him. They both felt their pulses beat faster.

"It's Mother!" Dickon said again when they met half-way. "I knowed tha' wanted to see her an' I told her where th' door was hid."

Colin held out his hand with a sort of flushed royal shyness but his eyes quite devoured her face.

"Even when I was ill I wanted to see you," he said, "you and Dickon and the secret garden. I'd never wanted to see any one or anything before."

The sight of his uplifted face brought about a sudden change in her own. She flushed and the corners of her mouth shook and a mist seemed to sweep over her eyes.

"Eh! dear lad!" she broke out tremulously. "Eh! dear lad!" as if she had not known she were going to say it. She did not say, "Mester Colin," but just "dear lad" quite suddenly. She might

have said it to Dickon in the same way if she had seen something
in his face which touched her. Colin liked it.

"Are you surprised because I am so well?" he asked.

She put her hand on his shoulder and smiled the mist out of
her eyes.

"Aye, that I am!" she said; "but tha'rt so like thy mother tha'
made my heart jump."

"Do you think," said Colin a little awkwardly, "that will make
my father like me?"

"Aye, for sure, dear lad," she answered and she gave his shoulder a soft quick pat. "He mun come home—he mun come home."

"Susan Sowerby," said Ben Weatherstaff, getting close to her.
"Look at th' lad's legs, wilt tha'? They was like drumsticks i'
stockin' two month' ago—an' I heard folk tell as they was bandy
an' knock-kneed both at th' same time. Look at 'em now!"

Susan Sowerby laughed a comfortable laugh.

"They're goin' to be fine strong lad's legs in a bit," she said.
"Let him go on playin' an' workin' in th' garden an' eatin' hearty
an' drinkin' plenty o' good sweet milk an' there'll not be a finer
pair i' Yorkshire, thank God for it."

She put both hands on Mistress Mary's shoulders and looked
her little face over in a motherly fashion.

"An' thee, too!" she said. "Tha'rt grown near as hearty as our
'Lizabeth Ellen. I'll warrant tha'rt like thy mother too. Our Martha
told me as Mrs. Medlock heard she was a pretty woman. Tha'lt be
like a blush rose when tha' grows up, my little lass, bless thee."

She did not mention that when Martha came home on
her "day out" and described the plain sallow child she had
said that she had no confidence whatever in what Mrs. Medlock had heard. "It doesn't stand to reason that a pretty woman
could be th' mother o' such a fou' little lass," she had added
obstinately.

Mary had not had time to pay much attention to her changing face. She had only known that she looked "different" and
seemed to have a great deal more hair and that it was growing

very fast. But remembering her pleasure in looking at the Mem Sahib in the past she was glad to hear that she might some day look like her.

Susan Sowerby went round their garden with them and was told the whole story of it and shown every bush and tree which had come alive. Colin walked on one side of her and Mary on the other. Each of them kept looking up at her comfortable rosy face, secretly curious about the delightful feeling she gave them—a sort of warm, supported feeling. It seemed as if she understood them as Dickon understood his "creatures." She stooped over the flowers and talked about them as if they were children. Soot followed her and once or twice cawed at her and flew upon her shoulder as if it were Dickon's. When they told her about the robin and the first flight of the young ones she laughed a motherly little mellow laugh in her throat.

"I suppose learnin' 'em to fly is like learnin' children to walk, but I'm feared I should be all in a worrit if mine had wings instead o' legs," she said.

It was because she seemed such a wonderful woman in her nice moorland cottage way that at last she was told about the Magic.

"Do you believe in Magic?" asked Colin after he had explained about Indian fakirs. "I do hope you do."

"That I do, lad," she answered. "I never knowed it by that name but what does th' name matter? I warrant they call it a different name i' France an' a different one i' Germany. Th' same thing as set th' seeds swellin' an' th' sun shinin' made thee a well lad an' it's th' Good Thing. It isn't like us poor fools as think it matters if us is called out of our names. Th' Big Good Thing doesn't stop to worrit, bless thee. It goes on makin' worlds by th' million—worlds like us. Never thee stop believin' in th' Big Good Thing an' knowin' th' world's full of it—an' call it what tha' likes. Tha' wert singin' to it when I come into th' garden."

"I felt so joyful," said Colin, opening his beautiful strange eyes at her. Suddenly I felt how different I was—how strong my arms and legs were, you know—and how I could dig and stand—and I jumped up and wanted to shout out something to anything that would listen."

"Th' Magic listened when tha' sung th' Doxology. It would ha' listened to anything tha'd sung. It was th' joy that mattered. Eh! lad, lad—what's names to th' Joy Maker," and she gave his shoulders a quick soft pat again.

She had packed a basket which held a regular feast this morning, and when the hungry hour came and Dickon brought it out from its hiding place, she sat down with them under their tree and watched them devour their food, laughing and quite gloating over their appetites. She was full of fun and made them laugh at all sorts of odd things. She told them stories in broad Yorkshire and taught them new words. She laughed as if she could not help it when they told her of the increasing difficulty there was in pretending that Colin was still a fretful invalid.

"You see we can't help laughing nearly all the time when we are together," explained Colin. "And it doesn't sound ill at all. We try to choke it back but it will burst out and that sounds worse than ever."

"There's one thing that comes into my mind so often," said Mary, "and I can scarcely ever hold in when I think of it suddenly. I keep thinking suppose Colin's face should get to look like a full moon. It isn't like one yet but he gets a tiny bit fatter every day— and suppose some morning it should look like one—what should we do!"

"Bless us all, I can see tha' has a good bit o' play actin' to do," said Susan Sowerby. "But tha' won't have to keep it up much longer. Mester Craven'll come home."

"Do you think he will?" asked Colin. "Why?"

Susan Sowerby chuckled softly.

"I suppose it 'ud nigh break thy heart if he found out before tha' told him in tha' own way," she said. "Tha's laid awake nights plannin' it."

"I couldn't bear any one else to tell him," said Colin. "I think about different ways every day. I think now I just want to run into his room."

"That'd be a fine start for him," said Susan Sowerby. "I'd like to see his face, lad. I would that! He mun come back—that he mun."

One of the things they talked of was the visit they were to make to her cottage. They planned it all. They were to drive over the moor and lunch out of doors among the heather. They would see all the twelve children and Dickon's garden and would not come back until they were tired.

Susan Sowerby got up at last to return to the house and Mrs. Medlock. It was time for Colin to be wheeled back also. But before he got into his chair he stood quite close to Susan and fixed his eyes on her with a kind of bewildered adoration and he suddenly caught hold of the fold of her blue cloak and held it fast.

"You are just what I—what I wanted," he said. "I wish you were my mother—as well as Dickon's!"

All at once Susan Sowerby bent down and drew him with her arms close against the bosom under the blue cloak—as if he had been Dickon's brother. The quick mist swept over her eyes.

"Eh! dear lad!" she said. "Thy own mother's in this 'ere very garden, I do believe. She couldna' keep out of it. Thy father mun come back to thee—he mun!"

CHAPTER 27
IN THE GARDEN

In each century since the beginning of the world wonderful things have been discovered. In the last century more amazing things were found out than in any century before. In this new century hundreds of things still more astounding will be brought to light. At first people refuse to believe that a strange new thing can be done, then they begin to hope it can be done, then they see it can be done—then it is done and all the world wonders why it was not done centuries ago. One of the new things people began to find out in the last century was that thoughts—just mere thoughts—are as powerful as electric batteries—as good for one as sunlight is, or as bad for one as poison. To let a sad thought or a bad one get into your mind is as dangerous as letting a scarlet fever germ get into your body. If you let it stay there after it has got in you may never get over it as long as you live.

So long as Mistress Mary's mind was full of disagreeable thoughts about her dislikes and sour opinions of people and her determination not to be pleased by or interested in anything, she was a yellow-faced, sickly, bored and wretched child. Circumstances, however, were very kind to her, though she was not at all aware of it. They began to push her about for her own good. When her mind gradually filled itself with robins, and moorland cottages crowded with children, with queer crabbed old gardeners and common little Yorkshire housemaids, with springtime and with secret gardens coming alive day by day, and also with a moor boy and his "creatures," there was no room left for the disagreeable thoughts which affected her liver and her digestion and made her yellow and tired.

So long as Colin shut himself up in his room and thought only of his fears and weakness and his detestation of people who looked at him and reflected hourly on humps and early death, he was a hysterical half-crazy little hypochondriac who knew nothing of the sunshine and the spring and also did not know that he could get well and could stand upon his feet if he tried to do it. When new beautiful thoughts began to push out the old hideous ones, life began to come back to him, his blood ran healthily through his veins and strength poured into him like a flood. His scientific experiment was quite practical and simple and there was nothing weird about it at all. Much more surprising things can happen to anyone who, when a disagreeable or discouraged thought comes into his mind, just has the sense to remember in time and push it out by putting in an agreeable determinedly courageous one. Two things cannot be in one place.

"Where you tend a rose, my lad,
A thistle cannot grow."

While the secret garden was coming alive and two children were coming alive with it, there was a man wandering about certain far-away beautiful places in the Norwegian fiords and the valleys and mountains of Switzerland and he was a man who for ten years had kept his mind filled with dark and heart-broken thinking. He had not been courageous; he had never tried to put any other thoughts in the place of the dark ones. He had wandered by blue lakes and thought them; he had lain on mountain-sides with sheets of deep blue gentians blooming all about him and flower breaths filling all the air and he had thought them. A terrible sorrow had fallen upon him when he had been happy and he had let his soul fill itself with blackness and had refused obstinately to allow any rift of light to pierce through. He had forgotten and deserted his home and his duties. When he traveled about, darkness so brooded over him that the sight of him was a wrong done to other people because it was as if he poisoned the air about him with gloom. Most strangers thought he must be either half mad or a man with some hidden crime on his soul. He was a tall man with a drawn face and crooked shoulders and the name he always entered on hotel registers was, "Archibald Craven, Misselthwaite Manor, Yorkshire, England."

He had traveled far and wide since the day he saw Mistress Mary in his study and told her she might have her "bit of earth." He had been in the most beautiful places in Europe, though he had remained nowhere more than a few days. He had chosen the quietest and remotest spots. He had been on the tops of mountains whose heads were in the clouds and had looked down on other mountains when the sun rose and touched them with such light as made it seem as if the world were just being born.

But the light had never seemed to touch himself until one day when he realized that for the first time in ten years a strange thing had happened. He was in a wonderful valley in the Austrian Tyrol and he had been walking alone through such beauty as might have lifted any man's soul out of shadow. He had walked a long way and it had not lifted his. But at last he had felt tired and had thrown himself down to rest on a carpet of moss by a stream. It was a clear little stream which ran quite merrily along on its narrow way through the luscious damp greenness. Sometimes it made a sound rather like very low laughter as it bubbled over and round stones. He saw birds come and dip their heads to drink in it and then flick their wings and fly away. It seemed like a thing alive and yet its tiny voice made the stillness seem deeper. The valley was very, very still.

As he sat gazing into the clear running of the water, Archibald Craven gradually felt his mind and body both grow quiet, as quiet as the valley itself. He wondered if he were going to sleep, but he was not. He sat and gazed at the sunlit water and his eyes began to see things growing at its edge. There was one lovely mass of blue forget-me-nots growing so close to the stream that its leaves were wet and at these he found himself looking as he remembered he had looked at such things years ago. He was actually thinking tenderly how lovely it was and what wonders of blue its hundreds of little blossoms were. He did not know that just that simple thought was slowly filling his mind—filling and filling it until other things were softly pushed aside. It was as if a sweet clear spring had begun to rise in a stagnant pool and had risen and risen until at last it swept the dark water away. But of course he did not think of this himself. He only knew that the valley seemed to grow quieter and quieter as he sat and stared at the bright delicate blueness. He did not know how long he sat there or what was happening to him, but at last he moved as if he were awakening and he got up slowly and stood on the moss carpet, drawing a long, deep, soft breath and wondering at himself. Something seemed to have been unbound and released in him, very quietly.

"What is it?" he said, almost in a whisper, and he passed his hand over his forehead. "I almost feel as if—I were alive!"

I do not know enough about the wonderfulness of undiscovered things to be able to explain how this had happened to him. Neither does any one else yet. He did not understand at all himself—but he remembered this strange hour months afterward when he was at Misselthwaite again and he found out quite by accident that on this very day Colin had cried out as he went into the secret garden:

"I am going to live forever and ever and ever!"

The singular calmness remained with him the rest of the evening and he slept a new reposeful sleep; but it was not with him very long. He did not know that it could be kept. By the next night he had opened the doors wide to his dark thoughts and they had come trooping and rushing back. He left the valley and went on his wandering way again. But, strange as it seemed to him, there were minutes—sometimes half-hours—when, without his knowing why, the black burden seemed to lift itself again and he knew he was a living man and not a dead one. Slowly—slowly—for no reason that he knew of—he was "coming alive" with the garden.

As the golden summer changed into the deeper golden autumn he went to the Lake of Como. There he found the loveliness of a dream. He spent his days upon the crystal blueness of the lake or he walked back into the soft thick verdure of the hills and tramped until he was tired so that he might sleep. But by this time he had begun to sleep better, he knew, and his dreams had ceased to be a terror to him.

"Perhaps," he thought, "my body is growing stronger."

It was growing stronger but—because of the rare peaceful hours when his thoughts were changed—his soul was slowly growing stronger, too. He began to think of Misselthwaite and wonder if he should not go home. Now and then he wondered vaguely about his boy and asked himself what he should feel when he went and stood by the carved four-posted bed again and looked down at the sharply chiseled ivory-white face while it slept and the black lashes rimmed so startlingly the close-shut eyes. He shrank from it.

One marvel of a day he had walked so far that when he returned the moon was high and full and all the world was purple shadow and silver. The stillness of lake and shore and wood was so wonderful that he did not go into the villa he lived in. He walked down to a little bowered terrace at the water's edge and sat upon a seat and breathed in all the heavenly scents of the night. He felt the strange calmness stealing over him and it grew deeper and deeper until he fell asleep.

He did not know when he fell asleep and when he began to dream; his dream was so real that he did not feel as if he were dreaming. He remembered afterward how intensely wide awake and alert he had thought he was. He thought that as he sat and breathed in the scent of the late roses and listened to the lapping of the water at his feet he heard a voice calling. It was sweet and clear and happy and far away. It seemed very far, but he heard it as distinctly as if it had been at his very side.

"Archie! Archie! Archie!" it said, and then again, sweeter and clearer than before, "Archie! Archie!"

He thought he sprang to his feet not even startled. It was such a real voice and it seemed so natural that he should hear it.

"Lilias! Lilias!" he answered, "Lilias! where are you?"

"In the garden," it came back like a sound from a golden flute. "In the garden!"

And then the dream ended. But he did not awaken. He slept soundly and sweetly all through the lovely night. When he did awake at last it was brilliant morning and a servant was standing staring at him. He was an Italian servant and was accustomed, as all the servants of the villa were, to accepting without question any strange thing his foreign master might do. No one ever knew when he would go out or come in or where he would choose to sleep or if he would roam about the garden or lie in the boat on the lake all night. The man held a salver with some letters on it and he waited quietly until Mr. Craven took them. When he had gone away Mr. Craven sat a few moments holding them in his hand and looking at the lake. His strange calm was still upon him and something more—a lightness as if the cruel thing which had been done had not happened as he thought—as if something had changed. He was remembering the dream—the real—real dream.

"In the garden!" he said, wondering at himself. "In the garden! But the door is locked and the key is buried deep."

When he glanced at the letters a few minutes later he saw that the one lying at the top of the rest was an English letter and came from Yorkshire. It was directed in a plain woman's hand but it was not a hand he knew. He opened it, scarcely thinking of the writer, but the first words attracted his attention at once.

> *"Dear Sir:*
>
> "I am Susan Sowerby that made bold to speak to you once on the moor. It was about Miss Mary I spoke. I will make bold to speak again. Please, sir, I would come home if I was you. I think you would be glad to come and—if you will excuse me, sir—I think your lady would ask you to come if she was here.
>
> > "Your obedient servant,
> > "SUSAN SOWERBY."

Mr. Craven read the letter twice before he put it back in its envelope. He kept thinking about the dream.

"I will go back to Misselthwaite," he said. "Yes, I'll go at once."

And he went through the garden to the villa and ordered Pitcher to prepare for his return to England.

In a few days he was in Yorkshire again, and on his long railroad journey he found himself thinking of his boy as he had never thought in all the ten years past. During those years he had only wished to forget him. Now, though he did not intend to think about him, memories of him constantly drifted into his mind. He remembered the black days when he had raved like a madman because the child was alive and the mother was dead. He had refused to see it, and when he had gone to look at it at last it had been such a weak wretched thing that every one had been sure it would die in a few days. But to the surprise of those who took care of it the days passed and it lived and then every one believed it would be a deformed and crippled creature.

He had not meant to be a bad father, but he had not felt like a father at all. He had supplied doctors and nurses and luxuries, but he had shrunk from the mere thought of the boy and had buried himself in his own misery. The first time after a year's absence he returned to Misselthwaite and the small miserable looking thing languidly and indifferently lifted to his face the great gray eyes with black lashes round them, so like and yet so horribly unlike the happy eyes he had adored, he could not bear the sight of them and turned away pale as death. After that he scarcely ever saw him except when he was asleep, and all he knew of him was that he was a confirmed invalid, with a vicious, hysterical, half-insane temper. He could only be kept from furies dangerous to himself by being given his own way in every detail.

All this was not an uplifting thing to recall, but as the train whirled him through mountain passes and golden plains the man who was "coming alive" began to think in a new way and he thought long and steadily and deeply.

"Perhaps I have been all wrong for ten years," he said to himself. "Ten years is a long time. It may be too late to do anything—quite too late. What have I been thinking of!"

Of course this was the wrong Magic—to begin by saying "too late." Even Colin could have told him that. But he knew nothing of Magic—either black or white. This he had yet to learn. He wondered if Susan Sowerby had taken courage and written to him only because the motherly creature had realized that the boy was much worse—was fatally ill. If he had not been under the spell of the curious calmness which had taken possession of him he would have been more wretched than ever. But the calm had brought a sort of courage and hope with it. Instead of giving way to thoughts of the worst he actually found he was trying to believe in better things.

"Could it be possible that she sees that I may be able to do him good and control him?" he thought. "I will go and see her on my way to Misselthwaite."

But when on his way across the moor he stopped the carriage at the cottage, seven or eight children who were playing about gathered in a group and bobbing seven or eight friendly and polite curtsies told him that their mother had gone to the other side of the moor early in the morning to help a woman who had a new baby. "Our Dickon," they volunteered, was over at the Manor working in one of the gardens where he went several days each week.

Mr. Craven looked over the collection of sturdy little bodies and round red-cheeked faces, each one grinning in its own particular way, and he awoke to the fact that they were a healthy likable lot. He smiled at their friendly grins and took a golden sovereign from his pocket and gave it to "our 'Lizabeth Ellen" who was the oldest.

"If you divide that into eight parts there will be half a crown for each of you," he said.

Then amid grins and chuckles and bobbing of curtsies he drove away, leaving ecstasy and nudging elbows and little jumps of joy behind.

The drive across the wonderfulness of the moor was a sooth-ing thing. Why did it seem to give him a sense of home-coming which he had been sure he could never feel again—that sense of the beauty of land and sky and purple bloom of distance and a warming of the heart at drawing nearer to the great old house which had held those of his blood for six hundred years? How he had driven away from it the last time, shuddering to think of its closed rooms and the boy lying in the four-posted bed with the brocaded hangings. Was it possible that perhaps he might find him changed a little for the better and that he might overcome his shrinking from him? How real that dream had been—how won-derful and clear the voice which called back to him, "In the garden—In the garden!"

"I will try to find the key," he said. "I will try to open the door. I must—though I don't know why."

When he arrived at the Manor the servants who received him with the usual ceremony noticed that he looked better and that he did not go to the remote rooms where he usually lived attend-ed by Pitcher. He went into the library and sent for Mrs. Medlock. She came to him somewhat excited and curious and flustered.

"How is Master Colin, Medlock?" he inquired.

"Well, sir," Mrs. Medlock answered, "he's—he's different, in a manner of speaking."

"Worse?" he suggested.

Mrs. Medlock really was flushed.

"Well, you see, sir," she tried to explain, "neither Dr. Craven, nor the nurse, nor me can exactly make him out."

"Why is that?"

"To tell the truth, sir, Master Colin might be better and he might be changing for the worse. His appetite, sir, is past under-standing—and his ways—"

"Has he become more—more peculiar?" her master asked, knitting his brows anxiously.

"That's it, sir. He's growing very peculiar—when you compare him with what he used to be. He used to eat nothing and then suddenly he began to eat something enormous—and then he stopped again all at once and the meals were sent back just as they used to be. You never knew, sir, perhaps, that out of doors he never would let himself be taken. The things we've gone through to get him to go out in his chair would leave a body trembling like a leaf. He'd throw himself into such a state that Dr. Craven said he couldn't be responsible for forcing him. Well, sir, just without warning—not long after one of his worst tantrums he suddenly insisted on being taken out every day by Miss Mary and Susan Sowerby's boy Dickon that could push his chair. He took a fancy to both Miss Mary and Dickon, and Dickon brought his tame animals, and, if you'll credit it, sir, out of doors he will stay from morning until night."

"How does he look?" was the next question.

"If he took his food natural, sir, you'd think he was putting on flesh—but we're afraid it may be a sort of bloat. He laughs sometimes in a queer way when he's alone with Miss Mary. He never used to laugh at all. Dr. Craven is coming to see you at once, if you'll allow him. He never was as puzzled in his life."

"Where is Master Colin now?" Mr. Craven asked.

"In the garden, sir. He's always in the garden—though not a human creature is allowed to go near for fear they'll look at him."

Mr. Craven scarcely heard her last words.

"In the garden," he said, and after he had sent Mrs. Medlock away he stood and repeated it again and again. "In the garden!"

He had to make an effort to bring himself back to the place he was standing in and when he felt he was on earth again he turned and went out of the room. He took his way, as Mary had done, through the door in the shrubbery and among the laurels and the fountain beds. The fountain was playing now and was encircled by beds of brilliant autumn flowers. He crossed the lawn and turned into the Long Walk by the ivied walls. He did not walk quickly, but slowly, and his eyes were on the path. He felt as if he were being drawn back to the place he had so long forsaken, and he did not know why. As he drew near to it his step became still more slow. He knew where the door was even though the ivy hung thick over it—but he did not know exactly where it lay—that buried key.

So he stopped and stood still, looking about him, and almost the moment after he had paused he started and listened—asking himself if he were walking in a dream.

The ivy hung thick over the door, the key was buried under the shrub, no human being had passed that portal for ten lonely years—and yet inside the garden there were sounds. They were the sounds of running scuffling feet seeming to chase round and round under the trees, they were strange sounds of lowered suppressed voices—exclamations and smothered joyous cries. It seemed actually like the laughter of young things, the uncontrollable laughter of children who were trying not to be heard but who in a moment or so—as their excitement mounted—would burst forth. What in heaven's name was he dreaming of—what in heaven's name did he hear? Was he losing his reason and thinking he heard things which were not for human ears? Was it that the far clear voice had meant?

And then the moment came, the uncontrollable moment when the sounds forgot to hush themselves. The feet ran faster and faster—they were nearing the garden door—there was quick strong young breathing and a wild outbreak of laughing shouts which could not be contained—and the door in the wall was flung wide open, the sheet of ivy swinging back, and a boy burst through it at full speed and, without seeing the outsider, dashed almost into his arms.

Mr. Craven had extended them just in time to save him from falling as a result of his unseeing dash against him, and when he held him away to look at him in amazement at his being there he truly gasped for breath.

He was a tall boy and a handsome one. He was glowing with life and his running had sent splendid color leaping to his face. He threw the thick hair back from his forehead and lifted a pair of strange gray eyes—eyes full of boyish laughter and rimmed with black lashes like a fringe. It was the eyes which made Mr. Craven gasp for breath.

"Who—What? Who!" he stammered.

This was not what Colin had expected—this was not what he had planned. He had never thought of such a meeting. And yet to come dashing out—winning a race—perhaps it was even better. He drew himself up to his very tallest. Mary, who had been running with him and had dashed through the door too, believed that he managed to make himself look taller than he had ever looked before—inches taller.

"Father," he said, "I'm Colin. You can't believe it. I scarcely can myself. I'm Colin."

Like Mrs. Medlock, he did not understand what his father meant when he said hurriedly:

"In the garden! In the garden!"

"Yes," hurried on Colin. "It was the garden that did it—and Mary and Dickon and the creatures—and the Magic. No one knows. We kept it to tell you when you came. I'm well, I can beat Mary in a race. I'm going to be an athlete."

He said it all so like a healthy boy—his face flushed, his words tumbling over each other in his eagerness—that Mr. Craven's soul shook with unbelieving joy.

Colin put out his hand and laid it on his father's arm.

"Aren't you glad, Father?" he ended. "Aren't you glad? I'm going to live forever and ever and ever!"

Mr. Craven put his hands on both the boy's shoulders and held him still. He knew he dared not even try to speak for a moment.

"Take me into the garden, my boy," he said at last. "And tell me all about it."

And so they led him in.

The place was a wilderness of autumn gold and purple and violet blue and flaming scarlet and on every side were sheaves of late lilies standing together—lilies which were white or white and ruby. He remembered well when the first of them had been planted that just at this season of the year their glories should reveal themselves. Late roses climbed and hung and clustered and the sunshine deepening the hue of the yellowing trees made one feel that one stood in an embowered temple of gold. The newcomer stood silent just as the children had done when they came into its grayness. He looked round and round.

"I thought it would be dead," he said.

"Mary thought so at first," said Colin. "But it came alive."

Then they sat down under their tree—all but Colin, who wanted to stand while he told the story.

It was the strangest thing he had ever heard, Archibald Craven thought, as it was poured forth in headlong boy fashion. Mystery and Magic and wild creatures, the weird midnight meeting—the coming of the spring—the passion of insulted pride which had dragged the young Rajah to his feet to defy old Ben Weatherstaff to his face. The odd companionship, the play acting, the great secret so carefully kept. The listener laughed until tears came into his eyes and sometimes tears came into his eyes when he was not laughing. The Athlete, the Lecturer, the Scientific Discoverer was a laughable, lovable, healthy young human thing.

"Now," he said at the end of the story, "it need not be a secret any more. I dare say it will frighten them nearly into fits when they see me—but I am never going to get into the chair again. I shall walk back with you, Father—to the house."

Ben Weatherstaff's duties rarely took him away from the gardens, but on this occasion he made an excuse to carry some vegetables to the kitchen and being invited into the servants' hall by Mrs. Medlock to drink a glass of beer he was on the spot—as he had hoped to be—when the most dramatic event Misselthwaite Manor had seen during the present generation actually took place.

One of the windows looking upon the courtyard gave also a glimpse of the lawn. Mrs. Medlock, knowing Ben had come from the gardens, hoped that he might have caught sight of his master and even by chance of his meeting with Master Colin.

"Did you see either of them, Weatherstaff?" she asked.

Ben took his beer-mug from his mouth and wiped his lips with the back of his hand.

"Aye, that I did," he answered with a shrewdly significant air.

"Both of them?" suggested Mrs. Medlock.

"Both of 'em," returned Ben Weatherstaff. "Thank ye kindly, ma'am, I could sup up another mug of it."

"Together?" said Mrs. Medlock, hastily overfilling his beer-mug in her excitement.

"Together, ma'am," and Ben gulped down half of his new mug at one gulp.

"Where was Master Colin? How did he look? What did they say to each other?"

"I didna' hear that," said Ben, "along o' only bein' on th' step-ladder lookin' over th' wall. But I'll tell thee this. There's been things goin' on outside as you house people knows nowt about. An' what tha'll find out tha'll find out soon."

And it was not two minutes before he swallowed the last of his beer and waved his mug solemnly toward the window which took in through the shrubbery a piece of the lawn.

"Look there," he said, "if tha's curious. Look what's comin' across th' grass."

When Mrs. Medlock looked she threw up her hands and gave a little shriek and every man and woman servant within hearing bolted across the servants' hall and stood looking through the window with their eyes almost starting out of their heads.

Across the lawn came the Master of Misselthwaite and he looked as many of them had never seen him. And by his side with his head up in the air and his eyes full of laughter walked as strongly and steadily as any boy in Yorkshire—Master Colin!

. . .

ESSAY

from *Happily Ever After:*
A Portrait of Frances Hodgson Burnett

BY

CONSTANCE BUEL BURNETT

Probably the most unusual aspect of Frances Hodgson Burnett's career was the uninterrupted flow of her work. Illness, grief, and disappointment could not stop her writing for any appreciable length of time. Personal troubles did not deplete her creative impulse, perhaps because trouble only heightened her capacity to feel, and in her case emotion was what compelled her to write. It was the crucible in which all her novels were shaped.

Her attachment to England was more than love of her mother country. England fed her talent as no other environment did. Its rich historical past, its feudal way of life, and its pageantry produced a climate in which her imagination thrived. Most of her books—certainly her best ones—have an English setting. She found in England an inexhaustible supply of subject matter and a proper balance for her triple need of stimulation, seclusion, and congenial contacts. . . .

No completely accurate record of Frances Hodgson Burnett's books exists, but it can safely be claimed that she wrote more than fifty novels. This does not include her short stories or the plays she constructed from books and stories, always sandwiched in between work she was already launched upon. Her books for children brought her her greatest rewards, though they were far fewer than her works for adults.

Brushing aside the honors showered on her when her books were most widely read, and the recognition accorded her by the most eminent people of her day, she used to say somewhat wistfully that her happiest years were those of comparative obscurity and struggle when, as a hard-working young mother, her two small boys were her closest friends and playfellows. To recapture this enchantment she would have to wait the arrival of grandchildren.

Her much-loved visits to England finally came to an end in 1914, when international events in Europe culminated in the opening phases of World War I. She happened to be in the United States at the time. Almost immediately England was deeply and tragically involved in the war, and Frances realized sadly that her return there from now on was unlikely. The war not only made travel impossible, but her English friends, now living under great stress and hardship, bitterly resented the fact that America did not come immediately to the assistance of the Allies.

As the war continued with growing ferocity the United States was eventually drawn into it, but Frances knew that the charming Victorian world she had loved and written about with such relish and intimate knowledge was gone forever.

It became obvious that the happiest plan she could devise for herself from now on would be to live near Vivian [her second son] and his family. She built herself a permanent home near the young people on Long Island, and there, except for regular visits to Bermuda each winter, she remained for the last decade of her life. . . .

Always sympathetic to the dreams and aspirations of the young, Frances once answered four questions put to her on the contributors' page of the *St. Nicholas Magazine*. Her advice contains as much wisdom for would-be writers today as it did then.

> *Question 1:* At what age did you first wish to take up work?
> *Answer:*   I began to write when I was seven years old.

Question 2: What characteristics do you consider the cause of your success?

Answer: The fact that I was interested in everything in the world—from emperors and prime ministers to swineherds and cats and dogs and every smallest blade of grass that grows. I *care* about them. I feel as if we were all part of each other. I try to understand why they do things and also why they don't. I always did.

Question 3: What led you to select your life's work?

Answer: I did not select it. It selected me.

Question 4: What special advice would you give me, a pupil of the eighth grade, wishing to take up the work of writing?

Answer: First, ask yourself *why* you want to do it. Then find out if you can do it. Try if you can tell a human story in human words, about some human thing. You can only do it knowing in your very soul that everything, however unimportant it may seem to the rest of the world, means joy or grief to the human being to whom it happens. *Everything* is a human story, if you can see it and feel it. But you cannot see and feel merely because you would like to write a book. I believe the power depends more upon what you *are* than upon what you would like to do. As for the rest, nobody needs to be told that to read and think about the best work the world has known and loved is part of the training.

I am answering your questions as a matter of conscience. When young people are contemplating taking up such a powerful and perilous weapon as a pen, it behooves one to try and say the right word. In your eighth grade may stand the coming great ones. Who knows? Why not? They are somewhere. Many a boy and girl wishes to be an author. . . . Some can and some

can't. Some ought and some ought not. Every-
one must find out for himself.

Frances Hodgson Burnett was keenly aware as she advanced in
years of the changing techniques in novel-writing during her own
time, and she was particularly aware of the cynical outlook that
permeated modern fiction. Wisely, she never tried to imitate these
trends. She gave what she had to give, even though she knew it
belonged to a vanishing era, and left this simple testimony to the
honesty of her purpose:

> "Long ago, even when I was a little girl writing in the
> attic room in the Ark at Knoxville, I began to feel that I
> could not have it on my conscience to make people un-
> happy, or make their minds foul with anything I had
> imagined or put on paper. There is enough of that in all our
> lives that we cannot get away from. What we all want is
> more of the other things—life, love, hope—and an assur-
> ance that they are true. With the best that was in me I have
> tried to write more happiness into the world."

Constance Buel Burnett (1893–1975), a writer, married Vivian Burnett,
Frances Hodgson Burnett's son, in 1914. Her works include *The Shoe-
maker's Son*, *Top Flight*, and *Happily Ever After: A Portrait of Frances
Hodgson Burnett*, from which this essay is excerpted.